Bernhard Tauchnitz

Strathmore Vol. 1

A Romance by Ouida

Bernhard Tauchnitz

Strathmore Vol. 1
A Romance by Ouida

ISBN/EAN: 9783741174513

Manufactured in Europe, USA, Canada, Australia, Japa

Cover: Foto ©Andreas Hilbeck / pixelio.de

Manufactured and distributed by brebook publishing software
(www.brebook.com)

Bernhard Tauchnitz

Strathmore Vol. 1

COLLECTION

OF

BRITISH AUTHORS

TAUCHNITZ EDITION.

VOL. 1169.

STRATHMORE BY OUIDA.

IN TWO VOLUMES.

VOL. I.

LEIPZIG: BERNHARD TAUCHNITZ.

COLLECTION

OF

BRITISH AUTHORS

TAUCHNITZ EDITION.

VOL. 1169.

STRATHMORE BY OUIDA.

IN TWO VOLUMES.

VOL. I.

STRATHMORE

A ROMANCE.

BY

OUIDA,

AUTHOR OF "IDALIA," "TRICOTRIN," ETC.

COPYRIGHT EDITION.

IN TWO VOLUMES.

VOL. I.

LEIPZIG

BERNHARD TAUCHNITZ

1871.

The Right of Translation is reserved.

There are depths in Man that go the lengths of lowest Hell, as there are heights that reach highest Heaven; for are not both Heaven and Hell made out of him, made by him, everlasting Miracle and Mystery that he is?

CARLYLE.

Oblivion cannot be hired —SIR THOMAS BROWNE's "*Urn Burial.*"

Good and evil we know, in the field of this world, grow up together almost inseparably; and the knowledge of good is so involved and interwoven with the knowledge of evil, that those confused seeds which were imposed upon Psyche as an incessant labour to cull out and sort asunder were not more intermixed.

MILTON.

TO THE READER.

A PREFACE too often provokes the reader to exclaim against it, what Cowley's silver pen wrote against the little word "but;"—that "it is *ærugo mera*, a rust that spoils the metal it grows upon." Nevertheless, as "but" may sometimes be the precursor of a clearer exposition of an argument, so a preface may perhaps be, here and there, the herald to a clearer understanding between a writer and his public. I have but a few words with which to prelude these volumes; and I do not entreat any critic to forbear divulging the plot in his remarks upon them. It is but a poor work which depends, like a conundrum, on the concealment of its catchword and secret, for the maintenance of its interest: whatever attraction may lie in this romance, I have preferred seeking to centre in the sketching of character, the development of temperament, and the issue of action. If it allure any reader, I would hope that such allurement will rest, not on the skeleton of its outline, but in the manner in which that outline is filled in and coloured.

I have given Strathmore purposely for what he is; a deeply erring man. I trust this will be remembered, and that people will not, therefore, express a supreme astonishment that he acts in consonance with such a character. If I wrote of a blind man, I could scarcely make him walk unerringly by the clear light of day; yet the public sometimes seem to look for such an anomaly, and expect a guilty man to act in all things like a demi-god. I have drawn in Strathmore one who, trusting in his own strength, fell by his own passions. I have screened nothing, excused nothing, palliated nothing. I have not softened the dark shadows that lie on a dark path. I have simply endeavoured to depict the insecurity of a haughty pride which held itself sufficient shield against all temptation; the inevitable steps by which one sin always leads onward to another; and the retribution, unseen of men, which rose out of the wilful guilt of a self-sustained and too-arrogant life.

If it be objected that in the woman who occupies a considerable place in these pages, crime wears too poetic and graceful a mask, I would answer that it is precisely this disguise in which it steals fatally into natures that otherwise would not succumb to it. Crime in its naked viciousness and coarseness has its least danger, and its open warning; I have sought to show that its darkest depths may underlie a bright seductive surface, as the volcanic line of the earthquake runs under a laughing and flowering landscape. The cruelty and the vices of Theodora did not prevent the loveliness of her face, nor the sway for nigh thirty years of her fascinations over Justinian. Women, perhaps, may resent the portrayal of Marion Vavasour; I regret that their sex has too often shown the truth of it. For the rest, I have no more to add; if there be any favour I would be inclined to ask of my reviewer, or my reader, it would be, not to judge of the work by any scattered fragments, but only as a whole: having followed it to the end, and having brought to its perusal the remembrance that human life is no flower of paradise, but a warped tree earth-stained in its growth, of which, as I have written later on, in the old well-known words:

> sed quantum vertice ad auras
> Ætherias, tantum radice in Tartara tendit.

London, May, 1863.

CONTENTS

OF VOLUME I.

STRATHMORE.

CHAPTER I.

White Ladies.

WHITE LADIES did not mean snowdrops, by their pretty
old English name, ghosts in white cere-clothes, or belles in
white tarlatan. It was only an old densely-wooded estate
down in one of those counties that give Creswick his cool
chequered shade and wild forest streams, his shallow sunny
brooks, and picturesque roadsides; but which, I am told by
superior taste, are terribly insipid and miserably tame, with
many other epithets I do not care to repeat, having a lingering weakness myself for the old bridle-paths with the boughs
meeting above head, the hawthorn hedges powdered with
their snowy blossom, and the rich meadow lands with their
tall grasses, and clover, and cowslips, where cattle stand up
to their hocks in fresh wild thyme, and shadows lengthen
slowly and lazily through long summer days.

White Ladies was an ancient and stately abbey, the last
relic of lands once wide and numerous as Warwick's ere he
fell at Gladsmoor Heath; a single possession—though that
lordly enough—where it had been but one among a crowded
beadroll of estates which had stretched over counties before
they were parcelled out and divided, some amongst the
hungry courtiers who fattened upon abbey lands; some among
the Hanoverian rabble, who scrambled for the goodly spoils
of loyal gentlemen; some, later on, among the vampires of
Israel, who, like their forefather and first usurer, Jacob, know
well how to treat with the famished, and sell us our mess of
pottage at no smaller price than our birthright.

In the days of Monkery and of Holy Church, White Ladies had been a great Dominican monastery, rich in its wealth and famous in its sanctity; though since then the great Gothic pile had been blasted with petronels, burned with flame, and riddled with the bullets of the Ironsides. Yet, when the western sun slanted in flecks of gold through the boughs of the wych-elms, and fell on the panes of the blazoned windows, or the moonlight streaming across the sward, gleamed through the pointed arches and aisles, and down the ivy-covered cloisters, the abbey had still a stately and solemn beauty, given to it in ancient times by the cunning hand of master masons, when men built for art and not for greed, and lavished love in lieu of lusting gold, when they worked for a long lifetime to leave some imperishable record of their toil, and were grandly heedless how their names might perish and be forgot. It stood down in deep secluded western valleys on the borders of the sea, shut in by dense forest lands which covered hill and dale for miles about it, and sheltered in their recesses the dun deer in their coverts and the grey herons by their pools; a silent, solitary, royal place, where the axe never sounded among the centenarian trees, and the sylvan glory was never touched by the Vandal of time and the Goth of steam, that elsewhere are swiftly sapping what Tudor iconoclasts spared, and destroying what Puritan petards left free.

Through the elm-boughs that swayed against the carvings with which Norman builders had enriched the pile; through the tangled ivy that hid where Cromwell's breach had blasted, and where Henry's troops had sacked; through the heraldic blazonries upon the panes, where the arms of the Strathmores with their fierce motto, "*Slay, and spare not!*" were stained, the summer sun shone into one of the chambers at White Ladies.

In olden days, and turn by turn as time went on and fortunes changed, the chamber had been the audience-place of the Lord Abbot, where he had received high nobles who sought the sanctuary because the price of blood was on their heads, or thriftless kings of Plantagenet who came to pray the aid of Mother Church for largesse to their troops ere they set sail for Palestine. It had been the bower-room of a captive queen, where Mary had sat over her tapestry thinking of the years so long gone by, when on her soft childish brow, fair with the beauty of Stuart and Guise, the astrologer had seen the taint of foreshadowed woe and the presage of death under the soft golden curls. It had been the favourite haunt of Court beauties where they had read the last paper of Spec, and pondered over new pulvillios, and rejoiced that the peace had been made at Utrecht, to bring them the French mode and Paris chocolate, and thought in their secretly-disaffected hearts of the rising that was fomenting among the gallant gentlemen of the North, and of the cypher letter lying under the lace in their bosoms from one brave to rash-ness, and thrice well-beloved because in danger for the Cause, who was travelling secretly and swiftly to St. Germain.

Now the Plantagenets had died out, root and branch, the tapestry woven by Mary was faded and moth-eaten, the Court beauties were laid in the chapel vault, and the oriel-chamber was scented with Latakia, Manillas, Burgundies, and liqueurs, while three or four men sat at breakfast with a group of retrievers on the hearth. The sun falling through the case-ments, shone on the brass andirons, the oak carvings, the purple silk of the hangings, and on the game and fruits, coffee and Rhenish, that were crowded in profusion on the table, at which the host and the guests of White Ladies lounged; smoking and looking over the contents of the letter-bag, peeling an apricot, or cutting into a foie gras, silent, lazy, and inert, for there was nothing to tempt them out but the rabbits, and the morning was warm, and the shaded room pleasant.

At the head of his table the host sat in shadow, where the light of the outer day did not reach, but left the purple hangings of the wall with the dead gold of their embroideries in gloom behind him. He was a man then of nine-and-twenty or thirty, but who looked something older than he was; he was tall and slightly made, and wore a black velvet morning coat. His face was singularly striking and impressive, more by expression than by feature—it was such a countenance as you see in old Italian portraits, and in some Vandykes, bearing in them power strangely blended with passion, and repose with recklessness; his hair, moustaches, and beard were of a dark chesnut hue; his mouth was very beautifully formed, with the smile generous, but rare; the eyebrows were dark, straight, and finely pencilled; the eyes grey. And it was in these, when they lightened to steel-like brilliance, or darkened black as night with instantaneous and pitiless anger, that an acute physiognomist would have inferred for him danger, and evil to himself and to others, which would arise from a spring as yet, perhaps, unknown and unsealed; and that an artist studying his face, in which his art would have found no flaw, would have said that this man would be relentless, and might have predicted, as the Southern sculptor prophesied of Charles Stuart, "Something evil will befal him. He carries misfortune on his face."

He lay back in his chair, turning over his letters, looking idly one by one at them, not opening some, and not reading wholly through any; many of them had feminine superscriptions, and scarlet or azure chiffres at the seal, as delicately scented as though they had been brought by some court page, rather than by the rough route of the mail-bag. They afforded him a certain amusement that summer's morning, and Strathmore of White Ladies—this man with the eyes of a Catiline and the face of a Strafford—had no care greater on his mind for either the present or the future just then than that his keepers had told him the broods were very scanty, and the young birds had died off shockingly in the early parts of the spring; that he was summoned to go on a diplomatic mission to Bulgaria to confer with a crabbed Prince Michel, before he cared to leave England; and that one of his fair correspondents, Nina Montolieu, a Free Companion, whose motto blazoned on her pretty fluttering pennon, was a very rapacious "*tout prendre!*" might be a little more troublesome than was agreeable, and give him a taste of the tenacious griffes now that he had tired of playing with the pattes de velours. He had nothing graver or darker to trouble him, as he leant back in the shade where the sunlight did not come, glancing out now and then to the masses of forest, and the grey cloisters, ivy-hung and crumbling to ruins, that were given to view through the opened windows of his chamber. His face was the face of a State-conspirator of Velasquez, of a doomed Noble of Vandyke; but his life was the easy, nonchalant, untroubled, unchequered life of an English gentleman of our days; and his thoughts were the thoughts that are natural to, and that run in couple with, such a life. "Born to calamity" would have been as little applicable then to Cecil Strathmore as it seemed to Charles of England, when he and Villiers looked into the long eyes of the Spanish donnas and drank to the loveliness of Henriette de Bourbon. But in those joyous, brilliant days of Madrid and Paris, the shadow of the future had not fallen across the threshold of Whitehall,—neither as yet had it fallen here, across the threshold of White Ladies.

He looked up and turned a little in his chair as the door opened, and the smile that was the more brilliant and the more attractive because extremely rare, lighted his face.

"You incorrigible fellow! the coffee is cold, and the claret is corked, and the omelettes are overdone, but it's no more than you deserve. Won't you *ever* be punctual? We were going down to Hurst Warren at nine, and it's now eleven. You are the most idle dog, Erroll, under heaven!"

"You were only down yourself six minutes ago (I asked Craven), so don't *you* talk, my good fellow. You have been reading the first volume of the 'Amours d'une Femme,' and sending the rabbits to the deuce; and I've been reading the second, and consigning them to the devil, so we're quits. A summer morning's made for a French novel in bed, with the window open and the birds singing outside; pastorals and pruriencies go uncommonly nicely together, rather like lemons and rum, you know. Contrasts are always *chic!*"

With which enunciation of doctrine the new comer sat down, rolled his chair up to the table, and began an inspection of some lobster cutlets à la Maréchale, taking a cup of creamy chocolate from the servant behind him, while Strathmore looked at him with a smile still on his lips, and a cordial look in his eyes, as if the mere sound of the other's voice were pleasant to him. The belated guest was a man of his own age, or some few years older; in frame and sinew he was superb; in style he was rather like a dashing Free Lance, a gallant debonair captain of Bourbon's Reiters, with his magnificent muscle and reckless brilliance, though he was as gentle as a woman and as lazy as a Circassian girl. He called himself the handsomest man in the Service, and had the palm given him undisputingly; for the frank, clear, azure eyes that grew so soft in love, so trustful in friendship, the long fair hair sweeping off a forehead white as the most delicate blonde's, the handsome features with their sunny candour and their gay sensuous smile, made his face almost as attractive to men as to women. As for the latter, indeed, they strewed his path with the conqueror's myrtle-leaves. His loves were as innumerable as the stars, and by no means so eternal; and if now and then the beau sexe had the best of the warfare, it was only because they are never compassionate on those who surrender to them at once, and whom they can bind and lead captive at their will, which the least experienced could do at one stroke with Bertie Erroll, as he freely and lamentingly confessed. The Beau Sabreur, as he had been nicknamed, à la Murat, was soft as silk in the hands of a beauty, and impressionable as wax when fairy fingers were at work. He had never in his life resisted a woman, and avowed himself utterly unable to do so. Have you ever, known the science that brought Laomedon to grief of any avail against the Lydian Queen?

"Letters! Why *will* they write them!" he said, as he glanced at the small heap of feminine correspondence piled beside his plate. "It's such a pity!—it only makes us feel bearish, bored, and miserably ungrateful; wastes an hour to get through them religiously, or hangs a millstone of un-performed duty and unexpiated debt about our necks for the livelong day, till post-time comes round again and makes bad worse!"

"Why *will* they write them?" echoed Strathmore, giving a contemptuous push of his elbow to Nina Montolieu's en-velope, a souvenir of the past season, with which he could very well have dispensed. "Our Brinvilliers poison us with patchouli paper, and stab us with a crowquill. One might like to 'die of a rose in aromatic pain,' but I would rather not die of three scented sheets crossed! Correspondence is cruel—with women. If you *don't* answer them, you feel sin-ful and discourteous; if you *do* answer them, you only supply them with ammunition to fire on to you afresh with fifty more rounds of grape and canister. They love to spend their whole morning skimming over a thousand lines, and winding up with 'Toujours à toi!' They love to write honey to you with one pen, and gall about you with another; they love to address their dearest friends on a rose-tinted sheet, and fold it to damn them on a cream-coloured one. Writing is wo-men's *métier;* but it is deucedly hard that they will inflict the results upon us!"

"It's an odd psychological fact that women will write on for a twelvemonth unanswered, as religiously as they wipe their pens, omit their dates, and believe in the acceleration of postal speed by an 'Immediate' on the envelope," put in Phil Danvers from the bottom of the table, helping himself to some Strasbourg pâté. "Some of them write delightfully, though—Tricksey Bellevoix does. Her notes are the most delicious olla podrida of news, mots, historiettes, and little tit-bits of confidence imaginable; she always tells you, too, mischievous things of the people you don't like, instead of scandalising people you do, after the ordinary fashion. Her letters are not bad fun at all when you're smoking, and want something to look at for ten minutes."

"I'll tell her how you rate them! She's going to Charlemont next week. See if you get any more letters, Phil!"
cried Erroll.

"My dear fellow, if we turned king's evidence on one another, I don't think we should get any more feminine favours
at all!" laughed Strathmore. "Very few of them would
relish the chit-chat about them if they'd correct reports from
the club windows and shorthand notes from the smoking-
rooms. Would you be let in again to the violet boudoir in
Bruton-street if Lady Fitz knew you'd told me last night that
she had the very devil's own temper! and would Dan be
called 'ami choisi de mon cœur,' if Madame la Baronne knew
that when he gets her notes he says, 'Deuce take the woman!— how she bothers,' audibly in White's! Try that
grilse, Langton—it was in the river yesterday."

"And is prime. It would have been worth Georgie's
trolling."

"Georgie lost all her rings last week in the Dee—two
thousand pounds' worth in diamonds and sapphires—serve
her perfectly right! What business has she with March
browns and dun governors!" said the host of White Ladies,
drawing a plate of peaches to him. "I cannot conceive what
women are about when they take up that line of thing. How
can they imagine an ill-done replica of ourselves *can* attract
us! A fast woman is an anomaly, and all anomalies are
jarring and bizarre. To kiss lips that smell of smoke—to
hear one's belle amie welcome one with 'All serene!'—to see
her 'bugle eyeball and her cheek of cream' only sparkle and
flush for a tan gallop and a Rawcliffe yearling—to have her
boudoir as horsy as the Corner, and her walk a cross between
a swing and a strut! Pah! give me women as soft, and as
delicate, and as velvet as my peaches!"

"Peaches!" put in Erroll. "Ominous simile! Your soft
women will have an uncommonly hard stone at their core,
and a kernel that's poison under the velvet skin, mon cher
Cis!"

"*Soit!* I only brush the bloom, and taste the sweetness!"

yawned Strathmore. "A wise man never lingers long enough over the same to have time to come to the core. With peaches and women, it's only the side next the sun that's tempting; if you find acid in either, leave them for the downy blush of another! How poetic we grow! Is it the Rhenish? That rich, old, amber, mellow wine always has a flavour of Hoffmann's fancies and Jean Paul's verse about it; it smells of the Rheingau! I don't wonder Schiller took his inspirations from it. I say, Erroll, I heard from Rokeby this morning. He doesn't say a word about the Sartory betting, nor yet of the White Duchess scandal. He is only full of two things; La Pucelle's chances of the Prix de Rastatt at Baden, and of this beauty he's raving of, something superb, according to him, a Creole, I think he says—Lady Vavasour! Really one's bored to death with ecstasies about that woman! Have you heard the name? *I* have lots of times, but I've always missed her."

"Vavasour? Vavasour? The deuce, I have—rather!" said Erroll, thrown into a beatific vision by the mere name of the lady under discussion, while he stirred some more cream into his chocolate.

"Who was she?" asked Langton, of the 16th Lancers, who was only just back from service in Bengal.

"More than I can tell you, my boy. I believe it's more than anybody knows. She sprang into society like Aphrodite from the sea-foam. One may as well be graceful in metaphor, eh? You mean a Creole, Strathmore, made a tremendous row at St. Petersburg—came nobody knew precisely whence —hadn't been seen till she appeared as Lady Vavasour and Vaux tooling a six-in-hand pony-trap, with pages of honour in lapis-lazuli liveries, that created a furore in Longchamps, and made the Pré Catalan crowded to get a glimpse of her. Ever since then all Europe's been at her feet!"

"That's the woman!" broke in Danvers. "Oh, she's divine, they say. Everybody goes mad after her, and can't help himself. Scrope Waverley raved of her; he saw her at Biarritz, and swears she's quite matchless. She's the most capricious coquette, too, that ever broke hearts with a fan-handle!"

"Hearts! Faugh!" sneered Strathmore; and, when he did so, his face was very cold—a coldness strangely at variance with the swift, dark passions that slumbered in his eyes. "My good fellow, don't give us a réchauffé of Scrope Waverley's sentimental nonsense! The man must be weaker than the fan-handle if he be ruled by it."

Erroll lifted his eyebrows, and sighed:

"May be! But the little ivory sticks play the deuce with us when they're well managed."

"Speak for yourself! Don't make your confessions in the plural, that their folly may sound general, pray!"

"Oh, *you*—you're a confounded cold fellow! Wear chained armour, wrap yourself in asbestos, and all that sort of thing, 'larva kisses' wouldn't melt you, and Helen wouldn't move you unless you chose!"

Strathmore laughed a little.

"Why should they? It is only fools who go in fetters. I can *not* comprehend that madness about a woman—to lie at her feet and come at her call, and take her caresses one minute and her neglect the next, as if you were her spaniel, with nothing better to do than to live in her bondage! It is miserably contemptible! What is weakness if *that* isn't one, eh!"

Erroll flung the envelope with the scarlet chiffre, lying on the table within reach of his hand, at his host and friend, as proof and reproof of the nullity of his doctrines.

"Most noble lord! you have the cheek to talk coldly and disdainfully like that, while you know you are in the net of the Montolieu, and Heaven knows how many others besides!"

.   Strathmore laughed again as the envelope fluttered down on the ground, falling short of him where he lay back in his fauteuil:

"*Bécasse!* that is a very different affair. Nina is a dashing little lawless lady, and knows how to pillage with both hands; one must pay if one dallies with the Free Companions. You don't suppose she ever held me in her bondage, or flattered herself she did for an hour, do you? No one was ever *in love* with that sort of women after twenty; one *makes* love to them in parenthesis as it were, of course, but that's quite another thing. It is how you lose your hearts, how you hang on a smile, how you let yourselves be marked and hit and brought down like the silliest noddy-bird that ever sat to be shot at, how you go mad after *one* woman, and that one woman with, nine times out of ten, nothing worth worshipping about her—it is that which I can't understand."

"Thank your stars!" said Erroll, softly, and with a profound sigh of envy. "Go about with your noli me tangere shield, and be piously thankful you've got it then. Only the 'haughty in their strength,' et cætera, you know—what's the rest of the scriptural warning?—unbelievers *do* come to grief sometimes for their hardened heterodoxy! This superb Vavasour, I want dreadfully to see her. They say she is the best thing we have had for a long time, since the Duchess d'Ivore was in her first prime."

"She must be the same I heard so much about in Paris last winter; she was passing the season in Rome, so I missed seeing her. She has the most wayward caprices, they say, of any living woman," said Danvers, turning over the leaves of the morning papers; "but the *caprices d'une belle femme* are always bewitching and always permissible. A great beauty has no sins; she may do what she likes, and we forgive her, even with the leopard claws in our skin. The pretty panther! it looks so handsome and so soft; its very crimes are only mischief."

"You haven't been in Scinde, Phil," said Langton, with the grim smile of a campaigner who hears those who have never suffered jest at scars; while their host, rather tired of this breakfast-chat about women, turned to his unopened correspondence, till his guests, having thrown their letters away, to be answered at any distant and hazardous future, having yawned over the papers, casually remarking that that poor devil Allington's divorce case was put off till next session, or that there was an awful row in South Mexico, rose by general consent, and began to think of the rabbits.

White Ladies was one of the pleasantest places to visit at in England. A long beadroll might have been cited of houses that eclipsed it in every point, but the Abbey had a charm, as it had a beauty, of its own. In the deep recesses of its vast forest-lands there were drives of deer that gave more royals in one day's sport than were ever found south of the Cheviots. In the dark pools, some of them well-nigh inaccessible, where they lay between gorse-covered hills or down in wooded valleys, the wild fowl flocked by legions. The river, that ran in and out, of which you just caught glimpses from the west windows, flashing between the boughs in the distance, was famed for its salmon, and had in olden days given char and trout to the tables of the monastery, whose celebrity had reached to royal Windsor and princely Sheen, and made the Tudor covetous for the land and water that yielded such good fare. Sport was to be had in perfection among the brakes and woods at White Ladies; and within, even in the very bachelor dens overlooking the cloisters, there were luxury and comfort; while fair women used to come down to White Ladies, sufficiently lovely to rouse the sleeping Dominicans from their graves, as they swept through the aisles of the chapel; and laughter would ring out from the smoking-room, when the men had their feet in the papooshes and their pipes in their mouths, loud enough to wake all the echoes of the abbey, and make the dead monks, lying under the sward, turn in their tombs and cross themselves, at the profanity of their successors and supplanters.

White Ladies was a grand old place, and Strathmore was envied by most of his friends and acquaintance for its possession. It had come to him by the distaff side, from his mother's father, who, failing heirs male in the direct line, had left it to him on condition that he assumed his name. Strathmore bore a close resemblance to his mother's family, whose name he had taken; he had nothing either in feature or in character in common with the easy, inert, sensual, placable,

Saxon Castlemeres, with their Teuton good humour and their Teuton phlegm, but he inherited in every point the type of the Strathmores, that courtly, silent, Norman race, swift and fierce in passion, dark and implacable in hate, keen to avenge, slow to forgive, imperious in love, and cold in hate; and with the features might go the character.

Others do not know, we do not know ourselves, all that lies latent in us, until the seeds of good or evil that are hidden and unknown, germinate to deed and blossom into action, and make us reap for weal or woe the harvest we have sown. If with the countenance, he inherited the character, of those who had ruled before him at White Ladies, there had been little in his life to develop the unroused nature. The darker traits might have died out with the darker times, as the mailed surcoat of steel had been replaced by a velvet morning coat, as the iron portcullis had been put away by a gold-fringed portière, as the culverin above the gateway had been removed for the soft, silken folds of a flag. Lions long kept in a tame life lose their desert instinct and their thirst for blood, so the Strathmores in long centuries of court life might have outworn and lost what had been evil and dangerous in them in the days of Plantagenet, of Lancaster, and of York. Or, if the nature were not dead, but only sleeping, there was nothing to arouse it; things went smoothly and well with Strathmore; he had birth, fortune, talents of a high order; he was courted by women, partly because he was very cold to them, chiefly, doubtless, because he was younger son of the Marquis of Castlemere and master of White Ladies. In a diplomatic career he had a wide field for the ambitions that attracted him—the ambition not of place, wealth, or title, but of Power, the deep, subtle state power that had in all ages fascinated the Strathmores, and been wielded by them successfully and skilfully. Life lay clear, brilliant, unruffled behind him and before him. If there ran in his blood the old spirit of the Strathmores, that had often worked their own doom and been their own scourge, that gleamed from their eyes in the old portraits by Antonio More, and Jameson, and

Vandyke, hanging in the vaulted picture-gallery at the
Abbey, and that made those who looked on them understand
how those courtly, elegant, suave gentlemen had been swift
to steel, and pitiless in pursuit, and imperious in ire,—if this
spirit still ran in his blood it was dormant, and had never
been wakened to its strength. Opportunity is the forcing-
house that gives birth to all things; without it, seeds will
never ripen into fruit; with it, much that might otherwise
have died out innocuous expands to baneful force. Man works
half his own doom, and circumstance works the other half.
Yet, because we have not been tempted, we therefore believe
we can stand; because we have not yet been brought nigh
the furnace, we therefore hold ourselves to be fire-proof!
Mes frères, the best of us are fools, I fear! The steel is not
proven till it has passed through the flames.

Sooner or later—though they may lie to it long, half a
lifetime, perhaps—I believe that men and women are all true
to their physiognomies; that they prove, sooner or later, that
the index Nature has writ (though written in crabbed, uncertain characters which few can read altogether aright) upon
their features is not a wrong nor a false one. Men lie, but
Nature does not. They dissemble, but she speaks out. They
conceal, but she tells the truth. What is carved on the
features, will develop, some time or other, in the career.
When Bernini made the prophecy that foretold ill for the heir
of England, could any prediction seem more absurd? Yet
Charles Stuart wrought his own fate, and the fruit of the past,
whose seed had been sown by his own hands, was bitter between his teeth when the foretold calamity fell, black and
ghastly, betwixt the People and the Throne. Strathmore's
life, cold, clear, cloudless as the air of a glittering, still,
winter's noon, was utterly at variance with his physiognomy
—the physiognomy which had the eyes of a Catiline and the
face of a Strafford! Yet, as time went on, and he passed of
his own will into a path which a man stronger in one sense,
and weaker in another, would have never entered, the spirit
that was latent in him awoke, and wrought his own fate and

wove his own scourge more darkly and more erringly, because
more consciously and more resolutely, than Charles Stuart;
making him eat of the fruit of his own sowing to the full as
bitterly as he of England, who might never have bowed his
head to the axe that chill January morning, when a king fell,
amidst the silence of an assembled multitude, if the first obstinate error which had seemed sweet to him had been put
aside, and the first wilful turn out of the right path been
avoided: the turn—so slight!—that led on to the headsman
and the scaffold!

CHAPTER II.

Under the Shadow of the Elms.

THE rabbits were tame in comparison with the drives for
which the forests of White Ladies were famed, and with the
bouquets of pheasants that the battues afforded later on in
the year; still they were better than nothing, and were pep-
pered *faute de mieux* that day. But the chief thing done by
the whole quartette, was to lie under the trees and drink the
iced champagne-cup and Badminton, brought there, with a
cold luncheon, on an Exmoor pony by the under-keepers about
two o'clock; which was, however, as pleasant occupation for
idleness on a sultry summer's day as anything that could be
suggested, while the smoke curled up through the leafy
roofing above head, and the dogs lay about on the moss with
their tongues out, hot, tired, and excited, and the mavises
and blackbirds sang in the boughs.

"Where the deuce is the Sabreur?" asked Phil Danvers,
when the rabbits had been slain by the score, and the chimes
of the Abbey, ringing seven o'clock with the slow, musical
chant of the "Adeste Fideles," came over the woods, and
warned them that the dressing-bell must be going, and that
, it was time to think about dinner.

"By George! I don't know," said Strathmore. "I haven't
seen him for the last hour. Didn't he say something about

the Euston Coppice! I dare say he is gone there after the rabbits; we must have missed him somewhere."

"It's easy to lose oneself in these woods of yours, Strathmore," said Langton, striking a fresh fusee. "The timber's so tremendously thick, and there are no paths to speak of; you never have the wood cut down, do you?"

"Cut down! Certainly not! My good fellow, do you think the woods of White Ladies go for building purposes? I wonder Bertie is gone off like that. Pritchard, have you seen Major Erroll?"

"I see the Major a going toward the coppice, my lord, about an hour ago, when we was beating of the Near Acre— a going down that ere path, my lord," responded Pritchard, the under-keeper.

"Queer fellow!" said Strathmore, as he gave his gun to one of the boys, and lighted a weed. "What did he go off for, I wonder? He must have missed us, somehow."

"Perhaps he's taken a wrong cut, and will wander miserably till the soup's cold and the fish overdone," suggested Danvers. "Lady Millicent is coming to-night, ain't she, with the Harewood people? He'll hang himself if he isn't in time to take her in to dinner; he swears by her just now, you know. The Sabreur's eternally in love! Who isn't, though?"

"*I*'m not," said Strathmore, with perfect veracity. It was somewhat his pride that he had never lost his head for any woman in his life.

"Because you're panoplied with protocols, and sworn to the State! You're a cursed cold fellow, Cis—always were!" interrupted Danvers, with a mixture of impatience and envy. "Bertie *has* lost himself, I bet you. I was benighted once, don't you remember? If he miss Lady Millicent, he'll hang himself, to a certainty! We must ask her for one of her rose ribbons to make the suicide effective!"

"I'll go round by the coppice home, and look for him," said Strathmore. "There are two hours before the people come. I shall be back in plenty of time. Au revoir!—you

and Phil want longer for your toilettes than I do, because
you'll dress for the Harewood women!"

It was a splendid evening—clear, sultry, with an amber
light falling through the aisles of the trees, and long shadows
deepening across the sward, while the wild fowl went to roost
beside the pools, and the herons dipped their beaks into the
dark cool waters that lay deep and still, with broad-leaved
lilies and tangled river plants floating languidly on their surface. Strathmore left his guests to take the shorter cut that
led direct to the side-door of the bachelors' wing, and strolled
himself through Euston Coppice, a wild, solitary, intricate
bit of the park, that had more of the luxuriant forest-growth
of parts of Lower Brittany than of the tamer, more cultivated
look of English woodlands. Some volcanic convulsion long
ages ago had rent and split the earth in this part into a
fantastic surface, the gaps so filled up by furze, hazel, and
yellow heath, and the rugged sides so covered that the right
track might very easily be lost. He walked onward, looking
about him; for he thought it possible that Erroll might have
missed the right path, and that he might fall in with him as
he passed homewards.

Bertie was the solitary person whom Strathmore could
ever have been said to have loved. His attachment was very
difficult to rouse; in the world, people, specially pretty
coquettes, called him without any heart, perhaps without any
feeling. It was true that he had never lost his head after any
of them; his indifference was no affectation, and his vaunted
panoply no pretence; the Strathmores had always better liked
state plot and subtle power than the women whose odorous
tresses had swept over their Milan corslets, and whose golden
heads had been pillowed on their breasts. To Erroll, Strathmore bore, however, a much deeper attachment than beauty
had ever won from him—the attachment of a nature that gives
both love and friendship very rarely; but when it gives either
gives instantly, blindly, and trustingly; the nature that had
always been characteristic of the "swift, silent, Strathmores,"
as the alliteration of cradle chronicles and provincial legends

nicknamed the race which had reigned at White Ladies since Hastings.   The friendship between them was the friendship closer than brotherhood of dead Greece and old Judæa—the bright truthfulness, the soft laziness, the candour, the dash, the verve, the hundred attractive, attachable qualities of Erroll's character, endeared him to Strathmore by that strange force of contrast which has so odd a spell sometimes in friendship as in love; and the bond between them was as close and firmly riven as a clasp of steel.   They never spoke of their friendship; it was not the way of either of them; it is only your loving ladies who lavish eternal vows, and press soft kisses on each other's cheeks, and swear they cannot live apart over their pre-prandial Souchong, to—slander each other suavely behind their fans an hour afterwards, and sigh away their bosom-darling's reputation with a whisper! They rarely spoke of it; but they had a friendship for one another passing the love of women, and they relied on it as men rely on their own honour, as silently and as securely.

Once, when they were together in Scinde, having both gone thither on a hunting trip to the big-game districts for a change one autumn, to bring home panther-skins and try pig-sticking, a tigress sprang out on them as they strolled alone through the jungle—sprang out to alight, with grip and fang, upon Strathmore, who neither heard nor saw her, as it chanced.   But before she could be upon her victim, Erroll threw himself before him, and catching the beast by her throat as she rose in the air to her leap, held her off at arm's length, and fell with her, holding her down by main force, while she tore and gored him in the struggle—a struggle that lasted till Strathmore had time to take aim, and send a ball through her brain; a long time, let me tell you, though but a few short seconds in actual duration, to hold down, and to wrestle in the grip of a tigress of Scinde. "You would have done the same for me, my dear old fellow," said Erroll, quietly and lazily, as his eyes closed, and he fainted away from the loss of blood.   And that was all he would ever vouchsafe to say or hear said about the matter. He had risked his life to save Strathmore's; he knew Strathmore would have acted precisely so for him.   It was a type of the quality and of the character of their friendship.

The evening shadows were slanting across the sward, while the squirrels ran from branch to branch, and the chesnuts lying on the mass turned to gold in the western sun, as Strathmore walked along with a couple of beagles following in his track. See Erroll he did not, and he wondered where the deuce he had gone; if he had been absolutely after the rabbits he would have taken some of the men, or the dogs at the least, with him; and it was odd he had chosen that night in especial to be belated, as among the people coming to dine at White Ladies in an hour's time was Lady Millicent Clinton, a beautiful blonde, tantalising, imperious, and bewitching to the highest degree, whom Erroll had watched for at Flirtation Corner, left the coulisses for at the opera, bought guinea cups of tea for at bazaars, and dedicated himself to generally, throughout the past season. He walked onwards, flushing the pheasants with his step, and startling the herons as he passed the pools, till they rose at the bark of the dogs, and sailed majestically away in the sunny silent air.   At last, as he went along the confines of the deer-park, towards the entrance of a long elm-walk, half lane, half avenue, that led round towards the Abbey, he saw, leaning over a gate against which his gun was resting, and talking to a woman, Bertie— in quest of other game than the rabbits.

He was at some distance, almost at the other end of the avenue; across which broad lines of yellow light fell through the trunks of the trees, while the elm-boughs meeting above head, thick with luxuriant leaf, threw chequered shadows on the turf below. He was standing by the stile which led into a bridle-path that wound up to the church a mile or so beyond, and was talking earnestly to his companion, who stood on the other side, and who, even at that distance, made a charming picture; much such a one as Aline, when Boufflers toyed with her at the woodland brook under the forests of Lorraine, with the butterflies fluttering above her head, and

the wild flowers hanging in her childish hands. She stood on
the lower step of the stile, so that as she reached upwards one
of her arms was wound about his neck, her face, soft, youthful, and fair, was lifted to his own, as his hand lingered on
her brow, pushing back from it the shining waves of hair,
while she nestled closely to him as a bird to the one who
caresses it, as a spaniel to the master it follows! It was a
scene to be interpreted at a glance, that golden sunset hour
under the shadow of the elms;—and *in* those hours who re-
members that the sun will set, leaving the dank dews of night
to brood where its beams have fallen; that the foliage above
us will drop off sere and withered like the "dark brown
years" of Ossian, into which we must enter and dwell; that
in the grasses the asp is curling, that in the west the clouds
are brooding? None remember, mes amis! neither did those
who lingered then beneath the elms before the sun went
down.

"*That's* his game! By George! I thought it was odd if the
rabbits alone made him too late for dinner! I wonder how
many he has shot in the coppice. Poor Lady Millicent! she
would die of mortification and pique," thought Strathmore,
as he looked up the elm-walk at its crossed light and shade,
with a smile in which there was a dash of contempt. He had
been loved by women who might well have claimed to haunt
his memory; proud, peerless beauties, who might well have
looked to rouse the swift imperious passion which, *when* they
loved—that unloving race!—the love of the Strathmores had
ever been; but he had cared for none of them, and this wasting of hours, this ceaseless adoration of women, this worshipping of a mistress's eyebrow, was incomprehensible and
somewhat contemptible in his sight. He never was so nearly
losing patience with Erroll as when he came in evidence with
the perpetual gallantries, the never-ending, ever-changing
grandes passions, as easily lit as cigars and as quickly thrown
aside, that were characteristic of the Sabreur, and his best
beloved pursuit. Strathmore would as soon have understood
consuming his time in constantly blowing soap-bubbles!—he

looked now with a certain disdainful amusement at them where they stood; then, unseen himself, he turned, and making the dogs quiet with a sign, crossed the avenue, and went along beside the sunken fence of the deer-park by another route homeward, so that he should neither spy upon nor interrupt them.

Such game was Erroll's especial sport, if he found it on the lands of White Ladies he was fully welcome to the preserves undisputed.   Strathmore did not envy him either the small amusement of slaying, or the inevitable trouble of the game when slain! A quarter of an hour later on, as he crossed the lawns that lay in front of the Abbey, while the chimes of the bells were still ringing the curfew with low mellow chants and carillons, he heard a step behind him, and as he turned faced the Sabreur, who came along smoking, blandly unconscious that he had been seen in his tête-à-tête under the elms.

"Had good sport in the coppice, mon cher! What did you mean by giving us the slip like this?" said Strathmore, as he swung round and waited for him.

"Pretty good; rabbits were rather shy," answered Erroll, with the meerschaum between his lips, and the most tranquil air of innocence that the human countenance ever wore.

"But la belle *wasn't!*—you seemed very good friends; is she an old acquaintance or a new? Is the game in the bag or only marked; hit or only just flushed? I expect the whole story in the smoking-room to-night!"

A certain dash of annoyance and discomfiture went over Erroll's face for the moment, but he laughed:

"Hang you! where did you see me?"

"Where you were very plainly to be seen! If you make open-air rendezvous, Bertie, you must be prepared for spectators. Who is she? If the game's been found on my lands, I think it is fair I should have an account of it. Is she an old love or a new?"

"Not new," laughed the Sabreur, pulling his Glengarry over his forehead, to keep the sunset glare out of his eyes.

"*Not* new! I thought you gave no more thought to old loves than to old gloves—the gloss off both, both go to the devil! I suppose you found her up last autumn, when you were down here in my place? I was in the East, so I am not responsible for what happened! You might have told me, my dear fellow; *I* shouldn't have rivalled you; pretty peasants never had any attraction for me; I like the *tournure* of the world, not the odour of the dairy. Give me grace and wit, not rosy cheeks and fingers fresh from the churn and the hencoop; the perfume of frangipane, not of the farm-yard. Petrarch might adore a miller's wife—it is not my line—and I think the flour must have made Laura's '*chiome d'oro*' look dusty: I never took a mistress from my tenantry! Who is she, Erroll?"

Erroll sent a puff of smoke into the air, and turned to Strathmore with his gay insouciant laugh, clear as a bell and sweet as a girl's, that had so much *youth* in it:

"I'll tell you some other time. Old story, you know, nothing new in it. We're all fools about women, and she beats any of those we shall have to-night hollow, Lady Millicent and all of 'em!"

Strathmore raised his eyebrows:

"An *old* love! and you're as enthusiastic as that? What must you have been in the beginning! Thank Heaven I was not here. Poor Lady Millicent! sal volatile by the gallon would never restore her if she knew a young provincial, smelling of the hayfield, with a set of cherry ribbons for a Sunday, and a week-day aroma of the cowshed (if not the pigsty), was said by the difficile Sabreur to beat her hollow! —and she a Court beauty and a Lady in Waiting! So much for taste!"

"Pigsty? Cowshed? You didn't see her just now, Cecil; you couldn't!" broke in Bertie, disgusted.

"I saw a woman, my dear Erroll; she was your property, and I noticed no more."

"For God's sake don't suppose me such a Goth that I should fall in love with a dairymaid, Strath!" said Erroll, plaintively. "She's nothing of that sort—nothing, I give you my honour! Let me clear my character, pray. *Should* I love a 'Phillis in a hazel-bower?' I hate cobwebs, dew, and ear-wigs; and I can't bear a coarse colour for a woman! I say, don't let out anything about it, though, will you? Don't tell the other fellows; there's no object, and they'd only——"

"Chaff you? Exactly!"

"No! I don't care a straw for chaff," said Erroll, medita-tively. "It's only boys who mind chaff, *we* don't. But they might get hunting her out, you see—would, I dare say, *I* should in their place—and I don't want that. I wish to keep the thing quiet. I have managed to do it hitherto; and she would cut up as rough at insult as Lady Millicent herself; you understand?"

"Not very clearly; but it doesn't matter; one doesn't look for perspicuity in love intrigues—nor for reason."

"Hang you! you know what I mean," murmured the Sa-breur, lazily.

"You mean, you don't want me to tell of your tête-à-tête, and set the men on to badger you about it when the women are gone? Very well! I'm silent as the dead!" laughed Strathmore. "What a wicked dog you are, Bertie, on my word, though. Country air ought to purify your morals; one naturally sins in cities, but——"

"Inevitably sins in villages! Just so, one's nothing else to do! In town, one sins from sociability; in the country, from solitariness—a safe indication that the soft sins are the natural concomitants of one's existence everywhere, and shouldn't be resisted!"

"Admirable theory!—developed in practice, too, by its preacher, which can't be said of all precepts. Arcadia and the Rue Bréda have more in common than one generally fan-cied then; but I shouldn't have thought *you'd* have taken to provincial amourettes, Sabreur! However, failing hot-house fruits, I suppose you take a turn at blackberries? What an odd state of existence it must be, not to be able to live

twenty-four hours without finding some woman's eyes to look
into!"

"Very natural, I think!—when women's eyes are the pleasantest mirrors there are, and framed on purpose for us. You
were never in love in your life, Strath."

"I was never the fool of a woman, if you mean that."

"You've brought over a prima donna, because, in a cold
sort of way, you thought her a handsome Roman," went on
Erroll, disdaining the interruption—"or you've taken up the
Montolieu, because she made a dead set at you; and because
one has a Montolieu as naturally as one has a cigar-case or a
pair of slippers—or you've made love to some grande dame
because it answered a political purpose, and advanced a
finesse to be in her boudoir when everybody else was shut
out of it; but as for *love*—you know nothing about it!"

Strathmore laughed:

"I know as much as any wise man knows. I know just
as much as flavours life—any more disturbs it. I like a
woman for her beauty, but I should be particularly sorry to
sup in raptures off a single smile, to tie my hands with a
golden hair, and to go mad after the shape of an ankle, as
you do with a dozen divinities in as many months. A week
or two ago you were wild about the Clinton, who *is* worth
looking at, I grant you, and now, I dare say, you've lost your
head just as completely for little Phillis yonder, with her
hands in the butter! My dear Bertie, it's positively inex-
plicable to me; I can fancy your kissing the lips, if they're
pretty ones, of all those goddesses, but I can't possibly understand your caring about the goddesses themselves!"

"Hold your tongue!—and, for Heaven's sake, don't suppose I'm in love with a human churn! Hands in the butter;
what an idea!" murmured the Sabreur, disgusted.

"Well! it must be a cabbage-rose this time, conservatory
ones don't grow about the home farms. Or if it isn't——"

Strathmore stopped, struck with a sudden thought, and
swung round, as they walked under the cloisters, his face as
he turned to Erroll softening with that smile which took from

it all that was cold, dark, and dangerous in its physiognomy, and gave to it an almost tender warmth—a warmth that as yet no woman had had the magic to waken there. He laid his hand on Erroll's shoulder with the old familiar gesture of their Eton days, as they came out of the aisles of the cloisters on to the lawn that stretched smooth and sunny before an antique grey terrace, with broad flights of steps hung with ivy, looking down on to thick avenues and long glades of trees, like the terrace at Haddon, where Dorothy Vernon fled in the summer moonlight to the love of John Manners.

"Erroll, I say, it is no entanglement, no annoyance, is it, this affair of yours?"

Erroll threw his cigar away, shook his head, and laughed:

"Not in the least; except—that my conscience smites me a little for it sometimes. That's all!"

Strathmore's hand rested still on his shoulder, lying there in the safe, cordial grasp of a friendship warm as the friendship of David for Jonathan.

"*Conscience!* How exceptional you are! The word's out of all modern dictionaries, and *rococo* from use. But what I meant was, if you had any difficulty of any kind—if you need to shake yourself free from any embarrassments—you would keep to your promise and let me serve you in all ways? Remember, old fellow, you gave me your word?"

He meant that Erroll would let him assist him more substantially than by advice. The Sabreur was a man about town, with little more to float him than a good name and a fashionable reputation, lucky Baden "coups" and dashed-off magazine articles; his debts were heavy sometimes, his embarrassments not a few, though on his gay sunny nature they never weighed long; he was, very literally, a "beggared gentleman," though his beggary was as joyous and insouciant a Bohemianism as might be; and Strathmore, who was generous to an extreme, and ascetically indifferent to riches, had always pressed him, and sometimes, though generally with the utmost difficulty, compelled him to accept his aid; without bond or payment.

His hand lay on Erroll's shoulder where they stood at the foot of the terrace steps, and the light from the west fell full upon his face as Strathmore looked at him—it was so frank, so glad, with a smile as bright as a girl's upon it, that many years afterwards Strathmore saw it in memory fresh as though beheld but yesterday.

"Dear old fellow! I know you would! *If* I needed, I would ask you as freely as though you were my brother;" and Erroll's voice was rich and full as he spoke, like the voice of a woman when she speaks of, or to, that which she loves: then he laughed with the gay carelessness of his temper. "But there's no need here; *I'm* not the sufferer. They are not panther griffes, like your Montolieu's or La Julia's, confound her! *I* play the tiger part if there be one in the duo. I say, Strathmore, what a confounded bore your going off to Servia—Bosnia, Bulgaria, where is it? Won't Prince Michel wait?"

"Prince Michel would willingly wait till doomsday rather than see *me*, but the F. O. won't. It *is* a bore; I didn't want to leave till over the First; however, *diplomatie oblige!* and there'll be a good deal of finesse wanted. It is an errand quite to my taste."

"Perhaps you'll see this adorable Vavasour and Vaux beauty on the Continent. Do try!"

"And report her to you, as game worth your coming over to mark or not, as the case may be? Your *paysanne* won't hold her ground long against the Peeress, if she's only a tithe of what Rokeby says. I will make note for you accurately *if* I see her; and I may come back through Paris in the spring. The deuce! it's getting very late. Those people will all be here before we are dressed for dinner," said Strathmore, as he crossed the terrace, entered the house, and went up to his dressing-room that looked out across the pleasaunce and the deer-park that lay beyond.

Lady Millicent came, haughty, lovely, and bewitching, with the Harewood people and several others, to dinner that night at White Ladies, in the great dining-hall that had been the refectory of the old Dominicans. Where travel-worn pilgrims and serge-clothed palmers, footsore and bronzed by Eastern suns, had sat and supped, telling of miracles of Loretto or persecutions from the Moslem to the listening brethren, pretty women with diamonds glancing in their hair, and smiles brightening in their languid, lustrous eyes, sat at the table, covered with gold plate, and Bohemian glass and delicate Sèvres, with rich fruits and brilliant exotics, and Parian figures holding up baskets odorous with summer blossom, while the wines sparkled pink and golden in their carafes, and flushed to warm, ruby tints in the silver claret-jugs. Where the white robes of the Dominicans had swept, the perfumed laces and silks of their trailing dresses as noiselessly moved; where the Latin chant of the Salutaris Hostia had risen and swelled, the low laugh of their musical voices echoed; where the incense had floated in purple clouds, the bouquet of Burgundies and the perfume of Millefleurs scented the air; where the silent monks had sat and broken black bread in the monarchical gloom of their woodland Abbey, Lady Millicent and her sisters flirted and smiled, and brushed the bloom off a hothouse grape, and trifled with the wing of an ortolan, while the light flashed azure-bright in their sapphires, and the opals gleamed in their bosom. Le Roi est mort. Vive le Roi! So To-day succeeds to Yesterday, and the dead are supplanted and the past is forgot! Where the viaticum last night was administered to the dying, the laugh of the living echoes gaily this morning, and in its turn the laugh will die off the air, and the chant of the tomb will come round again. Such is life and such is death, and the two are ever fused together and twisted in one inseparable cord, the white line running with the black, side by side, crossed and recrossed, following each other as the night the day!

"You incorrigible fellow, what would your wood-nymph have said to you if she'd seen you making such desperate love to Lady Millicent to-night?" said Strathmore, as he and Erroll passed down the corridor to the smoking-room, as the last roll of the carriages echoed down the avenue.

"The deuce!" laughed Erroll. "If they had a lorgnon long enough to let them see any of us when we're away from them, the tamest Griseldis would have little to say to us when we went back to her! Those poor women! they're shockingly cheated."

"They have their revenge, mon cher. If we're their first instructors in mischief, they take to the lesson very kindly, and improve on it fast enough!" laughed Strathmore. "If M. son Mari deceive Lucretia, Lucretia soon turns the tables, and dupes her lord. They are quits with us, and don't want any pity. I wish your luckless wood-nymph had seen you go on with the Clinton to-night! I am curious really to know how you get up the steam fresh every time; now with a duchess, and now with a dairymaid, now with a blonde, and now with a brune!"

"Afin de varier les couleurs!"

quoted Erroll, appropriately, wrapping about him his seed-pearl broidered and sable-lined dressing-gown, dainty and costly enough for Lady Millicent's wear.

"Caramba!" broke in Strathmore. "I have a good mind to punish your inconstancy by betraying your incognita. Such a monopoly of the wild game and the tame birds at once isn't fair. I'll tell Danvers the whereabouts of your preserves."

"No, no! Don't! there's a good fellow," interrupted Erroll, quickly. "You see—it would only bother one—and——"

Strathmore laughed as he opened the door of the smoking-room, and the flood of warm light streamed out from within:

"We don't like poaching in neglected preserves even! I understand, my dear fellow. Bag your big game and your small, make love to your Court belle and your country girl both at once, and just as you like! *I* won't set the beaters after either. Have I not said I'll be silent as death? Entrez! Bah! there is Phil smoking those wretched musk-scented cigarettes again; they are only fit for Lady Georgie or Eulalie Papellori. What taste, when there are my Havannahs and cheroots!"

CHAPTER III.

The Vigil of St. John.

IT was the Vigil of St. John in Prague.

The stars were coming out one by one in the clear violet skies, that were still yellow in the west with the beams of a setting sun; and the dews of the evening were moist upon the thick foliage of the Lorenziberg and the vineyards of the Anlagen, encircling the city with their fresh green zone. The lights, already lit upon the bridges, were mirrored in the waters of the Moldau, or the Veltava, as it is called by its softer Czechen name that ran like a broad smooth silver band beneath their arches; and the glare from the western skies fell on the gilt crosses of the Teyn church, making them blaze and sparkle with fiery brilliance, while the mosque-like spires of a thousand towers stood out clear and delicate as fairy handiwork in the warm golden haze, as the measured chant of litanies, sung by gathered multitudes, rose and fell with slow sonorous rhythm on the hush of the coming night. For many nights and days before, the hum of collecting people and the weary tramp of tired feet had been heard throughout the city, as devotees of every stock and province had flocked far and near, from wild Silesian forests, from remote Bavarian mountains, from Saxon hamlets buried in their pine-woods, and charcoal-burners' châlets in Moldavian wilds, and Czechen homesteads nestled in their cherry orchards, to the great Festival of Holy Johannes of Nepomuk, at whose most sainted martyrdom, as Legend and Church record, five stars arose and glittered in the waters where the Saint sank, a thousand years ago, and gleamed in golden radiance, heaven-sent witnesses to innocence.

At the Cathedral and in the Platz, before the stars and statue on the bridge, and around the bronze ring in St. Wenzel's Chapel, at every smaller shrine and lesser altar through the city, the dense crowd of pilgrims knelt, all their heads bowed down in prayer, as the numberless ears of wheat in a corn-field bend with one accord before the sweep of a summer breeze. There is something oddly touching, pathetic, majestic, almost sacred in the sight of a surging sea of human life! What is it that is grand and impressive in a dense silent crowd, collected together, no matter whether that crowd be a mass of troops in the Champ de Mars, the gathering of the people upon Epsom Downs, or a countless assembling of peasants in Prague on a Holy day? What is it? Taken individually, the units of each are unimpressive, grotesque, common-place; a French chasseur, an English touter, a Sclavonian glass engraver, have no sublimity about them taken singly. But in their aggregate, there is that same strange, nameless, mournful solemnity which brought hot, unbidden tears to the eyes of the man who, while the Magi offered libations to the manes of the Homeric heroes, sat on the white throne at Abydos, looking down on the crowded Hellespont, and the countless thousands that were gathered by the shores of Scamander, beneath the shadow of Mount Ida, while the sunlight glittered on the golden pomegranates of the Immortal Guard, and the gorgeous robes of the Thracians fluttered in the winds. Perhaps with him, we vaguely, unwittingly, involuntarily compassionate these vast multitudes, of which in a century there will not be one who has not been gathered to his tomb; and the depth of the sadness lends a sanctity to these crowds, whose goal is the grave, which the chill and shallow philosophies of an Artabanus cannot whisper away: for we too are wending thither in their company, we too must turn our steps from golden Abydos, and lay us down to die at Salamis!

It was the Vigil of St. John. Pyramids of gas-jets flared up to the skies, the Five Stars commemorative of the Saint of Nepomuk glittered on the parapet in the evening air: there was no sound but the swelling melodious cadence of the Latin litanies, chanted by a million voices in solemn and regular rhythm, filling the night with music, full, rich, mournful as the glorious harmonies that peal from cathedral choirs at a midnight mass. And an Englishman strolling through the

city on foot (for no carriages are permitted in the Platz and
Bridge at the Vigil and Festival of St. John), looked down on
the kneeling multitudes with a smile on his lips, a smile that
had perhaps a little of the sadness of the Persian as he gazed
down on the Ægean, and more of natural disdain for these
superstitions before him, which were but type of the bigotries
of a wider world, where difference from *him* is your neighbour's measure of your difference from Deity, and where we
are bidden to accept our creed, as in the time of the Moli-
nistes they were bidden to accept the Pouvoir Prochain, by
no better rule than that "il faut prononcer le mot des *lèvres*
de peur d'être hérétique de *nom!*"

As he strolled down Wenzel's Platz, in the centre of which
sprang a tree of gas, with a myriad of burning luminous
leaves, that threw their glare on the kneeling devotees as they
bowed in adoration before the holy shrines, a carriage that
had come into the square against all rule —for the best reason,
that the horses had broken away, frightened at the music, the
lights, the crowds, and had taken their own way thither, beyond their driver's power to pull them in—dashed down the
Platz at a headlong gallop. The crowd of pilgrims were too
densely packed to have power to move to save themselves by
separation or by flight; they fell pêle-mêle one on another,
the stronger crushing the weaker, according to custom in
every conflict, calling on Jesus and the Mother of God and
Holy Johannes to preserve them from their fate, shrieking,
praying, sobbing, swearing; while the horses, maddened by
the tumult and the gas glare, tore across the square, dragging their carriage after them like a wicker toy. Nothing
less than a heavenly interposition, miraculously great as the
Five Stars of Holy Johannes, could save the people in their
path from death and destruction; the carriage rocked and
swayed, its occupant clasping her hands and crying piteously
for help; the horses dashed through the kneeling multitude,
knocking down aged men and sobbing children and shrieking women in their headlong course; the oaths and prayers
and screams rose loud and shrill, half drowned in the rich

sonorous chant of the litanies from priests and pilgrims beyond, that swelled out uninterrupted from every lighted shrine and blazing altar.

Death was imminent for many—death in the hour of prayer, death on the eve of glad festivity;—the horses, snorting, plunging, flinging the white foam from their nostrils, trampled out a merciless path through the close-packed crowd, and trod down beneath their hoofs what they could not scatter from their road. The blaze of gas, the loud swell of the chants, the glitter of the altar lights, the wild tumult and uproar about them, terrified and maddened them. Death was in their van, and in their wake, for all the multitude kneeling there in prayer; but—as they neared the spot where the Englishman was; who had not moved a yard, and calmly waited their approach, he stood firmly planted, as though made of granite, in their path, and catching them, with a sudden spring, by their ribbons close to the curb, checked them in full flight with a force that sent them back upon their haunches. It needed what he had, an iron strength and perfect coolness; even with these to aid him it was a dangerous risk to run, for if they shook themselves free, the infuriated beasts would trample him to death.

They reared and plunged wildly, flinging the foam, tinged with blood, over their chests and flanks, and into his eyes, till it blinded him with the spray; they lifted him three times up off the ground by his wrists with a jerk sufficient to wrench his arms out of their sockets, with a strain enough to make every fibre and muscle break and snap. Still he held on; they had met their master, and had to give in at last; they were powerless to shake off his grip; and, tired out at last with the contest, they stood quiet; panting, trembling, passive, fairly broken in, their heads drooping, their limbs quivering, blood where the curbs had sawn their mouths, mixed with the snowy foam that covered them from their loins to their pasterns. He let go his hold; his face was pale, and calm, as though he had lounged out of a ball-room; but his eyes glittered and gleamed dark with a swift, dangerous passion—a passion that was evil. He stretched his hand up, without speaking, to the coachman for his whip; the man stooped down and gave it to him: and, clearing the crowd wide with a sign, he lashed the horses, pitilessly, fiercely— lashed them till the poor brutes, spiritless, powerless, and trembling, stood shaking like culprits before their judge. That merciless punishing done, his passion had spent itself; the horses were broken down to the quietness of lambs, and might have been guided by a young child; letting go his hold on them again, he approached the carriage window, and lifted his hat as carelessly and indifferently as though he were bowing to some acquaintance in the Ride or the Pré Catalan.

"Madame, you must be very much terrified, but I trust you have not been hurt?" he said, in German, to the single occupant of the carriage, who, leaning out, eagerly, and with grateful empressement, stretched to him two delicate, un- gloved, jewelled hands.

"Monsieur! Mon Dieu! how brave you have been! You have saved my life—and at the risk of your own! What can I say to you? How can I thank you?"

As the glare from the gas-pyramid near and the lights burning on the shrine fell upon her face, he saw that it was one of rare and exceeding loveliness, and smiled slightly as her warm white hands touched his own, that were aching and throbbing with pain:

"Madame, I am thanked already—*par un regard de vous!* Is there any way in which I can have the honour to assist you?"

Before she could reply, the carriage moved. The driver, a rough, ill-mannered Czech, who wasted no words and no time, started off his trembling horses afresh; he was impatient to be out of the crowd, who, recovering from their terror were swearing bitterly at him in a hundred guttural dialects, and screaming vociferous indignant wrath; and he was afraid, moreover, of the arrival and the fury of police officials. With- out awaiting orders, he started off back again through the square, and the carriage rolled away down the Platz, bearing its occupant out of sight; a broidered handkerchief she had dropped, as her hand met her deliverer's, was the only relic left of her, where it lay on the stones at his feet. The pilgrims, closing over the vacant spot as the vehicle rolled away, crowded round the Englishman who had saved two-thirds of them from imminent death, with impetuous, demonstrative, enthusiastic gratitude, the vivacious Sclavonians calling on the Mother of God and Holy Johannes to bless and reward him, showering down on him a thousand valedictions in harsh Saxon and vehement Czechen; the women holding up their children to look at him, and remember his face, and pray for him for ever; the terrified peasants kissing his clothes in frantic adoration, canonising him then and there, and calling down upon his head the blessing of the whole heavenly roll of saints and angels; while through the multitude ran a breathless whisper, that their deliverer was none other than St. John of Nepomuk himself, descended on earth in human form to save and champion his faithful people, keeping watch and prayer at his Vigil in Prague!

To be canonised was very far from his taste, and the vehement gratitude lavished upon him was an infinite bore. The vociferous worship of the crowds could very well have been dispensed with, and signing them off to leave him a clear path, he pushed them away, and breaking free from their eager clamour with some difficulty, he walked down the Platz, striking a fusee and lighting a cigar as he went—an act that slightly disturbed the pilgrims who had canonised him, and shook their faith as to his saintship: Holy Johannes would never have smoked!

As he moved from the spot, he saw the handkerchief lying at his feet, and stooped and raised it; it was of gossamer texture, bordered with delicate lace; it was subtilely perfumed, and in the corner, broidered with fantastic device, was a coronet and an interlaced chiffre, whose initials were too intricately interwoven for him to be at the pains to decipher them. It was a woman's pretty toy; some men would have kept it in souvenir of this Vigil of St. John when a face so marvellously lovely had beamed upon them; he was not one of those; it was not his way. For a moment he took it up to thrust it in the breast of his waistcoat, more without thought than from any motive in the action; but as he did so he was passing a pretty Bohemian glass-engraver, whose bright black eyes sparkled with eager longing as her pretty brunette's face looked out from her yellow hood, and she saw the dainty scented handkerchief in his hand. He threw it to her, dropping the little gossamer toy, with its broidered coronet, into her bosom.

"It will please you better than me, little beauty," he said carelessly, as he went on through the thickly-packed crowd, smoking, and not taking in return the caress she would willingly have allowed; as the pilgrims returned to their prayers, closing over the vacant spot, and the chanted orisons, broken off for a while, rose again in slow-measured harmonies, the litanies ringing out into the silent air, the lights burning on the blazing altars, and the dense crowds bowing down before the shrines throughout the city, while the golden cross of the Teyn church glittered in the light of the stars, and the hushed skies brooded in the twilight of the coming night over the towers and the palaces, the river and the vineyards, the lighted altars, and the frowning fortresses of antique and historic Prague.

CHAPTER IV.

A Titian Picture seen by Sunset-Light.

"MOUTON qui rêve, are you thinking of Prague and of me?"

A cumbersome Czechen boat was dropping down the Moldau, its sails idly flapping in the sultry June night, in which not a breath of wind was stirring, while the mournful music of some of the national lays broke on the air from a little band of musicians playing in the aft of the vessel, wild, sweet, and harmonious, as though they were the melodies of legendary Rübezahl and his Spirit Band. The boat was chiefly filled with peasantry going by water to a fair at Aussig, and bright-eyed glass-engravers, with yellow or scarlet kerchiefs on their black-haired heads, were laughing merrily with each other, and casting mischievous glances at the sailors as they passed them. It was such a summer night as you may see any year in Bohemia; the lazy, silent hour when the hot, toilsome, blazing day is sinking into the warm, still, tranquil night; when the peasantry leave their field-work, chanting fragments of Sclavonic songs; when the engravers put aside their little graving-wheels, and lean out for a breath of air from their single window under the eaves; when the cattle wind homeward down the hill-side paths, and in the doorways of the Gasthof, under the cherry-trees, the gossipers drink their good-night draughts of Lager and Bayerisches. The orchards, white with blossom, bowered gaily-painted homesteads; the dark red roofs peeped out of châlets half hidden under holly-hocks; the poppy grounds glowed scarlet, catching the last gleam of the setting sun; and over the rye-fields a low western breeze was blowing from the fir-covered hills as the vessel floated down the stream, passing green wooded creeks, and pine-woods growing between the clefts of riven rocks, and golden glimpses of hazy distance from the banks through which the Moldau wound its way.

"Mouton qui rêve, are you thinking of Prague and of me, mon ami?"

The voice was low, and sweet, and rich—that most ex-cellent thing in woman; and the speaker was worthy the voice, where she sat leaning amongst a pile of shawls and cushions with which her servant had covered the rough bench of the boat, as an Odalisque might have leaned amongst the couches of the Odà, with as much Eastern grace and as much Eastern languor. A *blonde aux yeux noirs*, her eyes were long and dark and lustrous, with a dangerous droop of their thick curling lashes, but her skin was dazzlingly fair, with a deli-cate bloom in her cheeks; the hair was not golden, nor auburn, nor blond cendré, but what I have only seen once in my life, the "yellow hair" of the poets, of Edith the Swan-necked, and of Laura of Avignon; the lips were beautiful—a trifle too full and too sensual, feminine detractors would have objected, but Béranger would have sung of them:

> pour ma lèvre qui les presse
> C'est un défaut bien attrayant!

and it was a mouth that surely smiled destruction! It was a face, brilliant, tender, marvellously lovely like a face of Titian or of Greuze, as she leant among her cushions, with a black veil over her hair, thrown there with the grace of a Spanish mantilla; and her white hands lying on the rough wooden edge of the vessel, with their rings gleaming in the sunset glare. Her eyes were dwelling on the face of a man who leant over the boat-side within a few yards of her, and who was looking down into the water, a cigar in his mouth, and his profile turned towards her;—dwelling with curiosity, admiration, satisfaction. A woman appreciated better than a man the peculiar and varied meanings of that physiognomy; women will not often see widely, but they always see microscopically; they cannot analyse, but they have invariably rapid intuition.

"It is a face of Vandyke! so much repose, with so much passion. I like it. It tells a story, but a story whose leaves are uncut," she thought to herself, as she leaned forwards, touched his arm with a branch of cherry-blossoms she held, and challenged him with her laughing words, "Mouton qui rêve!"

He turned; he had not seen her there before, though both had been on board some half hour; and as the light blow of the cherry-blossoms struck his arm, scattering their snowy petals, and her low, soft laugh fell on his ear, he recognised the face that he had seen a few days before in the gas glare of the Vigil of St. John, whose broidered handkerchief he had dropped into the bosom of a Bohemian peasant girl, instead of treasuring it in recollection of one so fair. Such a woman would have won courteous welcome and recognition from a Stagyrite or a nonogenarian; and he took the hand she extended to him soft, warm, and small, with sapphires and pearls gleaming on its ungloved fingers, lifting his hat to her with answering words of gratified acknowledgments. He had *not* been thinking of her, but Diogenes himself would not have had discourtesy enough to have told her so; and on a summer's evening, dropping down a river in a slow, tedious passage, such a rencontre to while away the time could not choose but be acceptable to any man.

"Ah, monsieur!" she said, softly, as he drew near to her, "how brave you were that night. To dare to stop those horses in full flight!—it was marvellous; it was heroic! You saved my life; how can I ever thank you well enough?—ever show you half my gratitude?"

"Hush, madame, I entreat you!" he said, with a smile, that was rather the calm conventional smile of courtesy than the warmer one she was used to see lighten at her glance. "You have thanked me abundantly; if you do more, you will make me ashamed of having served you so little. Few men would not envy me so rich a recompense as lies in having won the smallest title to your gratitude!"

La blonde aux yeux noirs looked up at him searchingly through her silky lashes, and laughed a pretty, mocking, airy laugh.

"Graceful words! but are they *meant?*"

"Ah, madame!" he answered, laughing, as he seated himself beside the fair stranger, into whose path accident had thrown him so agreeably. "Perhaps that is a question that it is always wisest never to ask of any words at all!"

"What an odd man!" thought the lovely Odalisque of the Moldau, letting her eyes rest on the countenance that had for her, as it had for most women, a peculiar fascination, while she laughed again. "Very true! Some women will tell you, monsieur, they do not like compliments—never believe them; it is only that the grapes are sour. *I* like flattery. I live on it as children live on bonbons; if it be not sincere, it is nothing to me, the blame lies on the bad taste of the flatterers. I must have my *dragées*, and, as long as they are sweet, what matter whether they are real sugar or only French chalk?"

"All offered to *you* must be genuine—you need have no fear!" he answered her—and he meant it. As he looked down on the dazzling incognita, whose insouciant freedom had yet all the grace and charm taught by the breeding of courts and beaux mondes, though critical and very difficult to please, he confessed to himself that he had never seen anything more lovely out of the pastelles of La Tour, or the dreams of Titian, than this young and brilliant creature found thus strangely out of place, and alone, in a Bohemian boat that was carrying a load of peasant passengers to Aussig Fair!

Who could she be?—a lady of rank, laissez faire and untrammelled, amusing herself with the romances and caprices of a momentary incognita; a Princess of the Tuileries, or of the Quartier Bréda; a Serene Highness of some Sesquipedalian-Strelitz, sans state and sans suite; or a Comtesse sans Châteaux (save en Espagne), with a face and a grace more fatal to her prey than her vin mousseux and her skilful écarté? As yet it was impossible to tell, and with a lovely woman so ungracious an interrogation can never be put as the insolent question, "Who are you?"

She looked up and met his eyes bent on her, as the light of the sun setting behind the pine-woods lit up her face and form, as she leaned among her cushions, into Rubens-like richness, with a bright touch of Fra Angelo and Carlo Dolce softness about the tableau.

"How strangely we meet, monsieur, on this clumsy little Czechen boat! I came by water, because the night was so warm; and you came from the same reason? Ah! *C'est le destin, monsieur!* We were fated to meet again."

"If fate will always serve me as kindly I will become a predestinarian to-morrow, and go in leading-strings with blind contentment!"

God help us!—how rashly we say things in this world. Long years afterwards we remember those idle, careless, unmeant words gaily uttered, and they come back to us like the distant mocking laughs of devils!—devils who tempted us, and now riot in their work.

"*C'est le destin!*" she said, smiling, her fair face, with its luminous eyes, looking the lovelier for that beaming coquettish smile. "But, monsieur, you have been my deliverer, may I not ask to know, who is it I have to thank for so daring a rescue as I owed to you in Prague?"

"Assuredly. My name is Strathmore—Cecil Strathmore."

"Strathmore?" she repeated, musingly. "It is a very pretty name, and a good one. Then you are English, monsieur? And if so, you are thinking, of course, what a strange incorrect whim of mine it is for me to be travelling alone with only my maid in a little Czechen boat in the evening? You English are so *raides*, so prudish!"

Strathmore laughed, as he wound the shawls about her that had dropped aside.

"The English are (though I am neither of the two, believe me), but they generally verify Swift's aphorism, that 'a nice man is a man of nasty ideas;' the chill icing is only to conceal dirty water, and they freeze—to hide what lies below! But may not I claim similar confidence, and entreat to know by name one for whom no name is needed, it is true, to make one remember her?"

She laughed, and shook her head in denial so charming that it was worth fifty assents.

"No, I am travelling incognita. I cannot reveal that secret. I like Romance and Caprice, monsieur, they are feminine privileges, and following them I have found far more amusement than if I had gone in one beaten track between two blank walls of Custom and Prudence. It may have made me enemies; but, bah! who goes through life without them?"

"None! and never those who awaken envy. Dulness and

mediocrity may live unmolested and unattacked, but people never tire of finding spots on a sun whose brilliance blinds them."

"Never!" she answered, with a naïve and amusing personal appropriation of his words. "If I had been born plain like some poor women, I should not have had so many *siffleurs;* but then, on the other hand, my *claque* would not have been so loud nor so strong; and the cheers always drown the hisses."

"You have had *siffleurs!* They must have bandaged their eyes, then, before taking so ungracious a rôle! Surely society hissed *them* for such atrocity!" said Strathmore, noticing the dazzling fairness of her skin and the exquisite contour of her form, and thinking to himself, "The deuce! she makes me talk as absurd nonsense as the Sabreur!"

"Of course it did, but *siffleurs* hiss on through all opposition, you know, monsieur——"

"Because it pays them!"

"No doubt. But, what do a few hisses matter, more or less, as long as one enjoys oneself in one's youth—one's delicious, irrecoverable youth? I suppose if I live long enough my hair will be white and my skin yellow, but I do not spoil my present by looking into the future. If it must come, let it take care of itself. It may never come—why mourn about it? Those people are *bécasses*, who work, and toil, and wear away all their good looks, and live hardly and joylessly only to hoard money to buy tisane, and nurses, and crutches, when all the zest of existence is gone from them, and given to a new generation that has pushed them out of their places? Doesn't Balzac say, that whether one sweeps the streets with a broom or the Tuileries with a velvet robe, it comes to much the same thing when one is old; the salt is equally out of the soup whether it is eaten in a Maison Dieu or in a ducal château!"

"Almost thou persuadest me to be an Epicurean!" smiled Strathmore, as he thought to himself, "Who on earth can she be!" and gazed down into her soft, laughing, lustrous eyes, languid yet coquettish, like the eyes of the women of Seville. "But *I* do not hold with you there, *ma belle inconnue;* to me it seems that with years alone can be gained what is worth gaining—power. The butterfly pleasure of youth can very well be spared for the ambitions that can only be reaped with maturity. A man has only become of real value, and able to grasp real sway, when he is near his grave."

"Ah, for your sex that is all very well, your youth lasts to your tomb, but with us—*nous autres femmes!*—with our beauty flies our sceptre. How can we reign after youth, without youth? You will not care for a mistress who is wrinkled!" cried the belle blonde, impatiently, the impatience of a lovely coquette incensed to be contradicted. "So, you think power the only thing worth having? Then you do not care for love, monsieur, I presume?"

"Well!—I must confess, not much."

It was rank heresy in the presence of so fair a priestess of the soft religion, it was a fatal challenge to the one who heard it, though Strathmore spoke the cold, careless, simple truth, and did not heed whether he offended or piqued a chance acquaintance of the hour by it.

"And yet that man *will* love, fiercely, imperiously, bitterly one day!" thought the Naiad of the Moldau, who, a stranger to him, as he to her, read his character by a woman of the world's clairvoyante perception, as he failed to read hers by a man of the world's trained penetration. "For shame!" she said, aloud, striking him a fragrant blow with her sprigs of cherry-blossom. "If you are heretical enough to feel so, mon ami, you should not be unchivalric enough to say so! Your bay wreaths will be very barren and withered if you don't weave some roses with them. Cæsar knew that. So you admire age because it will give you power; and I loathe it because it will rob me of beauty—what a difference! I wonder how we shall both meet it! But, bah! why talk of these things! The wind will be chilly, and the green leaves brown, and the ground frost-bound in six months' time; but the butterflies playing there above our heads are too wise to spoil the sunshine by remembering the snows. *They* are Epicureans; let *us* be so too!"

To such a doctrine, expounded by such lips, it was impossible to dissent. The sunset faded, the purple mists stole on down the slopes of the hills, the west wind rose, bringing a rich odour from the pine forests; the Bohemian musicians, for a few coins, sang airs sweet enough to have been played by the legendary music-demons of a land where Mozart rules; the boat dropped slowly down the stream in the evening twilight, and Strathmore leant over the vessel's side, talking on to his chance acquaintance, and looking down on to the exquisite Titian-like picture that she made, reclining on her pile of cushions, with the black mantilla of lace thrown on her yellow hair, and her dark lustrous eyes gleaming softly and dreamily in the light of the summer stars. He was singularly critical of the beauty of women, and coldly careless of their wiles and charms; yet even he felt a vague dreamy pleasure in floating down the river in the sultry moonlit night thus, with the echo of this sweet silvery voice in his ear, and a face on which he looked in the gloaming, soft as the music that lingered on the silent air. He would not altogether have found the voyage wearisome though it had lasted till the dawn; but—pardieu, mes frères! one never drops *long* down any river, real or allegorical, with a smooth current and Arcadian landscapes, under the shade of pleasant woodlands, beneath which we would willingly linger till sunrise, but that we are safe to be soon startled by the rough grate of the keel on the sand, that breaks the spell for evermore!

It was so now; the boat ground in a shallow bit of the water where red sunken rocks made the navigation troublesome for a vessel so cumbersome, and boatmen so clumsy, as were those who now steered it down the Moldau's course. No harm was done that could be of serious account, but the boat was stuck hopelessly fast between the rocks, and could not proceed to Aussig that night, at all events; while its passengers had no choice but to remain where they were till the sunrise, or to disembark at a landing-place which was luckily easily to be reached by a plank between the vessel and the shore, where, buried in the favourite cherry orchards of Bohemia, with a gaudy sign swinging under its dark red roof, half hidden in a profusion of giant hollyhocks, with linden-trees in full flower before the door, and the pine-covered hills stretching behind it, stood a little river-side Gasthof. The unknown, into whose society and in whose protection he was thus in a manner forced, laughed brightly, and made light of the contretemps when Strathmore explained it to her. "We must wait here?—very well! I like the smallest soupçon of an adventure. I will dine under those limes. I suppose they can find something to give us; but I must go on to-night if there be a vehicle procurable," she said, gaily and good-humouredly enough, without any feminine repining, as she gave him her hand to be assisted across the plank.

She was not altogether sorry to be able to retain as a *détenu* an English aristocrat, with a face like the Vandyke pictures; who was coldly indifferent to the soft creeds of which she was a head-priestess, and was a renegade and dis-believer in their faith. "Destiny throws us together, monsieur! We must be good friends. Dieu le veut!" she laughed, as Strathmore lifted her from the plank on to the landing-place, while the white soft hands lay in his, and the delicate fragrance of the perfumed hair floated across him, as the lace of her mantilla brushed his shoulder.

"I am the debtor of destiny, then!" he whispered, in answer, noting as she stood by him in the starlight the sweet grace and luxurious outline of her perfect form, that even the dark drapery of her travelling-dress, wrapped about in long voluminous folds, could not avail to hide.

Brothers mine!—it is well for us that we are no seers! Were we cursed with prevision, could we know how, when the idle trifle of the present hour shall have been forged into a link of the past, it will stretch out and bind captive the whole future in its bonds, we should be paralysed, hopeless,

powerless, old ere ever we were young! It is well for us that
we are no seers. Were we cursed with second sight, we should
see the white shroud breast-high about the living man, the
phosphor light of death gleaming on the youthful radiant
face, the feathery seed lightly sown bearing in it the germ of
the upas-tree, the idle careless word gaily uttered carrying
in its womb the future bane of a lifetime; we should see these
things till we sickened, and reeled, and grew blind with pain
before the ghastly face of the Future, as men in ancient days
before the loathsome visage of the Medusa!

CHAPTER V.

The Bonne-Aventure told under the Lindens.

CONTRETEMPS generally have some saving crumbs of con-
solation for those who laugh at fate, and look good-humouredly for them; life's only evil to him who wears it awkwardly,
and philosophic resignation works as many miracles as Har-
lequin; grumble, and you go to the dogs in a wretched style;
make mots on your own misery, and you've no idea how
pleasant a *trajet* even drifting "to the bad" may become.
So when the Czechen boat grated on the land and stuck
there, coming to grief generally and hopelessly, fortune was
so propitiated by the radiant smile with which its own scurvy
trick was received by the loveliest of all the balked travellers, that what would, under any other circumstances, have
been the most provoking bore, became a little episode picturesque and romantic, and took a *couleur de rose* at once under
the resistless magic of her sunny smile. It was a beautiful
night, starry, still, and sultry; the river-side inn stood like a
picture of Ostade, hidden in its blossomed limes; the pine-
woods stretched above and around, with the ruddy gleam of
gipsy fires flashing between the boughs; and with such a
companion as hazard had given him, Strathmore could hardly
complain of the accident, though he was a man who found
the gleam of women's eyes in a cabinet particulier of a

café, or a cabinet de toilette of a palace, far better than in all
the uncomfortably-romantic situations in the world, and held
that a little gallantry was infinitely more agreeable and
rational in a rose-tendre-hung chamber than *à la belle étoile*
in a damp midnight under the finest violet skies that ever
enraptured a poet.

The little hostelry was already full of travellers. Some
English *en route* to the waters of the Sprudel, some Moravians
and Bohemians on their way to or from Bucharest or Aussig;
and the arrivals from the boat filled it to overflowing, for its
accommodation was scant, and its attractions solely confined
to its gaily-painted and blossom-buried exterior. There was
but one common sitting-room, but one common supper-table,
and the guests, whether gräfins or glass engravers, were
treated without distinction: a Bohemian Gasthof is about the
only place upon earth where you see the doctrine of equality in
absolute and positive practice. The Sclavonians, accustomed
to it, took it unmurmuringly; the English tourists grumbled
unceasingly; preserved (the ladies in especial) a dead silence
to companions for whose respectability they had no voucher;
scorned the sausage, the baked pie, the cucumber-soup, and
the rest of the national *menu*, and solaced themselves with
gloomy consumption of hard biscuits from their travelling-
bags; while without, under the lindens, on the sward before
the door, Strathmore's Albanian servant making a raid upon
the Gasthof larder with the celerity of long continental experience, spread on a little table the best fried trout, Teplitz
and other fare that the inn afforded for the refreshment of the
fair traveller with the Titian face, who, refusing to enter the
hostelry, sat on a bench under the limes, leaning against the
rough bark as gracefully as amongst velvet cushions, looking
upward at Strathmore with her soft Orientalesque eyes, while
the leaves and flowers of the boughs swayed against her yellow hair.

She gave a Tokay flavour to the Lager, a Vatel delicacy
to the trout, a strange but charming spice of petits soupers
to this primitive supper under the limes; an unsuitable but

delicious aroma of Paris to the solitary river-side hostelry in Bohemian pine-woods. "Who could she be?" he wondered in vain; for on that head, under the most adroit cross-questioning, she never betrayed herself. She talked gaily, lightly, charmingly, with some little wit, and a little goes a long way when uttered by such lips. With something, too, of soft graceful romance, probably natural to her, perhaps only learned second-hand from *Raphael*, and *Indiana*, and *Les Nuits d'Octobre*; and Strathmore, though the light gallantries of a Lauzun had little charm for him, and the only passion that could ever have stirred him from his coldness would have been the deep, voluptuous delight, fierce and keen as pain, that swayed Sulla and Cimon, could not refuse his admiration of a picture so perfect as she sat in the light of the midsummer stars, leaning her head on her small jewelled hand, the lime-boughs drooping above her, and the dark, dimly-lit room within forming a Rembrandtesque background, while the river below broke against the rocks, and the heavy odour of the lindens and pines filled the air.

"How cold he looks, this handsome Strathmore, does he dare to defy me?" she thought, as she glanced upwards at him where he leaned against the trunk of the linden when the supper was finished, and while she herself still lingered under the limes as the stars grew larger and clearer in the May skies, and the purple haze of night deepened over the hills. He was the only man who had not bowed down at her feet at her first smile, and his calm courtesies piqued her.

"Do you like music, monsieur?" she asked him, with that suddenness which had in it nothing abrupt, but was rather the suddenness of a fawn's or an antelope's swift graces. Then, without awaiting a reply, without apology or prelude, inspired by that caprice which rules all women more or less, and ruled this one at every moment and in every mood, she began to sing one of the sweet, gay, familiar canzoni of Figaro, with a voice at which the nightingales in the linden-leaves might have broken their little throats in envying de-

spair.   Then, without pause, she passed on to the sublime
harmonies of the Stabat Mater—now wailing like the sigh
of a vesper hymn from convent walls at evensong, now
bursting into passionate prayer like the swell of a Te Deum
from a cathedral altar.   She sang on without effort, without
pause, blending the most incongruous harmonies into one
strange, bizarre, weird-like yet entrancing whole, changing
the Preghiero from Masaniello for one of Verdi's gayest
arias, mingling Kücken's Slumber Song with some reckless
Venetian barcarolle, breaking off the solemn cadence of the
Pro Peccatis with some mischievous chansonette out of the
Quartier Latin, and welding the loftiest melodies of Handel's
Israel with the laughing refrain of Louis Abadie's ballads.

Out on the still night air rose the matchless music of
voice, rich, clear, thrilling, a very intoxication of sound;
mingling with the ebb and flow of the waters, the tremulous
sigh of the leaves, and the rival song of the birds in the
boughs.   Those sitting within in the darkened chamber
listened spell-bound; the peasantry, laughing and chatting
under the low roof of the hostelry, hushed their gossip in
enchanted awe; the boatmen in the vessel moored in the
shadow below looked up and left off their toil; and—as suddenly as it had rung out on the summer air, the exquisite
melody ceased, and died away like the notes of a bell off the
silence of the night. She looked up at Strathmore, the starlight shining in the dreamy, smiling depths of her eyes, and
saw that he listened eagerly, breathlessly, wonderingly, subdued and intoxicated even despite himself by the marvellous
magic, the delicious intricacies, the luxurious richness of this
voluptuous charm of song, with a spell which—the moment it
ceased—was broken.

"You like music?" she asked him, softly; "ah, yes, I see
it in your face.   You Englishmen, if you be as cold as they
call you, have very eloquent eyes sometimes.   Are you not
thinking what an odd caprice it is for me to sing to you—a
stranger—at ten o'clock at night, under lime-trees?"

"Indeed, no; I am far too grateful for the caprice. Pasta

herself never equalled your voice; it is exquisite, marvellous!"

She laughed softly.

"Do you think so? And yet, I imagine, you are very difficult to please! When I sing some of those airs, the Inflammatus or the Agnus Dei, they make me think of the old days in my convent at Valladarra; how I used to beat my wings and hate my cage, and long to escape over the purple mountains. Why is it, I wonder, that a gloomy past often looks brighter than a brilliant present?—what is there in the charm of Distance to give such a golden chiar'oscuro?"

"Valladarra? Are you a Spaniard, madame?" he asked her, catching at any clue that might enlighten him as to the whence and the whither of the bewitching creature.

"A Spaniard? What makes you think so?"

"Because it is usually said, belle amie, that a Spanish blonde is the greatest marvel of beauty that the world ever sees," said Strathmore with a smile.

She laughed.

"Je vous remercie! Well, perhaps I am Spanish. You would like to know? Ah, bah! what a slander on my sex it is to say that Eve monopolised all curiosity!"

"Curiosity!" repeated Strathmore. "There may, surely, be a deeper interest that bears a better name, madame? When one lights on a matchless gem, or on a rarely lovely foreign flower, it is not unnatural that one may seek to know where it has come from, and where we may see it again."

"You are a courtier, M. Strathmore, and turn your phrases very prettily," said this most *provoquante* of all women, with the slightest possible shrug of her shoulders. "But it *is* curiosity, for all that; and, by all the rights of womanhood, I claim my title to the first indulgence of the privilege. Your name is Strathmore, and your servant calls you 'My lord,' and if asked about your country, you would answer, 'Civis Romanus sum,' with true Britannic bombast, I dare say. Well! England *is* figuratively rather like Rome, for it slays its Senecas, gorges its Vitelliuses, and is often garrisoned by ganders! But one more thing remains to know. *What* are you?"

Leaning her arms on the table, her chin on her hands, and resting her eyes upon him, she asked the point-blank question with the most charming insouciance and assurance of command; and Strathmore could not fail to satisfy her demand, though he was not fond of talking of himself; his egotism was of a much loftier sort.

"Ah! a diplomatist!" she said, raising her eyebrows. "Mon ami, I know your order: but you will not content yourself with settling internecine squabbles, and writing Cretan labyrinths of words, and being 'sent home,' like an expelled schoolboy, if your two countries quarrel for a split hair, will you? You will want the triumph of the *monstrari digito*, and the guidance of the helm through stormy waters, and you will pine for the old Medici and Strozzi days, when a stealthy arm could stretch and strike far away in a distant land, and a subtle brain could compass the supreme rule, and wield it, troubled by no scruples."

"Madame," said Strathmore, with a slight laugh, his laugh was usually cold, "if you draw such a sketch of me at first sight—though I don't really deny its accuracy—I fear I cannot have impressed you very favourably?"

"Why so? You are ambitious, by your own confession that you covet age for the sake of power; and ambitious men are all alike. If you had your own will, you *ambitieux* would check at no flights; and if we don't have the Medici and Strozzi secret murders in our day, I am afraid the virtue that refrains from them is nothing very much better than fear of the analytical chemists."

As she spoke, with a certain smile on her rose lips, and in the mocking light of her gazelle eyes, something in this brilliant and witching creature struck upon Strathmore as dangerous—almost as repulsive—and made him think of those women who gleam out from the pages of Guicciardini and Galluzzi, who dazzled all men who looked on them with the shine of their *tresse d'oro*, or the languor of their Southern eyes, yet whose white hands shook the philtre into the loving-cup, and whose title was "Opra d'incanti è di mala fattura." But the momentary impression passed off as she looked up laughing.

"Bah, M. Strathmore! Ambition is a weary work at its ripest; epicurean enjoyment is far better: 'gather your rosebuds while you may.' Old Herrick is the true philosopher!"

"Spoken by such lips, his theories are irresistible," smiled Strathmore; "only if one has the bad taste not to care much about the roses, how then? There can be nothing for it but to entreat some fair priestess of the creed to take one's conversion in hand."

"But converts have to pass through fiery ordeals; if you are wise you would not brave them. You despise love, mon ami; it will be the worse for you some day."

"I shall have no fear for the future; if I escape to-night untouched, I must, indeed, be clad in proof," smiled Strathmore. But the smile, like the compliment, did not please her; its flattery was contemptuous and derisive of her power. With quick intuition she saw that Strathmore had never been in love in his life, and would have defied any woman to make him so; and she smiled as she leant her head upon her arm, silent for once, playing with one of the lime-blossoms, and knowing that the moonlight was shining on a perfect picture which could not be improved, which might be broken by, speech. Strathmore was silent too; busied in restless, vague conjecture as to who and what this brilliant, capricious, dazzling, graceful creature could be, here thus alone, at night, travelling through Bohemia. While his eyes rested on her where she sat in the starlight, her beauty well befitting the sultry night, that was odorous with the fragrance of the limes and musical with the murmurs of the waters, breaking below against the rocks, the voice of a Zingara broke on his reverie and hers, as a gipsy-girl—one of a party camped among the pine-woods at the back of the Gasthof—drew near the group of lindens in the moonlight; a wild, dark, handsome Bohe-

mian, with a scarlet hood over her jetty hair, and her glittering eyes fixed longingly on the jewels that sparkled on the
hands of the fair inconnue, as she said, in a compound of
Czechen and Romany,

"Will you hear your fortune, fair lady? Let the Gitana
tell you your future."

The blonde aux yeux noirs, whose head was resting
thoughtfully upon her hand, started, and looked up in surprise as the handsome black-browed Arab, who might have
sat to Murillo or Salvator, approached her in the moonlight from the wooded shadows of the pine-forests behind
them.

"Let me prophesy for you, fair lady! I can look on the
palm of your hand and foretell you all things that will come
to you; the predictions of Redempta, daughter of Phara, can
never fail," chanted the Zingara, in a wild, monotonous recitative, that sounded hoarse and sad in the still summer
night as she drew nearer, her eyes glistening longingly on
the sapphire rings.

"Non, merci!" laughed the bright incognita, looking upward at the strange picturesque form of the Gitana, standing out in the starlight against the dark woods behind. "I
know my past and my present—it is plenty! I do not trouble
myself a moment for the future!"

"But in the past and the present lie the seed to bear fruit
in the future!"

The words spoken in Czechen sounded ominous and
mournful, falling from the lips of the Gitana like an augury
of ill; and the other shuddered a little as she heard, though
without comprehending, them. "What does she say?" she
asked of Strathmore. He translated them to her, and spoke
to the gipsy-girl in her own tongue, bidding her move away;
but the capricious songstress, whom the fancy of the moment swayed as completely as it sways a kitten or a child,
laid her hand on his arm as he stood beside her.

"No, no! don't send her away! She is like a picture of
Murillo. Let us hear some of her prophecies first. What

would she say to you, I wonder! I have a great curiosity to know your fate, my lord; the fate of a man who desires age and despises love! It must be an odd one! Come! cross her hand, and let her tell your *bonne-aventure.* Obey me at once! It is my whim and my pleasure, monsieur. Give her some silver and ask her your destiny!"

A lovely woman is never to be disobeyed without discourtesy, and pretty caprices are commands. With the white jewelled fingers lying on his arm, with the perfumy hair shining in the starlight, with the fair dazzling face upraised in the shadow of the linden-boughs, the sternest stoic could not have refused to chime in with her fancy, and please this charming tyrant in her most airy nonsense. Strathmore laughed, dropped a gold coin into the Gitana's brown hand, and, leaning against the trunk, stood awaiting his destiny from the coral lips of the handsome Arab in the silence of the summer night, while the distant lights of the gipsy fires gleamed fitfully through the dark pine-woods. The Zingara looked not at his hand, but up at his face, as the white, clear rays of the moon fell on it—on the aquiline outline of the features and the varied meanings of the physiognomy, on the proud and generous sweetness of the mouth, contradicted by the dark passions in the eyes and the cold straight line of the brows. She looked at him long and fixedly in silence, with a dreamy, vague stare in her own fathomless eyes, while her hands moved over the beads of a string of Egyptian berries:

"There will be love, and of the love sin, and of the sin crime, and of the crime a curse. And the curse will pursue with a pitiless bitterness and an unslackened speed, and when atonement is sought and made, lo! it may turn to ashes and to gall. The innocent may taste thereof, and share the doom they have not woven. Your woe will be wrought by your own hand, and you will eat of the fruit of your own past, and through you will come death. Redempta, the daughter of Phara, has spoken!"

The words fell slowly and sadly on the silence of the night, while the river-waves beat against the rocks with monotonous murmur, and the sough of the wind arose in the pine-forest, sweeping with a sudden chill through the sultry air; and as he heard them, a momentary shudder ran through Strathmore's veins at the destiny that the Gitana vaguely shadowed forth; an irrepressible coldness, like that which comes from the touch of a corpse, passed over him where he stood. And the incognita clung closer to him, her white hand closing on his arm, and her laughing lips turning pale:

"Mon Dieu! what a terrible fate!　Send her away.　She makes me tremble!"

Strathmore laughed, the impression of the ominous prophecy passing off as soon as it was made; and he threw another gold dollar to the Zingara:

"My handsome Arab! you might have been more courteous, certainly. If you wish your predictions to be popular, you must make them a little more lively.　Be off with you! Go and frighten the peasants yonder!"

"Redempta can say only that which she sees," murmured the Gitana, sadly and proudly, as she stooped for the gold where it shone on the turf, and turned slowly away, till her form was lost in the dense gloom cast by the shadow in the woods.

"What a horrible destiny!" said his companion again, not able so quickly to shake off the vague terror with which the sing-song chanting recitative of the Zingara had haunted her.

"She has terrified you?" laughed Strathmore.　"I am sorry for that, madame; you shouldn't have tempted prophecy in my behalf.　All seers from the religious world to the gipsy camp must make their predictions ominous, or they would carry no weight; and evil is so generally predominant in this life, that to croak is pretty sure to be on the right side."

"Ah, mon Dieu! do not jest!" cried the belle inconnue, with a little shiver of pretty terror.　"It is no laughing matter, such a horrible future."

"But it *is* a laughing matter, such a horrible *bonne-aventure*," said Strathmore, smiling, and thinking how lovely she looked as she shivered with pretty pretended fear, and clasped her hands, on which he noticed a mass of brilliant rings that might have belonged to an empress's toilette-boxes, but which didn't tell him much, since paste is very glittering, and defies detection by moonlight. "She deals in the Terrible—prophets always do, or what sway would they have over their dupes? You should have let her have told yours, madame; she would have given something better to the lines in so beautiful a hand."

"Ah, bah!" cried the incognita, shaking off her superstition with a sweet silvery laugh. "I know my future! I shall triumph by my beauty till that goes, and then I shall triumph by my intellect, which won't go. I shall tread my way on roses, and rule as Venus Victrix till grey hairs come and I have to take to enamelling; and then I shall change my sceptre, and begin écarté, embroglie, prudence, and politics. But I don't count on the change; I am not like you, and do not court Age——"

"Because you are not like me, and need not wait for Age to bring you Power; *your* power lies in a glance of the eyes and in all the 'purpureal light of youth'!" laughed Strathmore. "I fancy our ambition centres alike in ruling men, but—with a difference!"

"You are very secure in your future, despite all the Gitana's foretelling?" she asked him, with a curious glance, half-malicious, half-interested.

"Surely! We can make of our future what we like. Life is clay, to be moulded just at our will; it is a fool, or an unskilful workman, indeed, who lets it fall of itself into a shape he does not like, or lets it break in his hands."

"But one flaw may crack the whole!" said the fair stranger, as Strathmore's valet drew near them to announce the immediate departure of a clumsy vehicle, the only one the Gasthof could furnish, that had been engaged before their arrival by English travellers, and in which, at her urgent instance, Strathmore had taken the sole remaining places for herself and her maid. "Are they starting? I am ready!

My lord, I owe you more gratitude still; how deeply I grow in your debt! But I forgot; if I take these two places, you must remain under that miserable little red roof till to-morrow. I ought not to have done it; *mais—je suis egoïste moi!*"

"No matter! I am most happy to relinquish anything in your service," said Strathmore, as he took the hand held out to him within his own. He did not care about women, but this one was specially lovely and specially captivating, and thrown as she was on his courtesy, he could not refuse it her. "I shall sleep under the pines; it will not be the first time I have camped out, but, I confess, I was tempted to make you a prisoner, madame, perforce to-night, by bidding Diaz let the car go without you. Give me some praise for my self-abnegation!"

His voice was very melodious, and had a softness when he was quite guiltless of intending it, while his features, with their cold, proud Velasquez type, on which the passions that had never been roused still threw their shadow, had always a fascination for women, who, by the instinct of contradiction ever dominant in their sex, always seek to chain a man from whose hands their fetters slip. Her bright, soft, dazzling eyes looked up to his almost tenderly in the light of the midsummer stars:

"I will thank you when we meet again!"

"*When!* But what gage do you give me that we may ever do so? You refuse me any name, any address, any single clue; you oblige me to part from you in ignorance even of——"

"Who I am! The first question you Englishmen ask before you give your hand in friendship, or speak to your neighbour at a table d'hôte," interrupted the bright *capricieuse*, with a low, ringing laugh. "No! I will not give you even a clue. I will be a Chinese puzzle for your ingenuity. When we meet (and we shall; we are both in the world; we are cards of the same pack, and shall some time or other be shuffled together!), I will thank you for all your courtesy and chivalry, and pay my debt—comme vous voudrez! Till then, you must submit to mystery. I may be a prima donna, a dame d'industrie, a princess incognita, a dangerous Greek—you may think me whatever you like. You will remember me better if you are left in perplexity; your sex always covet the unattainable, and there is a golden charm in mystery that shall veil me—till we meet!"

"But I—what a cruel caprice! what an indefinite probation!"

"Do you good, mon ami! Perhaps you have never had to wait before; I fancy so! There! *they* are waiting, and we must part, monsieur. Adieu and au revoir!"

Tantalising, obstinate, capricious, wilful, wayward, but bewitching; all the more bewitching for that very quintette of faults—she let her hand linger in his where they stood in the shadow, with the moon shining on her upraised face, and the lime-blossoms swaying against her hair, delicately scented as the fragrance of their flowers, as he stooped towards her in farewell: a soft, subtle, amber-scented perfume, such as the tresses of Lesbia might have borne as she came from her odorous bath, or wound the roses amongst them at the banquet—a perfume that as he caught it had something of the same soft intoxication as her voice had carried with it in her song.

Another moment, and the hand that had lain in his, soft and warm as a bird, had unloosened its clasp, and the clumsy covered cart of the Gasthof, laden with its passengers, had rolled slowly from the door beneath the roofing of the lime-boughs, *la blonde aux yeux noirs* leaning out from its heavy tarpaulin, and looking at him with a gay farewell smile—leaving according to her vow, with the golden veil of mystery flung over her lovely, dazzling face, soft with Eastern languor, and bright with the brilliance of youth, that disappeared from his sight as the car, creaking slowly over the moss, was lost in the shadows of the pine-woods as it turned a bend in the hills, and left him behind—alone.

"Who the deuce can she be! Something very out of the common, talking to one at first sight about love, and singing

to the nightingales, au clair de la lune!   I never saw a lovelier creature in my life, nor a more nonchalante one; and yet
she isn't exactly Quartier Bréda style; she has more the look
of a court than a casino. Who the deuce can she be?" wondered Strathmore, as he threw himself down on the moss
under the limes, smoking and throwing stones idly into the
river that flowed below. He knew most courts and most
cities; he lived chiefly abroad, and thought he knew every
beauty in monde or demi-monde, sovereigns of the left hand
as of the right.   The numberless anomalies in this dazzling
inconnue piqued his curiosity—the first of her sex who had
ever so far excited him. Strathmore thought romance simply
insanity, and had lived at too thorough a pace to care to
twist a chance into an adventure, and make poetic material
out of a rencontre with a stranger, as other men might have
done.   But he thought of her, and of little save her, where he
lay smoking, while the river broke against its overhanging
banks, and the heavy odours of the pines rolled down from
the hills above. And as he mused over the bright capricious
mystery that had come and gone suddenly as a swallow
comes and goes through the air, and listened to the distant
chimes of churches and monasteries, tolling out the short
summer hours as the night wore away, to the villages sleeping below, he only thought once, as he caught the gleam of
the camp-fires flashing fitfully in the darkness from the gloom
of the pine-woods, with the dark lurid glare of a Rembrandt
scene, while their flames leapt up through the fan-like boughs
of the firs, of the destiny the Zingara girl had foretold him;
and then he smiled as he remembered the prophecy the
Gitana had made.

CHAPTER VI.

The White Domino powdered with Golden Bees.

"NOT seen La Vavasour!—mon cher, you have yet to live!" yawned Arthus de Bellus, Vicomte and Chambellan du Roi.

Cards and gold lay on the table in confusion in Strathmore's room at Meurice's; four or five men had been dining with him, and had been playing baccarat for the last hour or two, as more piquant than the olives and more tasteful than the Burgundies they had trifled with and left.

It was about twelve months since his run down the Moldau; affairs threatening to the peace of the Principalities had kept him much longer than he had imagined, and this was the first night of his arrival in Paris, free for a little time after his negotiations with Prince Michel, though he meant to leave again as soon as the races were run at Chantilly, where his own chesnut, Maréchale, stood a good second for the French Derby.

"*Yet to live!*" he said, lying back in his arm-chair and curling a leaf round his cigarette. "My life don't hang in women's eyes, thank Heaven! I can exist very comfortably without seeing your divine Vavasour for the next twenty years, if that's all, and by that time I suspect nobody will care much about seeing her; your superb Helen will be like most other Helens of a certain age then; décolletée to a disadvantage, ruddled with rouge, jealous of her daughters, and fat (or scraggy), *à faire frémir!*"

"Blasphemer, hold your tongue!" cried Bellus. "What a future for La Vavasour! She would poison herself with a bonbon, or die of a bouquet of heliotrope, before she'd exist for such a degradation!"

"Très cher, she *may* be a spoiled beauty, but she can't change the laws of nature. Briedenbach and Bulli haven't the *Breuvage de Ninon* in their treasury, and to be steeled

against and disenchanted with the loveliest mistress, one
has only to remember—*what she will be!*"

"Or—to see what she *is*, sometimes, even will do,"
laughed the Vicomte. "Full dress, what lovely figures they
have! but the embonpoint is dreadfully fictitious with certain divinities we know!"

"And so is the bloom! However, so as they look well
that's all they think about," laughed Strathmore. "I always
make up my mind, though, to enamel, &c.; I should die of
a mistress who was *bête*, and their wit's rarely worth much
till they've come to their first touch of rouge."

"The Lady Vavasour is alone an exception; her bloom is
her own—as yet; but her mots are perfection. You must see
her, Strathmore; she'll make you recant that heterodoxy."

"I don't the least think she will," said Strathmore, giving
a spin to one of the gold pieces. "My dear Arthus, I have
seen so many of those divine beauties, those dames du
monde, those Helens à la mode. I admire them; they are
delightfully bred; they are perfectly *gantées, chaussées, coiffées,
tirées à quatre epingles;* they are charming to talk to in their
own boudoirs, where the light is half veiled, and your eyes
are the same; they are admirable when you want a little
love *à discretion*, with Cupid delicately scented with *bouquet*,
and with pleasant platonics as elastic as india-rubber. I
admire them; but I have seen so many; there can be nothing so *very* new in the salons! Your exquisite Marchioness
may be the best of the kind, but then—one knows the kind
so well! Who was she, by-the-by?"

"Well! nobody knows exactly," said Lyster Gage, of the
British Legation, reluctant to admit such a flaw in this idol
as that she had not a pedigree to flutter in the face of the
world, blazoned with bezants of gold, and rich in heraldic
quarterings. "When she appeared at St. Petersburg, you
know, she was already Marchioness of Vavasour; it was said
that the Marquis had married her in the Mauritius when she
was fifteen—those Creoles are women so early. I never
heard anything more definite, but his sixteen quarterings

are quite wide enough to cover any deficiencies, and her divine beauty did the rest; she became the fashion at once, and she has reigned the queen of pleasures, caprices, and the salons ever since, here. Her circle is as exclusive as the Princesse de Lurine's; it is only plain women who dare to hint her as "adventuress.' "

"Adventuress!—adventurer! That is the name the world gives any man or woman who dares to be clever, brilliant, or successful out of the old routine! The world must have its revenge! Society falls down before the Juggernaut of a Triumph, but, *en revanche*, it always throws stones behind it. I detest Creoles—those black-browed, lazy, inert women, who have fattened on sugar-canes, and learned to scold slaves instead of to spell! I shall not admire your matchless Peeress."

"Peste!" said the Chambellan du Roi, settling the diamond stud in his wristband. "If you *don't*, you'll be the first man in Europe who's braved her. The utmost any of them can do is to only let their eyes be dazzled, and not lose their heads. As Tilly said of Gustavus, 'c'est un joueur contre qui de rien perdre est de beaucoup gagner.' It is lucky Lord Vavasour is no Georges Dandin!"

"Bah! So he gave her his rank, and gets rewarded with dishonour! It's always the way! That's the common coin in which wives pay their gratitude," laughed Strathmore, with a dash of disgust.

"Dishonour! Fie, fie, Strathmore!" cried the Earl of Lechmere, a good-natured fellow, in the Coldstreams. "Nobody uses those coarse, ugly dictionary words now-a-days, except when one wants to get up a duel. Vavasour's a wise man. They sign a mutual Roving Commission, and don't trouble each other to know where the cruise extends. Besides, madame's amitiés *may* be only friendship; some say so, and swear she's so heartless, that her pretty, dainty brodequins dance fireproof over red-hot ploughshares that would sear tenderer feet to the bone."

"I don't believe in miracles, thank you!" said Château-Renard, of the Guards. "She must get scorched *en passant;*

at any rate. You'll see her to-night, Strathmore, I expect, but if she don't unmask——"

"The sun will stay behind a cloud. Very well! I shall endure it. I never exist on that sort of rays at any time. I'm getting tired, too, of Mondes one confounds so easily with Demi-Monde, and Aristocrates that are so near allied to Anonyma. I should rather have liked those old times when dishonour got a taste of cold steel. *Now*, your husband is as obliging as Galba to Mecænas!" yawned Strathmore. "The lady goes to Baden 'till the gossip's blown over,' and her lord is discreetly silent, and doesn't trouble himself to notice what goes on before his eyes. Unless, indeed, he thinks he can turn the scratch on his scutcheon to pecuniary account, and make out of the crim. con. a neat little sum to stop the hole in his exchequer, or cover his Goodwood debts; *then* he becomes as anxious as his counsel to prove his own dishonour, and takes the co-respondent's money with a chuckling compassion for the poor devil that's bought the damaged article and doesn't know very well what to do with it! That's the style in England, and these Vavasours are 'of us.'"

"*Que le diable te prenne*, Strathmore!" cried Bellus. "Don't be so bitter! *You're* much more fit for the Middle Ages than you are for the present day."

"I think I am. Things were called by their right names then; men sharpened their steel, and struck a straight, swift blow; now they sharpen their pen, and wound in the back, sheltered under a shield of anonymity. Then they had 'honour,' and held it at the sword's point; now they've mock 'morality,' have lawyers to defend it (which is something like giving an artificial lily to a sweep to keep unsoiled), and trade in their shame, and ask for 'costs' for every stain, from a blackened eye to a blasted name! Caramba! this claret is corked!"

"Uncommonly inconvenient times; your favourite ones, though, old fellow," said Lechmere. "One would be in perpetual hot water. Fancy an inch of cold steel waiting for us at the bottom of every *escalier dérobé*, and an iron gauntlet dashed on our lips every time we laughed away a lady's reputation. Where *should* we all be? It would be horribly troublesome."

"No doubt! We're much wiser now. We chat amicably in the clubs with the husband after leaving madame's dressing-room. I don't dispute our expediency; it's a quality in the highest cultivation in the age; even Aspasia now-a-days takes the Communion to wash away her sins in Sacramental Tent. A propos of Aspasia, Vernon-Caderousse is fettered hand and foot by Viola Vé; she boasts that she will ruin a Peer of France every *trimestre*. Take care of yourself, Bellus!"

"Yes, for she'll keep her boast, the little demon!" laughed the Vicomte. "She might begin with a more profitable speculation than the 'Duca senza Ducati,' as La Marillia calls him; Caderousse is all but 'gone.' I wish he would smash quite; I should bid for that Petitôt snuff-box of his, the Ariadne à Naxos."

"So much for friendship! Take a pinch out of my snuff-box to-day, and bid for it to-morrow; sup with me on Monday, and speculate on my sales on Tuesday. I think you'll have your wish, Arthus. Vé would ruin a millionnaire, and will make very short work of Caderousse. She should net Tchemcidoff; Russians are the best prey; the Rosières revel in their roubles, and the lords of the serfs are the slaves of the serail," said Strathmore, as his guests rose to leave and dress for a bal masqué in the Faubourg St. Germain, at the Duchesse de Luilhier's, an inauguratrix of a thousand modes that passed the time for her own thorough-bred set, and served for talk for half Paris. "What are you all going for? It's so early yet—only twelve."

"Horrid bore!" yawned Lechmere; "but one's on the treadmill, and one must tramp along with it, that's the worst. Everybody goes to the Luilhiers."

"Stay and play, Lechmere," said Strathmore. "You're all off, I do believe, for the sake of this Vavasour. For shame, Bellus; et tu Brute! I *did* think better of you, on my life. I never dreamt that sort of thing survived in anybody after twenty."

"You haven't seen her," said the Vicomte, pettishly. "Bah! she does what she likes with one."

"A very self-evident fact, très cher! If you like to be slaves of a domineering, lazy Creole, *be* it; I don't understand your taste, that's all; but then I suppose I'm exceptional altogether; I don't like olives, and I don't care about women."

"Quite right," swore the Earl, under his moustaches; "both of 'em make you buy the nice rose flavour with too salt a bitterness."

"I don't know anything about the bitterness, thank God; I never travelled to that stage," laughed Strathmore; "but olives tempt one to drink, and women tempt one to weakness, and when either the love or the brandy's taken too strong, we lose our heads and tell our secrets; and, on the whole, I think two bottles less detrimental than one woman! Wine steals our wits, but Delilah does worse;—because she's a tongue to ask questions."

"Devil take your philosophy."

"Much obliged. I don't wish any devil to take it, male or female, Belphegor or Melusine. 'My mind to me a kingdom is.' I should be specially sorry for any raids to be made on it."

"I bet you fifty to one, Strath, you adore la Vavasour when you see her."

"*If!* This Vavasour tyrant. I bet you a thousand to one I don't even admire her."

"In Naps?—done! It's a heavy bet, mon ami," said Château-Renard, entering the wager in a little dainty jewelled book, a gift of S. A. R. the volage, and somewhat indiscreet Princesse de Lurine.

"And a very safe one for me," said Strathmore, with a slight yawn. "If you don't make your wagers more discreetly, Armand, it's not much to be wondered at that you come to grief at Sartory and Chantilly as you do. Au revoir, if you will go.   We meet again at Philippi, I suppose, in an hour?"

"I promised the Sabreur to give him correct notes of the Vavasour. I must notice her if she comes here to-night," thought Strathmore, as he lay back in a dormeuse before the fire, when he was left alone, finishing his cigarette, while the firelight danced on the marble bronze and ormolu of the mantelpiece, and the gas shone on the gold lying on the table, and on the wines that stood in a dozen decanters on the console. "I can picture her perfectly—a tawny, large, black-browed, voluptuous woman, silent, sensual, handsome, heavy, with a brow of Egypt, a Juno figure, and a West Indian languor. She *takes* because of her luxurious outline and her Creole indolence, and because she's a new style, and has done two clever strokes of diplomacy, by persuading an English Peer to marry her, and a thorough-bred set to make her Queen of the *ton*. She must have been very adroit—these silent, still-life women often cover matchless finesses; nobody suspects them of the manufacture till the web is woven. What could the Marquis be about? However, he was three parts a fool, they used to say, I think, and woman make idiots of wiser men if once they're allowed to have their own way. I dare say his yacht anchored off Martinique, and one day, when he was very hot and very languid, intensely bored, and had drunk a good deal of brandy, this woman had him alone in a verandah, where she lay fanning herself amidst a pile of flowers, with the air scented with pastelles, and everything planned to take him in a moment of weakness, and looked so handsome that she did what she liked with him, and made him say what he couldn't unsay. So much is done in that sort of way; there would be no marriages at all if men kept their heads cool always, but they're taken at a disadvantage, just after dinner, when they're lazy, and would consent to anything, or after the champagne at supper, when they talk nonsense they'd never have committed themselves to at noon; or in the whirl of a waltz, when the turns of the dance turn their heads! If we were always what we are between break-

fast and luncheon, we should never love at all. We're cold
after our matutinal mocha, but we're easily fooled after our
dinner coffee. What we defy in the morning light, we yield
to in the moonlight. Women know that; this Lady Vavasour,
I dare say, lured her lord into his declaration when the stars
were shining on the mango-groves and on the green sea-
vines, or perhaps—more likely—she was a *nouvelle riche*, and
brought him money. Men barter their good blood now-a-
days; soiling the scutcheon don't matter if they gild over
the dirt; we don't sell our souls to the Devil in this age,
we're too Christian, we sell them to the Dollar!"

With which satirical reflection on his times, and his order,
drifting through his mind, Strathmore's thoughts floated onward to a piece of statecraft then numbered among the delicate diplomacies and intricate embroglie of Europe, whose
moves absorbed him as the finesses of a problem absorb a
skilful chess-player; and from thence stretched onwards to
his future, in which he lived like all men of dominant ambition far more than he lived in his present. It was a future
brilliant, secure, brightening in its lustre and strengthening
in its power with each successive year; a future which was
not to him as to most wrapped in a chiar'oscuro with only
points of luminance gleaming through the mist, but in whose
cold glimmering light he seemed to see clear and distinct, as
we see each object of the far-off landscape stand out in the
air of a winter's noon, every thread that he should gather up,
every distant point to which he should pass onward; a future
singular and characteristic, in which state-power was the
single ambition marked out, from which the love of women
was banished, in which pleasure and wealth were as little
regarded as in Lacedæmon, in which age would be courted
not dreaded, since with it alone would come added dominion
over the minds of men, and in which, as it stretched out before him, failure and alteration were alike impossible. What,
if he lived, could destroy a future that would be solely de-
pendent on, solely ruled by, himself? By his own hand alone
would his future be fashioned,—would he hew out any shape

save the idol that pleased him? When we hold the chisel
ourselves, are we not secure to have no error in the work? Is
it likely that our hand will slip, that the marble we select
will be dark-veined, and brittle, and impure, that the blows
of the mallet will shiver our handiwork, and that when we
plan a Milo, god of strength, we shall but mould and sculp-
ture out a Läocoon of torture? Scarcely! and Strathmore
held the chisel, and, certain of his own skill, was as sure of
what he should make of life as Benvenuto, when he bade the
molten metal pour into the shape that he, master-craftsman,
had fashioned, and give to the sight of the world the Winged
Perseus. But Strathmore did not remember what Cellini
did—that one flaw might mar the whole!

The rooms were filled when he ascended the staircase
and entered the first of that suite of superb salons where
Madame de Luilhiers gathered about her her own particular
and exclusive set, and reigned supreme. Her ball was a
replica of a *bal de l'opéra*, with a dash of the brilliance of the
Regency, a time the Duchesse loved to resuscitate; scandal,
indeed, said that she loved it so well that she enacted the
rôle of the Marquise de Parabère with a descendant of Monseigneur d'Orléans; but—*taisons nous !*—scandal is ever indiscreet, and never true, we know, save here and there, when it
hits the defenceless, or besmears the fallen, or so delicately
stabs our bosom friend that we haven't heart to forswear it!
The low hum of many voices, that sound which, subdued and
harmless as the musical hum of gnats, yet buzzes away the
peace of entire lives, and murmurs death-blows to a myriad
of reputations, filled the rooms as he moved slowly through
the throng of glittering dominoes, broidered with gold or
studded with jewels, while brilliant eyes smiled recognition
on him through their masks, and witty badinage was whispered to him by fair incognite.

"Deucedly like life, mon cher—eh? People take advantage of disguise to slander at their ease, and under a
mask the dastard grows daring and whispers a scandal, or—
what's as bad—a truth! Very like life! Under the domino

how suavely they stab their foes, and unrecognised in the vicinity of his dear friends how secure a man is to overhear them damning his name!" laughed Strathmore to Château-Renard as he passed him in the vestibule, and went on to chat with the Comtesse de Chantal, a bewitching little brune, who had confided to him the colour of her adorable rose domino, and would quickly have been recognised without any other guide than her bright marmoset eyes.

"The domino gives one the privilege of *laissez-faire* and *laissez-parler;* it would be very pleasant if the world were one long bal masqué," said Madame la Comtesse, letting the eyes in question rest on him with coquette brilliance, for Strathmore was much courted by the sex he contemned.

"Madame! I think it *is* one. Who is there in it without a disguise?" he answered her, laughing, as they moved on to the ball-room through the crowd of titled maskers, while the music echoed from the distance, and the lights gleamed on the gorgeous dresses of those bidden to the Duchesse's fête à la Régence.

" Who, indeed! Not even Lord Cecil Strathmore, since he disdains women, yet he flirts with one!" murmured a whisper at his side.

"Who spoke, Cecil?" said the Comtesse, slightly disgusted with the style of the attack.

"Some one of your court jealous of my distinction, madame," laughed Strathmore, as he thought to himself, " I would swear the voice was a woman's," and turned to see who had recognised him with his mask on. Among the crowd of dominoes near, the one closest to him was white, powdered with golden bees.

"*Fi donc!* it was a woman: a man would have attacked *me*, not you," said Madame de Chantal, giving him a blow of her fan, a little jealous of the domino that Strathmore's eyes were tracking; more jealous still, when dexterously disentangling himself from her, he left her with Bellus, and followed the white domino in its swift passage through the crowd, that would have been a crush in any other salons than

those of the Hôtel Luilhiers: followed on an impulse vague
and irresistible, as he had never before followed the voice of
a woman. With whatever swiftness and dexterity he traced
her, she perpetually eluded him; though she never turned
her head, he would have sworn she knew he was pursuing
her (women, like flies, know all that goes on behind them),
and she seemed to take a perverse delight in winding in and
out interminable mazes, and in letting him approach her only
to escape him; the white folds of the domino, with its glittering golden bees fluttering in the light, ever within tantalising
reach, and ever at provoking distance. At last, when he was
tired of the chase, and on the point of giving it up, her own
passage was obstructed; he pushed hastily forward and
overtook her in the Pavillon de Flore, a winter garden,
where Louise de Luilhiers had the tropics reproduced under
glass in all their Oriental heat and Oriental fragrance, and
in which the maskers were moving, amidst the broad leaves
and glowing creepers of the East, while the falling waters of
innumerable fountains cooled the air, and subdued lights
gleamed through the dark tropical foliage, like fire-flies in
a palm grove.

"If I disdain all women, I have followed one. Belle
dame, whoever you be, I may trust your reproof to me shows
some sign of interest in him you condemned," whispered
Strathmore in her ear.

Though she had penetrated his disguise, he could not
penetrate hers; shrouded in her domino she defied detection, and by her voice he could not recognise her in the least.
He only saw, as she turned her head, that her eyes laughed,
shining brightly as stars, and that the lovely mouth below
her mask had the bloom of youth on its lips, like the soft
bloom on an untouched peach.

"Not at all! You are far too presumptuous, and if you
disdain all women, you cannot care what one of them thinks
of you. You have only pursued me because I eluded you;
we beat you best '*en fuyant comme les Scythes.*' Montaigne is
perfectly right."

Her voice had a sound in it familiar to him, but not familiar enough to be recognisable in her disguise. She baffled all detection, provocative as were the luminous eyes shining on him through her mask, and the laughing lips, like two roses d'amour, which were all that the envious masquerade gave to view.

"I have pursued you to learn who honours me, by forbidding me to flirt. Presumption or not, belle inconnue, I shall construe its interdict as it flatters me most. You recognised me even in domino; there must be some elective affinity between us!"

"None whatever. I knew you by your eyes, Lord Cecil. What does your legend say?—

> Swift, silent, Strathmore's eyes
> Are fathomless and darkly wise:
> No wife nor leman sees them smile,
> Save at bright steel and statecraft wile;
> And when they lighten, foes are ware,
> The shrive is short, the shroud is there!"

The words startled him, spoken by the lips of the fair mask in the gay salons of the Hôtel Luilhier; they were the burden of a rhyming chronicle, old as *Piers the Plowman*—a wild, dark legend, still among the cradle-songs of his county, and the chronicles of his own household. It was strange to hear here, in Paris, in the gay revelry of the fête à la Régence, words which he thought had never travelled beyond the woods of White Ladies, which he had never remembered since the days of his boyhood! Who could she be who knew him so well?

"Belle amie," he said, bending his head to her as they passed under the fragrant aisles of the winter garden, "you flatter me more and more! I must, at least, have some interest for you, since you know by heart my family legends and the look of my eyes! We cannot possibly be strangers——"

"Perhaps we are enemies!" interrupted the mask, the sapphires gleaming here and there on her domino, flashing their azure beams in the light. "The instinct of enmity is quicker than that of friendship or of love, you know, all the world through. How did you bend Prince Michel to your will a few months ago?—by playing on the subtlest and surest of human passions—revenge!"

"The deuce! is she a witch or a clairvoyante!" thought Strathmore, fairly astounded. The policy he had pursued had been closely kept, if ever the tactics of diplomacy had been so. Who had betrayed them to this Domino Blanc? Who was this Domino Blanc that she knew them? The only woman who could have penetrated their intricacies was that modern De Longueville, the Princesse de Lurine; but the Princess was a brune, an olive-cheeked daughter of Sardinia, and the delicate chin of the mask, which (save the rose lips) was all he could see of his clairvoyante unknown, was white as the skin of the fairest blonde.

"Did you think your state secrets were unknown, Lord Cecil?" she whispered rapidly, her bright eyes dancing with malicious amusement. "Bah! even a swift, silent Strathmore cannot defy a woman, you see. If we are not good for very much in this world, we are good for meddling and for espionage. We are the best detectives in the world, only we can't hold our tongues —we can't keep the secrets when we have learned them. We are so proud of our stolen nuts that we crack them *en plein jour*, instead of keeping them to enjoy in the darkness of night, as you wise men do!"

"Caramba, madame!" laughed Strathmore, looking down into her glittering eyes. "I think it is a popular error that your sex cannot keep a secret; you guard your *own* most admirably for a lifetime, if you deem it politic; it is only the secrets of others that you betray!"

He had no under-meaning, no hidden innuendo in the satire on her sex, but, for an instant, the bright eyes of the White Domino were clouded and angrily troubled. Perhaps he had struck, without knowing it, on some jarring chord; perhaps she was startled for the moment lest she should have

encountered clairvoyance, *en revanche*. Then—she laughed,
a gay, fantastic chime of mellow laughter..

"Those who are wise trust us; those who are unwise pique
us by drawn veils and forbidden fruits. A woman is never
so exasperated as when she is refused—of course it spurs
her to her mettle, and into what is bolted and barred from
her she will enter by a chink, coûte que coûte. Seal a letter,
and we look into it by a corner; shut a door, and we pass
through it by the keyhole; tell us a thing is poison, and we
taste it, as if it were elixir. No book is so eagerly read as
one you forbid us; no secret is so quickly found out as one
you taboo to us. If you do not wish me to learn all about the
Voltúra embroglio, you will tell me, with a good grace, what
private instructions D'Arrelio received from Turin; you were
with him this morning!"

She whispered it very softly, where they stood beside
one of the fountains, falling with measured murmur into its
marble basin, and casting its silvery spray high up amongst
the scarlet blossoms and the luxuriant foliage of the Eastern
creepers. The Voltura embroglio! that intricate knot of
Anglo-Franco-Italian intrigue, whose slightest threads had
never been dropped save in the privacy of the most secret
bureaux! Who the deuce could she be, and how could she
come by that! Witch, clairvoyante, political intrigante,
whatever she might be, he would have defied her to have
probed that most secret of diplomatic secresies, and to know
of a visit paid to the envoy of Turin by a side-door and an
escalier dérobé! This mystic *magicienne* baffled him utterly!
She knew his own movements—she knew his own thoughts—
she even knew the secret moves of the great chess-players,
who had Europe for their chess-board! Strathmore was
piqued, excited, provoked; he had never been so impatient
in his life; he could almost have forsworn all the courtesies
of masquerade, and have torn off by force the envious black
mask which hid from his sight the face of his mysterious
clairvoyante, and which shrouded every feature, save the

sweet, sensuous, mutine mouth, that only made concealment
the more cruel.

"The sure way to win whatever you wish, and hear whatever you seek, ma belle, would be to promise removal of your
cruel mask as a recompense; none could resist such a bribe,
let their probity be what it would!" he whispered her,
eagerly.

He by no means intended to confess to the accuracy of
her Voltura knowledge; it might be but the clever guess-
work of a feminine politician, flung out to entrap him hap-
hazard.

"How rash you are!" cried the Domino Blanc, interrupt-
ing him mischievously. "I may be wrinkled, haggard, and
enamelled, for anything you can tell; I may be a Ninon of
seventy, a Du Deffand coquetting in my eightieth year, a
female Mirabeau pitted with small-pox and yellow with
dyspepsia. Unmasked, I should have lost the charm that
only goes with the Unseen. Thank you! I am too wise to
part with it!"

"I am anything but rash, and you are anything but wise,"
persisted Strathmore. "One guesses the perfection of the
statue by the little that is unveiled; the beauty of the volume
by the grace of the vignette that peeps through the uncut
leaves! Enamel, madame, could no more have given the
bloom to your lips than their bloom to those blossoms, and
those eyes would not be so dangerously eloquent unless they
were washed with the morning dew of their dawn!"

"Charming compliments!" laughed the mask, striking
him on the arm with the jewelled sticks of her fan. "But
you only flatter my beauty to have your curiosity gratified.
It is not to see my face, Lord Cecil, but to find out who
whispers to you of your tête-à-tête with Arrelio that you
would like my mask off. *M. mon diplomat*, I take your flattery at its worth!"

"Then you do injustice to yourself and to me," whispered
Strathmore, urgently, tantalised and provoked to the last degree by a woman who knew so much of himself and would

let him know nothing of her. "Your hand alone is insignia and type of what the tout ensemble would be were it only unmasked. Those Titania-like fingers must have face and form to match with them. Do you not think your mask is as cruel as the closest veil of the Odalisque, since, like that, it only shows us enough to make us wistfully dream of all we are denied?"

"Gracefully turned! were it only sincere!" answered the White Domino, her low, musical, mocking laugh echoing softly where they stood by the fountain, where the light of the lamps was shaded by the fantastic ferns and fan-like leaves of the profuse Oriental foliage that drooped around. "But with Lord Cecil Strathmore it is only flattery, adroit and diplomatic, to find out who has the clue to his secret interview with Arrelio! Neither the mask nor the veil are cruelties to you; you care nothing for what they shroud; and as for dreaming of what is denied to you, you would disdain so poetical a weakness, unless the denial involved a state secret; then, indeed, it *might* haunt your sleep a little! Listen, Lord Cecil! I know your diplomacies, see if I know you personally. You are ambitious, but with a singular and lofty ambition, in which wealth has no share. You disdain gold as the *dieu du roture*, and seek power alone. You are cold, and proud of your coldness, as of the polish of steel that has never been dimmed. You prize friendship, but disdain love as the plaything of fools and the dalliance of dotards. You look on life as the clay, and on men as the plaster through whom you, master-craftsman, will fashion the shape that pleases you without a flaw, ductile and plastic to every turn of your hand. You love finesse, sway, dominance; you are independent of sympathy; you are perfectly and presumptuously self-reliant; you have the profound subtle intellect of the old Italian statesmen; perhaps you have their swift, dark, relentless passion too; but, if so, it slumbers—as yet, as it slumbered with them till it was time to strike. You are like the Strathmores of White Ladies, line by line, feature for feature, and with their physiognomy inherit their character. *Now*, am I clairvoyante or not? Tell me!"

She spoke in a low, sweet whisper, bending towards him with her luminous eyes shining on him through her mask, while the sapphires flashed their azure rays in the light, and the mystical, monotonous music of the fountain murmured on and on, and the scarlet flowers of the Eastern creepers swung against the glittering, snowy folds of her domino. With something of the strange, startled wonder with which Surrey saw his love shadowed out on the Mirour of Gramarye, Strathmore heard his character drawn in the unerring words of the mysterious mask. A moment before he would have sworn that no living creature, save, perhaps, Bertie Erroll, could have known him so well; and the portraiture, exact to the life in every line, startled him as we may have been startled coming suddenly upon an unseen mirror that gives us back our own reflexion in every trait and in a strong light. He stretched out his hand to her, his grasp involuntarily closing on the folds of the domino.

"Clairvoyante or not, you are an enchantress! and I must know who has studied me so miraculously before we part. Unmask, ma belle. I cannot let you go unknown. I will not!"

She laughed the laugh sweet as music, that had something menacing and mocking in its soft, subdued carillon.

"But you *must*, by the rules of all masquerades. I am like Eros, I must be adored unseen; bring light to unveil me, and I shall take wing! Will you lament as sincerely as Psyche? Adieu!"

With a swift, sudden movement, ere he could detain her, the white folds slid from his hand, and she had fluttered away, as though she literally took wing like the Eros she spoke of, floating off under the tropical foliage like some rich-plumaged bird, the gold-flowered domino brushing through the dark glossy leaves as she passed. As swiftly Strathmore pursued; but before it was possible to overtake her, a group of dominoes had surrounded her, and on the arm

of one of them she had passed so rapidly out of the Pavillon
de Flore, that ere he could follow she was lost in the
throng.

Who could she be? Who could know him so well while
she was unknown to him? Her air, her voice, her eyes were
half familiar while yet strange, and the mask might have
effectually disguised his best-known friend. Yet, as he recalled those who alone could have spoken thus to him, he
rejected them all; this mysterious clairvoyante could be none
of them. The lost White Domino piqued him. Soft voices
challenged him with witty mots, fair maskers kept him talking to them that light, brilliant badinage that women live
on, as humming-birds on farina, and bees upon honey; eyes
dazzling as hers wooed him tenderly through their masks;
but Strathmore was haunted by one woman, to the exclusion
of all the rest; he sought her unceasingly through the Luilhiers' salons, but always in vain. The sweet, sensuous mouth,
the luminous eyes, the thrilling, musical voice and laugh,
which would have had magic in others, were not what piqued
him; it was the strange knowledge that she had of himself,
the unerring fidelity with which she had sketched traits in
his character that he himself even had known but in in-
distinct shadow till the light of her words had streamed in
upon them. Had he believed in clairvoyance he would have
sworn to it now!

He sought the White Domino persistently, ceaselessly,
through the crowds that filled the rooms for the Duchesse's
fête à la Régence—sought her always in vain. At last,
giving up in provoked despair his bootless chase of the azure
sapphires and golden bees, that only flashed on his sight in
the distance to perpetually elude his approach, he leant
against the door-way of one of the conservatories, where a
breeze reached him, cooling the air that was hot with the
blaze of the myriad lights, and heavy with the odour of perfumes and flowers; and stood there looking down the long
suite of salons, glittering with the moving throng of dominoes,
and holding his mask in his hand, so that the light fell full

upon the peculiar Vandyke-like character of his head, rendered the more striking by the dark violet of his masquerade dress and the diamonds that studded it. He was provoked, impatient, interested more than ever he had been in his whole life—save once—and he was annoyed with himself that he had so mismanaged the affair as to let the Domino Blanc slip from his hands. He was annoyed with himself, and not less so when, as he stood there, snowy folds swept past him, the jewelled handle of a fan struck his arm, and a soft voice was in his ear:

"*Rêveur!* you look like a portrait of the Old Masters! Are you thinking of the Voltura affair, or of me? You will be foiled with both; Arrelio will not sign, and I shall not unmask! Good night, Strathmore! Perhaps I shall haunt your sleep this morning, as I know a state secret!"

The words were scarce whispered before she had passed him! Again she eluded his detention; again, swift as lightning, he pursued her, this all-mysterious and all-tantalising mask; but destiny was against him. The throng parted them, an Austrian Baroness detained him, the trailing folds of a rose domino entangled him; *she* was perpetually at a distance as he followed her through the salons, which she was then leaving on the arm of a black domino to go to her carriage, the golden bees glittering, the snowy dress fluttering, just far enough off to be provokingly near and provokingly distant, as, detained now by this, now by that, he threaded his way through the interminable length of the salons, ante-chambers, cabinets de peinture, and reception-rooms in her wake, and passed out into the staircase at the very moment that she was descending its last step! She had a crowd about her, following her as courtiers follow their Queen, and her sapphires were gleaming and her white domino glittering as she crossed in a blaze of light the marble parquet of the magnificent hall of the Hôtel Luilhiers.

"A white domino, powdered with gold bees!—can you tell me whose that is, Arthus?" asked Strathmore, eagerly,

where he stretched over the balustrade as Bellus came out
of the vestibule, while below, with her masked court about
her, she passed on to her carriage.

"A white domino with golden bees!" cried the Vicomte.
"Pardieu! you have seen her, then?"

"Seen *her!* Seen whom?"

"Did she take off her mask?" went on Bellus, not heed-
ing the counter-question. "Did you see her face? Did you
look at her well? What do you think of her?"

"Her! *Whom?* I ask you who the white domino is. Look
—quick! you will catch her before she has passed out of the
hall. Whose domino is that?"

"*That?* Nom de Dieu! that is HERS!"

"*Hers!* Curse your pronouns! She must have a name!
Whose?"

"Peste! Lady Vavasour. You have seen her, then, at
last!"

CHAPTER VII.

Two Night Pictures—by Waxlight, and by Moonlight.

MARION LADY VAVASOUR AND VAUX sat before her dressing-room fire (which she had lighted in summer or winter),
watching the embers play, nestled in the cozy depths of her
luxurious chair, with a novel open in her lap, and her long
shining tresses unbound and hanging in as loose, rippled
luxuriance as the hair of the Vénus à la Coquille. No toilette
was so becoming as the azure négligé of softest Indian
texture, with its profusion of gossamer lace about the arms
and bosom, that she wore; no chaussure more bewitching
than the slipper, fantastically broidered with gold and pearls,
into which the foot she held out to the fire to warm was
slipped; no sanctuary for that belle des belles fitter and
more enticing than the dressing-room, with its *rose tendre*
hangings, its silver swinging lamps, its toilette-table shrouded
in lace, its mirrors framed in Dresden, its jaspar tazze filled
with jewels, its gemmed vases full of flowers, its crystal

carafes of perfumes and bouquets, its thousand things of luxury and grace. Here, perhaps, Marion Lady Vavasour, who had rarest loveliness at all hours, looked her loveliest of all; and here she sat now, thinking, while the firelight shone on the dazzling whiteness of her skin, on the luminous depths of her eyes, on the shining unbound tresses of her hair; and on the diamond-studded circlet on her fair left hand that was the badge of her allegiance to one lord, and the signet of her title to reign, a Queen of Society and a Marchioness of Vavasour and Vaux. Her thoughts might well be sunny ones; she was in the years of her youth and the height of her beauty; she had not a caprice she could not carry out, nor a wish she could not gratify. Her world, delirious with her fascination and ductile to her magic, let her place her foot on its neck and rule it as she would; she was censed with the purple incense of worship wherever she moved, and gave out life and death with her smile and her frown, with a soft whispered word or a moue boudeuse. From a station of comparative obscurity, when her existence had threatened to pass away in insular monotony and colonial obscurity, her beauty had lifted her to a dazzling rank, and her tact had taught her to grace it, so that none could carp at, but all bowed before her; so that in a thorough-bred exclusive set she gave the law and made the fashion, and conquests unnumbered strewed her path "thick as the leaves in Vallambrosa."

On her first appearance as Lady Vavasour and Vaux, which had been made some six years before this at St. Petersburg, women had murmured at, and society been shy to receive, this exquisite creature, come none knew whence, born from no one knew whom, with whom the world in general conceived that my lord Marquis had made a wretched mésalliance; the Marquis being a man *sans reproche* as far as "blood" went, if upon some other score he was not quite so stainless as might have been. But the world in very brief time gave way before her: with the sceptre of a matchless loveliness, and the skill of a born tactician, she cleared all obstacles, overruled all opponents, bore down all hesitations, silenced all sneers. She created a furore, she became the mode; women might slander her as they would, they could do nothing against her; and in brief time, from her début by finesse, by witchery, by the double right of her own resistless fascination, and the dignity of her lord's name, Marion Marchioness of Vavasour and Vaux was a Power in the world of fashion, and an acknowledged leader in her own spheres of ton, pleasure, and coquetry. "Woman's wit" can do anything if it be given free run and free scope, and with that indescribable yet priceless quality of her sex she was richly endowed. How richly, you will conceive when I say that, she had so effectually silenced and bewitched society, that in society (save here and there, where two or three very malicious grandes dames, whom she had outrivalled, were gathered together for spleen, slander, and Souchong) the question of her origin was never now mooted. It would, indeed, have been as presumptuous to have debated such a question with her, as for the Hours to have asked Aphrodite of her birth when the amber-dropping golden tresses and the snowy shoulders rose up from the white sea-foam. Lady Vavasour was Herself, and was all-sufficient for herself. Her delicate azure veins were her sangre azul, her fair white hands were her seize quartiers, her shining tresses were her bezants d'or, and her luminous eyes her blazonry. Garter King-at-Arms himself, looking on her, would have forgotten heraldry, flung the bare, lifeless skeleton of pedigree to the winds before the living beauty, and allowed that Venus needs no Pursuivant's marshalling.

She sat looking into the dressing-room fire, while the gleam of the wax-lights was warm on her brow, and played in the depths of her dazzling eyes; a pleased smile lingered about her lovely lips, and her fingers idly played with the leaves of her novel—her thoughts were more amusing than its pages. She was thinking over the triumphs of the past night and day; of how she had wooed from the Marquis d'Arrelio, for pure insouciant curiosity, state secrets that honour and prudence alike bade him withhold, but which he was powerless to deny before her magical witchery; of how Constantine of Lanaris had followed her from Athens, to lay at her feet the sworn homage of a Prince, and be rewarded with a tap of a fan painted by Watteau; of the imperial sables Duke Nicholas Tchernidoff had flung down à la Raleigh on a damp spot on the Terrace des Feuillans, where, otherwise, her dainty brodequins would have been set on some moist fallen leaves, as they had strolled there together; of the pieces of Henri Deux and Rose Berri ware, dearer to him than his life, which that king of connoisseurs, Lord Weiverden, had presented to her, sacrificing his Faïence for the sake of a smile; of the words which men had whispered to her in the perfumed demi-lumière of her violet-hung boudoir, while her eyes laughed and lured them softly and resistlessly to their doom; of all the triumphs of the past twelve hours, since the doors of her hotel in the Place Vendôme had first been opened at two o'clock in the day to her crowding court, to now, when she had quitted the bal masqué of her friend Louise de Luilhier, and was inhaling again in memory the incense on which she lived. For the belle Marquise was a finished coquette, never sated with conquest; and it was said, in certain circles antagonistic to her own, that neither her coquetries nor her conquests were wholly harmless. But every flower, even the fairest, has its shadow beneath it as it swings in the sunlight!

"He did not remember ME!" thought the Venus Aphrodite of the rose-hung dressing-room, looking with a smile into the flames of the fire, which it was her whim to have even in so warm a night as was this one. "My voice should have told him; it is a terribly bad compliment! However, he shall pay for it! A woman who knows her power can always tax any negligence to her as heavily as she likes. How incomprehensibly silly those women must be who become their lovers' slaves, who hang on their words and seek their tenderness, and make themselves miserable at their infidelities. I cannot understand it; if there be a thing in the world easier to manage than another, it is a MAN! Weak, obstinate, vain, wayward, loving what they cannot get, slighting what they hold in their hand, adoring what they have only on an insecure tenure, trampling on anything that lies at their mercy, always capricious to a constant mistress and constant to a capricious—men are all alike; there is nothing easier to keep in leading-strings when once you know their foibles! Those swift, silent Strathmores, they are very cold, they say, and love very rarely; but *when* they love, it must be imperiously, passionately, madly, tout ou rien. I should like to see him roused. Shall I rouse him? Perhaps! *He* could not resist me if I chose to wind him round my fingers. I should like to supplant his ambition, to break down his pride, to shatter his coldness, to bow him down to what he defies. Those facile conquests are no honour; those men who sigh at the first sight of one's eyebrow, and lose their heads at the shadow of a smile; I am tired of them—sick of them! Toujours perdrix! And the birds so easily shot! Shall I choose? *Yes!* No man living could defy *me*—not even Lord Cecil Strathmore!"

And as she thought this last vainglorious but fully warranted thought, Marion Lady Vavasour, lying back in her fauteuil, with her head resting negligently on her arm, that in its turn rested on the satin cushions, with that grace which washer peculiar charm, as the firelight shone on her loosened hair and the rose-leaf flush of her delicate cheeks, glanced at her own reflexion in a mirror standing near, on whose surface the whole matchless tableau was reproduced with its dainty and brilliant colouring, and smiled—a smile of calm security, of superb triumph. Could she not vanquish whom and when and where she would?

That night, far across the sea, under the shadow of English woodlands that lay dark and fresh, and still beneath the brooding summer skies, a woman stood within the shelter of a cottage-porch, looking down the forest-lane that stretched into the distance, with the moonbeams falling across its moss-grown road between the boles of the trees, and the silent country lying far beyond hushed, and dim, and shrouded in a white mist. She was young, and she had the light of youth —love—in her eyes as she gazed wistfully into the gloom, vainly seeking to pierce through the dense foliage of the boughs and the darkness of the night, and listened, thirstily and breathlessly, for a step beloved to break the undisturbed silence. The scarlet folds of a cloak fell off her shoulders, her head was uncovered, and the moon bathed her in its radiance where she stood; the branches above her, as the wind stirred amongst them, shaking silver drops of dew from their moistened leaves on her brow and into her bosom. She loved, and listened for that which she loved; listened patiently, yet eagerly and long, while the faint summer clouds swept over the dark azure heavens, the stars shining through their mist, and the distant chimes of a church clock from an old grey tower bosomed in the woods tolled out the quarters, one by one, as the hours of the night stole onward.

Suddenly she heard that for which she longed—heard ere other ears could have caught it—a step falling on the moss that covered the forest road, and coming towards her; then —she sprang forward in the darkness, the dew shaking from her hair, and the tears of a great gladness glancing in her eyes, as she twined her arms close about him whom she met, and clung to him as though no earthly power should sever them.

"You are come at last! Ah, if you knew how bitter your absence is, if you knew how I grudge you to the cruel world that robs me so long, so often of you——"

Erroll looked down fondly on her.

"Lucille! I am not worth your worship, still less worth the consecration of your life, when I repay it so little, recompense it so ill."

She laid her hand upon his lips and gazed up into his eyes, clinging but the more closely to him, and laughing and weeping in her joy:

"Hush, hush! Pay it ill! Have I not the highest, best,

most precious payment in your love! *I* care for no other, you know that so well."

He stroked her hair caressingly, perhaps repentantly (few men can meet the eyes of a wife who loves them purely and faithfully, after a long absence, without some pangs of conscience, without some contrast of the quality of her fidelity and their own), and kissed the lips uplifted to his own; the love that he read in her eyes, and that trembled in her voice, saddened him, he could not have told why, even whilst he recognised it as something unpurchasable in the world he had quitted, where its strength and its fidelity would have been but words of an unknown tongue, subjects of a jeer, objects of a jest.

"And you have seen none who have supplanted me since we parted; none of whom I need have jealousy or fear!" she whispered to him, with a certain tremulous, wistful anxiety—he was her all, she could not be robbed of him!— yet with a fond, sunny smile upon her face as it was raised to his in the faint sheen of the starlight, the smile of a love too deeply true, too truly trustful to harbour a dread that were doubt, a doubt that were disloyalty to the faith it received as to the faith it gave.

He looked down into her eyes, and pressed closer against his own the heart that he knew beat purely, wholly for himself.

"My precious one! you need be jealous of no living thing with me. None have twined themselves about my heart, none have rooted themselves into my life as you have done. Have no dread! No rival shall ever supplant you, I swear before God!"

He spoke the oath in all sincerity, in all faith, in all fervour, speaking it as many men have so spoken before him, not dreaming what the day will bring forth, not knowing how fate will make them unwitting perjurers, unconscious renegades to the bond of their word, as they are lured onwards, and driven downwards, powerless, almost one would say blameless, in the hands of chance.

And the woman that nestled in his arms and gazed up into his eyes sighed a low, long sigh of gladness. He was her world; she knew of and needed no other.

Then he loosened her from his embrace, and led her under the drooping branches of the trees that hung stirless in the warm air, into the house hidden in the profuse and tangled foliage. Their steps ceased to fall on the moss, their shadows to slant across the starlit path, their whispered words to stir the silence; the woodland country lay beyond calm and still in the shade of the night, the fleecy clouds drifted slowly now and then across the bright radiance of the moon, the winds moved gently amongst the leaves; in the lattice casements shrouded in the trees the lights died out, and the church chimes struck faintly in the distance their hours one by one. On the hushed earth three angels brooded—Night, and Sleep, and Peace.

CHAPTER VIII.

The Kismet that was written on a Millefleurs-scented Note.

"Meurice's, Paris.

"MY DEAR ERROLL,—To keep faith with you, I must tell you that I have seen Lady Vavasour! Rather, to speak more properly, have heard her, for she was masked, and I saw nothing except, what I freely confess to be, as lovely a mouth and chin as the devil ever gave his special aides-de-camp, the daughters of Eve, for a weapon of slaughter and a tool of perdition. I met her at Madame de Luilhier's bal masqué, and she has her full share of Eve's curiosity; for though, to my certain knowledge, I have never seen her before, nor she me, she informed me of everything about myself, and a little more besides! She repeated one of the old White Ladies chronicles—where could she get hold of it?—and was up to some diplomatic tricks, whose juggling we all thought had been done strictly *in petto*. I suppose the Nazarenes, who lie in the lap of the titled Delilah, let her coax their secrets out of them. The ass that Samson in all ages ought to smite is Himself! *You* will think her divine, I dare say; fascinating I can very well believe that she is, by the wiles she tried upon me to-night; and she's gifted with the sex's true genius for tantalising. I like nothing I have heard of her, and I should say it is particularly lucky the Marquis is of elastic conjugal principles! I never remember seeing him, do you? I don't envy him his wife, though I admit she is half a sorceress, and has a very pretty mouth; but it is a mouth that would whisper too many infidelities to please me, were I *he!* What the deuce are you doing with yourself? Carlton tells me you said 'you were going out of town—*c'était tout.*' Out of town in the middle of the season! You surely are not turning pastoral, and getting *entêté* of provinciality? The Beau Sabreur a Strephon! What a vision! I dare say a woman's at the bottom of it; but Aspasia was always your game, not Phillis, except, indeed, with that mysterious White Ladies inamorata, whom you wouldn't be chaffed about. But it can't be she, because *that* love's twelve months' old now to my knowledge, and must have been rococo long ago. I will pique Lady Millicent till she badgers you out of your secret. Good night, old fellow. I shall be heartily glad to see you again. When will it be? Can't you run over here? I expect I shall get the French Derby, though Lawton's confounded love of a close finish lost me the English one. The betting's quite steady here on Maréchale, always five to one. I shall start him for the St. Leger, and send him over to Maldon to train through August and September. Nesselrode's a good second. They don't offer freely at all on Tambour, and I half think he'll be scratched. The Abbey's at your service, of course, as it always is, to fill as you like for the First. You will oblige me very much by keeping the old place open, and knocking over the birds, whether I come or not.

"Yours as ever,
"CECIL STRATHMORE."

Strathmore, having written those last words as the morning sun streamed in through the persiennes of his bedchamber, addressed his letter to Major Erroll, 19A, Albermarle-street, London (where that debt-laden Sabreur had a suite of rooms, dainty and luxurious enough to domicile Lady Millicent), and lying back in his chair, stirred the chocolate Diaz had placed at his elbow, and sat smoking, while the smooth Albanian moved noiselessly about, laying out the clothes that might be needed through the day, polishing an eye-glass, rubbing up a diamond, refilling a bouquet-bottle, or performing some other office of valetdom. Carelessly and cavalierly as he had dismissed the Domino Blanc in the letter he had just been writing, the tantalising mystery of the night before was not so easily to be dismissed from his memory.

Lady Vavasour!

For once Strathmore's keen penetration and diplomatist acumen were baffled and at fault; he could fathom neither the means nor the motive of the dazzling Peeress's interest in, and attack upon him. How could a woman, whom he had perpetually missed, and never met during the seven years that she had sparkled through society, know him, as he would have taken his oath his eldest friend could not do, and photograph his character with a realistic accuracy that he himself, limning it from analysis, could barely have attained?

The belle Marquise lying back in her fauteuil, gazing dreamily and nonchalantly at herself in the mirror, with her shining hair falling over her arm, and a smile of superb consciousness on her rich curling lips, might have exercised a mesmeric power of will the night before, so persistently had she haunted him from the time that he saw the last flutter of the snowy folds of her domino. Is there any electro-biology so potent as beauty?

A vague prejudice had associated Lady Vavasour in his eyes with a dangerous and disagreeable aroma; he had mistrusted, without knowing her, this woman who fooled fools at her will; she had been a mésalliance, and he abhorred més-alliances; she was a Creole, and he detested Creoles; she was

a coquette, and he was always impatient of coquettes. If
Strathmore had ever wasted his hours in imagining an ideal
mistress (which he most assuredly never did), his ideal would
have, probably, clothed itself in some form, pure, stainless,
lofty, of a soilless honour, and a grave and glorious grace,
such as Hypatia, when the sunlight of Hellas fell on her white
Ionic robes, and her proud eyes glanced over the assembled
multitudes. This malicious mask, this tantalising clairvoyante, was certainly of an order its direct antipodes! But
despite all that, perhaps because of it, Lady Vavasour, seen
yet unseen, unknown yet knowing so much, haunted him,
piqued him, usurped his thoughts; and when a woman does
that, what use is it for any man to send her to the deuce, to
consign her to the devil? Heaven knows, not one whit! Ana-
thema Maranatha only incenses the sorceress, and the more
she is exorcised the more she persists.

To dismiss her troublesome memory, he took up one out
of a pile of letters Diaz had placed on a salver beside him.
It was a delicate cream-coloured Millefleurs-scented billet,
fragrant with the odour of the boudoir, breathing of a buhl
writing-case, and a gemmed penholder, and white jewelled
fingers; it was only a note of invitation, pressingly worded, and
signed Blanche de Ruelle-Courances, asking him to join the
party gathered at her château of Vernonceaux, now that Paris
was growing empty and detestable, and the country and the
vine-shadows were à la mode. The Comtesse de Ruelle was
a charming leader of his own set, English by birth and tint,
Parisienne by marriage and habit; there was no more agreeable place in Europe to visit at than Vernonceaux, and she
always had about her as amusing and as *chic* a circle as the
fashion of the two nations afforded. He read the note; not
inclined to accept the invitation, but intending to go across
the Kohl, in common with most other European Dips and dé-
corés, to the pet Bad of ministers and martingales, congresses
and *coups de bonheur*, Chevaliers of the order of honour and
Chevaliers of the order of industry, king-like Greeks and
Greek-like kings. His weighing of the merits of Baden

v. Vernonceaux, and fifty other places open to him, was interrupted by Diaz approaching him from the ante-room:

"M. le Comte de Valdor demande si milord est visible?"

Strathmore looked up, setting down his chocolate:

"To him—oh yes! Show M. le Comte up here, if he have no objection."

The Albanian withdrew (Diaz was soft, sleek, noiseless as a panther, and obeyed implicitly—four inestimable qualities in a valet, a wife, or a spy!), and, in a few minutes, ushered Valdor in; a very young man, not more than four or five-and-twenty, slight, graceful, animated, delicately made, the beau-ideal, as he was the descendant, of those who turned back their scented ruffles, and shook the powder from their perfumed locks, as they went out with a mot on their lips to the fatal *charette* while the tocsin sounded.

"Valdor, très cher, forgive my receiving you *en négligé*," laughed Strathmore. "We don't stand on ceremony with one another. I'm later than usual, and you are earlier. It isn't twelve, is it?"

Valdor looked at his little jewelled watch, the size of a fifty-centime, and answered a trifle *à tort et à travers* as he sank into a dormeuse, and played with *Galignani*.

"If you come out at noon like this, Valdor, you'll soon lose your reputation; you'll tan your skin, disenchant your lady worshippers, and sink among the ordinary herd, who are deep in business before we've had our coffee, and trade in their coupons before we've thought of our valets," laughed Strathmore, noticing his unusual absence of manner, for Valdor was generally the most insouciant of *blondins*, and boasted that he never reflected but on two subjects—the fit of his gloves, and the temperature of his eau-de-Cologne bath.

Valdor laughed too, and stroked his moustaches with a hand as small and as delicate as that which the White Domino could boast.

"It *is* horribly early; friends are great bores in the morning; nobody's mot's good till the luncheon wine has washed it; indeed, I don't think a decent thing's ever said before dinner. I'm sure Horace himself was prosy before he had sat down to the *cœna*; wit must have starved of famine on a date! I owe you fifty excuses, Strathmore, for intruding so soon, but —I wanted to see you alone."

"I am most happy to see you, my dear fellow. If you are going to be unamusing, it's the prerogative of friendship to prose, as of marriage to bore one you know; every virtuous thing is dull; a preacher and a prig from time immemorial!" said Strathmore, playing with the dainty Millefleurs-scented note. "What's the matter, Valdor—anything? Are you ruining yourself for Viola Vé, like Caderousse? Has Nesselrode gone lame? Has some *brave du roture* been copying your liveries, or has some ugly Serene Princess fallen in love with you, and left you vacillating between the horrors and the honours of the liaison? What is it, eh?"

"Only this—once for all, I'm ashamed to say I must keep in your debt a little longer——"

"That all!" cried Strathmore, stopping him before he could finish the sentence. "My dear fellow! never trouble your head about such a trifle; I had forgotten it, I assure you; oblige me by doing the same."

Valdor shook his head, the colour in his face deepening, as he tossed the *Galignani* with the nervous gesture of a man embarrassed and mortified:

"I can't forget so easily; I would not if I could. You are too generous, Strathmore; you lend to men who have nothing. I never dreamt I should be unable to pay you; I made sure that by this time—but Lascases refuses to renew my bill; I cannot get money anywhere just yet, and——"

Strathmore stopped him with a gesture, and stretched out his hand; he liked young Valdor, and his own wealth, as I have said, he held in superb disdain, save in so far as it conduced to Power. He gave freely and royally; evil there might be in his nature, but not a touch of meanness; at that time he would have succoured his darkest foe from his purse; the virtues, as the errors of this man, were all naturally in extreme; petty things were not alone beneath him, but impossible to him.

"You would get into Lascases's debt to get out of mine? For shame! Trust your friend rather than that beggarly Jew, surely! You will repay it when you can, that I am certain of; meantime, give me your honour you will never renew the subject unless I do. It was a trifling affair, and you were most welcome to it!"

As he spoke, the generous smile, which gave much of sweetness to his face, came on it, softening what was dark, relaxing what was cold; and Valdor, as his hand closed on Strathmore's, saw all that was best, all that was most attractive, in a nature that was an enigma in much even to itself. He spoke a few hurried words of thanks; he, a bel esprit of the salons and the circles, was now at a loss for speech—now that he *felt;* and Strathmore stopped him once more.

"Not a syllable more about it! If ever the time come that I have to ask *you* to do anything, I know you will do it for me— *c'est assez.* Are you going to Vernonceaux this year, Valdor?"

He spoke carelessly, laughingly, to cover whatever embarrassment the other might feel in accepting his generosity; he little foresaw what the service would be that he would call on his debtor to render him.

"You are? Well! there isn't a more charming châtelaine than Blanche anywhere. She invites me, but I shall go to Baden after the race week," went on Strathmore, brushing a fly off the rose Cashmere sleeve of his dressing-gown. "I shall meet Arrelio there, and you get a man's meaning out of him in chit-chat as you never do in a conference. If congresses were held *en petit comité,* with a supper worthy Carême, they might come to something, instead of ending, as they always do now, in cobwebs and in moonshine. Why do the English always get cheated and fooled in a European congress, I wonder? Not because they *can't* lie, it is the national trade. Because they lie too much and too barefacedly, I think; and no *gobemouche* is ever tricked into even suspecting them of—the truth! A wise man never lies; I don't mean because he's moral, but because he's judicious: 'On peut être plus fin qu'un autre, mais pas plus fin que tous les autres.' Somebody always finds out a falsehood, and, once found out, your credit's gone! I say, Valdor, do you know my compatriote, Lady Vavasour?"

"Lady Vavasour? Bon dieu! I think I do! What a cold-blooded question to ask anybody in that indifferent way! Who doesn't know her, rather?"

"*I* don't. What sort of woman is she?"

"Peste, mon cher, you ask a folio. I couldn't tell you. She is divine——!"

"Divine? Well! 'a woman *is* a dish for the gods if the devil dress her not,' Shakspeare says; but I think the devil generally has the dressing, and serves up sauce with it so very piquante that it's all but poison; it's a dish like mushrooms, dainty but dangerous; with the beau sexe as with the fungi, it's fifty to ten one lights on a false one, and pays penalty for one's appetite! Is she a malicious woman, your divinity?"

"Malicious! No! Malice is for *passées* women, pinched, sallow, and hungrily jealous; for dowagers who nod their wigs over whist and their neighbours' character; for *vieilles filles* who vacillate between sacraments and scandals! Malice is a vinegar thing that belongs to a 'certain age!'—it has nothing to do with her. She's a little tantalising, if you like——"

"Distinction without a difference! I thought she was! And a coquette?"

"To the last extent!"

Strathmore laughed:

"To the *last*! I dare say!—when women once pass the boundary line they generally clear the ramparts. I suppose the Marquis gives the latitude he takes—just, at any rate. We're not often so on those points; we take an ell, but we don't give an inch. That's the beauty of vesting our honour in our wives; it's so much easier to forbid and dragonise another than ourselves! What a droll thing, by the way, it is, that an Englishwoman piques herself on being THOUGHT faithful to her husband, and a Frenchwoman on being thought unfaithful; their theory's different, but their practice comes to much the same thing!"

"They're like schismatics in the Churches, they split in semblance and on a straw's point, but, *sous les cartes*, agree to persecute and agree to dupe! As for Lord Vavasour, he's a detestable gourmand, invents sauces, bores you horribly, and has but one virtue—a great conjugal one!—he never interferes with his wife! He's a semi-sovereign with a lot of parasites, a mauvais sujet with a *ton de garnison*, and just brains enough to be vicious without enough to be entertaining."

"A very general case, my dear fellow! Vice is very common, and wit is very scarce; fifty men make mischief to one that makes mots. We can fill our cells with convicts, but not our clubs with *causeurs*. I wonder governments don't tax good talk; it's quite a luxury, and they might add *de luxe*, since so many go without it all their lives, in blessed ignorance of even what it is! Where does your belle Marquise go this year? I suppose you know all her movements! She must be leaving now."

"Peste! don't you know? I thought you were asked to Vernonceaux?"

"Well! if I be, what has that——"

"To do with it? She is going there too. She leaves Paris to-day."

"*There?*" The word had a dash of eagerness in it, different to the uninterested, careless tone with which Strathmore had asked all his other questions.

"Yes. She and Madame de Ruelle are sworn allies; they are constantly together. Go there and you'll see her. Do, Strathmore; parole d'honneur she is worth the trouble. She is exquisite, and for you, you icicle, she can't be dangerous."

"Dangerous!" said Strathmore, with his most contemptuous sneer. "Thank God, no woman was ever yet dangerous to me; a man must be a fool indeed who is snared by the ready-made wiles of a coquette."

"Antony was no fool."

"No, but he was a madman, and that comes to the same

thing; besides, Antony must have had very extraordinary tastes altogether, to be in love with a woman forty years old, and as brown as a berry."

"Yes," said Valdor, pathetically, "I do wish, for his credit, Cleopatra had been half her years, and a shade or two fairer. Actium would have been very poetic then."

"Poetic? Pitiable, if you like, as it is now. I say, Valdor—to go to a better theme—those steel-greys of Lee Vivian's went for nothing at the sale yesterday; they were splendid animals, and the pigeon-blue Arab mare was knocked down for five thousand francs! The wines will be worth bidding for, too; he had some of the best comet-hock in Paris. Poor fellow! one drinks his wines at his table one month, and discusses them in a catalogue the next. Ars longa, vita brevis!—one's connoisseurship survives one's friendship; Orestes must die, and Iolaüs must dine! Damon must go to the dogs, and Pythias must season his dishes! Because our brother's in the Cemetery, that's no reason why we should neglect our Cayenne!"

With which remark upon friendship, which was with him as much serious as satirical (since Strathmore was an egotist by principle and profession, habit and nature, and had never had any death touch him as he had never had any life wind round him), he began to discuss the news of the day with his guest, and it was not till Valdor had left that he took up the letter from Vernonceaux again, and drew a sheet of paper to him to answer it now,—by an acceptance.

In the little Millefleurs-scented billet lay, unknown to its writer as to him, the turning-point of his life. God help us! what avail are experience, prescience, prudence, wisdom, in this world, when at every chance step the silliest trifle, the most common-place meeting, an invitation to dinner, a turn down the wrong street, the dropping of a glove, the delay of a train, the introduction to an unnoticed stranger, will fling down every precaution, and build a fate for us of which we never dream! Of what avail for us to erect our sand-castle when every chance blast of air may blow it into nothing, and drift another into form that we have no power to move? Life hinges upon hazard, and at every turn wisdom is mocked by it, and energy swept aside by it, as the battled dykes are worn away, and the granite walls beaten down, by the fickle ocean waves, which, never two hours together alike, never two instants without restless motion, are yet as changeless as they are capricious, as omnipotent as they are fickle, as cruel as they are countless! Men and mariners may build their bulwarks, but hazard and the sea will overthrow and wear away both alike at their will—their wild and unreined will, which no foresight can foresee, no strength can bridle.

Was it not the mere choice between the saddle and the barouche that day when Ferdinand d'Orléans flung down on second thoughts his riding-whip upon the console at the Tuileries, and ordered his carriage instead of his horse, that cost himself his life, his son a throne, the Bourbon blood their royalty, and France for long years her progress and her peace? Had he taken up the whip instead of laying it aside, he might be living to-day with the sceptre in his hand, and the Bee, crushed beneath his foot, powerless to sting to the core of the Lily. Of all strange things in human life, there is none stranger than the dominance of Chance.

CHAPTER IX.

The Warning of the Scarlet Camellias.

WHERE the grey pointed towers of the Château of Vernonceaux rose above the woods among the vine-shadows of Lorraine, the air seemed still perfumed with the amber, still echoing with the madrigals of Gentil-Bernard, still rustling with the sweep of robes à la Pompadour, still filled with the mots of *abbés galants*, and the laughter of pretty pagans of a century ago. For Vernonceaux was near to Lunéville—the Lunéville of Stanislas, of Voltaire, of la belle Boufflers, the *replica* of Versailles, the pleasant exile of forbidden wit, the Lunéville of a myriad memories!

Vernonceaux stood as secluded in its forest as the castle of the Sleeping Beauty—so tranquil and so shaded, that the gay sinners of Lunéville might have been chained there in enchanted slumber, like the Moorish court under the marble pavements of the Alhambra; but if, without, there was a sylvan solitude, broken but by the song of the vintagers or the creak of the oxen-drawn waggon, within, when the Comtesse de Ruelle went there for the summer months with a choice selection from her ultra-exclusive Paris set, there were as much luxury, wit, and refined revelry as ever the Marquise de Boufflers, a hundred years before, had presided over at the little palace of Lunéville.

No sound broke the silence, save the ring of his horse's feet, as Strathmore drove the mail phaeton that had been sent to meet him through the park to Vernonceaux, on his way to the visit for which he had abandoned Baden. There was not a thing in sight but the rich country beyond and the dense forest-growth about him, until, as a break in the wood brought into view the grey façade of the building, a riding party rode into the court-yard by opposite gates to those by which he would enter, looking like some court cavalcade of Watteau, some hunting group of Wouverman's, and breaking suddenly in with life, and colouring, and motion on the solitude of the landscape, as they were thrown out in strong relief against the ivy-hung walls of the château. "I'm in time for dinner," he thought, noticing how well one of the women rode who was teazing her horse with sharp strokes of her whip, and making him rear and swerve, before she sprang from the saddle: the distance was too far for him to make out who she was, and, as he dropped his eye-glass, he wished for a lorgnon.

The saddle-horses were being led off by their grooms, and the first dressing-bell had just rung when he drove into the court-yard. At the moment of his arrival all the world was dressing, and Strathmore, as he went straight to his room, passing along the Galerie des Dames, consecrated from time immemorial to the repose of the beau sexe, heard a handsome *brune* coming out of one of the rooms say to another lady's-maid, apparently her sub-lieutenant in office, " Va vite chercher les camellias roses, dans les serres chaudes. Madame désire des fleurs naturelles, c'est sa *whim* comme disent les Anglais. Ah ma foi !—qu'elle a des caprices, Miladi Vavasour !"

This name was the first he heard at Vernonceaux! *As* he heard it, Strathmore, the last man in the world who was ever troubled by regrets or haunted by forebodings, who ever descended to the weakness of vacillation, or paid himself so ill a compliment as to imagine any step he took, however great, however trivial, could by any possibility be *unwisely* taken, wished for the moment, on an impulse he could not have explained, that he had gone to Baden instead, and left the Mask unmasked, the White Domino unknown. It was the first time a woman had ever influenced him, and he resented the influence. His prejudice against Lady Vavasour came back in full force as he heard her maid order the fresh scarlet camellias! The flowers were harmless, surely, and yet (perhaps it was association with *La Dame aux Camellias!*) with them she reassumed a dangerous aspect, as of a sorceress unscrupulous in her spells, a coquette merciless in her wiles, a woman who lived upon vanity and adored but herself, a creature like the Japan lilac, lovely to look on, but to those who lingered near, who touched or who played with her, certain destruction. By what force of argument he could not have told—trifles play the deuce with us, oddly sometimes, but by some irrepressible instinct, all his old dislike and mistrust of Lady Vavasour came back with that innocent and luckless hot-house order.

"Who are here, Diaz—do you know?" he asked the Albanian, as he dressed after his bath and a cup of coffee.

The inimitable *modus operandi* of that priceless person had mastered the whole visiting-list of Vernonceaux, though he had, on the whole, but about three minutes to himself for the process.

"Marquis and Marchioness of Vavasour, please your lord-ship," began Diaz.

"A stupid pigeon and a clever snarer!" thought Strath-more, as he held out his wrist to have his sleeve-links fastened.

"Lady George Dashwood and her sister——"

"Pretty precisians, naughty as Messalina, who go to church, like Marguerite, to meditate on Faust!" reflected Strathmore.

"My Lord Viscount Blocquehedd and M. de Croquis."

"One a fool, who writes slangy, burlesqued travels, that sell because hundreds in coroneted carriages drive up to his publisher's doors to get a copy in public and enjoy a laugh in private; and the other, a magnificent fellow, who'd have been fit company for Scipio at Liternum, but who can't send a sheet of copy to press without a 'caution' and a chance of Cayenne," thought Strathmore, perfuming his beard.

"Lady Fitzeden, my lord," pursued Diaz.

"Who gives ball-vouchers for other people's 'unimpeach-ability,' but couldn't on oath give one for her own!" reflected his master.

"Monsignore Villaflôr and M. l'Abbé de Verdreuil."

"A brace of priests, who have intrigues and absolutions in their hands, make penitents and shrive them, hide the *roué* under the *rochet*, and Cupid in the confessional. I know the race," thought Strathmore.

"M. le Vicomte de Clermont, Lord Arthur Legard, Colo-nel Dormer, and M. de la Rennecourt," pursued Diaz, in profound ignorance of his master's mental commentary.

"Very good fellows all of them; dress better than they talk, shoot with truer aim than they think, bore one rather at everything but billiards, and bestow more on their hair than on the brains underneath it, *comme il faut* but common-place," said Strathmore to himself, with the contempt of a clever man for men who are only educated, of an ambitious man for men

who are only *à la mode*, of a man who but makes society his
stepping-stone for men who never see or soar beyond it.

"Madame de Saint-Claire, H.S.H. Hélène of Mechlin,
and Lord and Lady Beaudesert, are here too, my lord," added
the Albanian, closing the list. "I think that is all—all I have
heard of at present, at least."

"A bas-bleu as mathematical and material as Madame du
Châtelet, a babyish blonde with a mushroom royalty and a
nursery lisp; a dashing brunette who smokes cigarettes and
has led the Pytchley. Well, there will be change, at any
rate. Blanche hasn't sorted her guests as she sorts her em-
broidery silks, in shades that suit; however, good contrasts
are effective sometimes. There's nobody I don't know, except
the priests and the Vavasours. That's a bore; new acquaint-
ances are much pleasanter than familiar ones; the varnish is
fresh, and the gilding is bright, and the polish is smooth, and
you only just touch the surface with friends an hour old.
Nothing wears so badly, and stands the microscope so ill as
Humanity. I suppose because we are all sham to one another,
and *les hommes se haïssent naturellement;* so the electro comes
off, and the hatred comes out, when we've been some time
together," thought Strathmore, as he left his room to go to
the drawing-rooms. No one was yet down when he was
ushered into the salons, and he threw himself on a dormeuse
with his back to a window opening on the terrace, playing
idly with the snowy curls of a little lion-dog, who, recognising
him, leapt on his knee, shaking its silver bells in a joyous
welcome. Strathmore did not care about animals; in truth, I
don't think he cared much about anything except—himself!
Not that he was an egotist in any petty sense of the word; he
would have shrouded no man's light, profited at no man's
cost, taken no man's right, but he was self-sustained and self-
absorbed; keen personal ambitions were dominant in him,
pure personal interests alone occupied him, and the instincts
and weaknesses—kindlier if you like, but more general and
less viril of most men—had no part in him. He was kind to
a dog, for instance, because it was helpless, and he would

have disdained to be otherwise; but to care for a dog's fidelity, to regret a dog's death as he had known Erroll do, were utterly incomprehensible to him.

He sat there some few moments listlessly twisting the ear of the Maltese, while the clock on the console near gently ticked away the time, and pointed to a quarter to nine; he did not hear a step approach towards the back of his chair from the terrace behind, he did not turn and see a figure that stood just within the window betwixt him and the faint evening light.

"Bon jour, Lord Cecil! Are you meditating on the Gitana prophecy, or on the Domino Blanc — which? Or is the Voltura affair absorbing you, pray, to the utter exclusion of both?"

That light, *méchante* voice that had mocked him from the mask struck on his ear like the gay, sudden chime of some silvery bell, and for once in his life Strathmore started! As he rose and swung round, the night under the Czechen limes came back swiftly and vividly to his memory;—how had that voice failed to recall it before?

With the scarlet coronal of flowers on her lovely amber hair, and the light of a sunny laughter beaming in her eyes; framed between the gossamer lace and broidered azure silk of the curtain draperies; a form bright and brilliant and richly coloured as any picture of Watteau's, thrown out against the purple haze of the air, and the dark shadows of evening that were veiling the landscape beyond; there stood the blonde aux yeux noirs of the Vigil of St. John, the White Domino of the fête à la Régence—Marion Marchioness of Vavasour! Strangely enough, he had never even by a random thought connected the two as one. Involuntarily, unwittingly, he stood a moment dazzled and surprised, looking at the delicate and glittering picture that was before him, painted in all its dainty colouring on the sombre canvas of the night; and she laughed softly to herself,—for one brief instant she had startled him from his self-possession. She guessed rightly, that no woman before her had ever boasted so much.

Then Strathmore bent to her with the soft and stately courtesy for which his race of steel had ever been famed— the velvet glove that they habitually wore over their gauntlets of mail.

"I merit a worse fate than the Gitana predicted me, for my blindness in not recognising the veiled picture by its eyes, in not knowing no two voices could have a music so rare! May I ask to be forgiven, though I can never forgive myself?"

She smiled as she gave him her hand:

"You may. You rendered me too daring and too generous a service, Lord Cecil, for me not to forgive you weightier offences than that. I am your debtor for a heavy debt—the debt of my life saved! Believe me, I am very grateful."

The words were few and simple; a young girl out of her convent could not have spoken more earnestly and touchingly than the woman of the world; where more florid, profuse, eloquently-studied words would have been set aside by him as the conventional utterances of necessity, these charmed and won him, these rang on his ear with the accent of truth.

"To secure so high a price as your gratitude most men would have perilled much more than I did," he answered her. "But I had not then the incentive that would tempt the world to any madness at Lady Vavasour's bidding. I had not seen what I rescued, I did not know whom I served!"

She looked up at him from under her black silken lashes as she sank into the chair he wheeled to her, and smiled.

"You compliment charmingly, Lord Cecil (you remember, I suppose, that I said I liked bon-bons), but then, how much is true? You are a diplomatist; it is your habit to speak suavely and mean nothing, it is the *spécialité* that will get you the Garter and give you an Earldom."

"Lady Vavasour—by everything I have heard of her— can surely never mistrust her own power to convert the most sceptical, and do with all men what she would?"

Her attitude, as she sank down into the chair, had all the

soft Odalisque-like grace with which he had first seen her lying amongst her cushions on the bench of the Bohemian boat; and he confessed to himself that this matchless and dazzling beauty, at once poetic and voluptuous, at once gifted with the loveliness of the sérail, and the tournure of the salons, might well play with men, and make their madness at its will.

"Ah!" she laughed—her airy, silvery laugh!—"but I do not profess to deal with people who desire age and despise love; they are not in my experience, or my category. I shall be a long while before I credit any compliment from you, mon ami. Did I not show you how well I knew your character at the *bal masqué?* Was it not sketched, now, as accurately, as any one of La Bruyère's?"

"It was, though it was not drawn altogether *en beau*. It was *so* accurate that it flattered me even by its unflattering points, since it showed that I must have been a subject of interest and of study to my unerring clairvoyante."

A momentary blush tinged her cheek, making her loveliness lovelier, and not escaping Strathmore, though he knew how *grandes dames* can blush, as they can weep at their will, when they need it to embellish their beauty, too well to be much honoured by it. She looked at him with the same glance that had flashed through her mask.

"Not at all! You are much too vain! I only wanted to puzzle you. If my shafts hit home, it was chance, not effort. Hearsay and penetration made my clairvoyance, as they make all. You were no stranger to me by name. I have heard plenty of you from others, though we had never happened to meet till that night in Bohemia. Come! tell me the truth. Do you not think it a terrible escapade to have travelled alone, at night, in that *inconséquent* manner, with only my maid?"

"I think it a '*caprice d'une belle dame*,' which became her far better than the common-place and the conventional, which have nothing in common with her," smiled Strathmore. And for once he paid a compliment that was sincerely meant.

"But why did you so cruelly refuse me your name, and condemn me to pursue '*un ombre, un rêve, un rien,*' in seeking to see again the phantom which had flashed on me, when, had I but known *whom* I sought, all Europe would have guided me to its idol!"

"Very gracefully asked, indeed!" said Lady Vavasour, with a sign of her fan, made eloquent in her hand, as in the hand of a Gaditana of Cadiz. "But, first of all, you never pursued the phantom at all, mon ami. You don't do those things! I wasn't a state secret, and I didn't carry despatches: sequitur, you were courteous to me while we were together because you were well bred, and I was a woman; but you never thought twice about me after we parted, except just that night, when I left you behind to smoke and sleep under the pines, when, perhaps, you said to yourself, 'Blonde with dark eyes—unusual! Travelling alone, too—very odd!' and then dismissed me to think of Prince Michel! Secondly, I refused you my name, because it was my whim to travel incognita; and down the river I dispensed with even my courier. I am as capricious as the winds, you know, and, like the winds, never change my caprices for any one's will!"

Before he could answer her the door of the salon was thrown open, and several people entered—his hostess among others, with that courtly, velvet-shod churchman, Monsignore Villaflôr. Strathmore had to rise, and his place was taken by the priest, who was a courtier, a connoisseur, and a *coureur des ruelles.* The rooms filled; dinner was announced and served as the little chimes of the clock rang nine, and to Strathmore's lot fell Lady George Dashwood, whose soft platitudes had never seemed more wearisome to him than to-night, when they discoursed of chamber-music, old china, Maltese dogs, new fashions, Elzevir editions, and altar-screens, in the same unvarying and perfectly-bred monotone, which had much the same effect as if a humble-bee had been perpetually humming in the flowers of the épergne before him. At some distance from him—too great for any conversation

with her—sat Lady Vavasour; and while keeping up his recitative with Lady George, Strathmore could not choose but
look at her, could not choose but think of her—this woman
who had been first so strangely thrown in his way, against
whom he still felt an unconquerably stubborn prejudice, yet
who exercised over him, when he was with her, a necromancy
of air, of glance, of tone, that surprised him, incensed him,
and yet beguiled him. Had he foreseen his future, he would
have flung aside every thought of this bright, brilliant beauty,
as he had flung aside her broidered handkerchief into the
bosom of the Czechen peasant girl in Prague; but—could
we foresee one step before another, would the lives of any
one of us be blasted, blundered, full of bitterness, and of evil,
as they are? Is not the misery of every life due to the band
that is bound fast on our eyes, which the wisest can do little
to lift, which makes us feel our way blindly, uncertainly,
erringly, stumbling at every step; which is never lifted, save
when our faces are turned backwards, and we are bidden to
look behind us at the land that we have quitted, which is
sown thick with graves; and at the gates that are closed upon
us, on which is written "Too Late"?

Amidst the hum of conversation, the bouquet of the wines,
the fragrance of the exotics, the numberless murmurs of
"Sauterne, monsieur?"—"Château Yquem?"—"Suprême de
Volaille?"—"Macedoine d'Abricots?"—"Beignets d'An-
nanas?" Strathmore throughout dinner let his thoughts be
usurped by the dazzling face, with its amber hair drawn
slightly back from the delicate temples, in masses and ripples
of yellow gold, which was but tantalisingly visible to him
through the clusters of gorgeous flowers, and behind the form
of an alabaster Ariadne that intervened between her and
himself. Is there any separation more exasperating than
the length of a dinner-table? I don't believe the Hellespont
was half so provoking! Leander could cross *that* if Hero
didn't mind receiving him au naturel; but what man, pray,
can move from his place at a dinner-party? He must say with
Claude Frollo, "*Anakthe!*" submit, and sit where he's put!

Strathmore found the dinner an interminable bore, and felt his prejudice giving way; his judgment in no way swerved from his settled conviction that Lady Vavasour was vain, spoiled, dangerous, and a consummate coquette, bent upon conquest, and not over-careful of her character—a glance told him that; but the rich, glad, luxuriant music that he had heard from her lips under the lindens by the river-side, now sweet as a bird's carol, now sad as a miserere, seemed to ring in his ear again, and he caught himself thinking a poetic sentimentalism worthy of the Sabreur—that she must have some of that music in her soul! Against the White Domino, the malicious Mask, he would have been prepared and steeled; the bright Odalisque of the Moldau, the songstress of the Spring night, took him unawares, and disarmed him.

As the women rose at length and swept out of the great banqueting-hall, where Guises had feasted Valois, she had to pass his chair, the lace of her dress brushing his shoulder, the subtle fragrance of her hair wafted to him like the odour of some hot-house flower. As she did so, a bracelet of cameo dropped from her arm (*really* dropped, she was too highly finished a coquette to need any such vulgar and common-place ruses); and as Strathmore bent for it and fastened it again on her arm, he noticed how snow-white and polished the skin was, like the skin of the unguent-loving and delicate Greeks, and confessed to himself that the smile on those sweet, laughing lips was the loveliest a woman ever had at command.

"Merci! We leave you, *à l'Anglais*, to olives and repose, politics and cigarettes, solitude and slander. How you will pick our beauty to pieces and legislate for the nations! Adieu!" she whispered, as she passed onward.

"By George! they did not overrate her; and that fool is her husband! Faugh! it is Caliban wedded to Miranda!" thought Strathmore, as he poured some Johannisberg into his glass, looking across at the Marquis of Vavasour. The epithet and the comparison were both somewhat overstrained, it must be admitted; but there are very few men, I think, who, ad-

miring a beautiful woman, are not disposed to think her lord
and master a contemptible fellow, and feel very much towards
him as you may have felt on a still grey day in September,
lounging along by the sunken fence of some splendid preserves
of which you have not the *entrée*, looking at the cover and
hearing the whirr of the birds, towards the owner, whoever
he be, for whom the game's set apart. And when M. le Mari
is a muff, or the owner no shot, your sense of injury is very
naturally redoubled in both cases, and your animus increased. Envy is a quick match, easily lighted, and needs
no spirit added to the wick to make it strike fire and flare
into flame.

The Marquis was not a Caliban, and not a fool, though
Strathmore, from the eminence of an acute, subtle, and
brilliant intellect, chose to call him so. He was a short, plain,
grey-haired little man, with small dark eyes, that leered and
twinkled viciously; a very sensual mouth, a good deal of
wickedness in the upper part of his face, and a good deal of
weakness in the lower; a man specially to enjoy taking the
world in neatly and slyly, yet a man not difficult to govern
by any one who knew his weak points. He had not very
many brains, and those he had had been spent chiefly in the
study of Brillat-Savarin, and the elucidation in theory of new
plats and sauces. He had taken no share whatever in public
life, had lived chiefly abroad, was principally noted for his
dinners, was considered rather an insignificant person by
those who stripped him of his strawberry-leaves; but being a
very great Personage to the world in general, had the kow-
tow performed to him to any amount, threw his ermine over
his emptiness, covered all cancans with his coronet, and
hushed all whispers with his wealth. He was the Marquis of
Vavasour—had livings for which the ecclesiastical saints
scrambled and truckled, granting him easy absolution for
such superior adowsons, and presenting him with a brevet to
heaven, as only a decent return for his rich presentations; he
had a considerable amount of family patronage, the eighth
cardinal virtue, for which a man will get loved more than for

all the other seven put together; he had a title of the highest
rank and longest date; therefore, though chiefly remarkable
for gourmandise and a certain monkeyish malice, this inert,
obstinate, sly, and rather demoralised gourmet gave the law,
had the *pas*, and was held in high honour and distinction by
all, save, indeed, by Strathmore, who thought again, as he
looked at his lordship, "Faugh! it is Caliban wedded to Miranda!" It was the first time that Strathmore had ever
thought a woman thrown away upon a man in marriage—
ordinarily his opinion was precisely the reverse! But the
Marquis *was* a provocative owner of anything half so lovely
as Marion Lady Vavasour, though it must be confessed he
was an easy one; the liberty he took he gave, he never
crossed her caprices, and there were invariably between them
that polite *bon accord*, that cool don't-carish, very-happy-to-
see-you never-interfere-with-you sort of friendship which is
the popular hue of "marriage in high life," and is decidedly
the best and least troublesome it can wear. If you have to
look long on *one* colour, let it be a well-wearing, never-
dazzling *nuance;* if you have to run in leash, don't pull at the
collar, it won't keep your companion from going her pace,
and will only gall your own throat for nothing. That discreet,
tranquil "friendship" of the Vavasours is an admirable thing ;
it's like a well-bred monotone, or a well-bred man that smooths
over all things and never makes a row. Galba, who shuts his
eyes and shakes hands with Mæcenas, is the wise fellow.
Menelaus, who raves, can't rouse his friends in *our* day; he'll
only get a sneering chuckle from them all, from Nestor in at
Boodles', to Amphimachus in at Pratt's, run the risk of a
Times leader, which is our modern substitute for the pillory,
and in lieu of Troy will only obtain—a "Decree Nisi, with
costs!"

CHAPTER X.

La Belle v. La Belle.

WHEN they entered the drawing-room, half an hour after, the first thing that met Strathmore's eyes was the woman who, more or less, had haunted his memory and excited his curiosity since the May night under the lindens, in the solitudes of Bohemia. Lady Vavasour was lying back in a dormeuse, glancing through George Sand's last novel; the full light from a chandelier above fell upon her, making the snowy camei dazzling, and the scarlet flowers glow; she looked like some rare and exquisite Sèvres figure as she sat there, with her cheek resting on her hand, and the lashes drooped over her eyes, the form perfect as a statuette of Coysvox, the colouring rich and delicate as an enamel of Fragonard. And yet—those cursed camellias! Was it the strange grouping of those scarlet flowers circling the dead gold of her hair that gave to her something startling with all her seductiveness, bizarre with all her beauty, dangerous with all her delicacy; something that made him involuntarily think of Lucretia Borgia, Catharine Medici, Clytemnestra, Frédégonde, Olympia Mancini, Gunilda, in a pêle-mêle chaos of every divine demoniac, every fatal facinatress that the world had seen since the world began; something which struck him with nothing less than aversion for the first moment that the glowing coronal on the amber hair met his eyes again; but which then forced him against himself into a dizzy, blind, breathless, admiration, such as no woman had ever wrung from him.

"That ever such beauty as this should belong to a creature good for nothing but to criticise sauces, smell the bouquets of wines, and gluttonise over green fat!" thought Strathmore, who held all gourmands in contemptuous disdain, and this one especial gourmand in particular, as he drew near her, and sank down in a low chair by her couch, regardless that Lady George looked chagrined, and that Lady

Beaudesert had signalled him with her fan. The bright beauties of his set rather resented his sudden and immediate desertion to another standard.

"Lady Vavasour, may I not trust to hear to-night the voice whose music drove the nightingales to despair under the limes?" said Strathmore, to the chagrin of Monsignore Villaflôr and a host of baser rivals.

She glanced at him under her silky lashes, and that under-glance was the most dangerous in the world.

"No! I sing to nightingales, but not to order, like a prima donna. The birds can appreciate me, the bores can't!" And her ladyship included, in a disdainful sign of her fan, the men whom Strathmore in his pride had classified as "*comme il faut*, but common-place"—a classification, by-the-by, which would fit, I fear, most of the members of "good society."

"But you sang to ME, and you will sing to me again!" said Strathmore, with the calm, appropriative, Brummellian nonchalance of tone that women always like. Women love an autocratic ruler; even your imperious coquettes, believe me, feel the charm, though they won't, I dare say, often own to it!

"Do not be so sure of that! I am not Malibran, whom you can hear any night for five guineas, and I did not sing to *you* under the limes; you are infinitely too vain! I sang *pour m'amuser*, and to scandalise those English women who grumbled at the cucumber-soup, and thought me 'evidently not a proper person!' The English are born-travellers. I wonder why they think it necessary to make one of the *spé-cialités du voyage*, a compound of ice and acid for every stranger they meet?"

"Because suspicion and reserve are to us what their shells are to cocoa-nuts; they make a little kernel look big, and if there's emptiness inside, conceal it," laughed Strathmore. "But you are very cruel to charge me with vanity. If I be vain, have I not food for it in knowing that I am such a sub-ject of interest to one whose tap from her fan is one of the *cordons d'honneur* of Europe, that she honoured me with

studying my character, learning my preferences, and even
making researches among my family legends? Lady Vavasour must not send me to Coventry when I remember the Domino Blanc!"

Her eyes laughed with malicious amusement.

"The Domino Blanc seems to have made a great impression on you, Lord Cecil! but only because she knew of the
Voltura affair, and you are curious to know *how* she knew it.
No woman ever makes you vain. What you are vain of are
things like your conduct of the Murat entanglement, when
your chief's à *propos* brain attack so obligingly left you alone
to steer through the troubled waters. Now, confess me the
truth, were you not glad when Lord Templetown had con-
gestion just at that juncture?"

"I believe I was! If a military man's friend dies who had
the step above him, his first thought is 'Promotion—deucedly
lucky for me!' His next, 'Poor-fellow!—what a pity!' always
comes two seconds after. I understand Voltaire. If your
companion's existence at table makes you have a dish dressed
as you don't like it, you are naturally relieved if an apoplec-
tic fit empties his chair, and sets you free to say, '*Point de
sauce blanche!*' All men are egotists; they only persuade
themselves they are not selfish by swearing so so often, that
at last they believe what they say. No motive under the sun
will stand the microscope; human nature, like a faded beauty,
must only have a demi-lumière; draw the blinds up, and the
blotches come out, the wrinkles show, and the paint peels off.
The beauty scolds the servants—men hiss the satirists—who
dare to let in daylight!"

She listened, and laughed her low, silver laugh. This was
not the conversation with which her courtiers usually entertained her, but, if only as a novelty, she rather liked it.

"Quite true! It is only here and there a beauty like *myself* who can brave the noontide, and a man who, like *yourself*, can stand the satire, who dare to admit it as true. *I*
don't want rouge yet, and *you* don't want ruses yet; but I

dare say we shall both come to them, and then we sha'n't like the blinds up better than any one else."

"Lady Vavasour needing rouge!—it is an impossible stretch of imagination. One cannot realise the doom of mortality thoroughly enough to picture that cheek of child-like bloom ever condescending to the aid of the dressing-box!" smiled Strathmore, his eyes dwelling on the bloom in question, that was softly faint, yet warmly bright, as the flush on a sea-shell.

"But a diplomatist needing ruses is not so difficult! You must condescend to the *blanc de perle* of the bureau—White Lies—or you will forsake your *métier*, or your *métier* you. If I can defy enamel, you won't be able to defy expediency, mon ami!"

Strathmore laughed:

"Enamelling *is* as much in favour in the cabinets as in the cabinets de toilette, I admit, and is very useful in both. Nations suffer for the cost in the one, and husbands for the cost in the other! But, for myself, I don't think I shall ever use the *blanc de perle* you predict. I am of Talleyrand's way of thinking, that the able man disdains so clumsy a tool as falsehood. It is the weapon of the bungler, not of the master. Take refuge in falsehood, and you have dealt a trump into your enemy's hand that he can play against you whenever he likes. The most adroit falsehood is but thin ice that may break any day. The true art is to know how to hold truth, and—how to withhold it; but never to deal with anything else."

"Then you can never humour men, and never flatter them! How can power be obtained without?"

"By using them and ruling them. Men are the wise man's tools, to be commanded, not his mutinous crew to be bribed and pampered!"

She looked at him as he spoke, and saw on his face the look of pitiless power, of imperious passion, of merciless will, that the Gitana had seen as she studied it under the Bohemian stars—that all saw who looked at the portraits of

the Norman Strathmores, when the western sun shone on
them through the stained windows at White Ladies—and,
while she was fascinated by it, thought to herself how she
would soften it, subdue it, break it down beneath her hands,
chain it there beneath her feet. Women delight to ponder
how "the dove will peck the estridge;" and the keener and
fiercer the hawk which is their quarry, the more they glory
in blinding him with the dazzle of their silvery wings, and in
disabling him with the music of their soft wood-notes! Shakspeare knew that women justified his metaphor, though fal-
coner's lore might not!

"You are very secure of your future," she laughed, while
the brilliant light above her head shone down on the waves
of her amber hair, and the scarlet coronal that wound round
them, in so startling and strong a contrast of colour—a contrast that no beauty less perfect, less delicate, less exquisitely
tinted, could ever have borne. "Doesn't the Bohemian's
prophecy make you tremble? How horrible it was!"

Strathmore laughed too, looking into the lustrous eyes
flashing on him sweetly and softly as an Oriental's:

"Yes! she gave me plenty of melodrame for my money,
but I don't see very well how it can come to pass. I'm not a
hero of romance, with a mysterious parentage or a hidden
murder; I sha'n't make a double marriage, discover a family
secret, or take anybody's life in hot or cold blood! All my
actions are patent to the world; I fear I shall never do anything to merit Redempta's romantic prediction! But that re-
minds me, when you talked to me that night, you talked only
in French, Lady Vavasour? I thought you were a Parisienne!"

"Of course you did. I would not give you a clue even
to my country."

"Which was very cruel, madame! But though you gave
me no clue, you gave me a promise, and I must claim its fulfilment."

"*I* gave you one? Indeed! I have forgotten it, then. A
year ago is an eternity to be called on to remember. Don't

you like those Maltese dogs! I think they are such pretty
snowy things."

"But *I* remember it," said Strathmore (indisposed to turn
the conversation from himself to the lion-pups), with a smile
that piqued his companion because she could not translate it.
"It was, that when we met again you would thank me for
my chivalry, as you honoured me by terming it, and would
pay your debt—*comme je voudrais!* I am tempted to be an
inexorable creditor!"

The lovely mouth made a *moue boudeuse*, but she gave
him the look that she had given him under the lime in Bohemia—soft with all its coquetry, tender with all its dazzling
brilliance.

"I dare say! Well! what would content you?" she
laughed, softly stirring her fan, while its motion floated the
subtle fragrance of her hair to him when he leant towards
her.

It was a dangerous question for such lips to put to any
man! He could scarce have but one answer rise to his tongue
within sight and touch of that tempting loveliness—an answer
that could not be uttered in the salons of Vernonceaux, to the
wife of a Peer, to Marion Lady Vavasour! Strathmore bent
down towards her till his voice could reach her ear alone, his
eyes darkening with that swift, instantaneous light which
showed—to any woman—that the passions he disdained did
but sleep, and might yet wake, like "giants refreshed from
their slumber."

"Some day, perhaps, I may dare to tell you—not here,
not yet!"

The words escaped him before he knew it. As the perfume of her hair reached him, as he met the glance of her
eyes, as he looked on her delicate dazzling face where the
light from the chandelier shone upon it, this woman's beauty
captivated him against his will, and made the blood course
quicker through his veins, as though he had drunk in the
rich bouquet and the subtle strength of some rare ruby wine,
warm from the purple clusters of the South. The faint rose-

blush, that was the most dangerous of all Lady Vavasour's
charms, since it was the one which flattered most, and most
surely counterfeited nature, came on her cheek, and her eyes
met his with a languid sweetness. It was the first whisper of
the syren's sea-song, that was to lead by music unto wreck
and death; it was the first beckoning of the white arms of
Circe, that were to wreathe, and twine, and cling, till they
should draw down their prey beneath the salt waves flowing
over the fathomless abyss whence there is no return.

Then with one of her rapid, coquettish mutations, one of
those tantalising *boutades* that were her most cruel and certain witcheries, she signed him away with a blow from her
fan, and laughed lightly:

"Lord Cecil, I have talked to you alone for full ten minutes. I never give any one a longer monopoly. Surrender
your place to Monsignore Villaflôr, and let the world in to
our conversation."

Strathmore leant back, and nestled himself more closely
in among his cushions with calm nonchalance:

"*Pardon, madame!* Monsignore can seat himself, and a
signal of your pretty toy will summon the world without my
moving. I am very comfortable just now!"

She glanced at him with a sparkle of malicious amusement.

"You are piqued, mon ami, *already!*" she thought, with
gratified triumph, as she arched her delicate eye-brows with
provoking indifference, and signed Villaflôr towards her.
Dormer, Legard, and Rennecourt gathered about her dormeuse the instant the signal permitted them; and for any
evidence she gave of remembering his presence, or even his
existence, Strathmore might have utterly faded from her memory as she dispensed the mischievous mots, the moqueur
smile, the silent dangerous glances that were the war-weap-
ons of the arch coquette whom Lord Vavasour had taken to
himself.

She knew that no possible mode of action could have
better impressed her on Strathmore's thoughts, the very an-

noyance it awoke in him with himself, retained her in his
mind; the momentary tenderness that had gleamed in her
eyes, succeeded by the tantalising indifference of her dis-
missal, he knew them well enough, they were the tactics of a
coquette, and he hated coquettes, "women who live on the cens-
ing of fools, and spend their time in fooling wise men!" he
thought, contemptuously, while, without moving so as to give
up his place to Villaflôr, or any one else, he began to play
écarté with the Vicomte de Clermont, at a table that stood at
his elbow. Strathmore was specially fond of that little witching French game; he was one of the best players in Europe;
he liked its tranquil, subtle finesses that were to be enjoyed
without stirring from his dormeuse; he liked its keen excitement bought for a few Naps a side, and he was tenacious of
his reputation in it. Clermont was almost the only member
of the Paris Jockey Club who claimed to equal him, and their
écarté was always a sharp contest of skill. Another time he
would have gone farther out of reach of the babble of conversation round Lady Vavasour's sofa; now, Strathmore did
not choose to let her think she could be any disturbing element at all. It was a dangerous neighbourhood for écarté,
or any game that hung on skill, thought, and finesse, where
every word of the silvery mocking voice was to be heard,
where every echo of the airy laughter rang on his ear, where
the fluttering motion of the fan, the gleam of her amber
tresses, the glitter of the camei on an arm as white as they,
caught his eye every moment. But Strathmore invariably
risked danger in little things as in great; he never avoided
it, he always disdainfully and self-reliantly lingered in it; it
was his strength or his weakness, whichever you like.

He played eight games as scientifically as though he had
been in a card-room, with not another face to distract him
from that of the king's he marked; and Lady Vavasour,
glancing at him, began to doubt her own power. Strathmore
leant back, his eyes fixed on the cards he held, his interest
centred in the game he played, and she might have been fifty
leagues away for any sign she could discover that she dis-

turbed him; the Voltura affair she *might* endure as a rival, states and princes were involved in that, but to be rivalled by écarté, by painted pieces of pasteboard and a few Naps a side!—never! She felt her character at stake—her vanity *was.* (There are plenty of people in this world, my good sirs, besides coquettes, who take the one thing for the other, and when they cry out their reputation's attacked, are in truth only snarling from their wounded conceit!) The eight games had been evenly won and lost, they were four all, and they began *la belle;* the Strathmores of White Ladies had never borne patiently to lose in anything, they were a race that dearly loved dominance, and took it, *coûte que coûte,* like imperious, unyielding Normans as they were; he did not choose that Clermont should beat him; this evening, in especial, defeat would have annoyed him unspeakably.

The luck of the cards had always been with the Vicomte, but Strathmore's play had more than balanced that; it was evident to all those who gathered near the écarté table that the game was in his hands. His hostess from a distance watched him over the top of her fan, while discoursing of turquoise céladon with H.S.H. of Mechlin; her name had some years before been entangled with his own in that gossip which is rife in those hotbeds of scandal, club-rooms and salons; the gossip had long given place to newer slander, yet the woman of the world could not wholly lose the tenderness that still clung about her heart for one whom she knew had never loved her—could not wholly keep down a sigh that rose to the lips, against which the gold-powdered down of her fan was pressed. The Marquis, lying half asleep, pondering on a new flavour for a salmi of woodcocks that he should have tried by his *chef* the first day of the season, looked through his shut lids at him with snarling envy. The Marquis always thought *"plus beau que moi—c'est un tort qu'il me fait!"* and the Norman physique of Strathmore specially attracted his attention. "That man's like a Velasquez picture, but he'll do something very bad some day," muttered Lord Vavasour, comforting himself with the detrimental rider with which we always qualify an admiration extorted from our envy. Most people in the room watched him as *la belle* began, catching the contagion of a skilfully-contested game, and the excitement of a chance so evenly poised that a single card would turn the scale.

Strathmore himself was entirely absorbed in it, entirely intent on it, keenly, eagerly, resolutely bent on winning. He would have lost fifty times the amount staked on it rather than have lost that game at écarté! He played indifferent cards with such superb skill, such matchless finesse, that *la belle* was all but won, when,—from where she sat near, on her dormeuse, Lady Vavasour leant towards him to look over his hand, to watch his triumph, the fragrance of her hair crossing him like the perfume of some exotic, her lovely lips, whose charm even he had admitted, so near his own that their breath fanned his cheek. He looked up and met her eyes; the dazzling beauty of this woman ran through his veins like subtle fire, and threw him off his guard, as though the air had been suddenly filled with the dreamy intoxicating odour of narcotic fumes, that bewilder the reason and charm while they weaken the senses. He played inadvertently—the wrong card. The false step was not to be retrieved (what false step is!); it gave the game into Clermont's hands, and for the first time for years Strathmore lost at écarté.

For the instant, trifle though it was, he hated the woman who had unnerved him and fooled him, as passionately, as bitterly, as though the wrong card had been some stain on his honour, the lost game some indelible shame on his name! The bad play he had been betrayed into incensed him enough, but that she should have had this power over him incensed him far more.

"I compliment you on your skill, Clermont. You played admirably. You have beaten *me!* They won't believe it at the Jockey Club!" he said, laughing, as he leant back again among his cushions. His annoyance only showed itself in his eyes, that darkened with the swift anger of his pitiless race, though the rest of his face never changed.

"When I came to look on at your victory, it was very uncomplimentary to entertain me with a defeat. I thought you were the best écarté player in Europe," said Lady Vavasour, maliciously, with a slight shrug of her snowy shoulders, and as much tranquil unconcern as though she were innocent and ignorant of having done all the mischief.

"Lady Vavasour, from Paradise downwards feminine Interference was never productive but of a losing game for man!" said Strathmore, in the tranquil *traînants* tones in which he always spoke his rudest things.

She laughed softly; it amused her; he had lost his game and she had won hers.

"*L'une belle te perdait l'autre, très cher,*" said Rennecourt to Strathmore, as they went to the smoking-room that night, when the women had deserted the drawing-rooms and gone to their chambers and their novels and their charming négligées in the Galerie des Dames.

Strathmore suppressed an impatient oath to himself; the libel, like most libels, was unpalatable because it was true. He hated the woman whose mere touch had so fooled him, and whose sway and whose spells, as he had seen her that night, he had been forced to confess the wildest rumours had not overdrawn. But for all that, though he owed her his defeat at écarté, and loathed her sudden and subtle power over him, as he lay on the couch of the smoking-room that night, while Baden favourites, new caprices of reigning lionnes, the hushed-up affair of the marked cards at Flora Dohla's, in which well-known names were involved, the *dernier débauche* of a Russian Prince, who was startling even Paris, were chatted over with the freedom that's only attained when the papooshes are on and the ladies are off, and is enjoyed like the ease of the dressing-gown after the restraint of the *grande tenue*, Strathmore felt a keener detestation still for his lordship of Vavasour and Vaux, as he glanced at the Marquis (who, wrapped in his luxurious Cashmere robes, looked something like an over-fed monkey, grizzled with age and pampered with eating, as his eyes leered and twinkled at a

grivois tale), and thought as he glanced, "Faugh! that Caliban to——!"

It was an envy and an impatience that many before him
had smarted under, looking at her lord and master, so made
and termed by marital right, and thinking of Marion Lady
Vavasour.

CHAPTER XI.

The Daughter of Eve in the Garden of Roses.

STRATHMORE very rarely got up early; usually he had his
chocolate brought to him, glanced through new novels, read
his letters, had his first cigar before he rose, and then lounged
down among the latest to breakfast. He was accustomed to
say, that your best *causeur* is dull over his coffee; with his
cutlets, a man thinks of consols and coupons, and with his
anchovy only finds relish for telegrams; in the oil of his sar-
dines his satire is swamped, and as he breaks his plover's
eggs he's only good for reading and speaking political platitudes; his head's admirably clear, but his wit isn't ripe.
Therefore Strathmore's rule always was, "Do your own business before noon; but don't be bored by your friends till
after. In the morning we're all cautious, not convivial: so
breakfast and write to your lawyer in solitude; congregate at
luncheon, and take *croustades* and conversation together!" It
was a very good rule, I think; letters written in the morning
never compromise you; mots made in the morning never
amuse you; and it was one he seldom broke.

But the morning after his arrival at Vernonceaux, when
Diaz entered his chamber to fill his bath, the breeze as it
blew in from the windows, which had been partially left open
through the hot night, came so pleasantly laden with the
fragrance of the rose-gardens, the pine-woods, and the vine-
covered hills, that it seemed for once more tempting than his
yellow-papered *roman* and his chocolat à la Vanille, which
had both a strong flavour of Paris; a flavour than which or-

dinarily *on ne peul mieux;* but Paris, like partridges, may want change sometimes, and pall—as what doesn't, from women to wine!—under the ruinous test of *"Toujours!"* For once Strathmore felt tempted to get up early; and he rose, dressed, and sauntered out by an *escalier* that led, without passing through any part of the building, from his wing of the château down into the gardens below.

"A device of some dainty châtelaine, some *dame des beaux cousins,* for her lover to pass up to her chamber without waking the seneschal, or risking his limbs by climbing," thought Strathmore, as he stood on the grey stone steps looking over at the gardens that lay before him. "Well! we have *escaliers dérobés* still! Licence may have gone out of the language, but it hasn't gone out of the manners; we've learnt to be hypocrites, but we haven't altered our tastes. To advance in Civilisation is, after all, only to perfect Cant. The nude figure remains the same delight to the precisian as the profligate; but he drapes her discreetly in public, while he gloats over her undraped *in petto.* Men don't change their natures, only their faces!"

With which, Strathmore sauntered down the steps, and took any way that hazard led him, which was through the bronze trellis-work gates that opened into his hostess's rose-gardens, mazes of blossom, where the birds sang under the roses, and the air was full of the rich fragrance of clusters of crimson bloom, as he strolled slowly along, profaning these sacred precincts, that were as consecrated to ladies as the gardens of Odalisques, with the scent and the smoke of his Manilla. There is something in the freshness, the stillness, the sunny calm of early morning, that has its charm, even when we are least inclined to give way to these things, and most inclined to sneer at them. Strathmore—essentially a man "of the world, worldly"—who lived in courts, clubs, and salons, who had never got up and come on deck to see the sun rise any day that his yacht was at anchor in the Bosphorus; whose manual was Rochefoucauld, and breviary Bruyère; whose life had been spent in an atmosphere scented with perfumes and pastilles, where daylight was never needed and never remembered, and a purer air would have lacked in excitement; even Strathmore, though nature was not much more to him than to Talleyrand or Grammont, felt the freshness, the tranquillity, the peacefulness of the hour. It was perfectly still and solitary round him, there was not a sound but of the wood-pigeons cooing from afar off, and the wind gently stealing through the fragrant aisles of the rose arcades, while the sun fell on the eastern side of the silent château, and on the terrace, with its grey balustrade covered by gorgeous creepers, that looked like the background of some Louis Quinze picture. He knew no one would have risen except the household at that early hour, and as he walked on, just under the terrace, that was at some considerable elevation above him, a voice startled him as it fell on the air:

"Since when have you become pastoral? I should not have fancied you had had sylvan tastes, mon ami!"

She stood immediately above him, leaning over the stone balustrade; behind her was the ivy-hung façade of the château, with its peaked *tourelles* and its long range of Gothic windows; beneath her sloped the ivy wall of the terrace, covered with the broad leaves of creepers and the profuse blossoms of the twining roses; the whole scene was like a landscape of Greuze or Lancret, and she who completed it added to its colouring of the Beau Siècle where she leaned on the parapet, looking down with a smile on lips that rivalled the half-opened roses. As he glanced upward, her loveliness swept over him like the intoxication of some dreamy perfume, now in the cooler judgment of morning, as at midnight, a few hours before, when the light of the chandeliers glanced on the scarlet camellias. Away from her he could criticise, condemn, displace, defy her; in her presence, with her eyes smiling down into his, with her voice vibrating on the air, he might resent, but he could not resist her. She enthralled him by the senses, so subtilely, so seductively, that she drew him within the charmed circle of her power, even while he hated her for her dominance over him.

"Sylvan tastes or not, would not any one, from an idler to an anchorite, be irresistibly drawn where the early morning proffers such a reward to all those who rise early?" said Strathmore, as he ascended the terrace steps to her side.

He had not seen her, until her greeting made him look upwards. But what man can tell the precise truth to a beautiful woman? She smiled as she gave him her hand, white, small, soft, with the jewels of an Empress upon it; a hand to close gently but surely on the life of a man, and make it its own; a hand to be raved of by poets, and hold sages in thraldom; to be modelled by sculptors, and coveted by courtiers.

"Last night you were quoting from Genesis to show the mischief done by a woman! How can you be so inconsistent as to seek one in Eve's special province of mischief—a garden? A diplomatist tasting the dew of the dawn, and sunning himself among roses!—you *are* an anomaly, mon ami. Is it your lost écarté which has dwelt on your mind, that you are wandering at such an unearthly hour?"

"It is more likely to be remembrance of the one who lost me the écarté!" said Strathmore, bending towards her.

His voice had an unusual softness, his eyes darkened and dwelt on her, fascinated by the voluptuous charm of her beauty, and the confession broke from him unawares. She arched her delicate eyebrows, and looked at him with mischievous amusement, where she leaned against the rose-wreathed parapet.

"Of M. de Clermont! You must be very deep in his debt for him to haunt you!—or perhaps you were meditating some sure, silent revenge on him?—that would be more à la Strathmore?"

"I thank you for the hint and the reminder, belle amie; I *will* revenge myself for the game that I lost on the tactician who threw me off my guard! But the revenge, like the payment I spoke of last night, must wait; it would be too great rashness to risk taking either as yet——"

He spoke softly, and with meaning; her power was winding itself about him, his senses were yielding themselves to the languid charm, the subtle spell of her beauty; Strathmore, who denied that any woman could be dangerous to him, might have known, then, how dangerous *one* might be! She blushed slightly, softly, and played with one of the rings of her left hand—the diamond-studded circlet that was the badge of her marriage—was it by hazard, or as a warning? Be it which it might, it served to recall to him that the woman he looked on was Marion Lady Vavasour, the arch coquette of Europe.

"I was unaware your tastes were à la Phyllis, Lady Vavasour," he went on, with the smile, slight, cold, half a sneer, which piqued her more than anything, since it perplexed her as to its meaning, and only gave her a vague idea that her game was foreseen, and—defied. "What charm can the early morning have for you? Your preferences, surely, are no more sylvan than mine, and there is nothing to be captivated but the bees and the birds! I have read in some old Trouvère song of a *breuvage* for perpetual youth and beauty, to be gathered from the first dew of roses—can *that* be your mission? If so, we must pity, as under De l'Enclos, generations unborn, who will suffer like us!"

"Don't use the first person!—*you* never suffer," she answered him, toying with the hanging sprays of the roses. "The charm that guided me was what rules me always—the caprice of the hour: I admit no other law! In Paris one never thinks the day is aired till two; but in the country—*c'est toute autre chose*—I heard the birds singing, the scent of the roses came through my windows, and——Ah, Lord Cecil, though we live in the world till we forget it, there are things better than pleasure, there is an air purer than the air of the salons! I am young, I am flattered, I reign, I love my sovereignty—who does not that has a sceptre to grasp?—and still, sometimes I wish that I were a peasant-child, playing with the brown chesnuts under the trees, and catching the butterflies in the sunshine!"

I have said that she had now and then a *tendresse*, a mournfulness, real or assumed; and at such moments, while the lids drooped softly over the black gazelle eyes, and a shadow of sadness stole the brilliance from her face, she was yet more resistless than in her most dazzling coquetry. Even Strathmore felt its charm, though, now, with the gesture that had recalled to him her title and her ownership, he had steeled himself afresh against her.

"Indeed!" he answered her, with the smile she mistrusted. "The world would scarcely credit you, Lady Vavasour; to play with men's lives must be more amusing than with fallen chesnuts, and to catch Princes and Peers in your net must be more exciting than the child's yellow butterflies! Who shall hope to be content if the envied of all wishes to alter her lot!"

"Ah! mon ami, those who envy us do not always know us. Among all rose-leaves there is one crumpled!" Her voice was saddened, the lustre of her eyes grew languid and softened, and her fingers unconsciously played with the diamond wedding-ring upon her finger, as it sparkled among the roses. Again the action spoke more eloquently than words. Besides her fascination, she tried now a charm more dangerous for him—she claimed his pity! "Look!" she went on, as she took one of the flowers and opened its fresh crimson leaves. "Look! as the rose swings in the sunlight, how lovely it is— the Queen of flowers! And yet, at its core lies a canker!"

"Is it so with *our* Queen of Flowers!"

He asked it involuntarily, bending lower towards her, till he saw the faint sigh with which her bosom heaved, under the gossamer lace that shrouded it.

"Hush!" she said softly, with a light blow of the rose spray on his arm. "You must not ask. I wear the badge of servitude and—silence!"

And silence fell between them; such silence as fell between Launcelot and Guenevere, when the first subtle poison ran through the veins of the man whom Arthur loved.

With a light laugh the silence was broken, as she flung the gathered spray off on the sunny air, and let her white hands wander afresh among the twining blossoms:

"I like roses, don't you? They are the flowers of poetry.

I don't wonder Cleopatra had her couch of them, and the Epicureans loved them showered down as they sat at banquet, and strewn upon the floors ankle-deep! They are the flowers of silence, of revel, of love; the flowers of the Greek poets and the Provence Trouvères; of the chaplets of Catullus and the lays of Chastelâr. Roses are for all time—while they bloom afresh with every summer, how can the earth fail to guard its eternal youth?"

While she spoke, she drew out one of the roses from the rest, crimson, and fresh, and fragrant, with the dew glittering still in its odorous core; and broke it off with its unopened buds and dark shining leaves.

"Is it not worthy Cleopatra?" she laughed, holding it up in the light before her eyes and his—his that followed her as she fastened the rose in her bosom with negligent grace, where it nestled half hidden, half seen, lying against the white skin that the tracery of the lace covered without wholly concealing, and contrasting its snowy beauty with its deep crimson petals. "Come! we have been talking mournfully, and I meant to teach you epicureanism—you who trample aside the roses of life, and covet only the withered yellow laurels of Age and Power. Adieu! I must leave you to finish your solitary promenades; I am going in to my chocolate!"

His eyes dwelt on her, on the rose, where it lay half hidden on her heart, on the hair lit to gold by the sunshine, on the antelope eyes that glanced at him through their black lashes, on the exquisite and voluptuous grace of her form. Though it had fastened fetters on him which had made him this woman's slave for life, he could not have resisted his impulse to follow her then; she fascinated him by the senses, and it was a fascination to which he chose to yield. What evil could lie in it for him? He was strong in his own strength, secure in his own coldness; he believed he could handle fire without feeling its flame; he believed he could let the whirlwind sweep over him, without being stirred by its breath; he believed he could meet the sirocco, and not be blinded, nor staggered, nor scorched by it. Actually, he would have called the man a lunatic who did these things: metaphorically, and quite as dangerously, he did them all. A scornful self-confidence made at once the grandeur and the weakness of Strathmore's nature.

As Lady Vavasour turned from the parapet and swept over the grey pavement of the rose-terrace to re-enter the château, the snowy folds of her dress gathering up the fallen crimson leaves, and her head slightly turned over her shoulder in adieu to him, he followed her, bending to her with a few low words:

"Who would not learn epicureanism or any other creed from such a teacher? You have given that senseless rose so fair a lodging; do not banish *me* utterly! I am going to my chocolate, too; must I take it in solitude? For the remembrance of our tête-à-tête meal under the limes, let us breakfast tête-à-tête this morning!"

The daughter of Eve had tempted him in the garden of roses, and while yet he might have turned away, he chose to follow and to linger with his temptress.

CHAPTER XII.

In Royal Broceliande.

In the breakfast-room every déjeûner delicacy was waiting, ready for such of the English guests at Vernonceaux as it might pleasure to come down stairs early. None had so pleased that morning save themselves, and this breakfast *was* tête-à-tête. He was alone with her, and in that solitude she ceased to be Lady Vavasour, whom he prejudged and mistrusted; she was the songstress, the incognita, the witching waif and stray of the Bohemian lindens. Almost *too* dazzling at night, with its exquisite tint, and its singular contrast of eyes and of hair, her loveliness, losing none of its brilliance, gained much in softness with the morning light. Moreover, you saw then how real was this youth, how wholly from nature this marvellous colouring; for, stream down on her as the

sun would, its strongest rays could never show a flaw or a
blemish.

Used to the women of Courts, no woman would have had
charm for Strathmore who had not had wit on her lips and a
finished grace in her coquetteries, and that nameless air
which the world alone gives; the fairest *bourgeoise* beauty he
would have passed unnoticed, and rustic loveliness was no
loveliness in his sight.

Condemned to love, he would have made his condition
like Louis Quatorze, "*qu'on m'aime mais avec de l'esprit!*"
Therefore, Marion Vavasour had her subtlest charm for him,
in that exquisite grace which empresses had envied her; in
that sparkling play which, if it were not wit, sufficed for it
from such lips; in that very worldliness which might have
chilled as heartlessness men less *petri* with the world themselves than Strathmore was. What had struck him the night
before as startling and bizarre, what even in his momentary
breathless admiration of her had repelled him, and made he
him think of Clytemnestra and La Borgia, had gone,—perhaps, with the scarlet camellias!

She was dressed simply, in snowy gossamer folds of
muslin, with floating azure ribbons here and there, and the
richness of her yellow hair, gathered back in its natural
waves and ripples, looked but one soft mass of dead gold
now it was unmixed with any colour. There was nothing to
mar the spells of her beauty, and those spells she wove to
her uttermost witchery as she sat daintily brushing the
bloom off a grape, or toying with her strawberries, adding
the cream to her chocolate, or touching the tiny wing of
some delicate bird.

With all her caprices, her coquetteries, her rapid wayward mutations, she was ever essentially feminine; too skilful not to know that the surest charm which a woman wields
over men is the charm of difference—the charm of sex; and
that half this charm is flown when Christina of Sweden wears
her hessians and cracks her whip; when her imitators of to-
day chatter slang with weeds in their mouths, and swing

through the stable-yards, talking in loud *rauque* voices of dogs with a "good strain!"

They were full an hour alone, and in that hour she led him far on a dangerous road; none the less dangerous because he knew her tactics and deemed himself secure to defy them. She was a coquette, therefore he was armed against her; she was a woman of the world, therefore he could trifle with her with impunity; she was Lady Vavasour, therefore he knew the worth of every smile, the value of every glance, which were but golden hooks flung out by skill to catch and fasten the unwary: so Strathmore reasoned—he who was a man of the world, and would lose his head for no woman!—and in his security lay his risk. For he felt that she had already a certain power over him—the power for which he hated her when he threw down his losing cards at écarté—the power with which her beauty had swept over him as he had come suddenly upon her in the sunlight of the rose-garden; but to have feared it would have been to confess that he might yield to it, and Strathmore held that he could evoke a storm and then arrest it with "Thus far shalt thou go and no farther;" he held that he could let poison flow into his veins and then eject it with "I do not choose to receive thee!"

The disdainful strength of the Strathmores had ever, I say, been their weakness; and the ruin that had come to them had ever been wrought by their own hand; the graven steel of their unyielding race ever the reed that bent beneath them.

The tête-à-tête breakfast was as seductive as any meal ever has been since She of the Golden Shuttle entertained the wanderer at Ogygia. Through the shaded windows the rose-scented air stole fragrantly in, while stray rays of sunlight streamed upon the amber grapes touched by her delicate fingers, and on the crimson rose lying hid in its snowy nest. Her moods were as variable as summer clouds, and her mood that morning was soft, subdued, gentle with all its gaiety, triste with all its coquettishness, and—it was the most bewitching of all.

"What is your White Ladies like—they say it is such a superb old place?" she said, when her mischievous witticisms ceased, as though tired with their own play and sparkle. "Charlie St. Albans—who told me your family legend, by the way, one day at Biarritz—raves about its beauty. It was an abbey, wasn't it?"

"An old Dominican monastery—yes. It has a beauty of its own, the beauty of that past when men sought rest as we now seek reputation, and found in solitude what *we* find in strife. May I not hope you will some day honour it with a visit, Lady Vavasour, and judge of it yourself?" he answered her, stroking her greyhound; his prejudice against her was quickly fading since he invited her to White Ladies—the daughter of Eve to the ancient Monastery!

She smiled the dazzling smile that had intoxicated wise men to worse than the madness of the opium-eater.

"Perhaps. Some day—some day. Ah, what may we all do 'some day!' You and I may be foes *à outrance* some day —who knows?"

"Foes? Nay, surely not. Did you not tell me 'destiny threw us together, that we must be friends?' *Dieu le veut!*"

"*Dieu veut ce que femme veut, mon ami!*" said the Marchioness, arching her eyebrows. "You know that; and on a man who disdains the love of all my sex I am not at all inclined to waste my own friendship!"

"Why, you had better rather cure me of my heresy in both. What teacher could convert me to her soft doctrines with such success? what rebuke could be at once more merciful and more convincing to me?"

A sadness, almost tenderness, shaded the dark gazelle eyes for a moment as they met his, and she was silent. Lady Vavasour knew the charm of silence when the eyes may be trusted to speak. A moment after she laughed coquettishly:

"Merciful? Perhaps not, monsieur, if I *did* take your conversion in hand."

"True. Perhaps the denial of your friendship is more merciful than its donation would be. Nevertheless, at all risks, I will seek it."

"You love risks?" she said, looking at him with a dash of tantalising malice. Strathmore laughed slightly—a laugh that sounded to her like contempt of her power.

"Well, I confess I do not fear many."

"Nor did Ragnar Ladbrog, mon ami, the northern Scalds tell us; sheathed in his armour of ice, what could attack him? How scathless he went for so long! And yet he came at last to his Hella, and he languished to death in the cave of the serpents. Take warning!"

Strathmore smiled.

"I am not quite so quixotic as the Bersaker, and before I handle serpents I take out their stings! Grasped rightly, no serpent can bite. But surely, belle amie, you do not pay yourself so ill a compliment as to compare the gift of your friendship with the fang of an asp? Though perhaps you are right—it may be as dangerous!"

"But a danger you smile at! Well, take it if you will. Shall we be friends, then, Lord Cecil?"

Her eyes were resistless in their witching softness, and a certain tremulous smile that seemed half born of a sigh was on her lip, as she held out in playfulness, yet in earnest, her white jewelled hand, as she leant slightly towards him. What man could have rejected the hand or the friendship?

Strathmore bent forward and accepted both: as he took the warm fingers within his own and met the glance that dwelt on him as they sat there alone in the shaded light, his pulses quickened, and his own eyes gleamed with something of the swift dark brilliance that she had sworn to lighten there—the dawn of the passion she had vowed to awaken in the nature that, by character imperious and unyielding, deemed itself by a fatal error to be also cold and calm. He released her hand suddenly, and threw himself back in his chair; the doors opened, and with Beaudesert and Clermont there entered Lord Vavasour and Vaux.

"Bon jour, messieurs," said the Marchioness, including her lord in her negligent, graceful salutation. "I suppose you have all been wasting the hours over cheroots and novelettes that I have been giving to the roses. Ah, if you were all to see the sun rise once in a way, what a deal of good it would do you! I will have a Trianon, and then, perhaps, you *will* learn to be pastoral. M. de Clermont, will you milk the cow like the Comte d'Artois? Vavasour, did I ever tell you that it was to Lord Cecil Strathmore I owed my escape that dreadful night at Prague? No? I ought to have done; then you have never thanked him?"

Her husband, thus apostrophised, turned to Strathmore, and addressed his thanks to him, complimenting him with as gracious a courtesy as that pampered, gouty gourmet, whose general manner was guilty of Valdor's impeachment, a "*ton de garnison*," could assume for any mortal. "Singularly striking-looking man—quite Vandyke!" thought the Marquis, while he uttered his gratitude for his wife's rescue; "but I am sure he will do something bad some day—come to a violent death, perhaps. That *physique*—very much so!" Which possibly was a complacent source of gratification to his lordship, as he had just come in on a tête-à-tête.

Strathmore received his thanks with that cold negligence which had the effect of making him cordially disliked out of his own immediate set, and lay back in his chair, playing with the greyhound, and joining now and then in the conversation. He knew that this woman's beauty stole on him despite himself; when her magic was off him he hated her for the food that she had made him give her vanity; but a seductive sensuousness allured him in her glorious loveliness, which, though he rated it lightly, should have made him place distance betwixt him and its subtle temptation—betwixt him and the wife of Lord Vavasour.

A weak man might have done this, and been strong; Strathmore, a strong man, stayed, contemptuous and defiant of the weakness. A man less cool, less keen, less nonchalant of all danger, might have taken warning; he saw no danger possible in it. One careless, over-confident turn of the hand may mar the whole of the statue which the sculptor deems plastic as clay to his will, obedient to every stroke of his chisel!

The statue that Strathmore at once moulded and marred was his Life: the statue which we all, as we sketch it, endow with the strength of the Milo, the glory of the Belvedere, the winged brilliance of the Perseus!—which ever lies at its best, when the chisel has dropped from our hands, as they grow powerless and paralysed with death, like the mutilated Torso, a fragment unfinished and broken, food for the ants and worms, buried in sands that will quickly suck it down from sight or memory, with but touches of glory and of value left here and there, only faintly serving to show what *might have been*, had we had time, had we had wisdom!

"Well, wasn't I right; isn't she divine, eh?" said Valdor to him that day, as they were playing billiards.

"She—who? My dear fellow, there are half a dozen divinities here who wear the cestus of Venus, or claim it at the least! Be a little more definite!"

"The deuce! Who should I mean? Nobody can hold a candle to her. Vavasour's in luck to have a wife that everybody envies him."

"Dubious luck!" said Strathmore, sticking his penknife through his cabana. "A wife of the first water, like a diamond of the first water, is rather a perilous possession. It's apt to be disputed by too many owners! You can't ever be sure the wards haven't been picked and the casket been rifled!"

"Exactly," said Legard. "Marriage is a disagreeable legal necessity for men with titles and entails, and the best colour for a wife's discreet plainness. No Bramah can protect you so effectually as an ugly choice; besides, I shouldn't think it's bad for yourself upon principle; if Lucretia's unlovely you must relish Lais and her graces all the more. One never enjoys a good omelette at Véfour's so much as after an ill-done one in the Grisons."

"There's something in that," said Valdor, reflectively. "But then—twelve hours with an ugly woman would kill one! Why *are* any of them ugly, I wonder? They were created on purpose for us. What's the good of giving us five out of six, as we don't like them? If they were all such as the Vavasour, now——" And Valdor paused, in mute contemplation of the delicious universal seraglio that might then be commanded.

"The Vavasour's something that comes once in a century. The deuce! how that woman does flirt!" interrupted Dormer, in the tone, half disgusted, half admiring, with which a man might say of some magnificent drunkard, like Piron, "How that fellow does drink!"

Strathmore sent his ball to make a *ricochet* with a certain impetus, as if the conversation annoyed him, and did not join in it.

"If fifty naughty stories ain't rife about her before next season, I'll bet you a thousand to one," went on Dormer, offering his wager generally, but nobody, it seemed, having sufficient confidence in her ladyship to be chivalrous enough to take it up! "They *do* say it's only flirtation—as yet; and I, believe she's as heartless as ice; but she does horrible mischief, if she's never absolutely 'compromised,' and I think *that's* open to doubt! At Biarritz, last year, she played the very deuce with Marc Lennartson; you remember him, don't you, Strathmore--Austrian Cuirassiers, you know? She drew him on and on, made him follow her about like a greyhound, fooled him before everybody, and then turned him off coolly for the Prince de Vorhn, and laughed at him with a blow of her fan. Lennartson had lost his head about her, and he shot himself through the brain! I know that for a fact; nothing but that woman at the bottom of it; and the very night she heard of his death she went to a fancy ball, fluttering about in her diamonds. By Jove! it was too bad, wasn't it?"

Strathmore made a hap-hazard cannon, with his coldest sneer upon his face: the story angered him.

"My dear Dormer! if a man's such a fool as to 'follow a woman about like a lapdog,' whether he goes out of the world or stays in it doesn't matter very much, I think. Yours is a romantic story; it would charm the women, but, *pour moi!* I must fancy there were some heavy debts hanging over Lennartson's head, or some more rational reason for your sentimental finale. I don't credit those things quite so easily."

"It *was* true, whether you like to believe it or not."

Strathmore lifted his eyebrows and dropped the subject; he would have said it did not interest him!

"What a voice of lamentation there was in Rama when Vavasour married her," said Beaudesert, who was betting on the game. "The women had made such hard running on him all over Europe; when the regular troops had always missed fire, it was a horrid blow to have an outside skirmisher knock him over!"

"Of course! Virtuous women love to take in hand the conversion of a sinner when the penitent can give them a coronet; they are very happy to be taken, like soda-water , after a debauch, if the debauchee excuses his past orgies with a page in Burke. There wasn't a *précieuse* in England that wouldn't have sold her pure soul to the devil and the Marquis, for his settlements. The morals of monde, and demi-monde, don't differ very much, after all, only the inferior goods are content with Rue de la Paix jewellery, and Lady Vavasour et Cⁱᵉ don't let themselves go under anything less than the family diamonds!" said Strathmore, with his coldest sneer. It gratified him to fling the sarcasm at that marriage of convenience where Helen of the antelope eyes had bartered herself for the gold and the titles of gourmand Menelaus; the flash and sparkle of the diamond circlet he had seen among the roses, added, by its memory, point to his irony.

"Quite right!" laughed Beaudesert. "And when we have to pay such a much heavier price to monde, and get so much better amused by demi-monde, how the deuce can they wonder we prefer ease to imprisonment, and *laissez-faire* to *il faut faire ?*"

"Perhaps they *don't* wonder, my good fellow, and in that lies the essence of their pique and the root of their philippics. If the debatable land's so agreeable, they know very well the time may come when the legitimate kingdoms will be left altogether," laughed Strathmore, as he went back to his game, and, Lady Vavasour not being there to spoil it, won it, as he piqued himself on winning most things that he tried for in life, from billiards upwards.

As he finished it, a servant entered to tell him that the horses were coming round; he had promised to make one of a riding-party at four o'clock, and left the billiard-room with Dormer to obey the summons.

"The pretty panther, how handsome she looks! She has merciless *griffes*, though, and her graceful play's death to those who play with her," said Dormer, under his moustaches, memories of Biarritz rising savagely within him as they passed out of the long gallery leading from the billiard-room into the great hall.

The "pretty panther," as he called her, was just at that moment standing on the grand staircase with some men about her, holding her jewelled whip in one hand, and the violet folds of her habit in the other, the light from the long range of stained windows falling on her, and on the tapestried arras, the damascened armour, and the dark oak carvings of the wall behind her. Strathmore glanced at her, and gave Dormer his coldest laugh.

"Fearfully poetic you are to-day, Will! Have you been scratched yourself?"

"No; but you're about to be."

"*I?* You don't know me much, my good fellow."

"But I know HER, and I bet you five to one that she is trying to play the deuce with you, Strathmore."

"Let her try! I have one bet pending already on that event, but I'm quite willing to take yours too."

"Glad to hear it; but forewarned's forearmed, you know."

"Thank you," said Strathmore, with that negligent cold-ness which was as chilly as ice, "but when I need counsel I ask for it, my dear Dormer. It is a dish I am not very fond of having offered me."

His eyes had lightened to the swift dark anger of his race; and Dormer, a good-natured, easy, indolent fellow, accustomed to be put down by him, and to be silenced by his sneer, held his peace with an obedience, the relic of their old Eton days; while Strathmore joined the group on the stair-case, and, by a nonchalant finesse, displaced the others, who had a prior claim as before him in the field, and leading her out into the court, assisted Lady Vavasour to mount the spirited Spanish mare that he had admired as it had reared with her, when he had seen the riding-party from the dis-tance the previous day. Assistance, indeed, she needed little; an inimitable rider, she sprang, lightly as a bird to a bough, to her saddle; but to have the foot beautiful as Pompadour's placed on his hand, the light weight leant upon him for an instant, the perfumed hair brush near him, the hand touch his as he put the reins within it, the lips softly thank him,— these made a service bitterly envied to Strathmore. As she dashed out of the great gates of the court, the mare rearing and plunging with the fire of its Spanish blood, Lady Vavasour had never looked, perhaps, lovelier, with her deli-cate cheeks flushed from the exertion of her strength, her light, defiant laugh ringing out, her eyes flashing with im-patient *will*. Yet for one moment as he saw her teeth clench tightly, her eyes gather a sinister light, her whip cut the mare with sharp, stinging strokes, it crossed Strathmore's mind that the real instinct, the true pleasure of this soft, dazzling woman might be, after all, Cruelty—the cruelty of the young cat that loves to see the wounded bird flutter and shriek and struggle for its liberty with the blood dabbling the broken wing, and to let it go for one fleet mocking mo-ment, and then to seize on it afresh, till the death-cry rings sharp and clear upon the air, and its own white teeth tear asunder the quivering flesh.

The fancy crossed him, and the aversion, amounting to almost the strength of hatred, which, mingled with the fascination that Marion Vavasour had for him, flamed up in all its bitterness. "She danced in her diamonds the night that poor devil shot himself!" he thought; "I dare say. What fools men are to let a woman play with them."

But twenty minutes after, Lady Vavasour turned her head towards him with her brightest smile. "Lord Cecil, you are our cicerone; which way leads to the Brèche du Gaston?" And as he spurred his horse to overtake her, and cantered on by her side, the wiser thought was forgot, the danger that was in this woman served but to give piquance to her beauty, as the thorns of the rose which pique those who admire to gather it; and as though she had divined the verdict that his reason was giving against her, she chained him to her side during the ride, and had all that softness of manner which, when she chose to assume it, would have made the testimony of men and angels weigh nothing against Marion Lady Vavasour!

"So, if I come to England this year, as Lady Beaudesert tries to persuade me, you will be prepared to do me the honours of White Ladies?" she said, laughing, to him an hour afterwards, as, having outstripped the rest of the party, they rode through a waggon-way that ran under the shelter of the hills, with the wild vine clustering in rich luxuriance from bough to bough, and the glowing lights slanting in, to turn the moss into gold, and burnish the ripening grapes into bloom.

"But too gladly! Since the Reine Blanche was received there the Abbey will never have sheltered so fair a guest. But Mary Stuart came to us as a captive; you will come as a captor omnipotent! Your sceptre rests on a sway that men cannot break, and your kingdom lies in a power more potent than mailed might——!"

"Ah!" she said, softly and mournfully, "but don't you

know the Reine Blanche had my sceptre and my kingdom too, and yet—her hair whitened and her head was bent to the block! She was a captive at White Ladies? and I dare say my lord of Strathmore was a courtly but a pitiless gaoler, had many a courtier phrase upon his tongue, but never relented to mercy! What a *triste souvenir!* I shall be afraid to come there; perhaps you will imprison me!"

Strathmore bent down in his saddle and loked into her eyes, while his own grew dark and brilliant, and the coldness of his face softened. Was it the warmth flung on it from above by the amber sunlight that was streaming through the vine-leaves and the purpling grapes?

"That I shall be tempted, I would not deny! Who could, who spoke truth?"

The reins drooped on their horses' necks, they paced slowly over the yielding mosses, their speed slackening, their voices softening, under the leafy boughs and the tangled tendrils of the drooping vines; the warm sun fell between the stems of the trees, the leaves were stirless in the sultry air, the birds sang with subdued music in the woodland shadow —and they rode onwards, as in the days of the past, Launcelot and Guenevere rode through the silent aisles and forest shades of Royal Broceliande.

CHAPTER XIII.

The Weaving of the Golden Shuttle.

BERTIE ERROLL sat at the head of the dinner-table at White Ladies with other spirits like himself, keeping the house open, as he had been bidden to do by his absent host in the first week of September. Dinner was just over, and the Sabreur lay back in his chair, lazily peeling a nectarine, recommending the Marcobrunn to Langley of the Twelfth, vowing it was deucedly warm, and lamenting pathetically that Strathmore would prefer the click of the roulette-ball to the glories of the open, the pleasures of pair et passe to those of the stubble, and forsake White Ladies thus perpetually for the Continent.

Some half-dozen men were down with him for the shooting; Strathmore had always bade him look on White Ladies as though it were his own home, to open to whom he would; and they were chatting over their grapes, peaches, and comet wines this warm, mellow September evening, while the last rays of the setting sun fell across Erroll's fair frank face as they slanted through the painted windows of the dining-hall, where the scutcheon of the Strathmores was blazoned, with their merciless motto, "Slay! and spare not!" radiant in gold and gules.

"We don't want women in September," Rockingham of the Guards was observing, with more truth, perhaps, than politeness. "They're delightful in their season, but when we're shooting we're better without 'em. Paullet took Valérie Brown and that lot down to Market Harborough last season, and we were positively ruined by 'em! Champagne suppers at two in the morning, and all the rest of it, put us shockingly out of condition; we were hardly in at a death, any one of us, all thanks to those confounded women——"

"Phyne v. the Pytchley! St. John's Wood morals spoiling Northamptonshire runs! You should write a 'Tract for the Times' on it; a 'Warning to the Pink not to trifle with the Rouge,'" laughed the Sabreur, pouring himself out some Rhenish. "Well, thank God, I'd suffer deterioration any day from that quarter. A bright-eyed brune is better than a brush any day, and two good things can't spoil one another. I say, Phil, did you see in the papers that Jack Temple's run away with Ferrar's wife?"

"Never read the papers, my good fellow," said Danvers. "Froth in the leaders, gall in the debates, acid in the on dits, and flummery in the court news, make an *olla podrida* that don't suit my digestion. Poor Jack! what could he be thinking of? She weighs nine stone, and is shockingly sallow in the daylight——"

Danvers stopped, the dogs gave tongue, the man handing

the coffee round paused in his duty, Waverley looked up from his olives, Rockingham dropped half a dozen almond soufflées on to a terrier's nose, Erroll sprang from his chair: "My dear fellow! By Jove! how glorious!" And, as the groom of the chambers flung the door wide open, Strathmore entered his own dining-hall, unannounced and unexpected.

"Keep your seat, old fellow! You or I, what does it matter which?" he laughed, as he shook the Sabreur's hand, and forced him back into the chair at the head of the table, looking on his old Eton chum with a warmer glance than women had ever won from him, as the other men gathered round to greet him. "How are you all? Who's shockingly sallow by the daylight, Phil? Nobody you've brought down here, I hope, is it? Sit where you are, Bertie. I'm your guest to-night, *s'il vous plaît!*"

With which Strathmore, refusing to take the head of his table, and looking with eyes of love upon Erroll, sank into an empty chair, told the servants to bring him some soup, and sat down at White Ladies as though he had never left it. He had arrived only some half-hour before, but had gone straight up to his own room, forbidding the groom of the chambers to disturb the dinner-party by announcing his arrival.

"My dear old fellow, this *is* prime! How are you, Cis?" said Erroll, lying back to look at Strathmore with an unutterable satisfaction, fully content to give up his *pro tempore* ownership of White Ladies to see his friend back again.

"All right, old boy. You're astonished to see me to-night, Bertie?"

"By Jove I am! I thought you were at Baden?"

"I *was* at Baden. I only left on Tuesday, and shouldn't have left then but I had asked some people here, and given them *carte blanche* to fix their own time, and they fixed it at such a short notice, that I had only just days enough to come over to receive them. It wasn't worth while to write, as I should have come with the mail-bag."

"Are there any women coming?" asked Rockingham, with prophetic *pitié de soi-même.*

"Some. Why?"

"Nothing, only I hate the sex in September," muttered the unlucky victim to Valérie Brown and "that lot" in the shires. "So your Jack of Trumps colt didn't win the Prix du Forêt Noir?"

"No; only came a good third. I rode Starlight myself for the Rastatt; we did the distance very nicely."

"By Jove you did, and gave Ninette a dress of your colours, I saw in the *Post.* How's the pretty *bouquetière?*"

"Handsome as ever. She asked for you, Erroll; I don't think there's one of the Jockey Club who cuts you out with her. She looked very charming in the scarlet and white. A poor devil of an Englishman shot himself on Monday night, after losing his last Nap, but all Baden was too occupied with Princesse Marie Volgarouski's desperate *engouement* of a young Tuscan composer to pay much attention. It's quite Pauline Bonaparte and Blangini over again. She's a striking looking woman, but I don't care for those Petersburg beauties, they're too olive."

"Ah, by George, Strath! you put me in mind," interrupted Erroll, with all the eagerness of a retriever scenting a wild duck—"you said you saw Lady Vavasour in Paris?"

"So I did."

"Well! What's she like? Have you seen her again?"

"Oh yes. She's been staying at Vernonceaux."

"The deuce she has! and you never said so? What do you think of her—how do you like her—what style ——?"

"My dear fellow, don't ask me to describe a woman!" interrupted Strathmore, indifferently. "They are like kaleidoscopes, and have a thousand phases, all pretty for the time, but never to be caught, and always changed when a new eye's on them."

"Hang you!" swore Erroll. "You wrote just enough to *intriguer* one about her, and now shove one off with an epigram! Come, *is* she the atrocious coquette they all say?"

"All women are coquettes, except plain ones, who make a virtue of a renunciation that's *de rigueur*, and hate their virtue (like most other people) while they brag of it!"

"Confound you! I don't ask about all women, only about one. You set out with a dreadful prejudice against her; you'd seen her at one masked ball, and wrote me word on the strength of it that you thought it particularly lucky that the Marquis was of elastic principles, and that you didn't envy him his wife, because her mouth, though perfection, would whisper too many infidelities to please you!"

A dark shadow of impatient, intolerant annoyance passed over Strathmore's face, and glanced into his eyes for an instant as the sun fell on it, slanting through the "**Slay! and spare not!**" of the motto blazoned on the painted panes; but there was no trace left of anger as he looked up and laughed slightly.

"I dare say it *is* particularly lucky the Marquis has elastic conjugal principles; it's lucky for any husband who has a handsome wife, and yet likes to live in peace with his brethren. Lady Vavasour is a very exquisite beauty, there's no disputing that; *you'll* rave of her, Bertie; at the same time, I never heard beauty reckoned as the best guarantee for marital fidelity!"

"The devil—not exactly!" said Scrope Waverley. "The Vavasour's the most abominable coquette—shocking, on my honour, isn't she, Strathmore? Be warm as the tropics on you one minute, and cold as the poles the next."

Strathmore looked at him with his chilliest contempt:

"Perhaps you have suffered! Acrimony generally bespeaks adversity. Not having been the subject of her ladyship's caprices, I cannot compare notes with you, Scrope, nor yet back your experience, though—in your case—I don't doubt any part of them, except that you ever basked much in the tropics!"

Waverley looked sulky as he picked over his olives, not

quite certain how to take the shot that had told in a very sore spot; while Erroll, ever good natured, and who could no more take pleasure in making a man smart than a dog wince, turned the subject, and postponing his own curiosity, asked Strathmore who the people were that were coming!

"Who! Oh, some of the Vernonceaux set," answered Strathmore, taking a Manilla out of the little silver waggon. "The De Ruelles, the Beaudeserts, Madame de Cevillac, your old friend Lady Camelot, and—Lady Vavasour."

He paused a moment before he added her name, but then spoke it indifferently enough.

"The Vavasour!" echoed Erroll and all the other men with him. "By Jove! Strath, you don't mean it!"

"Why should I not mean it?"

"The Vavasour! By Heaven!" ejaculated the Sabreur, stroking his moustache in beatified astonishment. "I thought you didn't like her, Cis?"

"I don't think I ever said so! *De plus*, she invited herself, and reigning beauties are like reigning fashions—one must obey them."

"Does the Marquis come too?"

"God forbid! At least, he comes for a day or two, but only en route to the Sprudel to cure his dyspepsia. Like the Roman, he goes to a bath that he may come back for a banquet."

"And leaves his wife a *droit de chasse* in his absence!" laughed Erroll. "But the idea of keeping that to yourself all this time, letting us talk of her and never telling us! What an odd fellow you are! You called her a sorceress, and said she tried her wiles on you at the Luilhiers' ball. Has she bewitched even *you*, old fellow?"

"Not exactly!" said Strathmore—his tone was more contemptuously cold than he had ever used to Erroll—"but I like beauty as I like a good Titian, a good claret, a good opera, a good racer. Who doesn't! To hear you, Bertie, one would certainly think no woman had ever been entertained at White Ladies since Mary Stuart! If Lady Vavasour wished to come here with Beatrix Beaudesert, could I say I wouldn't have her? Besides, I had no wish to say so; she is very charming. By-the-by, Phil, who was that you were talking about when I came in? Who's sallow in the daylight?—most blondes are that, though, after twenty."

He spoke so carelessly, as he lay back in his chair, that not a man present guessed that the name of Marion Vavasour was anything more to him than the names of fifty fair women, who had been, season after season, recipients of the stately hospitalities of White Ladies: except, indeed, Erroll, who looked at him with a puzzled look clouding his clear azure eyes, and drank his coffee in silence. He, the sworn Squire of Dames, who worshipped everything feminine that crossed his path, felt a vague dislike rise up in him against this witching beauty, whom Strathmore denied had had charm for him, and yet who was bidden beneath the roof of White Ladies.

That night, when they had left the smoking-room, Strathmore, sitting alone in his own room, thoughtful yet listless, with a restless indifference which had grown on him of late, and which he had vainly doctored with very heavy betting at Baden, and dangerous *coups de hasard* at roulette, threw open his despatch-box and took out a little note—a note which was not very many lines, which placed his title before his name, and which was chiefly gay, mischievous badinage and pretty command, with but here and there touches of something deeper, and these only deepened to friendship. Yet this letter had sufficed to bring him from Baden at its bidding; it had been looked at many times, where no other note addressed to him had ever served for any other purpose than to light his cigar, and it had a fascination for him which no words written by a woman's hand had ever claimed, for it was signed—"Marion Vavasour and Vaux." Letters have a strange glamour!—with this, the sweet mocking voice echoed in his ear, the smile of the dark antelope eyes laughed into his, the fragrance of the amber hair floated past him, and he flung the note back into its resting-place with a fierce oath— he hated the senseless paper! For he hated the hot, insidious passion that was creeping into his blood, and that, in night and solitude, wreathed round him as the serpent folds round the Laocoon, sapping his strength, and only twisting closer and closer with each effort to thrust it aside; the passion that would make him the slave of a woman, the vassal of a smile, the bond-servant of a kiss!

In the simplest trifles Strathmore was remarkable for an unswerving tenacity to truth, too proud a man not to hold his word his bond even in ordinary colloquial intercourse; yet that night, when denying to Erroll that she had any sway over him, he had for the only time in his life *lied.* It was the first trivial unnoticed step of the downward course that he was even now commencing, as the first unperceived loosening of the snow is the signal for the downward sweep of the avalanche.

Marion Vavasour had a power over him such as no woman had ever gained before her; the strange force with which absolute hatred of her mingled with the charm her beauty had for him, served only to heighten it and give it a sting which excited and enthralled a man whom a tamer or wiser love would never have governed. Strathmore had stayed on at Vernonceaux, voluntarily remaining in the danger, which a weaker man would, or might, at least, have fled from while there was yet time; finding in this new beguilement, this woman's intoxicating loveliness, a spell, subtle and resistless, the same dazzling, sensuous delight as lies in a soft Bacchante of Coustou's golden chisel, or a voluptuous *rêveuse* warm with the rich varied colours of the canvas of Greuze. Constantly in her society, meeting her alone in the freshness of the early morning, strolling with her at evening under the trellised roofing of the vines, bowing to the sway of her coquetries in the salon where she held her gay omnipotent reign, Strathmore did not dispute the "destiny" which she had said had decreed them to be friends.

For him, too, she had her most certain and most dangerous charm: capricious, mutable, scattering her coquetries *à pleines mains*, as the Hours of Corregio scatter their roses;

she had a softness, a sadness, a tenderness, *I* call it—*she*
termed it a "friendship"—for and with Strathmore which
seemed to bespeak that something warmer than vanity, something deeper than mere pride of conquest, might be awakened
in her. Amidst the largesse of adoration that she levied from
all who came within sight of her brilliant banner, which fluttered with its audacious motto, "*Je règne partout,*" from north
to south, from east to west, she made a distinction towards
the man who had saved her life at the Vigil of St. John,
which gave good ground for attributing a preference that
every man, from Monsignore Villaflôr downwards, bitterly
envied him as they began to yield place to him as of necessity,
and to couple his name with hers in the card-room or smoking-
room, when neither he nor the Marquis were present. The
latter was the only one at Vernonceaux who never troubled his
head which way his Marchioness's caprices might be turning;
it was a matter of profound indifference to him, and he dozed,
and read French novels, and played écarté, and discussed
l'art de goût, and let his wife go on her own ways, like a gentleman of breeding who did as he would be done by.

Half hating her, half beguiled by her, one hour accredit-
ing to her all the velvet treachery, the wanton cruelty of the
panther; the next, subdued by that charm which he had little
wish and less will to resist; one instant, bitterly contemptuous
on the witchery that made his pulse beat quicker at the mere
fragrance of a woman's hair; another seeking with all the
skill the world had taught him, to make the softened glance of
her eyes deepen into tenderness;—so the golden shuttle of a
woman's power had woven its woof and wound its web around
Strathmore, and so he had courted, even while he rebelled
from, its enchanted toils. And just at the very moment when
the surest meshes of its twisted threads were entangling
round him, when he was first beginning to feel it a necessity
to be in her presence—just then, Lady Vavasour left Vernonceaux. Without announcement, without preparation, she
went; carefully avoiding any *tête-à-tête* farewell, bidding him
"*au revoir*" with laughing negligence in a crowded salon, with

an indifference which Strathmore was not slow to simulate in imitation. Yet that adieu, by its very avoidance of him, by its very abandonment of that *tendresse* which she used as her habitual weapon of war, told him, by his experience of women, might equally mean one of two things: that she felt nothing, or—felt too much! *Which?*

The question was left open, and pursued him ceaselessly; nothing in his life had ever haunted him so persistently as that single doubt. I believe that weeks, months spent in her presence, would not have rooted her in his memory so firmly as that well-timed absence, that insoluble uncertainty. Away from her, it was in vain that he contemned, as he did with bitter irony, with pitiless rancour, her coquetries and her caprices; or mercilessly dissected her faults, her foibles, and her fascinations: her power had begun! *Insecurity* is to passion as the wind to the flame—without the cold breeze wafted to it, the embers would have faded fast, and never flared up into life; with the rush of the cooler air the fire leaps into flame, and its lust is not sated till it has destroyed all before it.

The Strathmores of White Ladies had never loved the women who had slept innocently on their hearts, and laid their pure lives within their keeping; the only passion that had ever roused them had been some fierce forbidden desire, and the guilty leaven of the dead race was alive in the man who bore their name and their features. From Vernonceaux Strathmore went to Baden, and if any feeling was strong in him towards the woman whose beauty, when the scarlet flowers bound her amber hair, had made him think of Frédégonde, of Sifrid, of Lucretia, of every living Circe who had drawn men downward by the witching gleam of her white arms till they lost all likeness of themselves, and sank into an abyss whence they could never more rise again into the pure light left for ever at her bidding, he would have said, and perhaps said rightly, that it was—hatred. If pity be akin to love, believe me passion is as often allied to hate! It would slay what it vainly covets; if it cannot kiss the lips it

woos, it would blur them out of all beauty by a blow; what it
seeks so fiercely, it loathes for the pain of its own unslaken
desire; and what it is forbidden to enjoy, it would thrust
away out of its own and other eyes, into the darkness of an
absolute or of a living death, with the hatred of Amnon, to
the tomb of Heloïse!

Such was the passion now wakening in Strathmore; which,
whilst it made him hate the woman who fascinated and
blinded him, because he knew that the softness of such hours
as that upon the rose-terrace was but a more fatal phase of
her brilliant and studied coquetries, were but the shadows
which, with a cunning art, she threw in to heighten a dazzling
picture; had still made him leave Baden the instant that the
note he now flung aside had reached him—the note which
accepted his invitation afresh, and selected White Ladies
from amidst a hundred other places that were open to the
honour of her ladyship's bright and sovereign presence.

In his own room that night he read over the delicate
fragrant letter that had made him leave Baden (and would
have made him leave Paradise!), and with an oath threw it
away from him, as though it were tainted with poison. He
hated the mad fool's delight that lay in it for him because
her hand had touched it, yet he longed with ungovernable
desire to feel that hand lie once more within his own; and
Strathmore, who held that he could mould his life like plastic
clay into any shape that pleased him, did not seek to inquire
whether the clay would break or harden in the fire which was
beginning to seethe and coil around it.

As he flung the letter away and rose, he pulled back the
curtains of the window nearest him, and threw one of its casements open. He felt impatient for the air, impatient with
himself, intolerant with all the world! The night was very
hot and he stood looking out for a while into the moonlight.
The scene was lovely enough, and the old monastic lands, as
far as he could see, were his own; but Strathmore, absorbed
in his own thoughts, looked little at the landscape. It was a

mere hazard that the figure of a man crossing the turf caught his eye.

"A poacher as near the house as that; impossible! That Knightswood gang *are* the very deuce for audacity, but even they'd never——" he thought, as he leaned out to get a good look at the intruder; in the clear white light the form, though distant, was distinct enough, and the red end of a cigar, as it moved through the gloom, sparkled like a glow-worm.

Strathmore looked hard at the mysterious shadow, till it had gone out of the moonlight into the deep shade of a cluster of elms.

"By Jove! Erroll, as I live! Another of my tenants' daughters come to grief, I suppose! What a fellow it is; if he's away from Phya of the Bijou Villa, he takes up with Phyllis of the Home-farm! I wonder how cider tastes, faulting champagne? Rather flat, and terribly homely, I should fancy; better than nothing, though, I suppose, for the Sabreur. Well, it's a very nice night for an erotic adventure. Byron's quite right—

> The devil's in the moon for mischief;
> . . . . . there is not a day,
> The longest, not the twenty-first of June,
> Sees half the business in a wicked way
> On which three single hours of moonshine smile—
> And then she looks so modest all the while!

He might have said, too, that in that respect the women who make the mischief are like the moon that looks on it! Chaste Diana of the skies, or of the sex, only veils that she may lend herself—to something naughty!"

With which reflection Strathmore shut the window down and rang for his Albanian, giving no more thought to Erroll's moonlight errand. Long afterwards, when it formed a link in that chain which his own passions forged about his life, the remembrance of this September night came back to him.

———

CHAPTER XIV.

Feathery Seeds that were freighted with Fruit of the Future.

"IT was a fine moonlight night last night, my dear fellow, and Hampshire 'moonrakers' do go fishing after contraband goods, *au clair de la lune*, but I didn't know *you* belonged to the fraternity, Bertie," said Strathmore, the next evening, as they walked home brushing through the ferns, after a good day out in the open.

Erroll turned with a certain dismay; though in the teeth of a convicted wickedness he would stroke his moustache with the blandest *plaît-il?* look of innocence, he was thrown a little off his guard, and confidence was such a habit with him with Strathmore, that it was difficult to get out of it.

"The deuce, Strath, you're as bad as a detective!" he murmured, plaintively. "Where did you see me?"

"Where you were very easily to be seen, my dear fellow, as I told you once before. If you walk about in the open air, as large as life, with a cigar in your mouth, I can't understand how you can very judiciously expect to go *unseen*, myself! What have you got about you, Erroll, to confer invisibility? You seem to expect it as your prerogative!"

"Bosh!" interrupted Bertie, striking a fusee. "But, by the way, my dear Cis, how came *you* to be looking at the moonlight last night? That isn't your line at all."

"Thank God, no! Who will may have the moon-rays for me: we can spend the night much more pleasantly than by looking at it! Who is she, mon cher? Such nocturnal depredations are poaching on my manor-rights; however, I don't grudge them to you. Katie or Jeanneton may make a very pretty picture with a broken pitcher or a gleaner's bundle for Mulready or Meissonnier, but in real life—no, thank you! No Psyche can lie on a hard pallet under a thatched roof. Bah! I thought better of you, Sabreur!"

Erroll laughed and didn't defend himself, but he looked a trifle thoughtful and worried for so insignificant an affair as a provincial *amourette*, which to that universal conqueror was usually something what knocking over a swallow with a stone, might be to a splendid shot, after the best bouquets of prime battues.

"Don't say anything about it, there's a good old fellow!" he said, carelessly, after a moment's pause—a pause apparently of some hesitation and indecision on a subject on which he seemed tempted to speak fully.

"Did I say anything about the other, last summer? If I were a man, now, who liked cabbage-roses, I should try my *droits de seigneur*, and turn you out from your monopoly. But on my life, Bertie, I don't understand your village liaisons," went on Strathmore, thinking no more about the matter than that Erroll's equal worship of Eros, whether the little god of mischief lived under a lean-to roof, or a ceiling painted after Fragonard, was not his own line of action, and seemed an unintelligible elasticity of taste. "'A Gardener's Daughter' and 'Jacqueline la Bouquetière' look very well in poetry and painting; so do rags and tatters; but, in real life, I can no more fancy making love to them, than taking to a beggar's clothes by choice. Love's born of the senses; then why the deuce take Love where half his senses must be shocked?"

"*L'amour est niveleur!*" laughed Erroll, a little more absent still than usual. "He's the only real republican, the only sincere socialist going, my dear Cis; he won't complain where you take him so long as he has a soft nest in a white breast, and can talk in his own tongue! What do you know about him? You only 'make love' languidly to some *grande dame*, who blinds him with sandal-wood and stifles him in lace; or some Champs Elysées Aspasia, who drenches his wings with *vin mousseux*, smothers him in *cachemires*, kills him with *mots*, and sells him for *rouleaux!* Your god isn't *the* god!"

"My dear fellow, will you tell me in what religion my god is ever *the* god according to my neighbour's orthodoxy?" said Strathmore. "I say, Bertie, didn't you lose a good

deal at the Spring Meetings? I told you that miserable bay
was worth nothing."

Erroll laughed gaily.

"I *did* drop a good deal, but I cleared a few hundreds after
at Goodwood, that put things a little square. Things always
right themselves: worry's like a woman, who, if she sees
she's no effect, leaves off plaguing you. Bills, like tears, are
rained down on you if they disturb you an inch, but, if you're
immovable to both, you see no more of either!"

"Comfortable creed! I never knew, though, that the un-
paid and the unloved were quite so soon daunted! But, Bertie,
you promised me that—that if——"

"My dear old fellow, I know I did!" broke in the Sabreur.
"If I were in any mess for money, I would tell you frankly,
and take from you as cheerfully as you'd lend——"

"Parole d'honneur?"

"Parole d'honneur! Won't that satisfy you?"

"No! I want to free you from those beggarly Jews. You
might let me have my own whim here. Name any interest
to me you like—a hundred per cent., if that will please you
—but only——"

"Sign a bond that you'd tear in two and scatter to the
winds, or thrust in the fire as soon as it was written! You
served me that trick once," muttered Erroll; but his eyes grew
soft with a grateful and cordial light as he looked at Strathmore. "Old fellow, you *know* how I thank you; but I can't
let you have your whim here, though you're as true as steel,
Strath, God bless you! I say, what does Paris think of Gra-
ziella? She's not worth half they rave of her in the Guards'
Box, and her ankles are so atrociously thick!"

"The deuce they are! She owes everything to her face;
her *pas de seul* would never be borne in public, only she's so
extremely handsome for a *pas de deux* in private! Carlotta
has ten times more grace; but Carlotta got a *claque* against
her from the first; she began by being—virtuous, and, though
she's seen the error of her ways, the imprudence will never
be forgiven her. Virtue is as detrimental in the Coulisses as

Honesty on 'Change! The professors of either soon get hissed down for such an eccentric innovation, and tire of its losing game before the sibilation!"

With which truism upon Life and Virtue, Strathmore walked on through the ferns, talking with Erroll of the topics of the hour, from the *carte* of the coming policies of Europe, to the best site for a new tan-gallop. That evening, as they strolled homewards in the mellow sunset, smoking and chatting, while Our Lady's bells chimed slowly and softly over woodland and cornland, over river and valley, in the Curfew chant, was the last hour in which they enjoyed, untainted, the free, frank, *bon camarade* communion of a friendship that was closer than brotherhood and stronger than the tie of blood. It was the last before a woman laid the axe to its root.

And even now their conversation lagged, and their voices dropped to silence, as the thoughts of both were occupied by her whom neither named—Erroll musing with an impatient curiosity, a prophetic prescience of distrust, on this sorceress-beauty which men attributed to the Marchioness of Vavasour and Vaux, yet which his friend averred had assailed him no more than the lifeless perfection of some Titian chef-d'œuvre; and Strathmore thinking of the hour, now near, when her hand should touch his, when the light of her eyes should glance on him again, when his own roof should shelter the loveliness which was fast shattering to the dust the proud panoply of his chill philosophies, and whose seductive sweetness had stolen into his life unperceived, from the first night that he had looked by the light of the spring stars on the *blonde aux yeux noirs* in Bohemia.

That evening Lady Vavasour drove through Paris; she had been staying with the Court at Compiègne, and was here but for a day or two in her favourite residence, which was peerless among cities as herself amidst womanhood. She and Paris both brilliant, sparkling, proud, without rival in their path, with their days one brilliant *fête de triomphe*, and their sovereign sceptre wreathed with flowers, suited and resembled each other—the Queen of Cities and the Queen of Fashion! And if in the Past and Future of the woman, as in the Past and Future of the city, there were cruelties which teemed with the ferocity of the tigress, lustful vanities which rioted with the licence of a Faustina, dark hours in which the Dis-crowned tasted of the bitterness of death, with both the Past was shrouded, and the Future veiled.

Paris, fair and stately, lay glittering in the sunset, with its myriad of lights a-lit, its song, its revels, its music; and Marion Marchioness of Vavasour and Vaux drove through the streets, her moqueur smile upon her lips, her silken lashes lazily drooped as she mused over a thousand victorious me-mories, her delicate form wrapped in costliest silks and laces, the very crowds doing homage to her as she passed through them, and they turned into the streets to glance after the loveliest woman of her day.

The carriage with its fretting roans, its mazarine-blue liveries, its outriders *à la Reine*,—for she passed through Paris with well-nigh as much pomp and circumstance as Montespan or Marie Antoinette,—halted before the doors of her hotel, and the people thronging on their way to the Boulevards and the Cafés-chantants, turned to gaze at the superb equi-page, and more at the loveliness which lay back upon its cushions, negligently indifferent to their gaze.

Among the crowd was a woman, a gipsy, at whom a Quartier Latin student, who lived on a pipe and three *litres* a day, and dreamt of high art when he was not drunk with absinthe, looked, thinking ruefully what a model she would have made had he had a sou to give her; for as the double light of the sunset and the *réverbères* fell on her, her vagrant dress was Rembrandtesque, and her olive features had the dark, still, melancholy beauty of an Arab's—that mournful and immutable calm which Greek sculptors gave to the face of Destiny and of the goddess Demeter, and which on the living countenance ever bespeaks repressed but concentred passions. And this woman, mingling among the passengers that thronged the trottoir, drew nearer and nearer the carriage as it stopped before the Hôtel Vavasour.

The horses pawed the ground impatient, the outriders pulled theirs up with noise and fracas, the Chasseur lowered the steps, and Lady Vavasour descended from her carriage, sweeping onwards with her royal, negligent grace, the subtle perfume of her dress wafted out upon the evening air. The Bohemian had drawn near; so near, that as she stretched forward this vagrant obstructed the path of the English peeress, and her heavy, weather-stained cloak, covered with the dust of the streets, all but touched the scented gossamer laces and trailing train of the Leader of Fashion!

"*Chassez-là!*" said Marion Vavasour to her Chasseur, as she slightly drew back;—she, for whom sovereigns laid down their state, and before whose word bowed princes of the blood, to have her passage blocked by a beggar-woman!

The Chasseur, obedient, struck the gipsy a sharp blow with his long white wand, and ordered her out of the way.

She fell out of the path, and Lady Vavasour went onward up the steps of her hotel, and passed at once to her own rooms to make, still more elaborately than usual, her dinner toilette—S. A. R. le Prince d'Etoile and his Eminence the Cardinal Miraflora dined with her that night, and ere bringing down royal stags she loved to know that all her weapons were primed and burnished. As she sank into her couch, and resigned herself into the hands of her maids, she tossed carelessly over the hundred notes that had collected in her absence, and were heaped together on a Louis-Quinze salver, chased by Réveil; she glanced at this, threw that carelessly aside, till she had dismissed dozens, scarce reading a line; at last over one she paused, with amused triumph glancing away the languor from her eyes, and a smile playing on her lips— a smile of success; while as she looked up from the letter to the face reflected in the mirror before her, the thought that floated through her mind was a fatal truth:

"My cold, proud Strathmore, who dared to disdain the power of woman!—you own it now, then, at last!"

And underneath the windows of her stately hotel the Bohemian still lingered, as though loth to leave the place, while the crowds brushed past her, and the carriage and the outriders swept away. When the blow of the Chasseur had struck her, and he had ordered her out of his path like a cur, the fixed, immutable melancholy of her face had not changed: she had spoken no word, made no sign, only her teeth had set tightly, and the light as of a flame had leaped for one moment into her eyes; this had been all. She lingered some moments longer, while the rush of the throngs jostled and moved her unnoticed: then she passed slowly away, walking wearily and painfully, with her head bowed, as the daylight faded, and the gas in the lamps glared brighter; while amidst the gay babble and the busy noise of Paris, her lips muttered to herself in the mellow Czechen patois of her people:

"My beloved! my beloved! Redempta has not forgot thee, Redempta will yet avenge thee! Her hireling struck me, at her bidding, like a dog—*that* was not needed *too*. Patience!—the lowliest stone may serve to bring to earth the loftiest bird that soars!"

CHAPTER XV.

The Charm of the Rose.

"She is divine—but she will destroy him!"

They were uncomplimentary words, and very harsh ones, for that devout adorer of the beau sexe; but as Erroll stood leaning against the doorway of the portrait-gallery at White Ladies, and looking down it to its farthest end, where Lady Vavasour was seated, while Strathmore bent towards her, on the morning after her arrival, a jealousy towards this woman stirred in a heart which never harboured any acrid thought or unjust envy to any living thing.

Is a man ever leniently disposed towards the woman whom his friend loves? Very rarely. She is his rival, and in lists, moreover, in which he can oppose nothing to her power. She

supplants him, she invades his supremacy, fifty to one she is
the cause of dispute between them; and he will see no good
in this soft-skinned intruder, this dangerous Nazarene: unless
he does what is worse—fall in love with her too!

And Erroll twisted his moustaches, and muttered to himself the first unflattering and mistrustful words that he had
ever uttered of a lovely woman, Bertie being generally given
to deny at all odds that the Ceinture could ever strangle; or
the "Drink to me with thine eyes!" ever be an invitation to
a cup of poisoned wine. Yet what he looked at was matchless, and dazzled his eyes even while he swore against it.

"Hate her!"—the germ of hatred might lie in it, but all
of impatience and aversion, that had crossed and checked
the witchery she had for Strathmore, were swept away the
moment that he touched her hand and received her beneath
his own roof. She came—the beauty of Paris, the Queen of
Fashion—where before her Mary Stuart had languished a
captive, and in ages yet farther the ascetic Dominicans had
dwelt, thrusting away from them, with the throes of an unnatural struggle, the mere thought, the mere memory, of her
sex. She came to White Ladies with the rest of a gay,
dashing, fashionable party from his favourite Paris set; and
the advent of Royalty could not have been received there
with more splendour than was the Sovereign of the Salons.
The State chambers were given to her, where the White
Queen and the Winter Queen had closed their soft Stuart eyes
in slumber before her, and where none save crowned heads
till now had been laid.

The witchery of this woman was on him, and to lend éclat
and honour to her I believe Strathmore would have dissolved
pearls in his wines, or scattered diamonds *à pleines mains*. He
did not realise it; told it, he would not perhaps have believed
even yet; but the web woven by the golden shuttle was drawing its charmed toils tighter and tighter about him, and he
was fast becoming the slave of Marion Vavasour: doubt had
but bound him closer, absence had but riveted her chains;
and Lady Vavasour laughed softly to herself when on the

night of her arrival she drew her hands through her amber tresses, as she leant her head on her arm and looked at her face in the mirror, thinking, "My cold Strathmore! you are *my* captive now!"

Was it love that she felt for him which set her heart so strongly on this triumph? It is as easy to follow the way-ward flight of a bird on the wing, or an April wind's wanton vagaries as it blows over field and flower, as to sift the reasons of a woman's will—of a coquette's caprices!

"That is your best friend, Major Erroll, isn't it?" she asked Strathmore, when they stood together in the deep embrasured window of the picture-gallery, her eyes glancing at the Sabreur, where he leaned against the doorway.

"My best indeed! You have been introduced to him?"

"Oh yes, you introduced me last night. I was anxious to see the only person out of the whole world to whom you are not indifferent! What charm has he about him?"

"What charm? Dear old fellow! None, save the gentlest nature and truest honour that I ever found in any man. He has the strength of a lion and the sweetness of a woman; he is game to the backbone, and frank as a boy!"

She raised her eyebrows. She was a little impatient of the warmth of his tone and the sincerity of his praise; a tyrannous, victorious woman is jealous of all influence not her own; and perhaps she foresaw here a power that might be opposed to hers. Lady Vavasour, with a woman's swift, unerring instinct, guessed that Erroll would be against her, in exact proportion to the sway she exercised over his friend.

" *You* admiring warmth of heart and the candour of boy-hood, Strathmore," she said, maliciously enough. "Why don't you cultivate them, mon ami, if you think them so admirable?"

At her tone all the strange, sudden hatred of her, which now and then flashed so ominously across the passion which was growing on him for this woman, stirred into life afresh for a moment; he smiled slightly, the smile which made his face sneeringly cold, and gave his eyes the look that, in a dog or a horse, we call *dangerous*.

"I am an Athenian, Lady Vavasour: I may admire what I fail to practise. Life makes us all egotists and dissemblers; but we may honour the nature which is such true steel that it resists and escapes the corroding. Erroll's is the only one *I* know which has done so."

Her impatience at Erroll increased. With the quick wit of her sex, she saw at once that Erroll would undermine her power if she did not undermine his, and she changed her tactics accordingly. She looked at the Sabreur, letting her lashes droop over her eyes, and lend them that glance of softened interest which was the most delicate flattery such eyes could bestow.

"I can believe it; his face tells one so. How singularly beautiful a face it is, too; a woman might envy him his golden hair and his azure eyes!"

And for the first time in his life, as he stood beside her—not for the praise of his personal attractions, such petty vanity and envy Strathmore was far above—but for the softness of her look as it dwelt on him, the softness which with imperious jealousy he loathed to see wake for any save himself, an ill-feeling stirred in him towards the man whom he loved closer than a brother. And Lady Vavasour glanced at him and smiled, amused and content; she had sown the larvæ of the cankerworm that would eat away friendship! It is a work at which the hands of women ever love well to be busy.

She had done enough to please her, and with one of her graceful, antelope-like movements she turned and looked upward at the portrait above her.

"Ah! a Vandyke and a Strathmore. Really you are wonderfully like one of those old pictures animated into life, Lord Cecil! My lord is quite right; he says you are a walking Velasquez. There are the eyes, 'fathomless and darkly-wise,' of the legend; you have them and the portrait has them; and in both they never soften, even to a woman!"

As she spoke, her own glanced at him with their most

enchanting mischief, and Strathmore, subdued to the charm
of her will, bent towards her:

"Looking down on *you*, the very portraits of the dead
might soften their glance. How then shall any living man
have power to resist? Have you not heard that the Strathmores of White Ladies have often disdained all, only as their
doom, to madly and vainly covet—one?"

And it was as he whispered those words that Erroll, not
catching even the sound of his voice, but seeing the meaning
warmth upon his face, the gaze which Strathmore fastened on
her, muttered, *sotto voce*, "She is divine; but she will destroy
him!"

Into him, too, entered—with a nature as different to
Strathmore's as the summer to the winter, as the sunny unruffled lake to the deep and silent sea—the subtle poison of
Marion Vavasour's beauty, mingled with a warning and prophetic hatred of her power.

There was a large party gathered by this time at the
Abbey, and the hospitalities she had recently quitted of a
Bourbon at Neuilly had scarcely been more brilliant than
those which welcomed her at White Ladies. There was
Blanche de Ruelle, that haughty dark-eyed beauty, who,
amidst all the homage she received, treasured bitterly and
wearily the memory of the love once whispered by a man
whom no love had touched—who was now her friend and her
host. There was Beatrix Beaudesert, that dashing *brunette*
who led the first flight in a twenty minutes' burst up wind,
and never funked at any bullfinch or double that yawned in
good Northamptonshire; but could have cleared Brixworth
Brook, and won the Grand Military, were the sex allowed to
enter either for the Steeple Chase or the Service. There was
the Comtesse de Chantâl, who wove half the intrigues of the
Tuileries, while statesmen and diplomatists wound her floss
silks, and who brewed *embroglie* for the Western Powers in
her dainty Sèvres coffee-cup. There was pretty Lady Alaric,
who was so very religious, and went on her knees before her

missal-like prayer-book before she floated down to breakfast to commence the flirtations, which always pulled up *just* short of a court and a co-respondent; of an error and an esclandre. There was Lady Clarence Camelot, leader of the most exclusive of the thorough-bred sets, who was cold and still as a rock-crystal, and proud as any angel that ever fell by that queenly sin; but whose nature was sweet as the sun of Sorrento, and whose heart was as mellow as a Catherine pear, for the few who had the fortunate sesame to either. There were these and others at White Ladies, but Lady Vavasour outshone them all: she was the Reine Regnante, and she used her sceptre omnipotently, and far eclipsed those whom most women found it a hard matter even to equal.

The Marquis—who came thither, *en route* to Spa, for a few days, chiefly because the venison and the char out of White Ladies' woods and waters had had such a celebrity for centuries that he was curious to test their reputed superiority—was blessed with the most gentlemanlike indifference to his lovely wife's vagaries. He knew she was always flirting with somebody—*who*, didn't matter much; perhaps when he did think about it, his chief feeling was a certain malicious pleasure in seeing so many of his fellow-creatures chained, and worried, and fooled, by the seductive tormentress whom he had let loose on the world, with her *droit de conquête* legitimatised by his coronet. The Marquis was a philosopher, and the very husband for his wife: their marital relations were admirably ordered for the preservation of peace and friendship; they saw little or nothing of one another (the secret recipe for conjugal unity), and, by mutual consent, never interfered, he with her *caprices de cœur*, nor she with his "separate establishments." When he had first married, people had said his lordship was madly *entêté* with his bride; but that inconvenient folly had departed with a few months' wear: and now—he was proud of her loveliness, but wisely and placably negligent on whom that loveliness might shine; a wisdom and a placability never more needed, perhaps, than now at White Ladies.

> "Lookest thou at the stars?
> If I were Heaven, with all the eyes of Heaven,
> Would I look down on thee!"

The words were very softly whispered, as Strathmore stood that evening on the terrace. It was late; the stars were shining, and the murmur of the waters flowing onward under the elm-woods was heard plaintively and monotonously sweet, as Marion Vavasour, whose whim was every hour changing, and who laughed at all feeling one hour, only to assume it most beguilingly the next, left the drawing-rooms, where she reigned supreme; and strolled out for a brief while in the summer night, followed by her host. The white light of the stars fell about her, glancing on the sapphires and diamonds that glittered in her hair or sparkled in her bosom, and shone in the depths of her eyes, as she raised them, and looked upwards at the skies above, where, here and there, some cloud of transparent mist trailed across the brilliance of the moon, or veiled the swift course of a falling star. She laughed, toying with the closed autumn roses that twined round the balustrade.

"Strathmore! you would do no such thing! If you had the eyes of Heaven, they would all be bent in watching conferences you cannot join, and in reading despatches you cannot see! There are three things no woman rivals with a man who loves any one of them; they are a Horse, a State secret, and a Cigar. We may eclipse all three, perhaps, for a little while, but, in the long run, any one of the triad outrivals us."

He bent lower towards her, with a soft whisper:

"Do not slander my sex, and belie the power of your own. Have there not been women for whom men have thought the world itself well lost?"

"There have been fools, mon ami; and that is how *you* would phrase it if you were out of my presence and in the smoking-room, and anybody advanced the proposition!" she laughed, with that *moqueur* incredulity with which at Vernonceaux she had so constantly tantalised and provoked him.

"Fools! It would be rash to call them so. Manuel was no fool, yet he found his Isles of Delight sweeter than the din and clash of triumph, and the fall of conquered citadels. Alcibiades was no fool, yet he found to look into the eyes of Aspasia better than the sceptre of the Alcmæonidæ and the wisdom of the Schools!"

Three months ago Strathmore would have sworn never to utter such words, save in derision: but now, as he stooped towards her in the stillness of the night, it was not either in jest or flattery, that he spoke them; the roses had the perfume for him with which they had wooed Manuel in the Isles of Delight; the eyes had the power to which the soft Greek had bowed and sunk. For with every year the roses bloom, and with every age men love!

Her sweet mocking laugh rang in the air—the laugh which had enthralled him under the lindens of Bohemia, and from behind the mask of the White Domino.

"*What!* you who acknowledge but one love—Power; and covet but one boon—Age; confess so much as that! You must be very suddenly changed since three months ago; your eyes, a Strathmore's fathomless eyes, actually soften at the mere memory of Aspasia!"

Her eyes laughed up into his, her hand touched his own where it wandered among the roses; the sultry air of the night swept round them, only stirred by the dreamy splash of fountains, and the rise and fall of her low breathings. He had no strength against her in such a moment, nor did he seek, or strive, or wish, to have.

"Changed! If I be so, the sorcery lies at your door. It is not the memory of Aspasia which evokes the confession; the daughter of Hellas has bequeathed her glamour to one who uses it to the full, as fatally, and as surely!"

A smile trembled on her lovely lips, which became half a sigh, while her hand absently toyed with the sapphire cross that glittered just below her throat.

"Ah-bah!" she said, with a laugh, whose gay mockery had in it for the first time a *timbre* of constraint, as of lightness assumed but unfelt. "I do not believe in such sudden converts; I do not receive them into my creed! Strathmore, am I, who read you so well while you were yet unknown, likely to believe in your suave words so quickly? Remember! I am clairvoyante. I know the sincerity of every one who approaches me, and I know the worth of your words, my diplomatist! I shall be a very long time before I accord to you the honour of any belief in them."

"If you be clairvoyante, you will no longer disbelieve; you will see without words what your sorcery works. You must know your own power too well to doubt it!"

Know her own power? In every iota! and she knew it now; knew that this man, who was steeled in his own strength, and held himself far above the soft foolery of passion, was fast bending to her will, fast drinking in the draught which she tendered to his lips, fast succumbing to her feet, to lie there, bound, and powerless to free himself from bondage; letting his life drift on as she should choose to guide it; losing all, forsaking all, risking all, so long as he could look upward in her eyes, so long as her white hand would wander to his own! Know her own power! Truly she did, and used it without mercy, without scruple!

Her eyes looked up and dwelt on his with the mournful languor which gave to their dark brilliance the softness as of unshed tears; the mockery of her smile faded; and the lips seemed charged with some unuttered whisper, as the roses she toyed were charged with the heavy sweetness of the clinging dew. If ever woman loved, Strathmore could have sworn she loved him then; and the scorching sweetness, the dangerous delight of a forbidden passion, stole over him, and swept round him, in the sultry air of the night, only heightened by the strange hatred of the power which enthralled him to her will, which ever mingled with the madness that was stealing on him. He bent towards her, his breath fanned her hair, his hand touched hers where it rested among the flowers, and touched—the diamond circlet that chilled him as with the chill of ice. It recalled to him that this woman was but fooling him; that this woman was Marion Vavasour! And as their hands met, she drew her own away; while a faint sigh stirred her heart beneath its costly lace.

"Hush! If they be not the words of flattery, they must not be the words of friendship! How beautiful the night is! I do not wonder that poets love it better than the day. The sunlight is for haste and care, and for men's toil and labour, and for the fret of daily life; but the night, when the flowers are closed, and the cities are silent, and the stars look into the chambers, where the living sleep peacefully as the dead, and shine upon the rivers, till the suicides who have sought their refuge wear a calm smile on their cold lips—the Night is the noon of the poets—the Night is for rest, for dreams, for——"

"*Love!*"

The word which paused upon her lips he uttered for her; and the soft rebuke, the gesture with which she repelled him, and recalled to him that there was a boundary which the language of homage must not pass, to the woman who was a wife, enthralled him more than any art she could have called forward, since in his ear it whispered:

"The woman who fears your homage, fears herself!"

As she spoke dreamily, mournfully, with that occasional earnestness which, when it succeeded her caprices and her brilliant mockery, had the charm of the Italian evening that follows on the dazzling day, Strathmore uttered, with a meaning new upon his lips, the word which had been his derision and disdain; the word before which she paused; the word which all the voices of the voluptuous night seemed to re-echo around them, while the moonlight streamed on the uncovered limbs of sculptured marble that wore all the repose of sleep, and the stars gleamed upon the winding waters, white with the snowy burden of innumerable lilies. Love! Strathmore would have flung away that word in disdain if spoken to him in the coldness of reason, in the pauses of judgment; but the insidious passion to which he gave no name, but which in her presence swept over him like a scorch of a sirocco, *was* love; love, if you will, in its most soulless, love in its most sensual, form, but that form the most alluring, the most dangerous, in which it ever steals into the life of man.

She shrugged her snow-white shoulders and pouted her lips with a *moue* of pretty contempt, while at the same time the faint sigh which was so little in unison with her beauty, yet gave it so rare a charm, heaved the sapphires where they sparkled in her breast.

"Bah! that is the 'pastime of fools,' too, and no more suits our world than the other. We do not believe in it; we only mimic it. It may do for Undine among the water-lilies yonder, but we have no faith left for those childish idyls. They are *contes pour rire* for us; we have outgrown them! Who loves in our world?"

For all its mockery the question was one of pitiless danger, spoken by her, as she leaned against the balustrade in the moonlight, gazing down on to the dark masses of foliage sheltering beneath; while her eyes were heavy as with some indefinite regret, as she pressed against her lips the leaves of a rose she had disentangled from the rest, which was wet and fragrant with the night dews. His lips brushed her hair, his breath fanned her brow, his words were whispered softly and wooingly:

"To answer you would be to risk rebuke afresh. The truth would neither lie in words of flattery nor of friendship."

"Then—those words must not be spoken!"

The reply was but like the cold breath which fans the embers into fire; uttered while her eyes dwelt on his without rebuke, while her lips parted with a breath that was so near a sigh, while half in sadness, half in coquetry, she silenced him with a light, fragrant blow of the roses, the words in their very forbiddance gave fresh fuel to the dawning madness they rebuked. In that moment he would have staked his life that he was loved by the woman he coveted, as he of Israel coveted the loveliness on which the eastern

sunlight fell, making it in his sight, while yet it was unwon,
more precious than palace treasure, or kingly sway, than the
good word of man, or than the smile of his God!

She turned from him with one of the swift movements
which had the charm of the antelope's grace, turned as a
woman might from the danger which she dreads and fears;
the jewels in her hair glancing in the starlight, the rose that
had been pressed against her lips, falling on the marble.

"Let us go in!—we have given time enough to the night,
we must give the rest to the world."

"And while the world claims you, even friendship may
at least claim this?" said Strathmore, as he stooped, and
lifted from the ground the rich fresh rose which had rested
against lips as fair and fragrant as itself. She laughed her
gay mocking laugh; but her eyes were saddened still as she
glanced at him while he held back the heavy draperies of a
window for her to re-enter the drawing-rooms.

"Ah, I know you too well: to-night the roses are taken
in flattery; to-morrow, withered and faded, they will be flung
away with a mot! You are a man of the world, Strathmore,
and all you prize is power. There is no State secret in the
core of that rose."

"But there is a secret more fatal in the charm of the lips
that have touched it."

Strathmore's eyes darkened as he spoke with the imperious and reckless passion she had rightly judged would
be the only love to which he would ever waken, and which
she had vowed to arouse in this man who held himself
sheathed in an armour of proof; his words, losing the softness of suave compliment, were hoarse with a deeper meaning, and as he followed her he thrust the rose into his breast
—the delicate leaves that had gained value in his sight,
because her lips had touched them!

That night he drank deep of the delirious draught of a
woman's witchery; that night, as he paid his gold to the
Marquis, at écarté, he loathed the man who had bought her
beauty with his title, and claimed her by right of ownership,

as he claimed his racing stud, his chef de cuisine, his comet
wines!—he loathed himself for having him at his table and
beneath his roof; for chatting the idle nothings of familiar
intercourse with him; and bidding the friendly good night
of host to guest, to the man whom he hated with the dark
hatred of the Strathmore blood, which was ever stronger than
their wisdom, and deeper than their love, and closer than
their honour. True! We seat our foes at our board, and
welcome what we hate to our hospitality, and eat salt with
those who betray us, and those whom we betray; wronged
Octavia smiles as she receives Cleopatra into heir house, and
Launcelot shakes hands in good-fellowship with Arthur, the
day after he has writ the stain on his friend's knightly shield!
It is done every day, and he was accustomed to such convenience and such condonation; but Strathmore, when once
roused, was a man of darker, swifter, deeper passions than
the passions of our day, and the leaven of his race was working in him, beneath the cold and egotistic surface of habit
and of breeding. As stillness fell that night upon his household, and sleep came with the hush of the advancing hours,
and he stood in the silence of his own chamber, hating the
husband, coveting the wife, knowing that both were now
beneath his roof; he thought of her where, like the Lady
Christabel,

> Her lovely limbs she did undress,
> And lay down in her loveliness:

till, with an oath, he pressed the broken rose-leaves to his
lips with a fierce kiss where her own had rested on them,
and hurled them out away into the darkness of the night.

Already—did he love this woman?

———

CHAPTER XVI.

"At her Feet he bowed and fell."

"I CONGRATULATE you on your fresh honours, old fellow. Bomont writes word the ministers have selected you for the Confidential mission to——.　Ticklish business, and a very high compliment," said Camelot, one morning at breakfast, when Lord Vavasour had left for Spa, and his wife had been some weeks the reigning Queen at the Abbey.

Strathmore went on stirring his chocolate.

"Bomont has no earthly business to tittle-tattle Foreign-office secrets; however, since he's let it out, I may confess to it."

"You accept, of course! You must leave at once—eh!"

"The affair's been on the tapis some time. I always knew I should be selected to succeed Caradoc. Try that potted char, Lady Beaudesert," answered Strathmore, avoiding direct answer to either of Camelot's inquiries, while among his letters lay one which selected him, in a juncture of critical difficulty, to occupy a post which older diplomatists bitterly envied him, and which gratified his ambition and signalised his abilities to the fullest. Questions and congratulations flooded in on him from the people about his breakfast-table, among whom Lady Vavasour was not; she usually had her coffee in her own chamber.

"You will draw us into a war, I dare say, Strathmore," laughed Beatrix Beaudesert. "You dips love an embroglio as dearly as journalists love a 'crisis'; and your race are born statesmen. Your *berceaunelles* must have been trimmed with Red Tape; and you must have learnt your alphabet out of Machiavelli's Maxims! You're not like Hamlet; you specially enjoy the times being 'out of joint,' that you may show your surgical skill in setting them right."

"Of course," laughed Strathmore. "If half a million slaughtered gets a General the Garter, what does he care

who rots, so long as he rises? Man's the only animal that
preys upon his species, and for his superiority calls himself
head of all creation. The brutes only fly at their foes; *we*
turn on our friends if we get anything by it!"

"*Fi donc!*" cried Madame de Ruelle. "You have just
received the Bath, and are appointed to a post which all the
diplomatic world will envy you. You ought not to be in a
cynical mood, Strathmore. It is those with whom life goes
badly, who write satires and turn epigrams; a successful man
always approves the world, because the world has approved
him!"

"True, madame; but at the same time there may be a
drop of *amari aliquid* under his tongue, because the world
has approved other people too!"

"Dear old fellow, how glad I am!" said Erroll, meeting
him in the doorway a quarter of an hour afterwards. "My
K.C.B.! a discerning nation does for once put the right man
in the right place. On my word, Strath, I *am* proud of
you!"

"Thank you!"

The two monosyllables were odiously cold after the cordial warmth of the other's words, and Strathmore crossed the
hall without adding others. He was conscious that he could
fling away power, place, fame, honour, if one woman's voice
would murmur, "Relinquish them—*for me!*" And the consciousness made him bitter to all the world, even to the man
who was closer than a brother.

"The deuce! How changed he is! It is all that woman's
doings, with her angel's face and her devil's mischief; her
gazelle's eyes and her Marcia's soul!" muttered Erroll.

"*Vous avez l'air tant soit peu contrarié, monsieur!*" said a
voice behind him, half amused, half contemptuous, as Lady
Vavasour, having just descended the staircase, swept past
him, radiant in the morning sunlight; her silk folds trailing
on the inlaid floor, and the fragrance of her hair scenting the
air. Perhaps she had heard his words?

Lady Vavasour, however, could very admirably defy him and his enmity, and anybody or everybody else. She played utterly unscrupulously, but equally matchlessly, with Strathmore; now avoiding him, till she made his cheek grow white and his eyes dark as night with anger; now listening with a feigned rebuke, which made it but the sweeter, to the whispers of a love, that while she chid, she knew how to madden with the mere sweep of her dress across him.

She was a coquette and a voluptuary. She loved with the shallow, tenacious, fleeting love, such as Parabère and Pompadour knew, while romance still mingled with licence, as their best *pointe à la sauce*. Strathmore's nature was new to her. To first rouse, and then play with it, was delightful to this beautiful panther; and she did both, till a very insanity was awakened in him. *Love* is by a hundred times too tame and meaningless a word for what had now broken up from his coldness as volcanic flames break up from ice. It was a passion born entirely from the senses, if you will, without any nobler element, any better spring; but for that very reason it was headlong as flame, and no more to be arrested than the lightning that seethes through men's veins and scorches all before it.

She heard of his appointment to conduct the mission to —— as though he were her brother, in whose career she was fraternally interested, and nothing more; and spoke of his coming departure to Northern Europe as if it were a question of going into the next county for a steeplechase or a coursing meeting.

"Ah! you are going to ——?" she said, tranquilly, when she met him in the library, trifling with a new French novelette. "It will be very cold! Give my compliments to M. le Prince de Vörn; he is a great friend of mine, though he is a political foe of yours. His wit is charming!"

Strathmore, standing near her, felt his face pale with passion to the very lips as she spoke. She had wooed, while she repressed; she had tempted, while she forbade his love, as a woman only does who knows that she has conquered where conquest is dear to her; and now—she heard of his departure for a lengthened and indefinite term as carelessly as though he told her he was going to visit his stables or his kennels!

He tried vainly that day to meet her alone; she avoided or evaded him from luncheon to dinner with tantalising dexterity. Letters to write, a game of billiards, chit-chat in the drawing-rooms—one thing or another occupied her so ingeniously, that not even for a single second did she give him the chance of a *tête-à-tête*. She knew he sought one, and pleasured herself by baffling and denying him, while her insouciant indifference tortured him to fury. Ambition had been the god, power the lust which alone had possessed him; with both within his grasp, he would now have thrown both from him, as idly as a child casts pebbles to the sea, only to feel the lips of Marion Vavasour close upon his own!

That night there was a ball given at White Ladies, one among the many entertainments which had marked her visit; it was to be, according to her command, a *bal costumé*, and as Strathmore went to dress he caught sight of the azure gleam of her silken skirt sweeping along the corridor to the State chambers. He crossed the passage that divided them, and in an instant was at her side; she started slightly, and glanced up at him:

"Ah! Lord Cecil, you try one's nerves! really, you are so like those Vandykes in the gallery, that one may very pardonably take you for a ghost!"

Strathmore laid his hand on her arm to detain her, looking down into her eyes by the light from above:

"I have sought a word alone with you all the day through, and sought it vainly; will you grant it me now?"

"Now? Impossible! I am going to dress. The toilette is to us what ambition is to you, the first, and last, and only love—a ruling passion strong in death! A statesman dying, asks, 'Is the treaty signed?' a woman dying asks, 'Am I *bien coiffée*!'"

Laughing, she moved onward to leave him, but Strathmore moved too, keeping his hold on her hand:

"Hear me you must! I told you once that I did not dare to whisper the sole guerdon that would content me as the reward you offered; *now* I dare, because, spoken or unspoken, you must know that the world holds but one thought, one memory, one idol for me; you must know—*that I love you!*"

The words were uttered which, old as the hills eternal, have been on every human lip, and cursed more lives than they have ever blessed. And Marion Vavasour listened, as the light gleamed upon the lovely youth which lit her face, and her eyes met his with the glance that women only give when they love.

"Hush, you forget," she murmured (and chiding from those lips was sweet as the soft wrath of the south wind!)—"*I* must not hear you."

But the eyes forgave him, while the voice rebuked: and Strathmore's love, loosed from all bondage, poured itself out in words of eager honeyed eloquence, with every richest oratory, with every ardent subtilty, that art could teach and passion frame. To win this woman, he would have perilled, had he owned them, twenty lives and twenty souls, and thought the prize well bought!

She listened still, her hand resigned to his, a warm flush on her cheeks, and her heart beating quicker in its gossamer nest of priceless lace; stirred with triumph, perhaps stirred with love. Then—she drew from him with a sudden movement, and laughed in his face with radiant, malicious mockery:

"Ah! my lord, you have learned, then, how dangerous it was to boast to a woman that you had but one idol--Ambition; that you desired Age, and despised Love! The temptation to punish you was irresistible;—you have learned an altered creed now!"

The silvery laughter mocking him rang lightly out upon the silence, and, ere he could arrest her, she had entered her chamber, and the door had closed. He stood alone in the empty corridor, stunned;—and a fierce oath broke from his throat. Had this woman fooled him? The echo of her words, the ringing of her laughter, stung him to madness; the taunt, the mirth, the jest flung at him in the moment when he had laid bare his weakness, and could have taken his oath that he was loved, was like seething oil flung upon flame. He swore that night to wrench confession from her of her love, or—or—— He grew dizzy with the phantoms of his own thoughts. But one resolve was fixed in him; to win this woman, or—to work on her the worst revenge that a foiled passion and a fooled love ever wrought.

As he passed out of the State corridor and turned towards his own chamber he came unhappily upon Erroll.

"Is it you, Strath? I want a word with you; may I come in for ten minutes?"

"*Entrez.*"

Strathmore's voice sounded strange in his own ears; he would have given away a year of his life to have been left alone at that moment.

Erroll followed him into his chamber, however, noticing nothing unusual, for Strathmore, with Italian passion, had more than English self-control; and Bertie, who had had bad intelligence of a weedy-looking bay on whom he had risked a good deal for the approaching Cesarewitch, came as usual to detail his fears and doubts, and speculate on the most judicious hedging with Strathmore. With a mad love running riot in him, and a fierce resolve seething up into settled shape, Strathmore had to sit and listen to Newmarket troubles, and balance the pros and cons of Turf questions as leisurely and as interestedly as of old! Apparently, he was calm enough; actually, every five minutes of restraint lashed his pent-up passion into fury.

The Newmarket business done with, Erroll still lingered; he had something else to say, and scarcely knew how to phrase it.

"Will all these people stay much longer?" he began; "they've been here a long time."

"I don't tell my guests to go away," said Strathmore,

with a smile. "Besides, the pheasants just now are at their prime."

"The pheasants! Oh yes, but I was thinking of the women. To be sure, though, you must leave yourself in a few days; I forgot! When must you start for——?"

"It is uncertain." The subject annoyed him, and he answered shortly.

Erroll was silent a moment; then he looked up, his eyes shining with their frank and kindly light:

"Strath, you wouldn't take wrongly anything *I* said, would you?"

"My dear Erroll! what an odd question. I believe I am not usually tenacious?"

"Of course not; still I fancy you'd let *me* say to you what you mightn't stand from another man; I hope so at least, old fellow! We have never been on ceremony with one another yet; and I want to ask you, Cis, if you know how yours and Lady Vavasour's names are coupled together?"

He could not have chosen a more fatal hour for his question!

"Who couples them?"

The words were brief and quietly said enough, but Strathmore's hand clenched where it lay on the table, and an evil light gleamed in his eyes.

"Oh, nobody in especial, but more or less everybody," answered Erroll, carelessly, whom the gesture did not put on his guard. "Your attention to her, you know, must be noticed; impossible to help it! Naturally the men joke about it when you're out of hearing; fellows always will."

"What do they say?"

The words were quiet still, but Strathmore's teeth were set like a mastiff's.

"You can guess well enough; you know how we always laugh over that sort of thing. Look here, Strathmore!" and Erroll, breaking out of the lazy softness of his usual tone, leant forward eagerly and earnestly, "I know you'll take my words as they're meant; and if you wouldn't, it would be a wretched friendship that shirked the truth when its telling were needed. If you called me out for it to-morrow, I would let you know what everybody is saying—that you are in-fatuated by a woman who is only playing with you!"

Strathmore leaned back in his chair, fastening his wrist-band stud, with a cold sneer on his face; it cost him much to repress the passion that would have betrayed him.

"The world is very good to trouble itself about me; if you will name the particular members of it who do the gos-siping, I will thank them in a different fashion."

"The better way would be to give them no grounds for it!"

"Grounds? I don't apprehend you."

"You do and you must!" broke in Erroll, impatiently; this smooth, icy coating did not impose on him. "Whether your heart be in the matter or not, you act as though it were. You are becoming the very slave of that arch co-quette, who never loved anything in her life save her own beauty; you, who ridiculed everything like woman-worship, are positively infatuated with Marion Vavasour! Stop! hear me out! I have no business with what you do; true enough! I am breaking into a subject no man has any right to touch on to another—I know that! But I like you well enough to risk your worst anger; and I speak plainly because you and I have no need to weigh our words to each other. Good God! *you* must have too much pride, Strathmore, to be fooled for the vanity of a woman!"

He stopped in his impetuous flood of words, and looked at his listener, who had heard him tranquilly—a dangerous tranquillity, thin ice over lava-flames! Strathmore only kept reins on the storm because it rose to his lips—to betray him.

"Pardon me, Erroll," he said, slowly and pointedly, "I will not take *your* words as they might naturally be taken, since you claim the privilege of 'old friendship;' but I must remind you that friendship may be both officious and im-pertinent. The office of a moral censor sits on you very ill; attention to a married woman is not so extraordinarily un-common in our set that it need alarm your virtue——"

"Virtue be hanged!" broke in Erroll, impetuously. "You don't understand, or you *won't* understand me. All I say is, that hundreds of fellows will tell you that Marion Vavasour is the most consummate coquette going; and that as soon as she has drawn a man on into losing his head for her, she turns round and laughs him to scorn. What do you suppose Scrope Waverley and all that lot will say? Only that you have been first trapped and then tricked, as they were——!"

"Thank you, I have no fear! Lady Vavasour makes you singularly bitter?"

"Perhaps she does; because I see her work. Near that woman you are no more what you were than——"

"Really I must beg you to excuse my hearing a homily upon myself!" interrupted Strathmore, as he rose, speaking coldly, intolerantly, and haughtily. "As regards Lady Vavasour, she is *my guest*, and as such I do not hear her spoken of in this manner. As regards the gossip you are pleased to retail, people must chatter as they like, if they chatter in my hearing I can resent it, without having my path pointed out to me; and for the future I will trouble you to remember that even the privileges of friendship may be stretched too far if you overtax them."

While he spoke he rang the bell for Diaz, and as the Albanian entered the chamber from the bath-room, Erroll turned and went out without more words. He was angered that his remonstrance had had no more avail; he was hurt that his interference had been so ill received, and his motive so little comprehended. Like most counsellors, he felt that what he had done had been ill-advised and ill-timed; while Strathmore, indifferent to how he might have wounded a friendship which he had often sworn worth all the love of women, was stung to madness by the words with which Erroll had unwittingly heaped fuel on to flame. Men saw his passion for Marion Vavasour! He swore that they should hopelessly and longingly envy its success.

The fancy ball at White Ladies was as brilliant as it could be made; the great circle at the Duke of Trémayne's, the

people staying at Lady Millicent Clinton's, and at other houses
of note in the county, afforded guests at once numerous and
exclusive, and the Royal women who had been visitors at
White Ladies had never been better entertained than was
Marion Vavasour. As he received them in the great recep-
tion-room known as the King's Hall, that night, women of
the world, not easily impressible, glancing at him, were arrested by they knew not what, and remembered long afterwards how he had looked that evening. He wore the dress
of the Knights Templars, the white mantle flung over a suit
of black Milan armour worked with gold, and the costume
suited him singularly; while it yet seemed to bring out more
strongly still the resemblance in him to all that was dark and
dangerous in the Strathmore portraits. His face was slightly
flushed, like a man after a carouse; his wit was courtly and
light, but very bitter; his attentions to the women were far
more impressive than his ever were—he might have been in
love with all in his rooms!—but his eyes, dark with suppressed eagerness, and with a heavy shade beneath them,
glanced impatiently over the crowd. Every one had arrived,
but *she* had not yet descended; his salons were filled, but to
him they were empty! This was no light, languid love, seeking a liaison as a mere pastime, which had entered into
Strathmore for another man's wife; it was the delirium, the
frenzy, the blindness, in which the world holds but one
woman!

At last, with her glittering hair given to the winds, a
diadem of diamonds crowning her brow, snow-white clouds
of drapery floating around her, light as morning mist, and
her beautiful feet shod with golden sandals, she came, when
all the rooms were full, living impersonation of the Summer-
Noon she represented. A crowd of *costumés* followed her
steps, and murmurs of irrepressible admiration accompanied
her wherever she moved; there were many beautiful women
there that night at White Ladies, but none that equalled,
none that touched her. The golden apple was cast without
a dissent into the white bosom of Marion Vavasour; and at

sight of her his reason reeled and fell, and his madness mastered him, as it subdued him of Brocéliande before the witching eyes and under the wreathing arms of Vivien,
while the forest echoed Fool!
His face wore the reckless resolve which was amongst the dark traits of the Strathmores when their ruthless will had fixed a goal, and underneath their calm and courtly seeming, the fierce spirit was a-flame which made them pitiless as death in all pursuit. His eyes followed the gleaming trail of her streaming hair, the flash of her diamond diadem, with a look which she caught, and fanned to fire with one dreamy glance of languor, one touch of her floating drapery. And yet, even while the passion devoured him, he hated her for its pain—hated her because she was another's and not his! Do you know nothing of this because it has not touched you? —tut!—the forms of human love are as varied and as controlless as the forms of human life; and you have learned but little of the world, and the men that make it, if you have not learned that Love, often and again, treads and trenches close on Hate.

It was as though she set her will to make her beauty more than mortal, and goad him on till he was as utterly her bond-slave as the Viking whom, as the Norse legend tells, twenty strong men could not capture, yet who lay, helpless and bound as in gyves of iron, by one frail, single thread of a woman's golden hair. That night his passion mastered him, and all that was most dangerous, in a nature where fire slept under ice, woke into life, and set into one imperious resolve.

It was some hours after midnight, when he passed with her into a *cabinet de peinture*. The wax-radiance streamed upon her where she stood like some dazzling thing of light, some dream of the Greek poets, some sorceress of the East, some diamond-crowned Priestess of the Sun. In the stillness of the night they were alone, and her eyes met his own with a glance which wooed him on to his sweet temptation. Ambition seemed idle as the winds; fame he was ready to cast aside like dross; at the most brilliant point in his career, he was

willing to throw away all the past, and cut away all the future, so that her voice but whispered him "Stay!" His honour to the man who had been a guest beneath his roof, the
bond which bound him to hold sacred the woman whom his
house harboured, were forgotten and left far behind him,
drowned in his delirium as men's wisdom is drowned in wine.
He saw, remembered, heeded nothing in earth or heaven
save *her*. And she knew the meaning of his silence as he
stood beside her.

"So you will leave England very soon, Strathmore?"

The words were light and ordinary: but her word is but
a tithe of a woman's language; and it was her eyes which
spoke, which challenged him to summon strength to leave
her; which dared him to rank ambition before her, and
claimed and usurped the dominion which power alone had
filled! It was the eyes he answered, only seeing in the midnight glare the fairness of her face.

"Bid me stay for *you*;—and I resign the Mission to-morrow!"

"What! desert your career, abandon your ambition, give
up your power, and at a *woman's* word, too! Fie, fie, Lord
Cecil!"

The sweet laughter echoed in his ear, and her face had all
its witching mockery as she turned it to him in the light.

"Hush! My God!—you know my madness; you shall
play with it no longer. Bid me stay, and I give up everything for you! But you must love me as I love; you must
choose to-night for yourself and me. If you are fooling me,
beware; it will be at a heavy price! Love me;—and I throw
away for you, honour, fame, life, what you will!"

The words were spoken in her ear, fierce with the passion
which was reckless of all cost; broken with the love which
was only conscious of itself, and of the beauty that it adored.
His face was white as death; his eyes gazed into hers, hot,
dark, lurid as the eyes of a tiger. This mad idolatry, this
imperious strength, made love new to her, dear to her, as its
costliest toy to a child; a richer gage of her power, a stronger

proof of her dominion. A blush warm and lovely, if it were but a lie, wavered in her face; her eyes answered his with dreamy languor; the diamonds in her breast trembled with the heavings of her heart, and even while she hushed him, and turned from him, her hand lingered within his.

He knew that he was loved!—and his whole life would have been staked on that mad hour. His arms closed round her in an embrace she could not break from; he wound his hands in the shining shower of her amber hair; he crushed this soft and dazzling thing which mocked, and maddened him, against the chill steel of his armour as though to slay her. Burning words broke from him, delirious, imperious, half menace, half idolatry, born of the strong passion, and the sensuous softness, of which his love at once was made.

"I sacrifice what you choose, for you; or—I hate you more bitterly than man ever hated! *Friendship* between *us!* My God! it must be one of two things—deadliest hate, or sweetest love!"

He paused abruptly, crushing her with fierce unconscious strength against his breast, gazing down into the face so fatally fair. Her eyes looked into his with all their eloquence of loveliness; her amber hair floated, soft and silken, across his breast; and his lips met hers in kisses that only died to be renewed again, each longer, sweeter, more lingering than the last.

CHAPTER XVII.

The Axe laid to the Root.

"YOU have written!" she said, softly, looking up into his eyes.

The whisper was brief, but as subtle and full of power as any words that ever murmured from Cleopatra's lips, wooing him of Rome to leave his shield for foes to mock at, and his sword to rust, and his honour to drift away, a jeered and worthless thing, while he lay lapped in a woman's love, with no heaven save in a woman's eyes.

It was some hours past noon on the morrow of the *bal cos-tumé*; she had not yet left the State chambers. Her hair was unbound, folds of azure, and lace of gossamer texture, enve-loped her; and she lay back on her low chair, resting her cheek on her white arm, and letting her eyes dwell upon his.

"You have written!" she murmured, softly, her hand lying in his, her lips brushing his brow.

For all answer he put into her hand a letter he had just then penned—a letter to decline the appointment offered to him; to refuse the most brilliant distinction that could have fallen to him; in a word, to resign the ambitions his life had been centred in, to destroy the career, and the goal, of his present, and his future!

Her head rested against his breast while she read it, her eyes glancing over the few brief lines which gave up all power and honour, the world and the world's ambitions, and flung away life's best prizes at her bidding, as though they were empty shells or withered leaves. And a smile, proud and glad, came upon her lips. Even she had scarcely counted on binding him thus far to her feet;—on chaining him thus utterly her slave. She read it, then she lifted her eyes, now sweet with the light of love, her warm breath fanning his cheek.

"You will not regret it, Cecil! Are you sure?"

"Regret! My Heaven! what room have I to dream even of regret *now?* My whole future would be a willing price paid down for one hour of my joy!"

The last words were spoken in a madman's heedless, headlong love! He stooped over her, spending breathless kisses on her lips, and passing his hands through the golden scented hair which floated on her shoulders. Every single shining thread might have been a sorcery-twisted withe that bound him powerless, so utterly he bowed before her power, so utterly he was blinded to all that lay beyond the delicious languor, and the sensuous joys, which steeped his present in their rich delight.

An hour afterwards, Strathmore descended from the State chambers by a secret staircase which wound downward to the library. He listened; the room was silent; he looked through the aperture left in the carvings, by those subtle builders of the olden days, for such reconnoissance by those who need secresy; it was empty, and, pressing the panel back, he entered. As it chanced, however, in the deep embrasure of a window, hidden by the heavy curtains, Erroll sat reading the papers; and, as he looked up, he saw Strathmore, before the panel had wholly closed on its invisible hinges, that were screened in a mass of carving. Erroll knew whence that concealed passage led.

"Why was she not dead in all her demon's beauty before ever she came here?" he muttered to himself; for Erroll had grown jealous of Marion Vavasour; and had, moreover, strange stray notions of honour here and there, better fitting the days of Galahad than our own.

"You here, Bertie!" said Strathmore, carelessly, very admirably concealing the annoyance he felt, as Erroll looked up from his retreat. "What's the news?"

"Nothing!" yawned the Sabreur, stretching him the *Times*. "They notice your appointment for——; very approvingly, too, for the Thunderer. When do you go, old fellow?"

"I do not go at all," Strathmore answered briefly. He was aware it must be known sooner or later, and, in the reckless rapture of his present, ridicule, remark, or censure, were alike disregarded.

Erroll looked quickly up at him:

"*Not go?*"

"No. I have requested permission to decline the appointment."

There was a dead pause of unbroken silence; then, with a sudden impetuous movement, Erroll rose, pushing back his chair, and flinging his fair hair out of his eyes with a gesture of impatient anger:

"Good God! Strathmore, have you sneered at every love all your life through only to become a woman's slave at last!"

The swift dark wrath of his race glanced into Strathmore's eyes. At all times he brooked comment or interference ill; now he *knew* himself the slave of a woman, and while in the sweet insanity of successful love his serfdom was delicious, and its bondage dearer than any liberty that had ever been his boast, the words were still bitter to him. To any but his friend they would have been as bitterly resented.

"That cursed coquette!" muttered Erroll between his teeth, as he paced impatiently up and down. "What! she enslaves you till you wreck your whole future at her word, let all the world see you in your madness, and forget your honour even under your own roof!"

The words broke out almost unconsciously; he was rife with hatred for the woman who had robbed him of his friend, and grown more powerful with Strathmore than honour or ambition; than the present, or the future; than the ridicule of the world, or the triumphs of his career.

Evil passions passed over his listener's face, flaming into life all the more darkly because the accusation bore with it the sting of Nathan's unto David — *the sting of truth.*

"By Heaven! no man on the face of the earth, save you, should dare say that to me and live!"

Erroll looked up, stopped, and halted before him, his sunny blue eyes growing cordial and earnest as a woman's:

"Dear old fellow, forgive me! I had no right, perhaps, to use the words I did, but we have never stopped to pick our speech for one another. No!—hear me, Strathmore. By Heaven! you *shall!* Your honour is dearer to me than it ever will be to anyone, and I only ask you now to pause, and think how you will endure for the world to know that you are so utterly a coquette's bond-slave that you lie at her beck

and call, and give up all your best ambitions at her bidding.
I am sinner enough myself, God knows, and have plenty to
answer for; but no passion should have so blinded me to
honour, let her have tempted as she would, that the wife of
an absent guest should have ceased to become sacred to
me, while trusted to my protection, and under my own
roof!"

He stopped: and a dead silence fell again between them.
They were fearless and chivalrous words, built on the code
of Gawaine and of Arthur; and the spirit of the dead
Knights, and of a bygone age, broke up from the soft indolence and easy epicureanism of the man, and found its way
to just and dauntless speech; but speech that on the ear
which heard it was useless as a trumpet-blast in the ear of a
dead man, as little heeded and as powerless to rouse! The
sting which lay in the Prophet's charge to him of Israel lay
here; but here it touched to the quick of no remorse: it only
heated the furnace afresh, as a blast of wind blows the fires
to a white heat.

For one instant, while Erroll's glance met his, Strathmore made a forward gesture, like that of a panther about to
spring; then with all that was coldest, most bitter, most evil
in him awake, he leant back in his chair, with a smile on his
lips.

"An excellent homily! Perhaps, like many other
preachers, you are envious of what you so venomously up-
braid!"

Over Erroll's face a flush of pain passed, as over a woman's
at a brutal and unmerited word.

"For shame! for shame!" he said, hotly. "You know
better than to believe your own words, Strathmore! I do not
stand such vile inuendoes from you!"

Strathmore raised his eyebrows, his chill and contemptuous
sneer still upon his lips; his anger was very bitter at all times
when the velvet glove was stripped off and the iron hand dis-
closed, which was a feature of his race.

"*Soit!* it is very immaterial to me! Pray put an end to

these heroic speeches. I have no taste for scenes, and from any other man I should call an account for them under a harsher name."

"Call for what account you will! But does our friendship go for so little that it is to be swept away in a second for a word about a woman who is as worthless, if you saw her in her true light, as any——"

"Silence!" said Strathmore, passionately. "I bear no interference with myself and no traducement to her! End the subject, once and for all, or——"

"Or you will break with a friendship of twenty years for a love that will not last twenty weeks!" broke in Erroll, bitterly. It cut him to the quick to be cast off thus for the mere sake of a capricious coquette; from their earliest Eton days they had had no words between them till now that this woman brought them in her train!

"It is the love which appears to excite your acrimony!" laughed Strathmore, with his chilliest scorn; that swift, keen jealousy stirring in him which is ever the characteristic of such passion as his, even in its earliest hours of acknowledgment and return, and which permits no man even to look wishfully after its idol unchastised.

As sharply as if a shot had struck him, Erroll swung round, righteous indignation flushing his face, and his azure eyes flashing fire.

"For God's sake, Strathmore, has your mad passion so warped your nature that you can set down such vile motives in cold blood to my share? I have no other feeling than hatred for the woman who befools you. *That* I will grant you is strong enough, for *I* see her as she is!"

"Most wise seer and admirable preacher! Since when have you turned sermonizer instead of sinner?" sneered Strathmore, coldly, the dark wrath of his race gleaming in his eyes. "It sits on you very ill!"

"Sermonizer I am not, nor have I title to be!" broke in Erroll, his gentle temper goaded fairly into anger; "but still in your place of host I might have paused before I violated the common laws of hospitality and honour to the wife of an absent man, let her have been my temptress as she would!"

In another instant words would have been uttered which would have cut down and cast away the friendship of a life-time; but the door of the drawing-room opened.

"Are you tired of waiting, Major Erroll? Never mind! Patience is a virtue, if, like most other virtues, she be a little dull sometimes!" said Lady Beaudesert, as she floated in—a picture for Landseer—with a brace of handsome spaniels treading on the trailing folds of her violet habit.

Her presence arrested, perforce, the words that were rising hot and bitter to the lips of both. But when the axe is laid at the root, what matter if its work be delayed a few hours, a few days, a few months? The tree which would have stood through storms is doomed by it, and will fall at the last!

The words Erroll had spoken that day had been just and true ones: but, like most words of truth in this world, they had been rash, and idle as the winds to carry one whit of warning, to stay for one hour's thought the headlong sweep of a great passion. Now that she had, like himself, forgotten every bond of honour, and cast aside every memory save the indulgence of a forbidden love, the semi-hatred which had so strangely mingled with Strathmore's fatal intoxication had gone: and with it the last frail cord which had held him back from falling utterly beneath the sway of her power. If in the bitterness of an unwelcome love he had been her slave, in the delirium of a permitted one he was more hopelessly so still. Erroll's charge of having violated the laws of hospitality stung him for one instant to the quick; but the next it was forgotten, as her smile lighted upon him, and her silvery laugh rang on his ear! He weighed nothing in the scale against her; he cast away all to stay in the light of the eyes where his heaven hung; he remembered nothing but the ex-ultant joy which lay in those brief, yet all-eloquent words: "he loved, and was loved!"

13*

She held him in her fatal web, as Guenevere held her Lover, when the breath of her lips sullied the shield which no foe had ever tarnished, and her false love coiled with subtle serpent-folds round Launcelot till he fell. But in Marion Vavasour would never arise what pardoned and purified the soul of the Daughter of Leodegraunce: those waters of bitterness which yet are holy — Remorse and Shame.

CHAPTER XVIII.

Guenevere and Elaine.

THAT night, when the men had left the smoking-room, and all was still, Bertie Erroll quitted the Abbey by one of those secret entrances which had been known to him, as to Strathmore from their childish days, and took his way across the park, treading the thick golden leaves under foot. A bitterness and depression were on him, very new to him, since he usually shook off all care, as he shook the ash off his cigar. After such words as had passed between them, he would not have stayed an hour under any other man's roof; but he loved Strathmore well enough not to resent it thus, though the breach in their friendship cut him more hardly than the sneers which had been cast at himself, as he paced on through the beech woods, that were damp and chill in the silent night, with white mists rising up from the waters in thin wreaths of vapour.

At some distance, just without the boundaries of White Ladies, a light glimmered through the autumn network of brown boughs and crimson leaves, from the casement of a cottage which stood, so shut in by wood from the lonely road near, that it might as easily have been overlooked by any passer-by, as a yellowhammer's nest on the highway. Its solitary little beam shone bright, and star-like, through the damp fogs of the chilly midnight; like the light which burns before some Virgin shrine, and greets us as we travel, way-

worn and travel-stained and foot-weary, down the rocky
windings of some hill-side abroad. The simile crossed Erroll's mind, and perhaps smote something on his heart; it
was the light of a holy shrine to him, but one from which
his steps too often turned, and one which now reproached
him.

He passed under the drooping heavy boughs, and over
the fallen leaves, across the garden of the little cottage,
drew a latch-key from his pocket, opened the door, and
entered. A light was left burning for him in the tiny cottage
entrance, which was still as death; he took the lamp in his
hand, mounted the staircase noiselessly, and turned into the
bed-chamber upon his left. It was small, and simply ar-
ranged, but about it, here and there, were articles of refined
luxury; and half kneeling beside the bed, as she had lately
knelt in prayer, half resting against it, in the slumber which
had conquered the watchful wakefulness of love, was a young
girl, delicate and fair as any of the white lilies that had
bloomed one brief hour, to perish the next, on the lake-like
waters of White Ladies. Her head rested on her arm, her
lips were slightly parted, and murmuring fondly his own
name, while

> her face so fair,
> Stirred with her dream as rose-leaves with the air.

His step was too noiseless to awake her, and he stood still
gazing on her in that slumber in which Life, becoming at
once ethereal and powerless, escaping from earth, yet lying
at man's mercy, so strangely and so touchingly counterfeits
Death. And while he looked, thoughts arose, filling him
with vague reproach; thoughts at which the women he had
just left, the women who knew him in intrigue, and in
pleasure, and in idle flirtations, would have bitterly marvelled,
and as bitterly sneered. The world in which we live knows
nothing of us in our best hours, as it knows nothing of us in
our worst!

They were in strange contrast!—the dazzling beauty of
Marion Vavasour, on which he had looked a few hours be-

fore, with a sorceress-lustre glancing from her eyes, and rare Byzantine jewels flashing on her breast; with this fair and mournful loveliness, which was before him now, hushed to rest in the holiness of sleep, with a smile like a child's upon the tender lips, and with a shadow from the lamp above falling upon a brow so pure that it might have been shadowed by an angel's wings. They were in strange contrast!—and he stood beside his Wife, as Launcelot stood and gazed upon Elaine, while the pure breath of a stainless love was still upon his soul, and while the subtle power of Guenevere only stole upon him in the fevered, vague phantasma of a fleeting dream, unknown and unadmitted even there.

He stooped over her, and his lips broke the spell of her sleep with a caress. She awoke with a low, glad cry, and sprang up to nestle in his breast, to twine her arms about him, to murmur her welcome in sweet, joyous words.

"Ah, my better angel," he whispered, fondly yet bitterly, as she rested against his the cheek which still blushed at his kiss, speaking rather to his own thoughts than to her, "why are men so doomed by their own madness, that they sicken and weary of a pure and sacred love like yours, on which Heaven itself might smile; and forsake it for a few short hours of some guilty passion, that is as senseless as the drunkard's delirium!"

And she believed he only spoke but of the sweetness of their own love, pitying those who had never known such, and smiled up into his eyes.

CHAPTER XIX.

The Silver Shield and the Charmed Lance.

"Is he to monopolise her for ever? He's kept the field a cursed long time," said a Secretary of Legation, dropping his lorgnon, one night at the Opera in Paris.

"The deuce he has!" said his Grace of Lindenmere.

"Madame is marvellously faithful; and they say he's as mad after her now as when he first——"

"*Taisez-vous!* A scandal six months old is worse than dining off a *réchauffé*," broke in the Vicomte de Belesprit. "A naughty story is like a pretty mistress; charming at the onset, but a great bore when it's lost its novelty. All Paris chattered itself hoarse over their liaison last December; what we want to know *now* is—when will it come to an end?"

"I dare say you do," chuckled the old Earl of Beaume. "But the succession there would be as dangerous as to the Polish Viceroyalty; a smile from her would cost a shot from him."

"Ah!—sort of man to do that style of thing," yawned the Duke. "Don't understand it myself, never should. But he's positively her slave—actually."

"Plenty of you envy him his slavery; white arms are pleasant handcuffs," laughed Lord Beaume. "But that woman's ruined him, and, what's worse, his career. He gave up the special mission to —— because it must have taken him where her ladyship could not go! A man's never great in public life till he's ceased to care for women!"

"Which is possibly the cause, sir, why the country, looking to you for great things, has always looked in vain?" said Lindenmere.

The Earl laughed, taking out his tabatière; he was good nature itself, and his Grace was a privileged wit, *c'est à dire*, one of that class who have made rudeness "the thing," and supply the esprit they lack by the impudence they love! The fashion has its conveniences—it is difficult to be brilliant, but it is so easy to be brusque.

Those whom they discussed were Lady Vavasour and Strathmore.

Their love had been the theme of many buzzing scandals the autumn before, when, on leaving White Ladies, she had returned to Paris accompanied by him; but the buzz had soon exhausted itself, and the liaison had become a fact generally understood, and but very little disguised. His place and right had been long unchallenged, however bitterly envied; and whatever rumour had said of her capricious inconstancy, as yet she had showed no disloyalty to her lover, whatever she showed to her lord. Either she really loved at last, or her entire dominion over the man who had scoffed at the sway of women satiated her delight in power; for no coquetries ever roused the jealousy, fierce as an Eastern's, which accompanied his passion, or flattered the hopes of those who sought to supplant him. If any magician had had the power twelve months before to show him *himself* as he had now become, Strathmore would have recognised the revelation, as little as we in youth should recognise our own features could we see them marked with the corruption they will wear in death.

Men who have been long invulnerable to passion ever become its abject bond-slaves when they at length bend down to it. Ambition was lulled to forgetfulness in the sweet languor of his love; had he been offered the kingship of the earth he would have renounced it, if to assume its empire he must have left her side! This man, who had long believed that he could rule his will, and mould his life, as though he were, god-like, exempt from every inevitable weakness or accident of mankind, had sunk into a woman's arms, and let the golden meshes of her loveliness enervate him, till every other feeling which might have combated or rivalled her power was drowned and swept away. Passion, often likened by poets unto flame, does thus resemble it—that, once permitted dominion, it can no longer be kept in servitude, but, mastering all before it, devours even that from which it springs. The strength which he had boasted could break "bonds of iron even as green withes" had ebbed away into a voluptuary's weakness: and under the even, brilliant, modern life he had led through these eight months in Paris, there had rioted in him the same guilty love which revelled in possession of the Hittite's wife, the same keen jealousy which slew Mariamne for a doubt in the days of old Judæa!

Lady Vavasour sat that evening in her loge at the Opera,

Strathmore in attendance on her, as he had been throughout
the winter wherever she went, the Duc de Vosges and Prince
Michael of Tchemidoff her visitors, for the *entrée* to her box,
closely as it was besieged, was ever a privilege as exclusive
as the Garter. Scandals, badinage, dainty flattery, choice
wit lying in a single word, rumours which answered the
"Quid Novi?" asked as perpetually in Paris as in the Violet
City, circulated in her box; and she sat there in her dazzling
youth, shrouded in black perfumed lace, like a Spanish gaditana, with the diamonds flashing here and there and gleaming starlike among her lustrous hair. Her coquetry of manner
she could no more abandon than could a fawn its play, than
a sapphire its sparkle; but, as I say, she never had fairly
aroused that deadly jealousy which lay in wait within him,
as a tiger lies ready to spring; though Strathmore, whose
love was a sheer idolatry, as enthralled by her now as in the
first moment when his kiss had touched her lips, begrudged
every glance which fell on another.

"Strathmore has the monopoly now; how long will he
keep it?" said the Duc de Vosges, as he left her box, while
S. A. R. the Prince d'Etoiles entered it. "There are women
who have *no* lovers perhaps (at least for our mothers' credit
we all say so), as there are women who use no rouge; but
when once they begin to take to either, they add both fresh
every day!"

"Peste!" said Arthus de Bellus, pettishly, "he has had
it a great deal too long. He must have bewitched her in his
old English château! If a whole winter is not an eternal
constancy, what *is?*"

"And this is May!" pursued the Duc, reflectively; "but
those Englishmen are resolute fellows; they hold their
ground doggedly in battle as in love; there is no shaking
them in either——"

"*Vrai*—! There is only shooting them in both! If one
picked a quarrel with my Lord Cecil, *par hazard*, and had
him out——"

"He would shoot *you*, mon cher, and stand all the better

with madame for it," said the Duc, dryly. "Strathmore is the crack shot of Europe; he can hit the ruby in a woman's ring riding full gallop—saw him do it at Vienna!"

"Look, Cecil! There is your friend!" said Marion Vavasour, lifting her lorgnon to her eyes and glancing at the opposite side of the house.

"What an indefinite description!" laughed Strathmore, lifting his slowly. "We all have a million of friends as long as we are happily ignorant of what they say of us!"

"*Tais-toi* with your epigrams! All social comfort lies in self-deception, we know that," she laughed, with that glance beneath her silken lashes which had first fallen on him under the midsummer stars of Prague, and which still did with him what it would. "There is your friend, your brother, your idol—the Beau Sabreur, as you call him—I hope he will not be shot like his namesake, Murat; he is far too handsome! Look! it *is* he yonder, talking with Lord Beaume!"

"Bertie! so it is. What has he come to Paris for, I wonder!"

Strathmore's eyes lightened with pleasure, and his brightest smile passed over his face as he recognised Erroll; his attachment to him was too thorough to have been cut away by those words, even bitter though they were, which had been exchanged between them in the cedar drawing-room at White Ladies.

She, glancing upward at him, saw the smile, and this woman, rapacious, exacting, merciless, with the panther nature under her delicate loveliness, permitted no thought to wander away from her, allowed no single feeling to share dominion with her! And she prepared his chastisement.

"What is he in Paris for? To see me, I dare say! *N'est ce pas assez?* Go and tell him to come here; he will not venture without," she said, carelessly, while she leaned a little forward and bowed to Erroll with an *envoi* from her fan, for which many men in the house that night would have paid down ten years of their lives.

How well she knew her lover, and knew her power over

him! The smile died off Strathmore's face, the dark, dangerous anger of his race glanced into his eyes.

"Pardon me if I decline the errand. I am not your *laquais de place*, Lady Vavasour!" he said, coldly, as he leaned over her chair. The answer was too low for those who were in the box to hear it.

She glanced at him amusedly and shrugged her shoulders slightly:

"Many would think themselves flattered by being even *that!* Since you are refractory, there are others more obedient. M. de Lörn, will you be so good as to tell Major Erroll he may come and speak to us here? There he is with Lord Beaume."

Lörn left the box on his errand, and Lady Vavasour turned to D'Etoiles. She was the reigning beauty of Paris still; none dared to dispute with her the palm of pre-eminence. Sovereign of fashion, she bent sovereigns to her feet, created a mode with a word, and saw kings suitors to her for a smile. She must have surely, they thought, loved Strathmore strangely well, with more than the fleeting, capricious passions rumour accredited to her, that she allowed him so jealous and undivided a sway over her; or—perchance it was that "the dove" still loved "to peck the estridge," to tame this imperious will to more than woman's weakness, and see this man, who boasted himself of bronze, grow pale if her glance but wandered from himself!

"For shame!" she murmured to him, as he bent for an emerald which had fallen from her bouquet-holder. "How rude you were. Do you not know my motto is Napoleon's: Qui m'aime me suit!"

"Yes," answered Strathmore, unsatisfied and unappeased; "but I do not see why you should care to be followed by so very many!"

She struck him a fragrant blow with her bouquet of stephanotis.

"If a vast crowd follow ever in vain, is it not the greater honour to be singled from so many? *Ingrat!*"

The idolatrous passion that was in him for Marion Vavasour, which bound him to her will, and made him hold his
slavery sweeter than all duty, pride, or glory, gleamed in
his eyes as he stooped towards her in the swell of a chorus
of the "Puritani," which drowned his words to any ear save
hers:

"Ay! but love grudges the idlest word that is cast to
others, the slightest glance that is bestowed elsewhere.
There is no miser at once so avaricious and unreasonable!"

"Unreasoning indeed! You are much more fit for the
days of Abelard and Heloïse than you are for these. No one
loves so *now*—save ourselves!"

For the sweetness of the last word, as it lingered softly on
her lips, murmured in the swell of the music, he forgave her
the arch mockery of the first; and the sirocco of jealousy
which, once risen, never wholly subsides, lulled, and passed
harmless away for the present.

Meanwhile, in Lord Beaume's *loge*, Erroll received his
message; received it with so much reluctance, almost re-
pugnance in his tone and on his face, that the Comte de Lörn,
who had only known him a Sir Calidore for courtesy and a
very Richelieu for women, stared at him and shrugged his
shoulders.

"Peste! the greatest beauty of the day sends for you, and
you are no more grateful to her than this! And one must
stand very well with her, too, to be invited to her box."

"I have no desire to 'stand well' with Lady Vavasour,"
said Erroll, impatiently, forgetting how strangely his answer
must sound, for memories of this woman as he had last seen
her at White Ladies stirred up bitterly within him; about
her, and her alone, passionate words had passed between him
and the man he loved; through her, and her alone, that blow
had been struck to their friendship, from which friendship
never rallies, howsoever dexterously the wound be healed.

"So much the better for you, for nobody has a chance of
rivalling your friend, it seems. Allons! you will hardly send

her such a message back as that!" said the Frenchman, as he thought, "Ah-ah! the fox and the grapes!"

Erroll wavered a moment, uncertain how best to evade her summons: he felt an invisible reluctance, in truth; did it not seem too exaggerated and cowardly a word, almost a dread to enter this woman's presence! He recognised her sorceress power, and feared it; he knew her influence over Strathmore, and resented it; he believed it wisdom to shun, foolhardihood to brave her; he abhorred her nature, and he acknowledged her loveliness. Down at White Ladies, even whilst he had hated her for the dominion she exercised over Strathmore, and loathed her for the wanton passions she veiled beneath her delicate and poetic language, her soft and refined grace, he had felt the dazzling charm of that divine beauty sweep over and stagger him, as though her eyes had some necromantic spell.

Now, with all the stories that were rife of the utter bondage in which she held Strathmore, abhorrence is scarce too fierce a word for what Erroll felt for Marion Vavasour. Had there been a plausible pretext for leaving the house to avoid her he would have taken it; already on his lips was an excuse to Lörn for his attendance to her *loge*, when, as she leaned forward to lorgner the prima donna, her glance met his, and he saw her, with the diamonds glancing in her bosom and her hair, and her lustrous eyes outshining the jewels. He hated her, condemned her, feared her, approached her with aversion; but that enchantment which Marion Vavasour exercised at will over temperaments the most diverse, hearts the most steeled to her, stole upon him as the syren's sea-song stole upon the mariners of Greece, though they turned their prow from the fatal music; as the fumes of wine steal perforce upon a man, though he refuse to put wine even to his lips!

It seemed impossible to evade her summons; he turned and followed the Comte de Lörn, as in this life we ever follow the slender thread of Accident which leads us to our fate.

"What has brought you to Paris? Anything special?" asked Strathmore, when Lady Vavasour, having given him a smile and a few words of negligent graceful courtesy, continued her conversation with D'Etoiles.

The hot words that had been passed between them had been allowed to drop into oblivion by both—freely forgiven by the one who had had right on his side; not so freely by the one who had been in error, for it was one of the worst traits among many darker that belonged to men of his race and blood, that a Strathmore *never pardoned*.

"My uncle's illness," answered Erroll. "He was knocked over at Auteuil by paralysis; they telegraphed for me some days ago, but this is the first time I have left him. It will prove a fatal, they tell me, though perhaps a lingering, affair."

"My dear fellow, I must be 'extremely glad and vastly sorry' in one breath—the first for your inheritance, the last for your uncle!" smiled Strathmore. "Poor Sir Arthur—I wonder I never heard of it; will he last long?"

"He may die any day; he may linger on for many months; so the doctors say at least, but they always hedge admirably in their prognostications, so that, whether their patient be cured or killed *they* are always in the right! I fear there can be no chance for him."

"Fear, Bertie!—on your honour, now?" said Strathmore.

All the old baronet's estates were willed by him to Erroll (his title he naturally succeeded to); a property not extensive, but of high value to a cavalry man in debt and in difficulties.

"On my honour! What will come to me will set me free in very many ways; but to rejoice in a man's death because you reap by it, would be semi-murder."

"My dear fellow," cried Strathmore, "we all break the Decalogue in our *thoughts* every hour with impunity, and in our acts, too, if we're not detected:

> Le scandale du monde est ce qui fait l'offence,
> Et ce n'est pas pécher que pécher en silence!

Tartuffe's the essence of modern ethics!"

"Ethics! Murder! Death! Quelle horreur! What *are* you talking about?" interrupted Lady Vavasour, catching fragmentary sentences, and turning her head, with her eyebrows arched in surprised inquiry, as the Royal Duke bowed his congé and left her to go to the box of a scarcely more notorious, though a less legitimate lionne, who had not a coronet to leaven her frailties. "What horrible words to bring into my presence! Are you going to quit the world and organise a new La Trappe, Major Erroll?"

"Not exactly! Though truly there are living beauties that might drive us to as fatal a despair as the dead loveliness of the Duchesse de Montbazon awoke in the Trappist founder!" answered Erroll, almost involuntarily.

The eyes that dwelt on him, the subtle spell that stole about him, seemed to wrench homage from him to this woman in the very teeth of his aversion and his condemnation of her, as if to justify the taunt and the suspicion that Strathmore had thrown in his teeth at White Ladies, and to make him by his own words prove himself a liar!

Strathmore's eyes flashed swiftly on him, and a contemptuous smile came upon his face. The thought that prompted it did Erroll as rank an injustice as evil judgment ever wrought in a world where its wrong verdicts are as many as the sands of the sea, and its restitutions so tardy that they are rarely offered, save—to the dead.

Marion Vavasour smiled—her moqueur, radiant, resistless smile.

"Well, it is a proof of woman's omnipotence that love for her was even the cause and the corner-stone of the most rigid monastic establishment that ever abjured her! Have you been long in Paris?"

"Only a few days. I am staying in attendance on an invalid relative at Auteuil."

"Auteuil! Ah, we go there in a week or so to my *maisonette*. We shall be charmed to see you, Major Erroll, whenever you can make your escape from your melancholy duty."

He bowed, and thanked her. For the few words of invitation many peers of France and England would have laid down half the trappings of their rank! He acknowledged them, but chillily; he could not pardon her for her work; he could not forgive her the estrangement between him and the man he held closer than a brother; he could not see Strathmore under the dominance, and by the side of the woman who ensnared and enslaved him, without bitterness of heart. He read her aright, this sorceress, who could summon at will every phase of womanhood; and his instinct and his reason alike allied to give out against her an uncompromising verdict.

With but cold courtesy he made his adieux, and left her box as soon as it was possible to do so, having satisfied the bare obligations of politeness her message had entailed on him. And yet, despite all this, as Erroll drove away from the Opera towards the Maison Dorée that night, the remembrance, which involuntarily uprose to him, of a pure and childlike loveliness, dedicated solely to him, which he had often watched when hushed in the repose of a sleep whose very dreams were haunted by no other image, and murmured of no other name than his own, was rivalled and thrust aside by what he strove to put away from him—the memory of the glance which had just met his, like the blinding rays of a dazzling light. Strong and close about him was the treasure of a warm and holy love; but if even such a love be a silver shield in hours of temptation to the man who wears it (though rarely, I deem, is it so, as poets picture and as women dream), it could not ward off the charmed lance of Marion Vavasour's fascination. Her memory followed him through the gas-lit streets to the Maison Dorée; her memory haunted him still when he left the laughing companions of his opera-supper, and drove through the grey dawn of the early June morning back to Auteuil. Are we masters of our own fate, or are we not rather playthings in the hands of circumstances and chance, floated by them against our will, as thistle-down upon the winds that waft it? It is an open question! Half

the world mar their own lives, and the other half are marred
by life.

"Now, Cecil, what cause was there for you to look as
stern as Othello, and to assert that you were not my *laquais
de place* to-night, when I merely paid an ordinary courtesy
to your friend because he *is* your friend? You are as jealous
as a Spaniard, and as ungrateful—as a man always is for
that matter, so there is no need for a simile!" said Lady
Vavasour that night, after her own opera-supper, when
Etoiles, the Duc de Vosges, and others who had formed
her guests at that most charming of all *soupers à minuit*,
had left.

The light shone down upon her where she leaned back
on a dormeuse, her perfumed laces drooping off her snowy
shoulders, and the diamonds glancing above her fair Greek-
like brow. They were alone; the Marquis was as polite a
host to Strathmore as the Marquis du Châtelet to Voltaire;
and Strathmore bent his head and kissed the fragrant lips
that mocked him with such sweet laughter.

"Ma belle! there is cold love where there is no jealousy!
Love waits for no *reason* in its acts; it only knows that it
hates those who rob it of the simplest word, and is jealous
of the very brute that wins a touch or a smile!"

She laughed as his hand pushed away from her a little
priceless toy dog, gift of the Prince d'Etoiles, which had
nestled in her lace.

"I tell you you are fit for the old days of Venice, when
a too daring look was revenged with the dagger! Nobody
loves so now; we are too languid, and too wise; and two
years ago you would have sworn never to love so yourself,
Cecil."

"Even so. But two years ago I had not met *you*."

"No. How strangely we met, too, those summer evenings in Bohemia! I told you it was Destiny."

He smiled.

"My loveliest! I do not think there is much 'destiny' in
this life beyond that which men's hands fashion for them-

selves, and women's beauty works for them. But if fate
would always use me as it did then, I would never ask other
guidance."

She laughed, that soft low laugh, which in its most mellow sweetness has always a ring of triumph and of mockery
difficult to define, yet ever menacing in its music.

"It was destiny! Let me keep to my creed. Bah! Life
is governed by chance, and each of us, at best, is but a leaf
that drifts on a hazardous wind, now in the sunlight, and now
in the shadow; and the winds blow the leaves hap-hazard together, for evil, for good, whichever it be."

And Lady Vavasour laughed again at her own careless
philosophies; a true epicurean, life had its most golden charm
for her, and turned to her its sunniest side; her foot was on
the neck of the world, and the world lay obedient, and enraptured by its enslaver; Emperors obeyed a sign of her fan,
how should Fate ever dare to turn rebel against her?

Then that sadness, which gave to her gazelle eyes their
most dangerous sweetness, came over them; she assumed by
turns, and at will, every shape and caprice, now heartless
and *moquante* as the world she reigned over, now tender and
full of thought, as the women of whom poets dream in their
youth.

"Ah, Cecil! I have taught you a better love than the Age
and the Power you once coveted? And yet—who knows?—
perhaps Ambition was the safer and the wiser, though not
the more faithful, mistress."

His eyes dwelt, with all the passion which she had
awakened in him, on the living picture before him, on which
the light of the chandeliers shone, enhancing all its wondrous
brilliance of tint, and its rare grace of form. His idolatry
outweighed the world, shrivelled ambition as a scroll of paper
shrivels in the flames, and filled his past, his present, and his
future, only with Herself!

"I do not know—I do not care!" he said, passionately,
whilst his lips were hot against her cheek. "For the love you
have taught me, I would barter life and sell eternity! Ambi-

tion—it is dead in me! *You* are my world. I have forgot all
others."

God pardon him! It was fatally true. And she looked
up softly in his eyes, his slavery was sweet homage to her
power, his insanity precious incense to her vanity; and as she
knew that she was all the world to him, so she whispered him
he was to her. She had vowed him so many times, with her
enchantress tongue, her fragrant lips, her eloquence of eye
and word—so she vowed him now.

"Ah, Cecil!" she murmured, with that caressing sweetness which was as resistless as the song of the serpent-
charmer, "we do not love the less, but the more, because the
world sometimes robs us of each other, and would sever us if
it could by its laws!"

CHAPTER XX.

Bella Demonia con Angelico Riso.

THE Bosquet de Diane was situated midway between
Auteuil and Passy, in one of the most charming retreats of
those pleasant places; nestled among sycamore and lime-
woods, catching from its terraces a distant view of the spires
of Paris, and a nearer of the windings of the Seine, with a
paradise of roses beaming in its gardens, and the luxury of a
sérail lavished on its interior. Hither, in the sultry heats of
early summer, when the thermometer was 38 deg. Réaumur,
came Marion Lady Vavasour after a lengthened Paris season,
with a choice *cohue* of courtiers and guests, to head a circle
scarce less brilliant than that adjacent at St. Cloud; to pass
her mornings, forming new sumptuary laws and despotic
edicts of fashion; to frame fêtes à la Watteau in her rose-
gardens, or in her private theatre; to spend her time as became the Marchioness of Vavasour and Vaux, and the Queen
of Society.

As it chanced, joining the grounds of her *maisonette*, lay
the grounds of a cozy bachelor-villa, that had been long in-

habited by an old English *bon viveur*, who, with very good taste, preferred Auteuil, and all to which Auteuil lies near, to his own baronial hall down in the dulness of Shropshire, where there was not a decent dinner-party to be had nearer than twenty miles as the crow flew.

The *bon viveur* was Sir Arthur Erroll, and the villa was, naturally, the Paris residence of his nephew, who had been summoned when a fit of paralysis threatened a sure, though a gradual, death for the baronet. The windows of the villa looked on to the glades of lindens and the aisles of roses, which formed the choicest portion of the grounds of the Bosquet de Diane; and, sitting in Sir Arthur's sick chamber, Erroll had full view of the Decamerone-like groups which strolled there in the luminous evenings, and had ever before him, as Lady Vavasour moved in the moonlight or the sunset radiance through the arcades of her orangeries, or down the length of her terraces, a living picture which united the rich glory of Giorgone with the aërial grace of Greuze. Perchance this constant, yet distant view of her, was more dangerous than closer neighbourhood; through it, perforce, she haunted his solitude, and usurped his thoughts.

Of necessity detained at Auteuil, he could not shut away what rose before his sight almost as regularly as the evening stars themselves. He avoided visiting at the *maisonette* as much as he could possibly do; to have constantly refused would have been to place himself in the absurd light of *censor morum* to Strathmore, and fostered rather than disabused the jealous error into which Strathmore had fallen, regarding the motive of his interference, the autumn before, at White Ladies. Still he went thither very rarely; but he could not walk through the Bois, or drive down the Versailles road, without encountering her carriage or her riding parties; and, when he sat beside the open casements of his uncle's chamber, he could not refuse his admiration to the brilliant and graceful form surrounded with her court, which came ever within his sight, when she swept slowly along the marble terraces, or beneath the avenues of her rose-gardens in the starlit

summer night. He ceased to wonder at Strathmore's infatuated passion—he ceased to marvel that, for this woman's
loveliness, he flung away fame, time, ambition, everything
that had before been precious to him, like dross; and, almost
unconsciously and irresistibly, Erroll ceased also to care to
drive over to dine at the Café de Paris, and sup in the Bréda
Quartier, as he had done hitherto, but stayed, in preference,
to sit beside the window of an old man's sick-room, with some
opened novel, on which his eyes never glanced.

Perhaps Lady Vavasour perceived how markedly her own
invitations were refused, yet how surely a lorgnon watched
her from the balcony of Sir Arthur's villa that was visible
through the limes; or perhaps she divined and resented the
verdict her lover's friend gave against her? "Major Erroll
is very rude. I have asked him to dinner three times, and
he has three times 'deeply regretted' &c. &c.—*Anglicè*, refused! I have shown him courtesy for your sake, Cecil; now
show him resentment for mine. I will *not* have you sworn
friends with the man; he does not like ME!" said her ladyship, laughingly, one morning to a lover with whom her
word was law, and who thought, as two scenes at White
Ladies arose to his memory, "Perhaps he but likes you
too well!"

The few phrases sufficed to sow afresh the doubt in
Strathmore's mind, and increased the coolness that had come
betwixt him and Erroll, whom Marion Vavasour treated with
an absolute indifference, though occasionally she watched
him with something of that curiosity which a flattered,
spoiled, and beautiful woman might well feel for the only
one who had ever dared to show her his disapprobation,
and been proof against her charm; and occasionally her eyes
lighted and dwelt on the rare beauty of his face with a
look which meant—it were hard to say what—perhaps a
challenge.

"Major Erroll, pray why do you persistently shun us?"
she asked him, suddenly, forsaking the negligence with which
she had hitherto habitually treated him, as was natural from

a proud and courted beauty to a man who had ventured to be ungrateful for her condescensions, and to show tacit rebuke of her conduct, without the prestige of a high rank to excuse him the insolence. It was one of those days when he had been compelled to come to the Bosquet de Diane, invited too publicly as he encountered them in the Bois, when riding there with one of Louis Philippe's equerries, to be able to refuse without drawing comment. They were for the moment almost alone, as they strolled through the gardens after dinner under the arcades of roses, while the starlight shone down on her, burnishing her hair to its marvellous lustre, and glancing off the Byzantine jewels above her brow, while the shadow of the night, half veiling her beauty, gave it a dream-like softness. She knew so well when it was at its rarest and its most resistless!

"Shun you?" he repeated. "Lady Vavasour can surely never do herself so little justice as to deem such a rudeness to her possible?" Courtesy demanded the reply, and he gave it only coldly.

"I deem it possible because it is the fact," she laughed carelessly. "Come, I never am refused or kept waiting, why do you do it?"

"It is much honour to me that you should even remark a discourtesy if I have been guilty of it," he answered, coldly still. He condemned and abhorred the nature which he read aright in her, and yet—his voice softened despite himself as he looked down upon her.

"You answer by an equivoque? For shame! I never permit evasions. Say frankly, Major Erroll, the truth—that you dislike me!"

As she spoke she turned her eyes full on him, their liquid darkness laughing with a light as of amusement that any mortal could be found so mad as to defy her power, so blind as to resist such loveliness; a light that flashed on him with its dazzling regard, challenging him to treasure hatred if he could, to preserve defiance if he dared, to Marion Lady Vavasour.

"Come," she repeated, a haughty nonchalance in her attitude as she turned her head towards him, while she swept through the fragrant aisles of her gardens, but with a mocking, amused smile about her lips—"come! the truth now, you dislike me!"

"Say, rather, Lady Vavasour, that I dread your power, and that—since you ask for frankness—I perhaps condemn its too pitiless exercise, its most pitiful results!"

They were rash and daring words to the pampered beauty, who heard the truth as rarely as a sovereign in her palace! They were spoken on the impulse of a frank nature and a loyal friendship, as Erroll's clear eyes turned on her steadily, with the first reproof that any living being had ever dared to offer to Marion Vavasour. From that moment his fate was sealed with her.

The glance she first gave him was one of grand amazement, of haughty indignation; then this woman, in whom was combined every fairest phase of woman's witcheries, and who could assume at her will any lying loveliness she would, looked at him with a faint blush wavering her cheek, and her lashes slightly drooping over her eyes, that lost their malicious laughter, and grew almost sad.

"Then you are unjust, and err in hasty judgment, a common error of your sex," she said, gently, almost mournfully. "Bah! you might as well condemn the sun that shone on the Ægean, because the blind and the unwise bowed down to it as God! You are prejudiced. *N'importe!* when you know me better you will not do me so much wrong."

And for the moment, as he listened, he forgot that she who spoke was the arch-coquette of Europe, was the avowed mistress of Strathmore; he forgot that those words on her lips were a graceful lie without meaning, only uttered as the actress utters the words of the rôle she assumes for the hour. They stood alone in the starlight, about them the heavy perfume of the roses that roofed the trellised aisle and strewed the path: and as she leant slightly towards him in the shadow, while her eyes seemed to glisten, and her rich lips to part with a sigh, words broke from him unawares, wrenched out against his will by this woman's sorceress' charm.

"Let us know you as we may, you do with us what you will! Lady Vavasour, for God's sake take heed—have mercy—you hold a fearful power in your hands!"

His tone bore more meaning than his speech, which was rapid and broken, and his prayer, in its very warning, only bore fresh incense to her triumphs. Her eyes dwelt softly on him, and the warm hue still lingered temptingly, flatteringly, on the cheek that had no charm so perfect as its blush. Then she laughed gaily as she turned away, the Byzantine gems gleaming in the star-rays. "Power? Bah! over an hour's rest, a moment's pique, an evening's homage! *C'est grand' chose!*"

With this careless, coquettish mockery she left him, and was joined by Strathmore and the Duc de Vosges; and Erroll, turning suddenly away, strode down the rose-walk in the moonlight at a swift, uneven pace, not to return to the Bosquet de Diane that night. Twelve months before, he had sworn, in that certain remorse which comes to all men when they return to one who has been faithful to them in absence, with a reading of fidelity which they have never followed, that no other love should ever supplant or efface his Wife, sworn it in all sincerity, believing that he should guard his oath sacred and unbroken. She was very dear to him still, dear as our purer thoughts, our better moments, our most holy memories are dear to us; he loved her fondly, truly, deeply; yet, the holier love was but a frail shield against the unholier, which swept on him with a sirocco's strength, hated yet insidious. *Mes frères!* did ever yet the silvery wings of your better angel so wholly enshroud you, that they made you blind to the laughing eyes of the bacchantes that beset your path, and banned from your sight the wreathing arms and wooing lips that lured you into error? Never, most surely, out of the happy fables of women's credence, and of poet's song.

POWER!

It was the idol of Marion Vavasour's religion, in one form;

as in another, ere she had supplanted it, it had been her lover's. She warped and used it pitilessly; and though she had disowned it, never exercised it more capriciously and mercilessly than over Strathmore, now that she had set her foot on his bent neck, and bound him into slavery. No toy was so dear to this tyrant as the imperious and unyielding nature she had bowed like a reed in her hands! No pastime so precious to her as to show, by a hundred fresh ingenuities, how pliant as straw to her bidding was the steel of his will and his pride!

"From whom is that letter, Strathmore?" she asked one evening in the rose-gardens, her favourite haunt, where she sat with him, the Duc de Vosges, and an English Viscountess.

The letter just brought him was from a British minister arrived in Paris for a European congress, and he passed it to her; his will had sunk so absolutely into hers that he neither seemed conscious of her dominion or his own degradation.

She arched her delicate brows as she read.

"This evening! You cannot wait on him this evening. We play 'Hernani.'"

"I fear it is impossible for me to avoid going; you see what is said," he answered her. "The Earl would take no excuse in a matter of so much import——"

"He *must* take it, if I choose you to send him one. You cannot go, Strathmore; I need you specially."

"But indeed, since he does me the honour to desire this interview, I could not refuse it without marked slight, not alone to himself, but almost to the Government at home."

Lady Vavasour made a *moue mourine.* She knew a lovely woman is never lovelier than when she will not hear reason.

"The Government! What is that to me! You are to play Hernani, and that is of far more consequence!"

"But I assure you——" began Strathmore, while Lady Mostyn listened amusedly, and he caught a smile on the face of the French Duke that he bitterly resented: his rivals

Strathmore kept utterly at a distance. *She* had him in thraldom, but they had not.

"Well? what? I cannot have my theatricals disarranged to pleasure your Earl, especially as he is a person I most particularly dislike. What would be the consequence, pray, of your neglecting his summons?"

"I have said, it would be little less than an insult to Allonby in his ministerial capacity, and——"

"Insult him, then!" cried her ladyship, with charming nonchalance. "And après?"

Strathmore stooped towards her and lowered his voice for her ear alone.

"Après? Very natural offence from him personally, and great injury to my own future career, from neglecting the opportunity he affords me."

"*Galimatias!* I cannot have my tragedy spoiled for the Ministry's farce," she answered aloud, with a slight shrug of her shoulders. "You must send an excuse to the Earl, or"— and she dropped her voice—"if you insult me with divided allegiance, Cecil, I shall receive none. You used to boast Age and Power were all you coveted. You may go back to your old loves if you disobey *me.*"

Perhaps it was that she felt jealous of her old rival, Ambition; perhaps it was merely to see her own power in its wanton completeness; but her eyes dwelt on him with the glance that, from her to him, commanded all things.

"Well!" she asked impatiently, "do you obey Lord Allonby or me? Which? I never share a sceptre."

A flush passed over Strathmore's face almost of anger; the look he caught on the face of Vosges reminded him for once of how completely he—a courtier, a diplomatist, a man of the world, who had sneered with his most bitter wit at love and all its follies—had become the slave of one passion, weak as water in the hands of one woman!

"Well? Which?" asked Marion Vavasour, with her charming petulance, and by the light in her eyes he knew that his capricious imperious tyrant would perchance resent disobedience in this trifle on which her will was set, more than a far heavier disloyalty. And so great was his idolatry, that even with lookers-on at his degradation, he—who had held his will as bronze, and had boasted his self-dominion as omnipotent—let her rule him even in this wanton caprice.

He bowed his assent to her:

"What Lady Vavasour wishes is a command."

It was a strange oversight which, for a mere frivolous tyranny, made Lady Vavasour detain him that night at the Bosquet de Diane.

An hour afterwards, when the sun had sunk, and the ladies had re-entered the *maisonette* to dress for dinner, Strathmore, at her request, remained behind them, and took his way to the stables to look at her favourite mare, which had been lamed in exercising that morning, and which she would not leave solely to the care of stud-grooms and farriers.

It was dusk, and the second dressing-bell had rung, when, as he returned from the stables through the thick shrubberies which filled that part of the grounds, he stumbled against a female form, which crouched upon the ground in a position so suspicious of some thieving design, that he laid his hold upon her clothes, and bade her get up with no very gentle epithet. The woman shook his grasp off by a rapid movement, rose with a spring like a young doe, and stood confronting him, without any sign of guilt or fear, though her gipsy look, and dusty dress, confirmed him in his opinion that her errand lay towards any costly trifles, or loose jewels, which the open windows and vacated rooms of the *maisonette* might let her make away with undetected.

She did not seem to hear the words he spoke to her; but her eyes dwelt on him curiously and earnestly, while a smile, half melancholy, half bitter, played about her lips; and as he scanned her face in the fading light, he recognised in its dark Murillo beauty the Bohemian woman who had taken his gold, and prophesied his future, under the Czechen limes. The prophecy and the prophetess would alike have been long forgotten, but for the one who had heard and seen them with him.

"What!" said the Zingara, in the Czechen patois, her mournful and monotonous tones falling dreamily on his ear—"what! the love is born already?—the yellow hair has drawn you in its net so soon! Take care! take care! Your kiss is not the first, nor will it be the last, on her lips——"

"Peace to your jargon!" broke in Strathmore, imperatively, catching enough of the words to incense him. "What are you doing here, an idle vagrant prowling about to steal?"

She threw herself back with a proud fierce gesture, the blood staining her bronze cheek, and a sinister light flashing in her eyes, that were darkly brilliant as those midnight stars from which, in olden days, her ancient race had prophesied to kings the fate of empires; by which now, in a strange travesty of their old fame and faith, they babbled to peasant-girls of love-predictions. "Steal!" she muttered in the Czechen dialect. "Steal—from *her* house! I would not drink a stoup of water that was *hers*, to save myself from dying."

The words were so fiercely spoken, that Strathmore, catching them imperfectly, thought he must have mistaken a language which, though known to him was unfamiliar, and laid his grasp upon her afresh.

"You must give some very good account of yourself, or I shall turn you over to the gendarmes. You are in private grounds at nightfall, and are here on no honest errand."

She turned her eyes on him half haughtily, half mournfully, with the same gaze with which she had studied his face under the Bohemian limes, and unconsciously his hand relaxed its hold and left her free. The regard, while it shamed the suspicion which accused her of low theft, struck him with the same chill as when her vague words had traced out his future in Bohemia. An artist would have given that look to the changeless and fathomless eyes of the Eumenides.

"I have no need to thieve," said the Bohemian, quietly

and proudly, "and my errand I will not tell you—now. In a
little time, when you hate where you still love, you may share
it—not yet.   The sin is fair in your sight, and the kiss is
sweet on your lips to-night; when the sin bears its curse, and
the kiss has turned to gall, come to me; Redempta will show
you your vengeance."

She turned swiftly, and had passed away in the gloom
through the trees before he could arrest her; taking advantage of the pause of involuntary hesitance which he
made, as he debated with himself whether this woman was
a maniac, or whether again he might not have misunder-
stood the Czechen dialect, rendered doubly unfamiliar as it
was by the gipsy patois she employed.

His eyes vainly sought her in the twilight. She was out
of sight; and, disinclined to enter on the chase himself, he
passed into the house, and apprising some of the servants
that a beggar-woman was loitering suspiciously about the
grounds, bade them have diligent search made for her. His
order was obeyed; but the Bohemian was nowhere dis-
covered. She had made her way through the twilight like
a night-bird, and left as little trace of her path.

CHAPTER XXI.

The Brooding of the Storm.

"HERNANI" was never better acted at the Français than it
was in the Marchioness's private theatre that sultry midsummer night. So many people were staying at the Bosquet
de Diane that no other audience was needed, and save one of
the Royal Dukes from St. Cloud, Erroll was the only *externe*
guest. A little note with but half a dozen lines in it had been
sent over to Sir Arthur's villa, signed "Marion Vavasour and
Vaux." That very morning Erroll had vowed to leave Auteuil
as soon as his uncle's death or recovery released him, and
while forced to remain there to go no more to the *maisonette;*
but—l'homme propose, et *femme* dispose! The few lines of

gracious courtesy and airy raillery on his eremite tastes invited him that evening, and broke asunder all his freshly-forged resolves!

From her bijou theatre, of which Lady Vavasour was singularly fond, actors and audience met again in the supper-room, decorated à la Louis Quinze, where she loved to revive the petits soupers that came in with the Regency and went out with the Revolution. These suppers were a peculiar charm of the Bosquet de Diane, and to-night one of the most brilliant of them followed on "Hernani," at which the sparkle of the wit might fairly have vied with the mots of Claudine de Tencin, Piron, or Rivarol; at which the Duc de Vosges, regarding his hostess, began to ponder that the advice of Arthus de Bellus might after all be the best, and that it would be well to shoot a lover whom there seemed no chance of supplanting; and at which Erroll's mots were so sparkling and his spirits so high, that some of the men there wondered to themselves if he were bent on eclipsing Strathmore.

The supper lasted long, every one loth to leave a table at which he was so well amused, and with the introduction of those perfumed cigarettes which Lady Vavasour permitted to be smoked in her presence, and which scented the air with a delicate Oriental odour, fresh jeux de mots seemed introduced, and it was very late when the Bourbon Prince took his departure. Son Altesse Royale was always cordially gracious and *en bon camerade* with Strathmore, whom he detained now at the door of his carriage, saying some last words relative to the Sartory Stakes, for which their horses were respectively entered; and when he rolled away, Strathmore stood outside the house a few moments, while Lord Vavasour left the entrance-hall after accompanying the Duc to his carriage. The air was pleasant, for the night was very sultry and oppressive, as with the near approach of a tempest; it reminded him of the one, now near twelve months past, when the first words of love had passed his lips to Marion Vavasour, and he had thrust into his breast the crimson leaves that had been pressed against her lips; it was she only of whom he thought now as he paced up and down, while the dawn broke above the woods to the east. His passion had this characteristic of a worthier love—that its success had not weakened, but tenfold strengthened it, and her memory alone filled his thoughts now in the hot, hushed stillness. She was his! and he would have driven out of his path the boldest that had dared to seek her love, he would have revenged with death the fairest rivalry, that had dared to usurp his place.

Some twenty minutes might have gone by when, as he turned to re-enter the *maisonette* by one of the French windows which stood open to the piazza, the figure of a man came between him and the moonlight, he did not see whether from the villa or the grounds, though a moment after he recognised Erroll. They met as the one left, and the other turned to enter, the house, met for the first time alone since the day at White Ladies, when words about a woman, rash on the one side, bitter on the other, had laid the edge of the axe at the root of their friendship.

In a clearer light, or when his own thoughts had been less preoccupied, Strathmore must have noticed the change that had come over Erroll in the short half-hour that had gone by from the time of the Duc's departure, when he had been laughing and talking at the supper-table with all his usual gaiety, and even more than his usual wit. Then, his mots had sparkled through the conversation, dropped out in his soft, lazy voice, and his laugh had rung as often and as clearly as a young girl's—now, his face was haggard and lined, and as he pulled the Glengarry over his eyes his hand shook slightly, like the hand of a man who has been drinking deeply, which was scarcely the case with him, since he had never left the society of titled women.

Strathmore, however, did not observe this; it was very dark just then, as the clouds swept over the moon, and the lights from Lady Vavasour's villa, which were streaming full in his own eyes, dazzled them, while Erroll stood with his back to their blaze.

"I thought you had left us, Bertie. Have a cigar?" he

began, holding out his own case. "What a hot night, isn't it? There's a storm brewing. We shall have it down in half an hour."

"It looks dark," said Erroll, briefly, as he struck a fusee.

"Mild word! How sweetly those limes smell; rather oppressive, though. I will walk across the grounds with you to Sir Arthur's; how is he to-day?"

"Not much better."

"Well, really that tyrannous old gentleman has lived quite long enough," laughed Strathmore, as he moved down the terrace steps. "I want you to have that Hurstwood property, the timber is magnificent. What do you think of Milly Mostyn?—lovely figure, hasn't she? Only, unluckily, some wicked fellows *do* say it is sadly fictitious, and disappears when her maid disrobes her."

"We're often tricked in that way," laughed Erroll. But the laugh was forced, and he pulled his cap down over his eyes as they walked on under the limes and across the lawn of Marion Vavasour's rose-gardens, Strathmore talking to a spaniel of hers, that had run after and leapt upon him—a beautiful creature with a collar of silver bells. Erroll glanced at the spaniel as they strolled on in silence farther, and a bitter, haggard smile came on his face. "She caresses you to-night—she will caress me to-morrow—and a German Prince or a French Duc the next day!"

Strathmore laughed slightly; his laugh had a peculiar intonation; it was not often that it warmed, but rather chilled.

"Poor Bonbon! How severe you are on her. What has she done to deserve such philippics?"

"Nothing! She merely made me think that she strangely resembles—her mistress!"

"Her mistress!" repeated Strathmore. He hated to hear the name of Marion Vavasour spoken by any. "Your remark is open to an odd construction, Erroll; what do you mean by it?"

Erroll swung round and paused where they now stood, under the limes in the midst of Lady Vavasour's gardens, nothing near them but the night birds, which swept with a swift rush through the foliage, fleeing to refuge before the storm —nothing watching them but the quick lustrous eyes of the dog, that glanced rapidly from one to the other.

"Strathmore! do you believe *now* in the love of that woman as you did twelve months ago?"

"To the full."

The answer was mild as yet, but Strathmore's eyes were beginning to glitter coldly and angrily. Of all things, he hated his personal feelings to be probed, his personal matters touched.

"What!" broke in Erroll; his manner was utterly changed from its usual soft and lazy nonchalance, and his words were spoken by hoarse, abrupt efforts. "What! you are as mad about her, then, as you were a year ago? You never see — you never think——"

Strathmore laughed a little again, more chillily than before:

"My dear Erroll! a year before you were so good as to intrude your counsels on me—pray don't be at the trouble to repeat them. I bore rather ill with your interference then, I may do so still worse now."

"Bear with it as you will! but do you mean to tell me, then, that, arch coquette as Marion Vavasour is, you are mad, blind, infatuated enough to believe she will for ever——"

" 'For ever' is a word for fools," interrupted Strathmore, with his chilliest smile; "even forbearance will not last, 'for ever,' if it be tried too far, as *you* take a fancy to try it to-night!"

"For God's sake, do not let our friendship be broken for *her!*" muttered Erroll, with so strange a vehemence and pain that the spaniel, Bonbon, jumped upon him, whining plaintively. "It will stay by us when all the women's love on earth has rotted out of our hands—do not let *her* destroy it!"

"Faugh!" said Strathmore, with contemptuous impatience. "If we had left the ladies' presence at supper, I should say our good host the Marquis's wine had got in your head, mon cher! The duration or rupture of our *entente cordiale* lies in your own choice; all I beg of you is, cease to meddle with my private matters. I must take the liberty to remind you, that you are neither my keeper nor my father-confessor!"

Strathmore's words were light, sneering, and cold: such, flung at a man in a moment of high excitement, keen suffering, and strong feeling, are like ice-water flung on flames; they came so now to Erroll, and on this spur he said, what else might never have passed his lips.

"You must be a madman or a fool, Strathmore!" he broke in hotly and quickly. "I do not want to be your confessor, to see that you are fettered hand and foot. It is no secret now, you never attempt to keep it so. You are the slave of her idlest caprice, you are utterly chained and infatuated by her—all the world sees it. It is a thing publicly and plainly known enough. Men jest and jeer over it!——"

"Because they envy it—as perhaps *you* do!"

"They ridicule you behind your back," went on Erroll, hurriedly, not noticing (or evading) the sneer, which was all the more cutting for its tranquillity. "I tell you what they —sneaks and cowards—only say out of your hearing. You have no will of your own with her—she rules you as she pleases. Great Heavens! can you make such a byword of your name, such a wreck of your ambition, for the sheer sake of this wanton adultress!"

"Silence!"

The word hissed out on the air like the ring of a bullet. The black, silent wrath of his vengeful race glared in Strathmore's eyes till they gleamed like steel, and he turned away with a smile that had darker meaning in it than the hottest fury, or menace, that could have shaped themselves in oaths or words.

"I should shoot any one else dead for that to morrow morning. I do not need to say our acquaintanceship ceases from to-night! *Bonbon, ma belle, allons-nous-en! Voilà la pluie qui tombe.*"

He moved away with a low and punctilious bow of contemptuous courtesy; but with a sudden movement Erroll swung round and stood before him in the path; in the yellow moonlight his face looked very pale, and the nerves of his lips twitched under his moustaches.

"Stop! we shall not part like that!"

They stood face to face in the middle of Marion Vavasour's paradise of flowers, while the first storm-drops fell among the leaves above head slowly one by one, and the garish light of the moon, which looked duskily red against the clouds, strayed in streaks across the darkness.

"Wait a moment!" Erroll's voice was thick as he spoke, and shook slightly. "I risked death for you once, I would do it again to-night. We have lived, and shared, and thought together, as though the same mother had borne us. We have not prated about it like boys, but we have held each other closer than men of the same blood do. We never had an evil word between us till *she* brought them. Strathmore! is all *that* to be swept away in a single night!"

The words were more eloquent by feeling than they were by rhetoric; they would have softened most men: Strathmore they did not even touch. He stood with his arms folded and his cigarette in his mouth, while his face wore its darkest, deadliest scorn. When his will was crossed, his wrath was roused, or his pride touched, the man was bronze; words could not scathe, pity could not stir, memory could not soften him. Once his glance grew a little gentler, it was at Erroll's first words; but it soon passed away, and the merciless scoff set on his lips again.

"You are admirably theatrical! but we are not playing 'Hernani' now, and I should prefer that we used the language of gentlemen. It is sad waste of stage-talent, and I should like fewer phrases and more rational ones! Lady Vavasour can in no way be charged with having caused the 'evil words' you speak of; you have only yourself to thank for them by your madman's conduct, and by your very marked insolence to me. Be so good as to oblige me by letting me pass?"

"Not yet," swore Erroll, between his teeth; a hot flush had come on his face, and his eyes were excited; Strathmore's words cut him to the quick, less for their insult, than their chill and mocking heartlessness. "You insult me for her sake —you turn against me because I tell you frankly what all your friends and enemies say with one voice behind your back—because I seek to warn you against your insane belief, your wretched slavery, with a wanton coquette, a titled courtesan? What if I told you she were faithless to you?"

For an instant the words struck Strathmore like a shot, and he made one fierce swift panther-like movement, as though to spring upon and rend limb from limb the man that dared to whisper this thing to him; then he restrained himself, and laughed a low, cold imperious laugh of contempt and of power; he took the cigarette leisurely from his lips, and his eyes, that glittered like a furious hawk's, fastened on Erroll with deadly significance.

"What!" he said, slowly, and gently winding a loosened leaf round the cigarette. "*What?* Why, you would give me your life for the lie, that is all."

"But if I could prove to you that it were true?"

"Prove it, then! You have dared to hint it, dare to make it good!" hissed Strathmore through his teeth, where he leaned forward as a boar-hound strains to leap upon his foes, while the leash holds him back from the death-grip.

The blood rushed to Erroll's face, staining it crimson; his head sank like a man suddenly and sorely stricken; he stood motionless in the still and sultry night.

"Prove it, if you are not the greatest dastard upon earth!" hissed Strathmore, his voice vibrating with the suppressed passion, which was worse in men of his blood than the darkest wrath of a more open and a quicker spent anger. "Prove it, I say, if it is not the vilest lie that jealousy ever spawned!"

"My God! it is the *truth* I spare you!"

The words wrung out from him, died on his lips too low to be overheard, as he forced them back to silence, by the might of a generous self-sacrifice which wrestled in conflict with a fiery temptation. He stood silent, stood to be branded as a liar! No other man would have uttered that word to Bertie Erroll and lived when the dawn rose.

Strathmore looked at him, in the uncertain shimmer of the moon that streamed fitfully between them through the boughs; and he laughed, tauntingly, scornfully, imperiously, while a cold exultant light glittered in his eyes, and a haughty scorn sat on his lips.

"You dare not? I thought so. Fie, sir, for shame! So this is cowardice as well as falsehood? You play in a new *rôle!*"

The words cut through the air like the swift whirr of the sabre, and Erroll—stood silent still. The veins swelled to cords on his temples; the blood left his face till it looked white and drawn like a corpse; he struggled with a horrible temptation. A word uttered, a word held back: in this lay the whole gist of a great self-sacrifice, and of a great revenge; in this lay the whole powers of his choice. With a word he could strike down the man who stood there in the yellow weirdly light, scorning, and taunting, and thrusting liar and coward in his teeth. With a word he could cast him out of the paradise where he had lain so long, cast him out of every one of its sweet hours, every one of its honeyed draughts; with a word he could turn his exultant idolatry to loathing hate, to bitter shame. With a word! And that word he was gibed and dared to utter!

It was a deadly struggle, but the past, with all its boyish memories, was closer knit about his heart than about the heart of him whose laugh was grating on his ear, and whose insults were falling on his brain like drops of fire. His head drooped, his lips moved faintly, and he muttered like a man in his extremity:

"God give me strength to keep silent!"

The words were very low, and were unheard, as the nightbirds cleft the air with a rushing sound, and the winds rising swept up with a moan through the trees—the moan of the storm afar off.

A moment more, and he lifted his head with a gesture of proud grace; he chose to endure insult, aspersion, wrong, rather than do what he held in his power to do now—lay the burden on the shoulders, and turn the steel back into the breast of the man who had been his brother in all save the ties of blood.

"Since you deem it a falsehood, hold it one—watch your own treasure! For the sake of the past, I let pass your words; *I* can afford to be called a coward.   Strathmore! if we must part, let it be in peace."

He held out his hand as he spoke, and his voice grew mellow as music; the moonlight fell full upon his face, with its fair and fearless beauty, while his eyes were soft with the wistful, forgiving, lingering gaze of a woman. The look, the words, the action, should have unlocked a flood of olden memories and thoughts of youth, and should have swept away, as the light of morning sweeps aside an evil dream, all the dark and pitiless passions which a few seconds had been long enough to beget and bring to birth.   But in the tangled web of Strathmore's nature ran one hell-woven thread—in anger he was pitiless, in revenge relentless.   With his sneer on his lips he signed aside the offered hand, and in the ghastly light his eyes looked into those which met him with gallant fearlessness and wistful tenderness: but his own neither changed nor softened.

"You might know me better—I never forgive!"

And with those brief, calm words he turned and passed across the sward, followed by Lady Vavasour's spaniel. Once, when he had reached the marble piazza of the villa, he turned and glanced at the night, as he called the dog to follow him. Erroll was out of sight. There were only the heavy darkness, which hung like a pall above the earth, and the angry moon, gleaming blood-red where she glared through the mist. The roar of the winds was rising louder, and from afar off the thunder broke, subdued and sullenly.

The storm was near at hand.

CHAPTER XXII

The Ashes in the Lamp.

THERE was no moment when Lady Vavasour was so re-sistless as in negligée in her own dressing-room. With half the pearls and diamonds of her regalia glittering on her in the presence-chamber of St. James's or the Tuileries, though perhaps more dazzling, she was less dangerous, than reclining among her cushions like the odalisque of a harem, with the light softly shaded and the air scented with attar of roses, with her shower of hair unloosed, and the folds of some texture, white as snow, or delicate in colouring as the blush on the opal, half enshrouding, half unveiling her, as the sea-foam the goddess. She was so lovely, then, at midnight or morning; and it was a privacy wherein so few saw her, while of even those few, each believed himself the only one!

Strathmore looked at her where she lay, with her feet softly sheathed in pearl-broidered slippers, and a slight smile of amused reverie just parting her lips. It was the morning after *Hernani*, and he thought of the hint that had been thrown out to him the night before, with disdainful ridicule, and bitter scorn of the man who had employed such methods to implant the lie he had not even dared repeat. Long ago at White Ladies he had suspected where the root of Erroll's bitterness upon her lay; in the last few weeks at Auteuil his suspicion had strengthened into certainty, and this morning, as he felt her hand wander over his brow where he lay at her feet, he repented that he had allowed the memory of any friendship to stay him, and that he had not washed out with fitter punishment the coward envy that had sought to revenge itself on him by the suggestion of a hideous suspicion. Truly all better things are swept away betwixt men, when once the face of a woman has come between them!

"What are you thinking of, caro?" she asked him, softly touching his hair.

"I was thinking—how many would make you faithless to me if they could."

"What a wide field for speculation—there are hundreds! Well, if they succeeded, I should not expect you to complain."

"Hush! Do not jest about that."

"Why not?" she laughed. "Love wisely taken *is* a jest, you know. You would have no right to complain, Cecil. One may be queen of all the world, but not sovereign of Oneself; and our hearts are like Ben Jonson's 'blow-balls,' now here, now there, wherever the winds of chance and caprice like to float them. Indeed, I should expect you to take your congé with the most tranquil grace. Come! what *would* you do if I said I loved you no longer?"

The question was asked with that mocking malice which was part and parcel of her nature; this delicate, youthful creature loved to torture! His passionate eyes looked up into hers with the jealous love of Othello.

"Do! God knows! Take your life or my own—or both!"

The answer was not wholly a jest, too deep a meaning lay in the look he fastened on her and the unconscious vibration of his voice; and, for once, she felt a vague terror at the force of the love she had delighted to excite and feed, till it lost all reason in its madness; for once she felt that she had roused what she could not so easily allay, and that the weakness she triumphed and tyrannised over, was a strength which might one day menace her, when no words of hers would be able to soothe it away. For the moment she feared the work of her own will, the next she gloried in her power, and laughed, her white fingers caressingly wandering among the dark chesnut waves of his hair.

"What a horrible answer, Cecil! One would think we were in the *Cinque Cento!* You swift, silent Strathmores have much more of the Italian in you than of the English nature. You ought to be a Colonna or a Malatesta, with the steel in

your sleeve, and the poison in your ring. What! has one love
become so necessary to you, that life would be unbearable
without it? Oh, Lucifer, Son of Morning, how art thou
fallen!"

"But my fall has opened heaven to me, not exiled me
from it," smiled Strathmore, as he lay at her feet. "Why do
you wonder at my answer? Love has turned to crime in its
agony more than once since the world began."

"Perhaps—but not in *our* world——"

"Where passion enters all worlds have the same law!
You have made me learn the same madness as an Israelite
learnt from Mariamne a thousand years ago, as twice a thousand a Spartan learnt from Cleonice."

"Who both taught it to be slain by it! What an ominous
souvenir! You would not slay *me*, Cecil?"

And the loosened tresses swept against his brow, and her
eyes looked laughingly yet lovingly into his.

"Almost I could, rather than other eyes should feast on
you. Ah, Marion! when men love as I love, they loathe the
very daylight to look on what they idolise."

"*Tu es fou*," she interrupted him, but the words were
spoken so softly that they were themselves a caress. "It is a
madness, Cecil! But why, I wonder, are men who love us as
you do, imperiously, avariciously, jealously, and would hate
us as pitilessly, always most dear to women? Why? It is
very *bête*."

"Why? Because you know no love, worth the name,
ever yet bore the shadow of a share in what it loved; because
you delight to feel yourselves the mistresses of a man's life,
and taste your power to give him misery or rapture, to yield
him a god's delight, or cast him out to worse torture than the
cursed! To learn how men can love, women must be loved
as I love you."

"Ah, my cold, proud Strathmore, what lava flames lay
beneath the ice!" she murmured, while the smile still hovered
on her lips. "You did not know your own nature till I loved
you!"

As she stooped towards him, her caress lingering on his brow, the forward movement dislodged a note which lay among the laces, silks, and Eastern stuffs piled on her luxurious couch, so that it fell, with its superscription upward, upon Strathmore's arm. He took it up to throw it towards a table which stood near, attaching no import to it, but Lady Vavasour with a quick movement interposed her hand, and as he gave it to her he caught sight of the handwriting. Coupled with the memories of the night that was just passed, it struck on Strathmore with a keener suspicion.

"You correspond with Erroll?" he said, quickly, keeping the note in his hand.

"I invite him to dinner, and he answers me," she said, carelessly, with a little half-suppressed yawn; "and I do it pretty often, since he is so adored a friend of yours."

"Is this a dinner acceptation?"

"No, a refusal. I fancy Milly Mostyn said something about his going back to England."

She had moved her hand again as if to receive the note, but had checked herself, and lay with her head resting on her arm, with negligent grace, and her lashes drooping languidly. Nothing could be more easily indifferent than her manner, but as his eyes fastened on her, a faint colour deepened the sea-shell bloom on her cheeks, and Strathmore noted it with the swift Moor-like jealousy that always runs in leash with such a love as his. On his impulse he would have wrenched the envelope open; honour and courtesy compelled him to restrain himself, but he did not give up the note.

"Will you permit me to read this? I have my reasons," he asked her. He believed she might resent, but could not refuse him.

"No!"

The single prohibition was uttered with disdainful nonchalance and haughty sovereignty; the superb and graceful indignation of a proud woman subjected to a doubt that is insult.

"*No!* Why not? You claim your right to my confidence, I claim my title to yours."

She raised herself upon her arm from her cushions, with questioning wonder in her eyes, and a smile of scorn upon her lips—she, Marion Vavasour, to be arraigned in judgment by a lover who was as wax in her hands, and whom she could have bent to any sin, or any folly, at her word! *She* to be doubted, questioned, opposed!

"Confidence!" she re-echoed, with a scornful curl on her lovely lips, and an angry light in her eyes, very new to them, for Marion Vavasour was by nature of a sunny, insouciant temper, rarely troubled by irritation or bitterness. "What confidence can be needed in such a trifle? You have lost your senses, Cecil, I think. Certainly, since you presume to disbelieve my word, I shall not allow you to insult me by verifying it."

"It is not I who have lost my senses, but you your memory, Madame," said Strathmore, the black jealousy in him leaping into sudden life. "Discourteous or not, I must doubt either your word or your recollection. This is a strangely lengthy 'dinner refusal.'"

The letter, which had half fallen from its envelope, was of four pages, closely covered with many lines. For an instant her colour deepened and then died out, leaving her cheek pale, her eyes sank beneath his, and her fluent tongue was silent. Strathmore rose to his feet, grasping the letter in his hand, a hideous suspicion coiling round him, and the jealous love in him working up in silence.

"Since you must be in error as regards its meaning, Lady Vavasour, do you *now* permit me to read this mere 'dinner refusal?'"

"No!"

And as the single word was launched from her lips in haughty denial, with the swift movement peculiar to her she raised herself from her pile of cushions, caught the note in her hand, twisting it by a rapid action from his hold, and held it to a spirit-lamp, that was burning liquid perfume on

the table, which stood, with her coffee, at her elbow. The
flame caught, it flared alight, and shrivelling in a second, the
note fell, a harmless heap of light grey ashes, into the jasper
saucer of the lamp, its words destroyed, its secret safe. Then
she laughed softly and amusedly at her own success—her
mood changing like a child's.

"Amico mio," she said, gaily, "never oppose a woman—
she will always outwit you! While you have but one mode
of Menace, we have a thousand resources of Finesse!"

Lady Vavasour was laughing, tranquil, at her ease again,
now that the note was floating among the liquid perfume in
ashes which could tell no tales. Done in one moment, ere he
could arrest her hand or avert the flame, the action literally
for that moment confounded Strathmore, and struck him
dumb; the next, the abhorred suspicion seemed written in
letters of flame before his eyes. His love, though an utter
slavery in its bondage, was imperious in its dark and bitter
jealousy; the blood rushed over his forehead, and his teeth
clenched hard, as he saw the ashes fall into the essence, and
heard her low, soft laugh of triumph.

"That letter holds a secret so dear that you destroy it!
So be it, then! I will wrench it out of the man who shares it!"

He moved to leave her presence, but, before he could
escape her, she raised herself from her couch, and laid her
hand on his arm—the hand that could hold him closely as a
chain of iron:

"Cecil, you must be mad! Wait and listen to me."

Every word of her voice he was used to obey as though he
had no law save her will; but the very weakness of the love
she had triumphed over, made its ferocity when crossed with
the looming shadow of the slightest rivalry; now he threw her
hand off him.

"Listen!—you have palmed one falsehood off on me, already, why wait for another! Your own secrets you must
keep as you will, but the man who shares them shall answer
to me——"

"You are mad, Cecil!" cried Marion Vavasour again, her

eyes lighting with pretty contemptuous anger, as of a spoiled beauty crossed in her will, while the slender hand closed still on his arm with a movement that, slight as it was, might betray anxiety. "I forbid you to do any such thing! *My* name disputed over, as over some dancer's, or rosière's! I forbid it—I will not have it!"

"Let me go!" said Strathmore, so rife with passion that he scarce knew or heeded what he said. "Let me go! You have lied to me, and I will know what made the need of a lie. You burnt the letter, lest I should even see one word; I have a right to know what those words were which must have been faithlessness to me; I cannot grind it from *you* by force—I will seek it where I can, and, by God, if——"

The words broke asunder unuttered; he could not put into plain speech the hideous thought which he would have disbelieved, in the teeth of all evidence on earth or heaven, save her own witness against her. His strength went down under the torture of the mere doubt that she could be faithless to him, and the oath died away on his lips, which were blanched as death; his love swept aside all beyond itself; to *her* he had no pride, and he threw himself beside her, twining in his hands her loosened hair, and scorching her brow with his breath.

"I *am* mad, if you will! My God! have pity on me. I never stooped to any living thing—I stoop to you! Give a thought to another you shall not—you cannot! For the love of Heaven, tell me what it is you hide?"

"No!"

And she thought with a woman's glad, pitiless idolatry of power how utterly this man loved her!

"Do not trifle with me," muttered Strathmore, incoherently twisting round his hands, in his delirious suffering, the golden meshes of her hair, as though with that frail bond to knit her to him through life and death. "Tell me the truth—the truth!—or I will wrench it from the coward who has robbed me. No man should thieve even a glance of yours, and live——"

The words were muttered in his throat, fierce in their menace, yet imploring in their pain; his very life—more than his life!—hung on this woman's love. She saw he was no longer to be played with; she saw that every syllable he said would be wrought out; she saw that *here*—with his jealous passions loosed—he was no more her slave, but had become her master, and Marion Vavasour shrank from his grasp and from his gaze;—she feared the strength of what she had invoked.

But she was a woman who knew well how to deal with the men she ruled. Her hand gently touched his brow, and she stooped towards him with a pitying, tender smile:

"Ah, Cecil! can you not trust me even in so little? Sceptic! you are unjust and cruel; I but burnt that letter to spare you pain!"

"To *spare* me pain! Quick!—tell me all—all!"

"No," she whispered, bending till her wooing lips kissed his brow; "let it pass. You know I love you—love but you? Let it pass, my dearest!"

"Never! Tell me—at once—or I seek him this moment."

She stooped lower still, while her fragrant breath was warm on his cheek, and her whisper stole on his ear:

"Then—then (let it stir no words between you, Cecil, for *my* sake!)—but—your friend was very treacherous to you, and that letter spoke a love which was as hateful to me as it was craven to you. That is all the truth! Forgive me its concealment; I would so gladly have saved you its pain!"

CHAPTER XXIII.

The Swoop of the Vulture.

AN hour afterwards, Strathmore quitted the Bosquet de Diane, and took his way across the grounds. He walked at his usual leisurely pace, he had a cigar in his mouth, and his manner was tranquil as usual. But a dog glancing at him would have shrunk whining and frightened away, and a stranger meeting him, and looking at the deadly glitter in his eyes under their drooped lids, would have thought, "that man is bound on a merciless errand." The hour was just mid-day, the birds had ceased from song, the scythe lay among the unshaven grass, the vintagers afar off had left their work, the very leaves hung stirless. All nature was calm and at rest—all, save the same passions which have drenched the laughing earth in blood, and mocked the sweet, hushed stillness of the summer skies, and made the fair day hideous with their riot, since the suns of Asia shone on the white, upturned face of the First Dead, and the curse was branded on the brow of Cain.

Strathmore crossed the gardens without haste in his steps, his hand closing on a little cane; the blood of his race ran unchanged in his veins, dark with that ruthless wrath which had never yielded to the memory of mercy, the prayers of pity, or the rights of justice, and which had scathed all out of its path, as the scythe sweeps the seeding-grass. To the woman he had quitted he had said but little; but he left her to revenge the coward who would have robbed him, by such chastisement as men do not speak of to women. Less fully told than hinted at, less gathered by deliberate evidence than grasped in all its broad, accursed meaning, the treachery stood out black and bare before him. In his revenge he would have spared no living thing that could have risen up betwixt him and it; had he known of any darker, fuller, fouler, which his birth and breeding could have permitted, or the age and the world allowed, he would have made the man he now hated drain it to the last drop. He had left her, soothing her fears, promising her no violence—left her, with the passions in his blood, that in darker ages far back, had trodden out human life pitilessly and recklessly, as so much waste water spilt, and had scored down with unrelenting bitterness the ruthless motto of a ruthless race, "Slay! and spare not."

He walked across the grounds alone—once he glanced up. The radiant day seemed hot with flame, and the cloudless heavens looked brazen in the light. But he went onward, still calmly, leisurely as before, but with the bloodhound's thirst growing stronger and stronger within him, and set but on one goal. What *are* our passions, once let loose, but sleuth-hounds freed from leash, which run down all before them, and hunt on even to the death?

A breadth of sward alone separated the *maisonette* of Lady Vavasour from the villa beyond. He opened the gates and passed on, leaving the paradise of roses behind him. Through the glades of trees the terrace which ran before the villa was visible, and a group of men were standing there. Three of them were strangers to him, the fourth was Erroll, who was standing with a brace of setters at his feet, behind him the open window of the dark oak library he had just quitted, be-fore him all the light of the summer noontide.

Strathmore saw him—and his hand clenched down on the cane he held, that dainty jewelled switch, fragile and costly enough for a lady's riding-whip. As the sun flickered through the branches on to his face it was calm and impassive, but there was a cruel smile about his mouth, and his grey eyes were black and lustrous, with a fierce, eager light.

The setters as he approached gave tongue, and Erroll turned. He was talking with them of Court beauties, of Blois races, of the baccarat at Lilli Dorah's, of all the trifles and the chit-chat of an ordinary Paris day; for we smoke and gossip and laugh and dine while our lives are making ship-wreck, and all we value is drifting away to the greedy, tide-less sea of a fathomless past, that will never give back its dead.

As he looked up his face brightened—he thought Strath-more was come for a tacit reconciliation. Enough had been said twelve hours before to have steeled him to any such feeling; but his nature was not capable of harbouring revenge: he forgave freely—as he would have forgiven now, even such epithets as men never pardon, for the sake of all those thou-sand memories of childhood, and of manhood, that were still warm about his heart, not even to be washed out, and tram-pled from remembrance, by the tide of a jealous love, or by the sting of a bitter feud.

He looked up, a smile of pleasure lighting his eyes, which had been heavy and worn before; and Strathmore saw him as he came up the turf terrace—the man who had once flung himself in his defence into the near grip of death, who had been with him in shifting scenes of danger, pleasure, revel, or privation, and who had trusted him and shared his trust, as though the same mother had borne them, since they had been children together playing with the fallen chesnuts, or wading in the shallow estuaries under the woods of White Ladies, far away in England. Strathmore saw him, and his hand closed tighter on the switch, with which he moved out of his path the curling tendrils of the clematis. The revenge of men of his blood had always been swift and silent, but they had always *tasted* it, slowly yet thirstily, drop by drop, with the fierce delight of the vulture, as it sweeps and circles above its prey before it swoops down to wrench and tear.

He went up the terrace-slope leisurely, and lifted his hat with suave courtesy, the soft ceremony in which the Strathmores of White Ladies had ever clothed their deadliest approach, the silky velvet glove which they had ever drawn over the merciless iron hand whose grip was death.

Erroll stood leaning against the side of the window; he could not make the first movement towards a tacit reconciliation, but he was ready to meet, to more than meet, one. He only needed his friend's hand stretched out to him in silence, to give his own, and mutely forgive the worst words which had been uttered twelve hours before.

"*Pardon, messieurs!*" said Strathmore, quietly passing the other men, while they parted to let him approach: as the sun fell on it, his face wore a strange look, out of keeping with the easy suavity of his manner. He moved on to the library window, where Erroll stood, with the sunlight full upon his face. Calmly, as though he tendered them a cigar, Strathmore glanced round him at the three other men, with a bitter evil scorn about his lips.

"Gentlemen! is there any answer save one customary to a lie?"

The men—young fellows—surprised and embarrassed, hesitated; Erroll looked up, the angry blood rushing hotly to his face; but he stretched out his hand with an involuntary gesture.

"Strathmore! you are in gross error! Come within here a moment; I must have one more word with you."

"*Words* are not my answer!"

And as the syllables left his lips, hurled out in blind and deadly fury, he lifted his right arm, the jewelled handle of the cane flashed in the sunlight, the switch swirled through the air like a flail, with a shrill sound, and in the swiftness of a second had struck a broad, livid mark across Erroll's brow, brutal as a death-stroke, ineffaceable as shame.

"*That* for your treachery to me. I will have your life for your love for her."

The words were hissed in Erroll's ear as the blow fell, low but distinct as the hiss of a snake, chill as steel, relentless as death. As he reeled back, for the moment staggered and blinded, Strathmore's eyes fastened on the swollen crimson bar, where the switch had cut its mark, with the steady, pitiless greed for revenge that, fed to the full, yet clamoured still for more. In the blazing glare of the hot noon the vile, ineffaceable insult seemed stamped on the living flesh in letters of flame, which nothing in past, or present, or future, could ever cover or wash out, for which blood alone could ever atone—he laughed a low, chill, mocking laugh. Breaking the switch in two, he threw the fragments down at the feet of the man he had struck, his eyes glittering exultant, the veins in his face black and swollen in the fury of his wrath, a scornful smile set about his lips, as he turned to the others with a slight bow of careless courtesy:

"Gentlemen! you are my witnesses——" but Erroll's hand struck his lips to silence with a force that would have sent a weaklier man hurled backward to the earth. "By God! you must answer this."

The oath rattled in his throat, his face was white, save where the red cut stood out across his brow; his voice was hoarse and his breath stifled as the words gasped out; the suddenness of the foul indignity seemed to have paralysed in him all save the sheer instinct of its revenge, and to have numbed and stricken even that.

"With pleasure!"

"Where?"

The single word came from Erroll's throat hoarse and suffocated with passion.

"In the Deer-park of the Bois, by the pond, if it suit you."

"Your hour?"

"At sunset to-night! I am engaged until then."

"I shall await you."

"*Soit!*"

With those few rapid words all was said; all had been done and spoken in less than sixty seconds, swift as thought and breathless as passion, staggering and bewildering those who looked on like the sudden flash of lightning in their eyes. Then he turned, bowed low to those standing by, passed along the terrace, and took his way across the lawn back to the Bosquet de Diane. He was well content. Half his vengeance was wrought, the rest could not now escape him. He thought of the brutal and ineffaceable insult he had given with pitiless delight; of all yet to come he thought as thirstily; the jealous hatred and the revengeful greed that were within him could only be sated with one requital—life! Life! which in a few hours' time would be in his hands and at his mercy. Mercy, I say?—the word has nothing to do with him; it was not in his blood nor in his creed. As ruthlessly as he had dealt out insult, he had it in him now to deal out death.

Once he glanced upward at the sky above-head, and as the hot beams fell on his eyes, across his pitiless and exultant thoughts, there strayed by some strange chain of memory, old familiar words, unheard, unread since childhood: "Let not the sun go down upon thy wrath."

The sun was high in the noontide heavens, shining without shadow on the day that was at its full—the day that had dawned to be weighted with the wail of new lives, and the sighs of dying lips, with the burden of crowding crimes, and the bitterness of human words, with the cry of the slaughtered in far-off battle-fields, and the pent breathing of the toilers in great cities. When the sun should sink and the day fade into night, who should call back warmth to the lips they had seen close for ever; who should render unsaid the words they had heard curse the living; who should have power to bid them return to restore the deeds undone, the sin unwrought, the graves unsealed, and yield back the hours garnered to the past?

The old words, with their grand simplicity of counsel and of warning, crossed his memory; words which mark the short day all too long for men's wrath to endure. God forgive him! Strathmore only thought how, when that sun should rise to light another day, there should be one lost from amongst the numbers of the living, one human life the less upon the peopled earth!

Furies' passions blinded him with their accursed lust, and his soul was set on vengeance—vengeance that would know no pity, and yield no shrive.

From the sultry glare of the terrace he passed by abrupt transition into the aisles of the rose-gardens, into the midst of gay groups gathered about Marion Vavasour; and, with a game of life and death to be played out before the sun went down, he joined in with the jests, the impromptu, the epigram, the graceful flatteries, as lightly and laughingly as any there. There was not a sign by which to tell his past errand, not a glimpse to disclose the purpose on to which his will was set; yet there was one whom the easy wit did not blind, whom the careless nonchalance did not deceive, and at first the bloom had wavered anxiously on her cheek, quickly, however, to be succeeded by an amused, exultant light in her gazelle eyes.

Like Cunigunde, she loved well to see those whom she had ensnared reel up to dizzy heights, and stagger downwards to yawning chasms, courting death, and wasting life, to feast her eyes with proof of her own power.

"Come to me in a few minutes," she said, in a low tone, as she passed into the house an hour or two after. Her idlest whisper was his law, and he obeyed, entering her boudoir, where the light stole subdued, and dreamy oriental odours filled the air.

She stood by an étagère of flowers, idly toying with their blossoms, and turned towards him as he approached, with the imperious grace that so well became her:

"Where had you been, Cecil, when you came into the rose-garden?"

"To the stables. I know how you value Mazeppa, too well to leave her to the stud-grooms."

The answer was careless and natural; there was nothing to indicate that the reply was even an evasion; but Lady Vavasour made a gesture of impatience.

"Mazeppa and I thank you much, but you came by the west gate of the gardens; the stables lie to the south. Never play with me, never evade me, it is utterly useless! You had been to Bertie Erroll?"

"Indeed, no. You are distressing yourself most needlessly, my dearest!"

Strathmore spoke softly and persuasively; he was solicitous to guard from her even a suspicion of what was unfitting for her ear and her sex in the work which was wrought by her own beauty.

"Hush!" she said, petulantly, her eyes glancing into his, with the gaze with which she knew she could have made him lay bare the dearest secret that ever locked in honour. "You are only deceiving me, Cecil. You have broken your word; you have taken revenge when you promised me to forbear it."

"Well!—I do not come of an over-forbearing race."

He spoke with a slight smile—a smile that, momentary as it was, struck a chill to her like the touch of cold steel. She shuddered for an instant as she caught a glimpse of what this man's revenge *might be;* shuddered as though with a prophetic dread of the future—that dread which romancists idly call "presentiment," but which is often only the reflected colour, thrown before our steps, from our own past acts and follies, as our shadow falls in advance of us as we walk.

"What did you say to him?" she asked, quickly.

And the light was so shaded, that the flush of a certain anxiety which came and went in her cheek escaped him. As great sovereigns have feared their most abject slaves, when the might of their own tyranny has roused proportionate might of passion in those who have long bent the knee to their word, so she now began to fear this man, whose love, now his weakness, might so soon become his strength—a strength to crush its tyrant.

"What did you say to him?" she repeated, impatiently. "I *will* know, Strathmore!"

He saw that she already guessed too truly to be evaded longer, and her will in its lightest caprice lay on him like an iron chain, dragging him where it would.

"I said nothing. I am not fond of words."

"What was it that you *did*, then?"

"Do not ask, my loveliest! These are not themes for a woman's ear."

"But I *will* know!"

"Why? It is not a subject for you. Be content, your name is involved in no way. You may surely trust me to guard against that!"

"But I WILL know!" There was all her wilful, imperious witching tyranny in the words, and in the gesture with which she spoke them. "What have you done?"

"I have treated him as I should treat a hound that bit me."

Even though he spoke to a woman, he could not restrain the pitiless passion that vibrated through his voice, and she understood without translation.

"And he?"

"He has but one course open. A coward would have to meet me, and he is not that."

An eager, exultant gladness lightened in her eyes, a flushed warmth came on her cheek, her graceful loveliness grew instinct, for one fleeting instant, with the fierceness of the panther as it rises for its spring;—for one instant, while it lent to her beauty a glow almost fearful, a life almost terrible, the dark revenge of a Theodora was given to a creature soft and radiant as the morning.

"You are right—you are right," she said, with nervous force. "*I* was wrong who bid you stay your hand. Revenge it! Revenge becomes your race! Could I think you would submit to such rank treachery; sit silent under such perfidious rivalry? Revenge it, Strathmore! You are right."

The fierce words came strangely from those soft lips, that only parted with sweet laughter, or gave a wooing caress. Her hand closed upon the rich blossoms among which it wandered, crushing and breaking them. She stood there, fatal in her dazzling loveliness, fascinating him, confirming to fresh strength every evil instinct in him, inciting to yet darker deed every worst passion of his soul, luring and tempting him to the impending crime which grew holier and dearer to him with every instant that drew him nearer to its act.

If he had loved her ere now, in this hour he adored her! The passion of his own nature found answering echo, spur, and unison in hers. In his mood then, a woman who had stood between him and his wrath would have been hurled out of his path, though he had worshipped her; the woman who spurred him to his revenge became thrice idolised, as her voice spoke the thoughts, and goaded the lusts, of his heart. He crushed her in a close embrace.

"Be content! No man should seek to rob me of your love, and live!"

"But—ah, my God!—I forgot. If your life should pay forfeit!"

The words died on her lips, her face was blanched, her eyes filled with the sudden terror of a horrible remembrance, the piteous fear of a ghastly thought—now she was but a woman, who loved!

"That I must risk. But whether my own life fall or not, my revenge will not escape me."

While he soothed and thanked her with his caresses, the answer, brief as it was, was pregnant with meaning. With the dews of death heavy upon him, and the mists of death blinding his eyes, he would still find strength to keep his grip upon his vengeance, and to take it standing on the brink of a yawning grave, which would, at the least, close over *both*.

"But Cecil—Cecil—your own danger!"

It was the anguished cry of a woman's love, imploring in its terror, yearning in its tenderness, shrinking in horror from the near approach of a fatal hour for him whom she holds dear, or,—it was the most marvellous and matchless acting with which the false breath of a woman's lips ever yet duped man?

"Do not think of it, my worshipped one; think as little as I! But—if it chance so, if I never look upon your face again, kiss my lips when they are cold, kiss my eyes when they are closed, that your love may be with me in my grave; and remember, my love for you was such, that when my life was at its sweetest, when my years were at their richest, I died to revenge one whisper which sought to steal you from me!"

The passionate answer broke from his lips, hoarse and tremulous with the hot tears that rose in his throat, and sprang unbidden to his eyes—the first which had ever gathered there—as he looked on her in her loveliness, and thought that when the morning rose her kiss might have no warmth to waken him, her voice no power to call him back to life, his eyes be for ever blind and sightless to her gaze. Her own tears fell upon his brow as she bent towards him; but her glance looked into his with responsive meaning, her face lightened with his own vulture-thirst for vengeance, a smile of superb triumph wantoned on her lips—triumph to thus sway, and give away at will, to death or life, this man's entire existence!

"Ah! this is to be loved, indeed, as poets have fabled and as women have dreamed! Strathmore, revenge yourself and me—revenge! It is meet and just. And death shall not scathe you, nor come nigh you, my beloved.   You shall return unharmed, untouched, to find your reward *here!*"

She pressed his hand to her heart, where it beat warm and quick beneath its costly lace. As she bent over him, her voice sank to all its wooing softness, but thrilling with a new and fiercer meaning, which fostered every darker passion in him, as tropic heat fosters the poison-plants to seed and blossom, tempting and goading him to the crime that was sweet in his eyes as the gold-haired Gunhilda in the old Norse days wooed Eric the Viking to the sin of Cain. These were the passions that she loved to rouse in men, and see run riot in their deadly course; when a whisper, a caress from her, might have slaked them, her lips only fanned the flame!

And here, an eager thirst for revenge craved its food in her as in him; here, this soft and radiant creature was *cruel* as any panther that ever crouched, any snake that ever reared its brilliant painted crest.

CHAPTER XXIV.

"And the Sun went down upon his Wrath."

THE sun was setting, descending beyond purple bars of cloud, and leaving a long golden trail behind it in its track—sinking slowly and solemnly towards the west as the day declined, without rest, yet without haste, as though to give to all the sons of earth, warning and time, to leave no evil rooted, no bitterness unhealed, no feud to ripen, and no crime to bring forth seed, when the day should have passed away to be numbered with hours irrevocable; and the night should cast its pall over the dark deeds done, and seal their graves never to be unclosed. The sun was setting, shedding its rich and yellow light over the green earth, on the winding waters, and the blue hills afar off, and down the thousand leafy aisles close by. But to one place that warm radiance did not wander, in one spot the rays did not play, the glory did not enter. That place was the Deer-pond of the old Bois, where the

dank plants brooding on the fœtid waters, which only stirred
with noisome things, had washed against the floating hair of
lifeless women, and the sombre branches of the crowding trees
had been dragged earthward by the lifeless weight of the
self-slain, till the air seemed to be poisonous with death, and
the grasses, as they moved, to whisper to the winds dread
secrets of the Past. There, the light of the summer evening
did not come, but only through the leafless boughs of one
seared tree, which broke and parted the dark barrier of
forest growth, they saw the west, and the sun declining
slowly in its haze of golden air, sinking downward past the
bars of cloud.

All was quiet, save the dull sound of the parting waters,
when some loathsome reptiles stirred among its brakes, or
the hot breeze moved its pestilential plants; and in the silence
they who had been as brothers, and who now were foes, stood
fronting each other: in this silence they had met, in it they
would part. And there, on their right hand, through the
break in the dank wall of leaves, shone the Sun, looking
earthward, luminous and blinding human sight like the gaze
of God.

The light from the west fell upon Erroll, touching the
fair locks of his silken hair, and shining in his azure eyes as
they looked up at the sunny skies, where a bird was soaring
and circling in space, happy through its mere sense and joy
of life. On Strathmore's face the deep shadows slanted,
leaving it as though cast in bronze, chill and tranquil as that
of a marble god's, each feature set into the merciless repose
of one immovable purpose. Their faces were strangely con-
trasted, for the serenity of the one was that of a man who
fearlessly awaits an inevitable doom, the serenity of the other
that of a man who mercilessly deals out an implacable fate;
and while in the one those present saw but the calmness of
courage and of custom, in the other they vaguely shrank from
a new and an awful meaning. For beneath the suave smile
of the Duellist, they read the intent of the Murderer.

The night was nigh at hand, soon the day must be gathered

to the past, such harvest garnered with it as men's hands had sown throughout its brief twelve hours, which are so short in span, yet are so long in sin.

"LET NOT THE SUN GO DOWN UPON YOUR WRATH!"

There, across the west, in letters of flame, the warning of the Hebrew scroll was written on the purple skies; but he who should have read them stood immutable yet insatiate, with the gleam of a tiger's lust burning in his eyes, the lust when it scents blood; the lust that only slakes its thirst in life.

They fronted one another, those who had lived as brothers; while at their feet babbled the poisonous waters, and on their right hand shone the evening splendour of the sun. Their eyes met, and in the gaze of the one was a compassionate pardon, but in the gaze of the other a relentless lust.

The duel was *à la parrière;* and the lot of the seconds' toss-up fell to Strathmore; giving him the right to fire first. They turned, and stood back to back; waiting the signal.

"One!"

The word fell down upon the silence, and the hiss of a shrill cicala echoed to it like a devil's laugh.

And the sun sank slowly downward beyond the barrier of purple cloud, passing away from earth.

"Two!"

Again the single word dropped out upon the stillness, marking the flight of the seconds; again the hoot of the cicala echoed it, laughing hideously from its noisome marsh.

And the sun sank slowly, still slowly, nearer and nearer to its shroud of mist, bearing with it all that lingered of the day.

"Three!"

The white death-signal flickered in the breeze, and the last golden rays of the sun were still above the edge of the storm-cloud.

There was yet time.

But the warning was not read: there was the assassin's devilish greed within Strathmore's soul, the assassin's devilish smile upon his lips; the calmness of his face never changed; the tranquil pulse of his wrist never quickened, the remorseless gleam of his eyes never softened. The doom written in his look never relaxed. He wheeled round—in seeming, carelessly, as you may turn to aim at carrion birds—but his shot sped home.

One moment Erroll stood erect, his fair hair blowing in the wind, his eyes full open to the light; then—he reeled slightly backward, raised his right arm, and fired in the air. The bullet flew far and harmless amidst the forest foliage, his pistol dropped, and without sign or sound he fell down upon the sodden turf, his head striking against the earth with a dull echo, his hands drawing up the rank herbage by the roots, as they closed convulsively in one brief spasm.

He was shot through the lungs.

The sun sank out of sight, leaving a dusky, sultry gloom to brood over the noxious brakes and sullen stagnant waters, leaving the world to Night, as fitting watch and shroud of Crime; and those who stood there were stricken with a ghastly horror, paralysed by a vague and sudden awe, for they knew that they were in the presence of death, and that the hand which had dealt it was the hand of his chosen friend. But he, who had slain him, more coldly, more pitilessly than the merciful amongst us would slay a dog, stood unmoved in the shadow, with his ruthless calm, his deadly serenity, which had no remorse as it had had no mercy, while about his lips there was a cold and evil smile, and in his eyes gleamed the lurid flame of a tiger's triumph— the triumph when it has tasted blood, and slaked its thirst in life.

"*Fuyez!—il est mort!*"

The words, uttered in his ear by Valdor, were hoarse and almost tremulous; but he heard and assented to them unmoved. An exultant light shone and glittered in his eyes; he had avenged himself and her! Life was the sole price that his revenge had set; his purpose had been as iron, and his soul was as bronze. He went nearer, leisurely, and stooped and looked at the work of his hand. In the gloom the dark-red blood could yet be clearly seen, slowly welling out and staining the clotted herbage as it flowed, while one stray gleam of light still stole across, as if in love and pity, and played about the long fair hair which trailed among the grass.

Life still lingered, faintly, flickeringly, as though loth to leave for ever that, which one brief moment before, had been instinct with all its richest glory; the eyes opened wide once more, and looked up to the evening skies with a wild, delirious, appealing pain, and the lips which were growing white and drawn, moved in a gasping prayer:

"Oh God! I forgive—I forgive.—He did not know——!"

Then his head fell back, and his eyes gazed upward without sight or sense, and murmuring low a woman's name, "Lucille! Lucille!" while one last breath shivered like a deep-drawn sigh through all his frame—he died.

And his murderer stood by to see the shudder convulse the rigid limbs, and count each lingering pang-calm, pitiless, unmoved, his face so serene in its chill indifference, its brutal and unnatural tranquillity, whilst beneath the drooped lids, his eyes watched with the dark glitter of a triumphant vengeance, the last agony of the man whom he had loved, that the two who were with him in this hour shrank involuntarily from his side, awed more by the Living than by the Dead. Almost unconsciously they watched him, fascinated by a dumb horror, as he stooped and severed a long flake of hair that was soiled by the dank earth and wet with the dew; unarrested they let him turn away with the golden lock in his hand and the fatal calm on his face, and move to the spot where his horse was waiting. The beat of the hoofs rang muffled on the turf, growing fainter and fainter as the gallop receded. Strathmore rode to her whose bidding had steeled his arm; and whose soft embrace would be his reward; rode swift and hard, with his hand closing fast on the promised pledge of his vengeance, while behind him, in the shadows of the falling night, lay the man whom he had once loved, whom he had now slain, with the light of early stars breaking pale and cold, to shine upon the oozing blood as it trailed slowly in its death-stream through the grasses, staining red the arid turf.

And the sun had gone down upon his wrath.

CHAPTER XXV.

The Message from the Dead.

THE golden curl of the dead man's hair lay in her lap, in pledge and proof that her bidding had been done, that his revenge was taken; and she stooped over her lover, this Messalina with her cheek of childlike bloom, this Circe with her glance of gazelle-softness, and wreathed her white arms about him, and leaned on his her fragrant lips. And he was happy!—ay, as the drunkard is in the reeling madness of his revel, as the opium-eater is in the delirious insanities of his excitation; he was happy with this guilt at his door, with this life on his soul, while the tresses of her hair swept soft against his cheek, and the languor of her eyes looked back into his own.

Remorse was not upon him,—she, even as she was his idol, became also his conscience and his God. His honour had bent like a green withe in her hands, and crime had no sting since it was just and sweet in her sight.

The past hour left no trail of its horror, the death summoned at his will followed him with no reproach; as he had been without mercy, so he was now without remorse: the ghastly breath of the grave did not chill him in the dreamy warmth of her kisses, and in his heart the plague-spot of crime was not felt while it beat upon hers. As a man after deep draughts of strong wine has all memory dizzily drowned, but every sense subtilely heated and roused, so the fierce passions of which he had drunk so deeply in one brief twelve hours had dulled all conscience, and fanned his blood to flame. For her sake, at her bidding, he had steeped his soul

in the guilt of murder; and so much the more deeply as it
doomed him, so much the sweeter grew his love. And the
silken gold of the dead man's hair lay there, wet and soiled
with the night dews; and he, the Living, gave it no glance
of pity, no shudder of remorse, but looked up only to the
eyes of the enchantress, and only drew her rich lips closer to
his own.

What though a hell had yawned before him for this
deed?—his heaven lay here in a woman's soft embrace.
What were God or man to him?—*she* smiled upon his sin.

"Strathmore!"

Low whispered, the name struck on his ear as he passed
the open window of a corridor leading back to his own room,
in the grey of the early dawn. The casement looked upon
the gardens, and in the faint light he saw the figure of a man
standing there below.

"Strathmore!"

At the second whisper he turned towards the embrasure,
and leaned out:

"Who are you?"

"I—hush!" said the speaker, in whom he now recognised
Erroll's second. "Wake no one, or they will wonder why I
come like a thief in the twilight. As I saw you pass the
window, I thought it better to call you than to rouse the
house. I came to tell you that to-night's affair may be the
subject of inquiry, and that it would be wise for you to get
out of France."

"Pshaw! All I do I defend."

He spoke carelessly and contemptuously where he leaned
against the embrasure, looking down on the speaker, who,
although his adversary's second, had been an acquaintance
also of his own.

"As you choose, I only tell you. Sir Arthur has rallied
enough to be furious in his grief. For myself, I shall go
across the frontier. I have no fancy to wait for the fracas."

"That will be as you please, but it cannot concern me."

The other looked up at him in the light of the new-risen sun, with something of that feeling, which had made him shrink from the man who had stood with a pitiless smile on his lips, to watch the death throes slacken and grow still. He was a soldier, and thought little of a life taken or spared, but even he shuddered at Strathmore's calm indifference, whilst as yet but the short space of one summer's night stretched betwixt so dark a tragedy and its author.

"No," he said, bluntly. "I believe you take no concern save in what touches *yourself!* But Erroll bade me, if he fell, give you this; it is all he left to my charge—save another for a woman in England."

He lifted his hand, standing on the stone coping, and held up a letter. Strathmore stretched and took it, and the other turned away, without more words, and strode back across the lawn in the gloaming.

The sun had risen high enough for the writing to be clear, and as his eyes fell on the superscription, where he stood alone in the deserted corridor while all around him slept, for the first time his own revenge recoiled back on him; he remembered how the life which he had taken had once been perilled for his own; he remembered how this man had loved him! The suddenness of this unlooked-for message from the dead, awoke memories which staggered his merciless and immutable calm. He crushed the letter in his hold unread, and, leaving the house, went out into the dawn instead of going to his chamber; in that moment he wished to shun even the gaze of hirelings—in that moment, ere he read what the hand now lifeless had written, he felt he must have about him the fresh clear air of morning. For,

> Our acts our angels are, or good or ill,
> The fatal shadows which walk by us still;

and already the doom, wrought by his own sin, was following in his trail.

He walked onward in the solemn stillness of that early day, fresh from the lascivious sweetness of a guilty love, and the furious delight in a brutal vengeance,—walked onward

through the warm white mists of the morning, through silent
solitudes of woodland, crushing the packet in his grasp unread, until the rapid rush of the river at his feet arresting his
course made him note whither be went. Then he paused,
and wrenched open the letter of the man who had fallen by
his hand.

And what he read was this :

"YOUR OWN ACT has made more words between us impossible; to a blow there can be but one answer. But I write
this in the hazard that in a few hours I may have ceased to
live; when I am dead you may hear without dishonour to me
that you have wronged me from first to last. Were it alone
for the sake of our past friendship, I would not let you go
through life holding me the liar and betrayer you now do; it
were to debase and pollute all mankind, in my person, and
in your sight. What you believe I see plainly, how you
were duped to believe it I can conjecture well enough; it is
sufficient that by your belief you do me the foulest wrong
that ever a lie worked. It is she who betrayed you, not I.
I loved her—true! with that vile passion which levels us to
brutes: but, before God, Strathmore, I write my oath to you
that to that love I never yielded; it was she who tempted, I
who resisted. In this must lie the root of the revenge upon
myself which she now takes in goading and duping your
jealousy, till you believe you see in me a rival who would
have treacherously supplanted you. Last night, in warning
you of Marion Vavasour's inconstancy, I spoke no slander as
you thought; when you taunted me for proof, I could have
given it you on the word of one who, as you well know, never
lied.   Only a few moments before I had been alone with her,
when the Duc left, in the supper-room; alone, with no shield
between my hateful passion, that sprang up unawares, ripe
as it was rank, and her own loveliness, that lured me with
glances, with smiles, with hinted words, with every devilish
divine temptation. . . . My God! you know the snare—you

succumbed to it. Pity me, forgive me, if, for an instant, I almost forgot all bonds of honour to you; if, for an instant, I fell so low as to remember nothing save that her eyes wooed my love and confessed her own—save, that what I loathed while I coveted it, might be mine at my will. Pity me, forgive me, you who know her accursed sorceress beguilings, her subtle tempting that lies in the languor of a glance, in the passing fragrance of her hair! My weakness endured *but* an instant; then I broke from her while I had strength; I left her while the first whispers of love stole from her lips. At the moment I encountered you, I strove to warn you of the worthlessness of the woman on whose love you staked your life and—fool that I was! when you gibed and taunted me for proof, I shrank from striking you the deadly blow; I chose rather to let you think of me as you would, than force you to own the right by which I spoke, since I must have bought my vindication at such cost to you. Early on the following morning her page brought me a note from Lady Vavasour. I send it to you; it will serve to show you how subtlely, how poetically, she shrouds her wanton infidelities, this double-traitress to her lovers and her lord! I wrote her back words that she will never pardon me. Suffice it, that they were such as stripped her amours of their delicate gloss, to show them to her in their own naked light; such as refused her love for your sake, and rebuked her treachery in your name and my own. Out of her presence, and in the calmness of morning, I had strength to do thus much in the right path: God knows I have wandered from it often enough! This is the brief entire truth. My lips never spoke a lie; my hand would scarce write one, when, for aught I know, I may be within an hour of my death. I write it because I could not endure that, throughout your life, you should hold my memory tainted with such thrice-damned treachery as you have attributed to me; and it will spare, rather than inflict on you, added pain, since sooner or later you must learn that this woman's passion has fled, though her pride of dominion over you still lingers, and you will suffer less to know it thus, than to track it first in the rivalry, and triumph, of some living foe.

"Now let me make you one request in as few words as I can; for though, after what has passed, I should compel you to meet me were you my brother by blood, I still choose rather to ask this boon of you than of any other. The young girl whom you once saw with me in the elm-walk at White Ladies—perhaps you have forgot the circumstance—was not my mistress, as you naturally thought, but my wife. Three years ago, we met by a strange accident, while I was staying at your house, during your absence. She was the daughter of an exiled Hungarian noble, who had taken refuge near the abbey, in obscurity and poverty. She was in the early grief of her father's recent loss, a mere child in years, singularly lovely, and almost destitute. I loved, and I soon taught her to love. To have offered her dishonour, in her trustful and defenceless innocence, would have *been* dishonour. I married her, but secretly, and have kept it secret even from you, partly for entanglements, that you know hampered me, partly because of my creditors, chiefly because, as you are aware, the knowledge of such a marriage would have ensured my certain disinheritance by Sir Arthur. She has lived at White Ladies, still under her father's name of de Vocqsal, and your almost constant absence on the Continent prevented your hearing whatever rumours might be afloat regarding our connexion. She is very dear to me; yet I have but ill recompensed such love as she has borne me. My death will leave Lucille and her child penniless and unprotected; what I would now ask of you is, as far as may lie in your power, to shield her from the bitterness she is so little fitted to brave. This, then, is the trust I leave you, Strathmore; you will let her find in you a sure and faithful friend; you will make to her atonement for the wrong you have done to me; and if her child, now in its infancy, ever live to womanhood, I would wish that in years to come you should speak to her sometimes of her father, but never let her become aware that it is by your hand I fell. Should it be decreed that I die thus, I will not say, 'Know no remorse,' for that were to wish you devil, not man; but I do say to you, believe this, that neither now nor in the most abhorred hours that your mad passion for the wanton adulteress who has parted us, ever caused me, have I felt bitterness to you. 'I would that it had been an open enemy who had done me this dishonour, and not thou, my brother, my guide, my own familiar friend;' but—since thus it has chanced—take my last words as you would take the oath of a dying man. I forgive you fully all that has already passed, all that may yet be to come. If I die, remember—it will be in peace with you.

"BERTIE ERROLL."

This was the message of the dead.

Standing in the morning light, whose reddening sun-rays, streaming on the page, lit up each word till it seemed written in blood, Strathmore read—read on to the last line.

Then a shrill, hoarse cry, shuddering rang through all the forest silence, greeting the early day as it uprose—the cry of a great agony—and throwing his arms above his head, he fell, like a drunken man, down upon the sodden earth.

CHAPTER XXVI.

"Whoso has sown the Whirlwind shall be Reaper of the Storm."

MARION VAVASOUR stood on the balcony of her dressing-room looking down on the rose-gardens below, and leaned her white arms upon the bronze scroll-work, and let her Eastern cymar of snowy silk float at will upon the summer wind, and with a sunny laughter sweetly glancing in her eyes gazed at the mists afar off, or downward to where her love-birds were shaking the dew from their wings. Yonder, beneath the roof that was within her sight, where the early sun-rays played about the lips that were sealed to silence, and the eyes which could never more open to their light, lay the dead, slain at her whisper, to sate her revenge;—yonder,

under the forest-shadows, whose outline she traced from her
rose-hung balcony, a living man wrestled with his agony, his
soul tainted with a murderer's guilt, because her kiss had
moved him to its work, her word aroused him to its hell-born
passions. But the knowledge did not cast one shade upon
her brow, did not scare away for one brief hour the smile
that wantoned on her lips; nay, the knowledge was dear to
her, since it was proof and tribute to her power. For in this
dazzling delicate creature was the cruelty of the beast of the
desert.

The full light of the day, now fully risen for some hours,
bathed her in its warmth, whilst clusters of her favourite
flowers clung above and below her in their perfumy profusion,
till she seemed framed in roses; her floating dress showed all
the voluptuous outline of her form; her rich hair lay lightly
on her shoulders, glancing in the sun;——and thus, in her
proud loveliness, she was seen by the man she had betrayed.

It had been better for her then that death had stricken
her in that hour. Woe as her beauty had wrought for others,
it had never worked deadlier destruction than that which it
now brought herself.

Suddenly, between her and the sunlight, a shadow fell.
She turned, with the gay challenge of her triumphant
smile, the silvery folds of her robes sweeping the leaves of
the roses till they fell in a fragrant shower; then, for the first
time in her shadowless life, the smile faded from off those
laughing lips, and the pallor of a ghastly terror blanched the
rich bloom from her face. She saw the man whom she had
fooled with the foul simulation of an undying love, and whom
her breath, with its traitorous caresses, had wooed to the
bottomless depths of crime. And she saw that he knew her
aright at last—saw that there are moments in human life
which transform men to fiends, leaving them no likeness of
themselves; moments in which the bond slave, goaded to
insanity, turns and rends his tyrant.

With a spring like a bloodhound's, Strathmore overleapt the barrier which parted them, and caught her in his grasp, bruising the white skin which he had once deemed too fair for the summer winds to breathe on as they blew. And a deadly fear came on her, for she knew that now her voice would have no power to quell the tempest—the voice which had lured him to crime! She knew that now her loveliness could have no sway to bring him to her feet—the loveliness which was but one fell lie!

As the bloodhound seizes on its prey, his hand crushed her there where she stood; his face was haggard, his eyes were bloodshot, and alight with lurid flame; his hair wet and clotted with the damp sweat of anguish; his dress disordered, and stained with the soil of the earth, and the dews of the morning. Few could have recognised him in the wreck one crime had wrought—one hour worked. In his agony he was mad—I speak it literally—mad; with its hideous riot surging in his brain, and reeling through his blood. And in the sunlight he saw the mocking accursed loveliness, which, even as a fiend in angel guise, had drawn him on into an abyss of infamy, and stained his soul with the curse of fratricide.

He crushed her in his arms, bruising her white bosom and her delicate limbs; and his voice, which had lost almost all human sound, broke out with a loud hissing whisper:

"Traitress—murderess! I will have life for life! It is the old Jew law—God's ordinance!"

Through the stillness of the summer morning his laugh rang with horrible mirth, his soul, drunk with one sin, was athirst for more—athirst to trample out this divine and devilish thing which he had worshipped, down into the darkness of the tomb; to avenge his own betrayal, and the betrayal of the dead, on the woman who had trepanned both, with her wanton's love, her serpent's cruelty. His hot breath scorched her face; his eyes, bright with the light of insanity, glared into her own; his hands twisted in the shower of her shining hair, that golden web which had meshed him in its toils; he held her powerless to break away from the worst that he might work, while

the fair hues of her face blanched white, and her voice rose
in a shriek of abject terror.

"Oh Heaven! I shall die—I shall die! *You* would not kill
me, Strathmore!"

Again, in its mirth, his laugh broke out; he was delirious
in his agony.

"Why not? Why not, if devils *can* die? You have done
murderer's work, you shall have a murderer's doom!"

Held in his grip, she could not free herself; clenched there
as in a vice of iron, she could not escape from whatsoever he
might mete out to her, and in his maddened cheated love, his
felon guilt, his tortures of remorse, he knew not what he did;
he was brutal and conscienceless as any beast of prey raven-
ing for blood. He only saw, in the burning glare of the
mocking sunlight, the beauty which had betrayed him; he
only felt the forest-brute's fierce craving thirst for life. And
she knew that she was in his power;—she knew that her slave
was now her master. Sickening with terror, trembling,
quivering, stifled, she wrestled in his grasp, while her voice
moaned out a piteous cry:

"Oh, Strathmore! My God!—have mercy, mercy!"

Closer and closer he clenched her in his anguish, her
amber hair tangled in his arms, her form pressed in his hold
until she moaned with pain, while his laugh rang out again,
like Damien's in the torture of the fires:

"I will give you such mercy as you gave:—no other!"

And she knew that death was nigh her now—death from
the hands of the man she had fooled, and goaded, and
betrayed; in his iron strength her delicate frame was frail as
flax which the winds can break in twain, and as helpless to
his will. One pressure of his fingers on her throat, and its
breath would be stilled for ever; one blow from his hand
upon her fair veined temples, and the death she had meted
out would be her portion.

With all the preternatural strength which is begotten
from a ghastly terror, she wrestled and panted in his hold, as
the bird in the hand of the snarer; as easily might she have

sought to escape from a vice of steel that had locked her in
its jaws, as seek to wrench herself free from the deadly grip
of the man whose outraged love made him a fiend, whose
vain remorse made him a madman.

A sickness of mortal fear came over her; a mist blinded
her eyes, shutting out the light of day; a loud noise surged
in her ear, and beat about her brain. He only saw in the
glaring sun-rays the face which he had worshipped—the face
which had lured him to his sin; he only knew but one brute
impulse to crush and trample out this loveliness, where never
more could it reproach him—where never more could others
gaze upon, and rejoice in, it. She was dying—dying by his
hand!—without power to summon all those who lay within
her call; without strength to break from him to where safety,
succour, defence were all close, only parted from her by the
velvet hangings of her door! There, without, lay the sunny
peopled earth; here, nigh at hand, was the household which
obeyed her lightest word: yet, powerless, voiceless, im-
prisoned in his grip, she must die, without a sign, without a
cry, like the fawn which is choked by the hound's death-
grapple!

And her eyes gazed up to him with a wild appealing pain;
—that look smote his strength like a sudden blow. He had
seen it when the sun had set, in the sightless eyes of the
dead.

His frame shivered, his limbs grew powerless, his sinews
paralysed, his nerves stricken strengthless; he threw her from
him with a sudden cry, hurling her fragile form from his
arms, as the winds hurl a broken flower from out their path.

"Death is too much mercy for you! You shall *live* to
suffer——"

And, leaving her where she lay in her bruised and quivering loveliness, Strathmore reeled out into the scorching sunlight, that seemed to glare upon his sight and scathe his brow
like fire—reeled, staggering like a drunken man, his eyes
blind, his reason giddy, with the horrible riot of threatening
delirium. For on his soul was the curse of Cain.

Marion Vavasour told none of that hour of jeopardy. When he hurled her from him she fell insensible, and her attendants, finding her thus, deemed it a swoon or syncope, and she let the error pass, undisputed. Too much was intertwined with that horrible conflict for her lips to be those which unfolded its story. And on the morrow, when she lay on her delicate couch shrouded in laces, and silks, and cashmeres, her eyes but the lovelier for the dark circle beneath them, her face but the fairer for its fragile whiteness and the languor of indisposition, Monseigneur le Duc d'Etoiles and Monsignore Villáflor, admitted to her cabinet de toilette, thought they had never beheld her more divine in her most dazzling moments, than in this illness, which she allowed that the tragedy in which her name was involved, had brought on her through its shock and its terror.

"Cecil Strathmore has killed his friend, you know? It is fearful—it is terrible! It has shattered all my nerves," she said, with a delicate shiver of terror, to the prince and the bishop. "That horrible story!—do not talk of it any more, I beseech you—I entreat you, sire. Poor Cecil! My lord always said he would commit some crime or other some day. They quarrelled about me, you say—perhaps! But it was *bien bête* if they did. And poor Bertie Erroll was so handsome! It is such a pity that the Strathmores' passions were always dangerous!"

And Marion Vavasour sighed, and shuddered again with that delicate *tressaillement*, and stirred her chocolate, and stroked the snowy curls of her lion-dog, and languidly tossed some perfume over her jewelled fingers, and asked what they thought of Scribe's new comedy and George Sand's fresh novel; while Monseigneur and Monsignore each alike congratulated himself that her long unbroken liaison was evidently snapped asunder with this Bois scandal, of which all Paris was talking, and that its rupture had left a fair field open to all new aspirants.

Remorse was not in her; she knew it not; and she was

well content that Paris should have nothing else to discourse
of, before midnight in the Salons, and after midnight in the
Cercles, but this tragedy in the Deer Park, whose fatal end
was but sign and seal of her power. Two countries babbled
of that Helen-like beauty which drove men to madness—

as when through ripen'd corn,
By driving winds, the crackling flames are borne.

What mattered it at what price her superb triumphs were
won?

It was but once or twice in solitude that, remembering,
with the icy dread of its awful danger shivering afresh
through all her veins, the peril of the death which had so
nigh encompassed her, she heard again hissing in her ear,
with its ghastly laugh, that menace of the future: "Death is
too much mercy for you! You shall *live* to suffer!" It was
only then that, vaguely and with a nameless dread, Marion
Vavasour, in her glad and glorious omnipotence, feared, with
prescient terror, that law inexorable which has written,
"Whoso sows the whirlwind, shall be reaper of the storm!"

CHAPTER XXVII.

Dies Iræ.

THE full sweet light of the summer day fell into the
chamber of the dead, where they had lain him down and left
him, in the deep stillness that no footfall stirred, no voice
disturbed, and no love watched, save that of a little spaniel
which had crept into his breast and flew at those who sought
to move her from her vigil, and crouched there trembling and
moaning piteously.

The sun of another day had risen, waking the earth to its
toil and the children to their play; lifting the drooped bells
of the closed flowers, and rousing the butterfly to flutter in
the light; giving back to the birds their song, to the waters
their sparkle, to the blue seas their laughing gleam; bringing
to all the world its resurrection from the silence and the

gloom of night. But here where the sun fell, touching his cheek to warmth, his hair to gold, it had no spell to waken: life was left to the insect stirring in the grasses, to the leaf flickering in the wind, to the spider weaving in the sunshine, —but life was robbed from him!

Through the long day the light found its way into the darkened room, and wandered lovingly about the limbs, with their superb and stately stature, which lay powerless and stricken; and about the face, with its rich, woman-like beauty, where the fair, luxuriant hair was clotted and soiled with the black trail of blood; and where the grey hue of that Corruption which knows no pity in its theft, no mercy in its march, already was stealing on its ghastly way.

The day was nigh its close when the hired watcher, dully sleeping at his post, started in affright as a voice fell on his ear:

"Let me pass!"

"Pass! Not *there*!"

"Yes—there."

At the reply the man looked up to scan the stranger who sought to enter the chamber of the dead; and as he saw his face, although it was wholly unfamiliar to him, shuddered at the look it wore, and at the light that glittered in the eyes.

"Why—why!" he faltered. "What claim have you! Who are you!"

"I am his murderer! Stand by!"

And at the hideous calmness of the answer the man involuntarily sickened and shuddered and fell back; and an iron grasp thrust him aside like a cowering dog, and closed the door upon him and barred him out.

Strathmore was alone with the dead.

And he stood by him, even as in the virgin years of the young world the First Murderer stood beside the brother whom he had slaughtered in his fair and gracious manhood, because the seething madness and the brutal hate of jealousy and vengeance had made a ghastly crime seem sweet and holy in his sight. The sin of Cain was on his soul—and even as Cain heard in the awful silence the voice of God calling on him for the life that he had hurled from earth, so he heard it now, as in his agony he shrieked aloud to the dead to waken, and free him from his curse!—to arise and live again, so that he should not bear this doom through life and through eternity! And his own voice, as it echoed back upon the stillness, left silence as the mocking answer of his prayer, that silence which must for ever stretch betwixt the dead and him.

He shuddered in the sultry warmth of day, like one who shivers in dank, icy waters; and stood looking down upon the white, serene face, and the hair that was blackened with blood, looking, with the dulled, paralysed stupor of remorse.

This man had loved him, had suffered for him, had borne with sacrifice and wrong for his sake, had cleaved to him closer than a brother,—and he had slaughtered him as we slaughter a brute!

Yesterday living, in all the fulness, the strength, the beauty, the rich rejoicing glory of his manhood, and to-day dead—dead!—carrion that lay sightless to the sunshine, senseless to all sound, powerless to lift his hand against the feeblest insect that should begin the fell work of the tomb, useless save to be thrust away by hasty hands out of the remembrance of men into the dark and brutal silence of the grave.

Standing there beside him, a terror, such as falls upon men in their own death-hour, when every forgotten sin stands out to damn them, fell upon his murderer; rending asunder the iron of a pitiless nature; striking to dust, as the lightning shivers steel, the unyielding strength which had refused to know remorse, and had gazed with a chill smile upon the agonies of death: smiting down upon his knees, as with the wrath of God, the mortal whose passions had usurped God's judgment and forestalled God's summons, who had dared to mete out life and death as though he were not Man but Deity.

Now for the first hour he realised what he had done:—
and struck by it as by a blow, he staggered and fell, his
head bowed, his arms stretched out, the dews of a mortal
anguish thick upon his brow, his brain on fire with the horrible surging of the blood, that, like a pent-up flood, seemed
bursting to break from bondage.

Suddenly in that dread silence where he knelt beside the
bier, there arose, joyous and melodious, the evening song of
the birds without, where they fluttered amidst the ilex leaves;
and the tender sound struck on his ear as a knife strikes upon
bare quivering nerves. In those frail things, born for a summer's span, which could be crushed by a young child's feeble
grasp, the great mystery of Life was left; and here—*here*—
his hand had shattered it for ever!   A lifetime of remorse
could not restore what he had destroyed, and trampled out,
in the brute fury of one crime.

That sound broke his stupor, and saved him from madness; his chest rose and fell as though heaving against bands
of steel; the blood beat and surged about his brain; the iron
of his nature broken asunder, yielded and gave way, and one
deep gasping sob quivered in the air as he sank forward,
calling in his blind agony on the name of the dead.

There, beside the man whom he had loved and murdered,
they found him when, far towards the night, they broke open
the barred door—found him lying senseless.

For two months the wise men who gathered about his bed
because he had gold and rank, and sought to drive away the
retribution which followed a fell crime, with the poor miserable herbs and poisons that their pharmacopœia taught them,
held his life in danger, and called his peril by a lengthy
name.

More briefly, it was still but the mad beating of the im-
prisoned blood, which, like the waves of a sea, flooded all the
chambers of the mind, already filled with distorted thoughts
and abhorred sounds, the offspring, not of the fantasia of
delirium, but worse—of the memories of guilt. Worse; for the

madman, or the fever-stricken, made sane, leaving his bed, leaves far behind him all which turned it into hell; but when the lurking fire in Strathmore's blood had, flame-like, of itself burned down into exhaustion (or, as the wise men better loved to phrase it, when "*they* had cured him"), with him arose every dread shape that had made night horrible and day sickly; and with him they passed out into the world, and mingled with the things of daily life, and followed him—denying him solitude, forbidding him rest. In those awful hours when but one of two issues had seemed inevitable for him—insanity or death—*these* had been ever before him; the Sorceress, with the wanton glamour of her divine loveliness, whose kiss seemed ever scorching on his lips, whose laugh seemed ever mocking on his ear; and the Dead whom he had slaughtered at her bidding, whose dying sigh quivered for ever on the air, and whose face, with the eyes wide open to the light, with their last look of wild appealing pain, for ever was before him.

When he arose and went forth again amongst men, with what seemed to the world, which had thrilled with the horror of his story, an unaltered bearing, an unnatural negligence and calm, these were with him still—spectres of the passion which had betrayed him, of the crime with which his soul was stained. Before the tribunal of God, in the horrors of night and solitude, when none were by to stand between him and the sin which made his conscience its own hell, between him and the anguish which rioted still for this woman's lost loveliness, his chastisement grew more ghastly with every day which dawned, with every hour that passed. It was like the chastisement of Orestes, followed by those dread shapes which tracked him through his doom, and lay beside him even on the threshold of the altar of God, watching him while he slept, so that his sleep was peaceless; while he waked, so that his day was joyless; while he prayed, so that his prayer was fruitless—those Eumenides which are but type and figure of the Passions.

There are natures which in their anguish seek the fellowship of their kind, as a wounded deer will seek his herd; there are others which shun it, as the stricken eagle soars aloft to die alone, howsoever the blood be dropping from his broken wings. Strathmore's nature, proud, tenacious, un-yielding as iron, was the last. Pitiless himself, he abhorred pity, and if he yielded little mercy to misery, he asked none for his own. Therefore the world, when he rose from his bed and entered it once more, marvelled at his heartlessness, and deemed him unchanged, untouched. So the world, great liar though it be, is oftentimes deceived!

Unchanged!—if the iron that has passed through the fire be unchanged after the furnace which has molten it in its scorch till it has bent like a river reed, then was he so: not else. All that was evil in him had leaped up like a lion from his lair, and now could never more be drugged to sleep; all of softness which his guilty love had lent his nature had been swept aside in the whirlwind, and its pitiless strength had centred in but one purpose, one desire, one craving: that of vengeance. For his character was one of those in which cruelty is twin-born with suffering, and which, having tasted of crime as the tiger blood, seeks more, and blots out sin by sin. His curse had been born of his vengeance; yet to crush out his agony he craved vengeance yet again. For this man, who had held himself his own god to mould his destiny at will, who had deemed he ruled his desires under iron curb, and who had looked on in cold disdain while others suffered or rejoiced, indifferent to joy as he was steeled to pain, en-dured tortures such as weaker, gentler natures never know— let them thank Heaven for their exemption! However guilty and born of the senses his love had been, he had worshipped to devotion the woman who had betrayed him; the very air she breathed had been sacred to him; he had loved her with passionate truth; he had been jealous of the very winds that played amongst her hair; he would have staked his life upon her fidelity, even as he did stake his honour and his peace. What marvel that *now* "the hate wherewith he hated her was yet greater than the love wherewith he had loved her!"

Her hand had hurled him into an abyss of guilt; her kiss had breathed upon his lips a curse that must for ever lie there; her tempting had allured and betrayed him into crime, which however the law and the world freed him from all stain, marked him out for ever in his own sight and in the sight of truth—a murderer.

And go where he would his curse pursued him. In the watches of night it wakened him, and he cried out in its agony with the cold sweat dank upon his brow. In the chill dawn it uprose with him, till the light of day looked hideous, and made him turn from it as from the gaze of an accusing angel. Passing the open doors of church or cathedral it pursued him, for the hot sun seemed streaming down upon the written Law which guards the sanctity of life, and forbids its golden cord to be cut asunder by the hand of man. Amidst the peopled world it haunted him, till the purple wine in his glass looked red with blood, and through the riotous laughter of brilliant revel he heard ever in his ear the piteous shiver of one dying sigh. In the gay glare of gaslight, or in the grey shadows of the twilight, in the rush of crowds or in the stillness of his chamber, he saw the face of the dead; he saw the shudder of the laboured breath, the anguish of the death-spasm, the life-blood winding slowly, slowly, in its dark and slimy trail amidst the grasses, and soaking the fair and trailing hair. Like Cain's had been his crime; like Cain's was now his chastisement. And the brand burned not the less, but the more, upon his soul because it was not written on his brow for men to read.

CHAPTER XXVIII.

Requiem Æternam.

IT was a damp, yellow autumn night, with the melancholy sighing of winds through the dense Druidic woods, and white vapours rising from the meres and estuaries to sweep chillily across the sward. A profound silence reigned over White

Ladies—a silence in which the "calling of the sea" could be heard from afar off, where the Western Ocean washed its time-worn reefs, and each fall of the yet green leaves trembled audibly through the stillness. And in this silence, complete as that of mountain solitudes, save for the moaning murmur of the restless seas and the weary lulling of the winds as they swept through the pathless forests, a man on foot, and alone, took his way through the woods on an errand that it is rarely given to mortals to fulfil: he went to atone to the Living for a wrong to the Dead. Fool!

We can destroy, but we cannot restore; and the soul may labour futilely through the length of weary years, to upbuild what one brief hour of its passions has sufficed to shatter into dust. Sin ever comes obedient to man's bidding; Expiation, fugitive and fleeting, mocking him, eludes his grasp.

He walked through the gloom of the descending night, with the pale skies above him, and in his hand the dead man's letter. It seemed to him that that which he must say to the one whom he had widowed in her youth would be better said beneath the shroud of night than in the garish day. He went on alone, while at intervals a water-bird started at his step, and the hoot of an owl pierced the silence; went on till he reached the dwelling to which they had directed him, where it stood shut away by forest trees from the lonely road. No living thing was near; the faint bark of a dog baying in the distance the only sound which broke upon the night, while the moon shone fitfully on the dark rustic porch and the lozenge-shaped panes of the casements. The door was slightly open, and since no one answered to his summons, he thrust it farther back and entered; the house seemed empty. There was no light save that of the moon's rays as they strayed in, and of a dim lamp burning above the staircase: the rooms on either side the entrance were deserted, though they bore the trace of recent occupance, and in one, as the moonbeams fell upon it, he saw the outline of an easel, and the white pages of a book open upon a music-stand. The house appeared forsaken, and he went slowly onward up the stairs, guided by the little oil-lamp that swung there, and bending his head to avoid the beams of the low ceiling. In a chamber to his left, as he mounted the staircase, he saw the glimmer of light, and followed it; he thought he had mistaken the dwelling, and here might find some who would direct him aright, for he knew but little of the by-roads and homesteads about.

He paused on the threshold of the bed-chamber, and struck lightly on the panels of the door; it was opened by a woman, who looked up at him alarmed and curious at the first moment, then dropped him a lowly reverence as she recognised the lord of the manor.

Strathmore uncovered his head and slightly advanced.

"I am Lord Cecil Strathmore. Can I see your mistress?"

She hesitated, and looked uncertain.

"I suppose so, my lord—if so be as you wish——"

"I desire to see her,—now."

The woman noticed that his voice was hoarse, and seemed to tremble slightly, and, in obedience rather to that sign than to his desire, or his rank, fell back to let him pass into the room.

"Will you walk hither, then, if you please, my lord?"

"Here?"

He followed her, wondering at the place chosen, into the dimly lit bedchamber, that to him looked as deserted as the rest of the dwelling. The woman preceded him, herself strangely silent and subdued, and drawing aside the muslin curtains of a bed which stood, in foreign mode, in an alcove, motioned him there, without a word, to her side.

At the gesture he paused involuntarily.

"Good God! is she ill?"

The servant looked at him surprised, and her voice sank to a whisper:

"Ill? I thought your lordship knew she died at dawn to-day?"

"*Died!*"

The word rattled in his throat, he staggered back against

the wall, and leaned there, his face covered, his breath thick
and laboured: another life lay heavy on his soul!

"A few weeks ago, my lord," went on the woman, while
her voice faltered and grew thick with tears, "a letter came
from Paris—leastways, it was that postmark—with a strange
writing on the envelope, and inside of it another letter from
Major Erroll. Mademoiselle Lucille read the note from my
master first, and as she read her face grew scared and awful,
with a piteous look in her eyes, like a lamb's they're leading
to slaughter. She seized the letter it had come in, and her
eyes had scarce fell on it before she gave a cry like a death-
cry, my lord, and sunk down, all cold and senseless and
crouched together."

The woman's voice stopped with a low gasping sob.

"We did all we could, my lord—indeed we did; but the
minute the doctor see her, he said as there was no hope; that
a sudden shock had shattered her brain, and that the cruel-
lest thing to wish for her was life. Oh, my lord! and so
young as she was! She never knew any one of us again, not
even the child, but lay there, weeks through, with no sense
or sight in her beautiful eyes. She sank slowly of sheer exhaustion, fading off like a flower. And, at length, at sunrise
this morning she died. I suppose your lordship will know
what has chanced to my master? His letter that she held
clenched in her hand, the doctor took and locked up with
other papers, but that in the strange handwriting was left,
and I made bold to read it. It came from a gentleman, who
wrote that Major Erroll had been shot in some duel at Paris,
and had bade him as wrote it enclose that letter to Mademoiselle Lucille if he fell. I know nothing else, my lord; I only
know that the news killed my mistress."

She ceased; and each of her homely words struck like
steel to the heart of her hearer, staining his soul with the
guilt of two lives blotted out by his hand from the Living.

Dead!

Had he known her and loved her well, the word could
scarce have echoed more hideously in his ears than now, when

it met him on the threshold mocking the atonement that he
came to offer, and striking paralysed and powerless the soul
which, in its presumption, had thought to strike the balance
with its sin, and cover crime by costless expiation. DEAD!
He leaned against the wall, with his head bowed in silence;
the direst agony that racks men in their hours of bereave-
ment was mercy to the remorse that Strathmore knew.

Then he raised his head slowly and moved towards the
couch, whilst the woman turned away so that she did not look
upon his face; she, who only had heard of his close friendship
with the dead man, thought he was moved by grief at his
friend's loss, and his rank made his sorrow sacred and unapproachable in her eyes. He drew near the bed, impelled by
some resistless impulse to look on the work that he had
wrought, urged by that strange self-chastisement which forces
us to drink to the uttermost dregs from the cup of retribution.
The pale lamp-light fell on the white and delicate couch, fit
bier and pall for the early youth thus early smitten to the
tomb, and on the bed she lay—dead in the opening summer
of her life—dead like a lily rudely broken in its bloom. The
love faithful in life was faithful unto death; she had gone to
rejoin her husband!

The lifeless form lay there in its ethereal and solemn
loveliness, her hands lightly folded on her breast, her eyes
closed as though in slumber, bearing no sign of the destroying hand, save in the hue that blanched the lips, on which,
even now, a sigh seemed set, a voiceless prayer suspended.
And in strange contrast with her mother's mournful and
motionless repose, her head pillowed on the heart that had
no throb for her, her brow resting on the arm that gave her
no embrace, her breath leaving its fresh warmth on the lips
that answered her by no caress, was a young child sleeping.
Life in its earliest bud, side by side with Life stricken in its
fullest bloom; the light gold locks mingling with the dark
unbound waves of her mother's hair, the flushed cheek, with
its rose-leaf hue, lying against the one now colourless and

cold, the soft and dreamless sleep of childhood beside the chill and hopeless slumber of the tomb.

"The child would not leave her, my lord," whispered the woman. "She sobbed herself to sleep there trying to waken her mother, and I had not the heart to stir her. Poor orphan! she is but an infant; scarcely two years old, and a love child! What will become of her!"

"Her future shall be my care."

His voice sounded dull and hoarse in his own ear as he answered the brief words; standing there, the vanity and the mockery of the atonement he had come to offer seemed to rise, and jibe and gibber in his face before the holy hush of death; and the hand of God seemed stretched to sever him from those whom he had slain, and bid him stand aloof, alone on earth, with no companion save his crime.

He was too late!

TOO LATE!

The words seemed wailing through the air—the eternal requiem of every sin; and as he stood there, with his head bowed in the faint lamplight of the chamber of death, the young child, waking from her sleep, stirred as from some joyous dream, and pushed her fair hair from her eyes, and laughed up in innocence and gladness in his face. With an involuntary gesture he spurned her from him as though some accursed thing had crossed his vision:—her lips wore her father's smile.

Stricken by that look as by the sword of an avenging angel, he turned and went out into the silent night; and in his ear the ceaseless moaning of the distant seas, and the weary cry of the winds, wandering and without rest, followed in his path with one eternal wail—"Too late! Too late!"

CHAPTER XXIX.

"Good and Evil as two Twins cleaving together."

"YOU drink the bitterness of Remorse! Taste the sweetness of Revenge."

The words stole softly to his ear in the stillness as he paced down the ruined cloisters of the Abbey, breaking in on the far-off lulling of the seas and the hoot of the nightbirds near. They pierced so strangely to the secret of his thoughts, broke in so suddenly on the solitude, in which no living thing was near him, that he started and looked up with, for one instant, what in a weaker man might have been akin to superstition. The fitful moonlight, slanting greyly in through the low pointed arches, fell across the figure of a woman leaning against the moss-grown pillar of the cloister-side; and in the dress, worn something as Arabs wear their garments, with the vivid colours which marked her tribe, and in the profound melancholy of the Sclavonian features, he recognised the Bohemian Redempta, who thus crossed his path for the third time like some fixed recurrent fate.

His steps were involuntarily arrested, and he paused, looking at her in the moonlight, whilst her gaze steadily met his, without boldness yet without fear, with something compassionate in its mournful fixity; and as she moved forward where a brighter streak of the moon-rays fell, he saw that the olive-bronze of her cheek had paled, and that her deep-set eyes were lit with a luminous gleam.

"Well!" she said, slowly, "does the kiss burn like poison now? Was sin born of the love, and a crime of the sin, and a bitter curse of the crime? Were the words of Redempta aright?"

He flung her out of his path with unconscious violence; the passions that were at work within him made this mocking travesty of them seem scarce so much insult as jibe.

"Out of my way, woman—devil—whichever you are!"

"More devil than woman, for, like you, I hate!"

The answer came slowly and bitterly from her lips with menacing meaning; the ferocity of his grasp and his words seemed to have swept unnoticed over her, and to have stirred her no more than the sweep of the forest wind past her cheek. Her intonation caught his ear, and he turned and looked more closely at her features, on which were written the dark passions of the Sclavonic character, masked by that melancholy composure natural to the Eastern blood which mingled in her veins. He saw that this woman's words were not the offspring of charlatanry if they might be those of a maniac's wanderings, and he paused, instinctively drawn by the fate which seemed to have interwoven her knowledge and her actions with his own.

Of that moment's pause she seized advantage, and leaned towards him, changing her slow and imperfect English for her own swift, mellow Czechen.

"Listen! You are an English noble, rich and full of power—I a wandering Czech, whom your laws call a tramp and your scorn calls a vagrant, and yet—yet—listen! I, the daughter of Phara, the gipsy, can give you what your wealth cannot buy nor your power command—I can give you your vengeance!"

By the faint yellow light she saw in his eyes rise the steel-like glitter of his dangerous wrath as he thrust her back.

"You are mad, or an impostor! Let me pass, woman! I am in no mood for fooling!"

A smile bitter as his own crossed her face, and she did not move from his path.

"Am I? Look in my face and see! Listen first, my lord, ere you judge! If the words of Redempta were error that she spoke to you long ago in Bohemia, then say she speaks falsely now;—if you did not find, as she foretold to you a brief while since in France, that your love, changed to hatred, will know no rest for its throes till it is slaked in revenge, then believe that she lies to you now. But if you found these things true, then judge her by them: as true is her hatred

for her whom you hate, as sure is her power to point you your
vengeance.   Say! were they truth or error? Say!"

She waited for his answer, and he was silent, where she
stood fronting him in the dim moonlight of the ruined cloister;
a bitter wrath was in his eyes, a haughty menace on his lips,
but the melodious appealing voice of the Bohemian carried
its own conviction, and in a measure disarmed his anger; her
words struck too closely home to the curse he bore within him
to be heard idly or with scorn, and the soul of this man, in
whom much that was great commingled with dark and evil
crimes, was too instinctively true to itself and to others to
sully itself by a lie even to a beggar. She saw the advantage
gained, and pursued it, her voice growing swifter, and sunk
to a whisper, whilst the untutored poetry of her natural speech
lent dignity, almost solemnity, to the Bohemian tongue in
which she spoke.

"They were truth!—and you have known their bitterness.
Listen, then! I have followed you here to your own country
to be heard, for what you vainly seek I can point out, what I
vainly crave you can work. Listen! The worm burrows,
where the tiger cannot reach; the tiger tears and rends to
death, where the worm would be trampled and crushed under
foot; let them both work together! Will you hold your revenge in your own grasp, to let its blow fall, slowly, surely,
sharply, at what hour you will?—will you shatter the jewels
from her breast, the smile from her lips, the laughter from
her eyes, the world from her feet?—will you hold her fate in
your grip, meting it out at your will, crushing all that wanton
loveliness which has betrayed you, as you might crush this
velvet-painted moth in your hand? If you will, then, my lord,
listen to the words of Redempta, who, though ahungered and
athirst, a wanderer on the earth, without home or people,
poor, and stricken, and desolate, will ask no reward of you
save one—one!—*to see her suffer!*"

Her voice sank lower and lower, stealing out in the hushed
night with a terrible and ghastly meaning; her hand clenched
unconsciously upon his arm, her eyes gleamed with a lurid

thirsty light, and the immutable and melancholy calm that veiled her features, as it veils the faces of the Easterns beneath the throes of strong emotion, only lent but a more deadly strength to the last words than the wildest curse of passion could have carried with them. To doubt her was no longer possible; and he answered her nothing where they stood in the sickly autumn moonlight, the air around them filled with the faint and mournful soughing of the sea, and the lull of the winds among the cloisters of the dead Dominicans.

"*To see her suffer!*"

It was the lust of his own soul—this merciless and brutal longing to draw within his grasp the vile and lovely thing who had been his madness and his curse, and watch his vengeance work, and fester, and eat its way into her very soul, whilst he stood calmly by, as men in ancient days stood to watch the lovely limbs of women stretched and broken on the rack. For Strathmore, who had been born pitiless, had now become cruel.

The Bohemian was silent also; she seemed to have lost all memory of his presence or her errand; and where she leaned against the broken archway, her eyes were vaguely looking onward into the darkening night, and as her hands moved unconsciously over her chain of Egyptian berries, her lips muttered still:

"*Thou* knowest how I have toiled to keep my oath. Grant me but this—but this! To see her suffer ere I die—suffer as she made *thee*. Vengeance is righteous!"

A smile more evil than the worst curse that ever lodged on human lips, came upon Strathmore's face where the watery light of the moon fell on it. Having tasted guilt, he had ceased to abhor guilt; racked by remorse, he still longed for added crime, and the fires that scathed his soul neither chastened nor purged, but only burned what was iron into steel.

"Righteous!" he echoed, while his voice was laboured with the passions roused by this woman's tempting, but suppressed by her presence. "No!—it is hellish! But what matter?— it is all that is left now! Answer me, impostor or devil, whichever you be—why do *you* hate?"

A weary smile, haggard as grief, crossed her lips for one moment, and a strange softness trembled over all her face.

"Why, why!" she cried, while the melancholy Czechen words rose plaintively upon the silence. "Why do women ever hate, sorrow, travail, rejoice, lament? Because they love! I loved—I—the vagrant, the gipsy, the fortune-teller, whom delicate women shrink from as from pollution, loved, what she—the aristocrat, the courted darling, the beauty of courts—robbed from me. I loved—oh God! it is not of the *past*. I love still! my beloved, my beloved!"

Her head drooped upon her breast with a low gasping sob, and her form trembled as though she shivered at the wind; then she threw back her head and stood erect with her stag-like gesture, the light glittering flame-like in her eyes, the dark blood burning flame-like on her brow.

"We met in Galicia. He was an Austrian soldier, a noble like yourself, and he found beauty in me, and I loved him, as the chill, pampered, luxurious women of his world never love. I was his toy, but he—he was my god! What others called my shame, was my glory; what others held my sin, was my crown; and I said in my soul, 'I have lived enough, since I have lived to be thus dear to him.' I quitted my tribe to become his mistress; and when Lennartson left the province, and went to Vienna, I followed him—and he loved me still, though where he once gave me days, he gave me hours. And when he went to Southern France, I forgot my people and my country, and followed him still thither—and still he loved me, though where he once gave me hours, he gave me moments. It is ever so with men's love! And there he saw HER. By night, as I crouched under the myrtle shrubs of her villa to see his shadow, where it fell, I saw him in her gardens; by day, hidden under the pines, watching for his horse's gallop, I saw them riding together. She beguiled him as she beguiled you; he loved her, and he was lost to me for ever!

For a while, I know scarcely how long, time was a blank to me. I remember nothing; people who tended me said afterwards that I went mad—it may have been so. The first thing I remember is, when I crawled out and found my way to his house, there was a crowd about—a crowd whispering and awe-stricken; and when I pushed my way through them, I saw him——"

A shiver ran through her frame, and her voice dropped; she waited one instant, then summoned back the proud and mournful calmness with which she spoke:

"I saw him, dead, shot by his own hand .... and those about him were saying how she had laughed and taunted him the night before, and how, maddened by her, he had left her presence and ended the life that she had made worthless. She had slain him!—and when they told her she felt no remorse for her work, but went to a ball in her diamonds and her loveliness with a laugh on her lips. And by his corpse, when it lay there, torn, pale, its beauty shattered, and its glory stricken, I took my oath to God and him to know no rest until I had revenged him!"

She paused again; and in the silence between them there sounded the melancholy lulling of the ocean like the endless ebb and flow of human passions, ever renewing, never at rest. Then her chanting and melodious tones took up their burden once more:

"And I have kept my vow. I joined my own people again; but, unseen, undreamt of by her, I have followed in her track, groping in the dark for some dropped clue, some broken thread to guide me to the redemption of my oath. She never saw me save once, when she bade her hireling strike me out of her path like a dog; yet I never let her escape me, but followed ever in her shadow, as her doom should follow a murderess. Oftentimes my errand seemed hopeless, and I said in my heart, 'Fool! can the field-lark cope with the falcon? can the emmet destroy the gazelle?— how then canst thou reach her?' Yet ever again I took patience and courage, since ever in my ear his voice seemed

crying, 'Revenge! revenge!' and when my soul fainted because of the weariness of its travail, I thought of him as I
had beheld him, driven to his death by her, with his beautiful
face shattered and ghastly, and bathed in its blood! Then I
gathered my strength afresh, and afresh pursued her, blindly,
but yet in security, for I believed that the hour would come
when the God of Vengeance at length would deliver her into
my hand. And lo! the hour at last is here. Yet now that I
have the knowledge my power is too weak to turn it against
her. I, poor and lowly, and whose voice would never be
heard, cannot use what I have found. But you, English lord,
can do with it what you will. I, the Vagrant, and you, the
Noble, both hate; let the great take the key to his vengeance
from the obscure. The worm has burrowed, let the tiger
rend!"

Her voice ceased, and there was silence again between
them, whilst the winds swept with hollow echo through the
arched cloisters where they stood, these strange companions
thus strangely drawn together, with the great chasm of social
difference yawning between them, only bridged by the community of hatred, which, like the community of love, binds
together those who are farthest asunder. He had heard her
throughout without interruption, and as the moonlight fell
about him she saw the varied passions that swept across his
face, and the tiger glare darkening his eyes. As dried wood
ready for the burning leaps up to the touch of flame, so the
lust of revenge which was within him leapt up to the woman's words,

"To see her suffer!"

He, too, was athirst for it. All that was evil and merciless latent in his nature—and there was very much—had
fastened on one desire: to wreak the fulness of some hideous
revenge where he had blindly doted. And he stood now
silent, while many thoughts coursed through his brain, larvæ
of evil which the hotbed of remorse was swiftly nourishing
to deed.

A profound and rapid reader of human character and

motive, this woman's soul was bare before him as a book, and in it he read—truth. Her history brought back to him that which had once been told him at Vernonceaux of Marc Lennartson's death and of its cause, and he saw that the heart of the Bohemian, untamed and untutored, knowing no god but its love, and no heaven but its hate, would make no erring flight to the quarry of its vengeance. He saw that this woman held, or believed she held, the key to the redemption of her oath; and he saw that, weak with her sex's tenderness, yet thereby strong as her sex ever is, ignorant, and malleable as wax in his guidance, yet with the tenacity of an Indian in tracking the trail she followed, she would be his tool to work as he would.

For one moment he paused; the pride of rank and of habitual reserve, rather, perchance, than any nobler principle, shrinking from association with the Gitana, rejecting the employment of one thus far beneath him, loathing his instrument because he must make it even with himself if he once stooped to use it. That moment passed; then he motioned her from him:

"I will hear you; follow me."

And she followed him in silence down the cloister as he went onwards to the entrance of the Abbey, which stood out, a grey, sombre, stately pile, in the moonlight that was shining white upon its delicate fretwork and its pointed windows, and leaving deep in shadow its masses of Norman stone and battled wall shrouded in their vast elm-forests.

An hour afterwards the dark figure of the Bohemian moved swiftly and silently across the park of White Ladies, taking the road which led to the little hamlet beyond the gates, and at the window of the library where his audience had been given to this strange, unfitting guest, Strathmore stood leaning out to catch the coolness of the autumn night —fire seemed on his brain, fire in his blood, for the hatred of men of his race had ever outweighed and outstripped the sweetness and the madness of their love. And as a sleuth-hound scents the trail of what he would hunt downward to its death, so he now saw shadowed out before him the sure track of a deadly vengeance.

Here, beneath the roof of the Dominican Abbey, which once had sheltered both, both seemed beside him: the woman who had betrayed him, the man whom he had slain. The sweat of a great horror gathered thick upon his brow—flee where he would these must ever pursue him, wander where he would for ever on his lips must burn the delicious lie of her guilty kiss, for ever in his path must rise the spectre of that death-agony which he had gazed on with a smile. For Conscience is God; and hide us where we will, it tracks us out, and we must look whither it bids, we must listen to that which it utters, we must behold that which it brings, in the reeling revel as in the silent dawn, in the dull stupor of sleep as in the riotous din of orgies;—from its pursuit there is no escape, from its tribunal there is no appeal.

And where he stood, while through the silence there seemed to echo the mocking music of Marion Vavasour's sweet, accursed laugh; and down the hush of night there seemed to tremble the dying sigh of him whom he had murdered at her bidding, good and evil strove together in his heart; the remorse that should have purified like fire, and the hatred which, like fire, would destroy.

Atonement!—his soul hungered for it. It had been shattered from his hand to-night; yet, later on, it might be wrested back. If he gathered, by his will and by his wealth, about the young child whom he had orphaned, all that earth can know of gladness, shelter, riches, tenderness; if, for her father's sake, and in her father's trust, he made her future cloudless as the life of the flower which but opens to the light to rejoice through the sunny length of a fair summer day, and made her lips only speak his name in gratitude and blessing, the sin might be atoned? He had loved the man whom he had brutally slain: through the young life given by the dead, should expiation to the dead be wrought.

Expiation to the dead;—but to the living Vengeance.

The lust for it was in his blood as strong as at that hour when his hand had been upon her throat, her life within his grasp:—and the power of vengeance lay now within his grip. "*To see her suffer*"—suffer, and plead for mercy, and be denied, even as she had denied it, and find her loveliness of no avail to shield her from the doom of an unerring and a pitiless fate! For this his soul was athirst; to its purpose his life was set; he saw it looming through the darkness of the future; the pursuit in which his speed would never slacken, in whose success his will would never relent.

In this hour, when he stood alone in the autumn night, with no companion save the distant lulling of the weary seas; of his remorse was begotten his atonement, of his hatred his revenge.

Twin-born, must not one strangle the other in the birth? Or, twin-nurtured into strength and life, could both prosper side by side?

CHAPTER XXX.

The frail Argosy which was freighted with Atonement.

FOR a year Strathmore was not seen in Europe.

Rumour, which must always lie rather than keep silence, babbled now and again remembrance of him; he had been seen in Thebes; he had been met on the Amazon, or the Ganges; he had been heard of as dwelling at Damascus, and studying the buried learning of the East; he had been slain in a midnight fray with dragomans close by the Gates of the Kings in Egypt; these were among the things that Rumour babbled of him, and that Rumour lied, for none were true. Those who knew him best deemed that he shunned the world, and had sought solitude; and these also erred. For Strathmore was of a nature which masked anguish with an iron strength and an impassive calm, and to which the artificial atmosphere, the feverish crowds, the profound ambitions of the great world, were the necessities of existence; of the air of the mountain and the valley he had ever wearied; his breath was the breath of cities. Whatever of returning peace the eternal calm of mountains and the freshness of trackless forests may lend to the man whom the world has wronged, they have none for the man self-doomed by a self-chosen guilt. *Now* solitude was abhorrent to him—to be alone with Nature, man must be at peace with Himself.

Solitude! while over the still, starlit, pathless ocean in the hush of night there seemed to steal the quiver of that dying sigh. Solitude! while the crimson glare of the desert sunlight, streaming from the brazen skies, seemed reddened with the blood that he had shed. Solitude! while in the fairest fall of the tropic night, there seemed to look into his those dying eyes with their look of blind, beseeching pain. *His* solitude was a hell.

Yet for a year he was absent from Europe, and though many babbled of him, none truly saw him, or knew whither he had gone. He was absent for a year. For he held, what had been ever the creed of those of his blood, that vengeance accomplished, is crime acquitted, and remorse dulled.

And patiently and ruthlessly as the sleuth-hound follows in the trail of its prey, he followed the track of his revenge. For his own agony had not taught him mercy, and in pursuit this man was untiring and inexorable.

In the betrayal of his love he had suffered enough to have chastened his sin to its full due; the most rigid moralist might have compassionated him beneath the tortures of his guilt-stained passion. It had not been *love* with Strathmore, it had been worship—blind and insensate, if you will; but one into which his whole being had been absorbed, which had cast down unheeding every sacrifice at her feet, which would have died for her, content if his last breath had been spent upon her lips, and which had laid waste his life as no merely sensual passion could have ever done, when he had learned that his love had betrayed him, her fealty forsaken him, that her kiss, her sigh, her smile, her loveliness were divine lies, as free to all the world as to himself! The hate wherewith he hated her was as mighty, therefore, as the love wherewith he loved her. Born with that certain taint of cruelty which often belongs to a character in which desire of power is dominant, and which an imperious, negligent egotism renders indifferent to all not touching on itself, the latent trait hitherto negative or dormant, rose under the pressure of maddened passion and grief, into an accursed thirst for retaliation. Ere this he would not have inflicted pain save when compelled to do so to clear his path, or to advance an aim; now, the germ grown into a tree, the seed sprung to a disease, the passive quality that had lain in his nature, grew active, inflexibility ripened into cruelty, and he set himself with pitiless purpose to work such ruin as he should watch and taste and prolong to slow protracted pain, and deal out as though his hand and his will had but to wield the iron flail of destiny.

Blindly as Othello had he worshipped what he loved; ruthlessly as Othello he now longed to crush her out with his own hand where none could gaze on the loveliness which had betrayed him; for there is no cruelty with which passion has not been allied; there is no vengeance so remorseless as that which has its birth in love that has turned to hate. And although his nature had been bowed and bent under the weight of its agony, as steel in the forging and the flame of the furnace, it had but grown like the steel in the ordeal, the keener to strike, the surer to slay. Because a ceaseless remorse ate like fire into his soul, he clung but the closer to his vengeance; because an anguish of regret smote his strength till it sickened and reeled in the torture of his lonely hours, he reared that strength but the higher, to gather afresh the reins of fate into his grasp, and build up with his own hand the structures of expiation and of chastisement.

Strathmore, great in much, weak in much, and guilty in far more, was very human; for human nature, with many touches of deity in it, has yet far more of devil, and is a tree of which

sed quantum vertice ad auras
Ætherias, tantum radice in Tartara tendit.

And of the few boughs which stretch to heaven, how many
fibres strike to hell!

Where the Atlantic waves wash on the western shore, and
the headlands are clad with ivy and trailing honeysuckle;
where the white surf foams up on the ribbed pearly sands,
and in the shadows of the hollowed rocks, ever sounds from
dawn to sunset the delicate music of birds' voices mingling
with the murmur of the seas; there was sheltered the young
life which Strathmore's crime had orphaned in its opening.
It was a fitting place for childhood to grow up in, free as the
winds which swept over the ocean, joyous as the white-
winged sea-birds which cleft their path through the sunlight;—this place on the western seaboard, with the melody
of its waves echoing through the day and night, with its
warm breezes blowing over golden gorse and purple heather,
with its snowy breakers dashing on the rocks, and with its
broad blue waters tossing seaweed in the light of a summer's noon.

There, where the boughs of the trees dropped almost to
the edge of the sheltered sunny bay in St. George's Channel,
and through the opened windows on a summer dawn came
the voices of the fishermen, and the sound of the sea, and the
piping of the waking birds, dreamily mingled in one pleasant
music, lived the one who filled her dead parent's place to Erroll's young child—Lady Castlemere. Although he had
given to her but negligent regard, a cold ceremonial of attachment, Strathmore's mother had loved him, not in his
childhood or his youth, for she had then been a political
leader absorbed in her great party, but proudly and warmly
now that she followed his career from her solitude by the
western shores, whither she had gone when age and delicacy
of health had made the great world distasteful, and had
softened that haughty chillness which came with her Norman
blood. A stately and noble woman still, with that which had

been unyielding in her nature rendered touchingly gentle under the hand of Time, which mellows whilst it destroys, she left the proud station of Marchioness of Castlemere to her elder son's wife, and merged her own ambitions into those of Strathmore, whom she saw seldom, but of whom the world told her much. She had bitterly mourned when she heard of the slavery into which a woman's beauty had fettered him, and had shuddered aghast at that deadly tragedy which the world passed over with a light forgiving name. But in his guilt she loved him more truly, perhaps, than she had ever done; and in his guilt his thoughts turned to her.

It was his mother to whom he had delegated, and who had accepted that trust which the death of the wife had rendered it alone possible to fulfil to the child; and in proportion to the remorse which gnawed to his heart's core with every remembrance of the man whom he had murdered, was his almost morbid craving to fulfil to its uttermost breadth and depth that which he looked on as a request to be obeyed sacredly and unceasingly, as the sole atonement that lay in his power to render to the dead.

If you have once known what it is to recall, in a too late repentance, cruel words spoken, harsh thoughts uttered, to one whom you loved well and who has gone from you for ever beyond hearing of your prayer; and to lavish your care—in your poor miserable futile longing for some atonement, or cleaving to some relic of, the dead—on horse, or dog, or flower that he or she had treasured, then you know in some faint shadow of its bitterness that which he now felt; that on which he now acted.

The heart of his mother yearned to him in his crime and his remorse. For his sake, and at his wish, she accepted the guardianship of Erroll's young child: he coupled it with the condition—first, that the child as she grew up should be taught to look upon him as her friend and guardian, and, again, that she should *never be told her father's name*. So, alone, could none unfold to her the history of her father's death; so, alone, could she grow up ignorant that the hand which fostered and sheltered her was stained with her father's blood.

It was easy to accomplish this. Erroll's marriage had been known to none; the clergyman of the obscure village where the ceremony had been performed was dead; his wife had still borne her maiden name; the servants, the doctor and the vicar at White Ladies had looked on the offspring of their union as a "love-child," and there were no others who even knew of her birth. Accordingly, when the young Lucille was secretly removed and placed with Lady Castlemere, under her mother's Hungarian name, as an orphan whom she had adopted, and to whom her son had been appointed guardian, into a matter of so little moment none inquired, and his mother's protection of her excluded any coarser supposition as to Strathmore's relationship to her, which, under other circumstances, might have been mooted, to her disadvantage in later years. On her he settled, independently of himself, a considerable sum, more than sufficient for all needs of her nurture and education, and, in the case of his death, provided that she should inherit largely of his wealth. He desired that if she grew to womanhood she should hold his name in love and gratitude, ignorant of the heritage of wrong she owed to him; he longed that there should be one innocent life on earth unaware of the guilt which lay upon his soul. And here, too, the will of the dead strengthened and sanctioned his own: Erroll had written, "Never let her know that it was by your hand I fell." A wish of his was now more sacred to the one who had slain him, than all the laws of God and Man which he had broken!

The arrangements with his mother had been all made before he quitted England, and the child had been a year in the dower-house of Silver-rest, happy as a joyous childhood ever is from the sunrise of its careless, cloudless days to the sunset of its peaceful, dreamless nights; happy with the sea-weeds for her treasures, and the yellow gorse for her wealth, and the hushing of the seas for her slumber-song, yet—it might have been whimsically fancied—with the regret of her mother's loss vaguely told in the wistful gaze of her fair eyes, and the shadow of her father's dark and early doom left in the touching and unconscious sadness, which stole like a fate over her young face in sleep or in repose.

She had been there a year, when, in the close of the summer, Strathmore's yacht, *Sea Foam*, bringing him, as most believed, from the trackless forests and buried cities of Mexico, came to anchor in the little western bay, after her long run across the Atlantic, before she went down Channel. He landed, and went on alone to Silver-rest in the morning light. Far as the eye could reach stretched the deep still waters of the bay; the white sails of his yacht and of the few fishing skiffs in the offing stood out distinct and glancing in the sun; over the bluffs and in all the clefts of rock the growing grass blew and flickered in the breeze; and as he crossed the sands the air was fragrant with the scent of wild flowers that grew down to the water's edge.

But to note these things a man must be in unison with the world; to love them he must be in unison with himself. Strathmore scarce saw them as he went onward; all that he beheld was the Future and the Past, the vengeance which should stand in the stead to him of all that he had forfeited, and the crime which gnawed unceasingly at his heart, as the vulture at the living entrails of the doomed. Outwardly, he was unchanged: the cold, urbane manner, the chill, keen brilliance natural to him were unaltered; he was a courtier and a man of the world; for twenty years to come he would not change perceptibly; but in character he had altered much; or rather—to speak more truly—his nature had leapt up from its repose like a lion from its sleep. An agony of repentance had shaken his soul to the dust, rousing it for ever from the calm egotism in which he had bade it lie; a guilty passion had swept over his life like a whirlwind, smiting from his hands for ever the curb with which he had boasted, god-like, to rein his passions at his will. The temple which he had built to himself had been riven to the ground by the thunderbolts of the storm: a holier from its ruins might yet have arisen, but that with his own hands he chose to fashion the twin structures of Retribution and Expiation. Briefly, Strathmore had grown at once more sensitive and more dangerous, and though the whole creed of his pride had been scattered, like leaves before the wind, before the test of a great temptation, though the strength which had haughtily held all human error aloof and in disdain, had succumbed to the first attack of passion, and had wrought a foul crime as calmly as a righteous act, Strathmore never altered in this: life was still to be moulded by *his* will, and by *his* decree he held still that he should rule fate even as Deity! Alas!

> Evil or good may be better, or worse,
> In the human heart, but the mixture of each
> Is a marvel and a curse!

This is the widest truth in human life, but it is one little remembered among men.

He went this morning where, in his yearning love for the man whose blood was on his hands, he had centred his sole chance and choice of expiation on the frail life of a young child. As he walked onward over the wet smooth sand he came into a sheltered semicircle in the rocks, part of the grounds of Silver-rest, where the trailing plants were thick and odorous, forming a hanging screen of flowers, through which the sun-rays played upon the pools, and on the boulders that glowed deep red where the water had splashed them wet; and here he stopped, for lying on the wild ivy full length, with two setters beside him, he saw a boy of some ten years old, Lionel Caryll, the son of one of his sisters by an ill-fated mésalliance, who, early left an orphan, had always been brought up by Lady Castlemere.

The boy started, rose, and stood shyly silent; he had seen but little of Strathmore, and of that little he was afraid. He was a handsome child of the Saxon type, with a fair, tanned skin, and a mane of fair, tangled hair. Strathmore put out his hand carelessly to him; he disliked and never noticed children.

"How are you, Nello?"

The boy, shy still, did not answer, and Strathmore passed onward, putting aside a quantity of creepers which, hanging from the shelf of rock above, obstructed his progress. But the boy sprang forward with an eager gesture:

"Stop! please—pray! you will wake her!"

"Wake what?"

"Wake *her!*—and she was so tired."

Strathmore instinctively looked down, deeming that the boy's care referred to some pet setter or retriever.

Amongst the long grass under the ledge of rock, with the sunlight streaming fitfully through the leaves upon her, with her arms above her head, and her limbs lying in the pliant, unconscious grace of childhood and of sleep, there at his feet lay the child he had last seen at the death-bed of her mother. Her clasped hands held a long trail of ivy, her fair hair was wreathed in with a childish crown of wood violets, and her face was turned towards him with the dark lashes resting on its warm, flushed cheeks, and in its loveliness, still almost that of infancy, the shadow of that unconscious sadness which seemed like the shadow of her father's fate; a presage, or a heritage, of woe.

Strathmore paused, and a shudder ran through his frame; again this young child, in her innocent sleep, seemed to him as his worst accuser, seemed to him at once her father's phantom and avenger; and again this time, as she slept, the smile that smote him to the heart parted her lips and passed over her face, the smile that he had seen so often on the lips of the Dead.

Lionel Caryll looked at him, awed and terrified, he barely knew why:

"Are you ill?" the boy asked timidly.

Strathmore signed him away:

"Yes—no. Go on and tell my mother I am here, Nello. I will follow."

The boy hesitated, and looked at the sleeping child who had been his companion in play.

"Will you take care of Lucille?"

Accustomed to deference, and intolerant of opposition, Strathmore signed him away:

"Go, and do as I bade you."

The boy wavered, looking wistfully at his companion, and doubtfully at Strathmore; then, instinctively compelled to obedience, he went like a greyhound over the sands, followed by his setters. Strathmore was left alone with the remorse which an infant's smile had sufficed to waken into all its anguish—such is the coward doom of Crime.

He stood in solitude, with the sound of the seas about him, and at his feet the sleeping child, with the violets tangled in her fair, floating hair; and as he looked on her young loveliness, which, so different yet so similar, bore so strange a likeness of her father's face, memories thronged upon him, starting from the haze of long forgotten years, and gathering around him, even as the pursuant Shapes gathered about the Slayer in Hellas, till the air, which was clear to the sinless, grew, to the accursed, darkened and crowded with their thronging, shadowy forms. He remembered Erroll, a young child, even as this, with the same fair, trailing hair, and the same smile like sunshine on his lips; he heard his fresh, glad laugh ring on the summer air; he heard his childish voice echo upon his ear; he felt the touch of his young hand; he lived again in those years that had long drifted by, forgotten in the whirl of years more evil, when in his own soul there was no sin, when the man whom he had murdered played beside him in the sunlight, when his life was guiltless as that on which he now looked, where it lay sleeping at his feet!

And a bitter cry broke from him where he stood on the solitary shore:

"My friend! My brother!"

Back upon his ear the echo of the rocks around wailed in return his own yearning, futile anguish, like a prayer fruitless and rejected of Heaven.

In the sunny stillness of the noon Strathmore bowed down his head upon his hands, and his frame shook with the throes

of the remorse which could not force back the sealed portals
of the grave, which could not call to earth the existence one
fleeting instant had been sufficient to destroy. He could not
have told how long he had sat there in the solitude, where
every stirring pulse of life, from the noiseless rush of the sea-
birds' wings to the faint shouts of the fishermen across the
bay, seemed like the voice of God calling upon him to answer
for the life he had hurled into the grave; moments might
have passed, or hours, when he was roused by the silken
touch of hair against his hand, and a voice which whispered
softly in his ear:

"You are not happy!—tell Lucille!"

He started and looked up; the young child, awakened
from her sleep, had come to him, and vaguely grieving for
the grief she could not comprehend, as spaniels do at sight
of human pain, was blindly striving, as a spaniel might, to
comfort him. Losing fear of a stranger in her child's compassion, she had drawn close to him, so that her bright hair
swept over his hands, and in her large soft eyes stood tears
half of terror half of pity for the suffering which she saw and
vaguely felt, with answering pain, as the spaniel the sorrow
of which he nothing knows. And her young voice, tremulous
but tenderly caressing, murmured in his ear, "Lucille is sorry
for you—do tell Lucille?"

With a gesture as though a serpent had stung him, Strath-
mord started, flung her off, and quivered like a man who has
been struck a death-blow.

"Child, child! hate me, curse me, reproach me, but—oh,
God!—do not pity me! Keep off; my hands are red with his
blood, *yours* must not touch them!"

The wild words died inarticulate in his throat, and his
teeth clenched as the anguish she had strung to torture rent
and tore his frame—the worst chastisement from the hands
of man would have been mercy to the reproach of those innocent words which *pitied him;* to the unconscious accusation
of those uplifted eyes gazing with a child's tender yet wondering compassion on the face of her father's murderer!

She stood apart awed and silent, the tears standing in her eyes, that were at all times wistful with a haunting, beseeching sadness; the fierce gesture which had flung her off she understood, the words she did not, they were unintelligible—indeed, unheard—but she waited, pale to her lips, and trembling like a young fawn after a cruel blow, yet drawn by a strange instinct of compassion towards this agony, which she seemed to know was brutal, not to her, but from its own blind pain. She waited, then grown more daring, and taught by those who instilled to her an infinite love for all who suffered, she drew near him again—nearer and nearer, till her hair swept once more on his hand, and a pathetic entreaty trembled in her voice:

"Speak to me—do speak to me! Lucille meant no harm."

Again at her touch and her voice he shrank and shuddered as under physical torture; this child came with caressing gentleness and plaintive pity to the one whose guilt had orphaned her, and to whose hands she owed the deepest wrong that life can owe to life! Then he lifted his head and looked at her; when his resolve was set his strength was iron to bridle himself or to coerce others, and it was his will that she should grow up holding him in love and gratitude, and ignorant ever of the crime which otherwise must stretch, a hideous and impassable gulf, between her and the assassin of her father. He passed his hand lightly over her fair silken hair, and answered gently:

"Lucille is very kind. I thank her. Tell me, you who are so pitiful to pain, are *you* happy?"

"Always."

Her eyes looked their mute surprise that any one could ask her such a question, and a smile played about her lips as she drew a long glad breath, recalling her own exhaustless treasury of joy—the joys born of sea, and bird, and flower, of a crown of forest violets, and a chase of summer butterflies! The joys which are pure, and cost no pang of shame, no purchase-gold of guilt, in their glad reaping!

Strathmore found in the simple answer the first seed of his atonement; it was much to him to learn from the child's fresh, truthful lips that she was "happy"—happy by his means, and in his fulfilment of the trust bequeathed him by the dead. His hand rested on her hair, and his eyes upon her face, as she leaned against him caressingly and without fear, as though he were known and dear to her, rather than, as he was, a stranger. Skilled in reading human features, he read the nature easily which was dawning here, the susceptibility to joy and pain suggested by the lips with their mournful lines in repose, and their sunny, laughing smile which sparkled and then died; the too early depth and poetry of thought which were written on the low, broad brow; the latent tenderness which lay in the sadness of the upward look, and in the liquid melancholy depths of the eyes, soft and dreamy as the night. These might have told him that to secure happiness to the Childhood was easy, with its fleeting pleasures centred in a bird's carol, in a dog's love; but to secure it to the Womanhood was a more perilous venture, which might chance on shipwreck.

At that moment a little toy-spaniel that was with him caught her eyes, and with a child's swift change of thought she uttered a laugh of delight, and threw herself upon the sands beside it, kissing its long ears, and bathing it fondly in her bright long hair. With a stifled cry Strathmore seized the animal from her arms: the dog was the one which had nestled in Erroll's breast, and refused to leave the side of the dead man; he could not see the child in her unconsciousness caress the brute whose fidelity had outlived his own, whose watch had been kept over her father's corpse!

She looked up at him, deeming that she had committed some great fault in touching a stranger's dog without his leave; and with caressing grace and penitence she leaned against him, lifting her dark, beseeching eyes:

"Lucille is sorry—Lucille was wrong! But he is so pretty, and he would love me—all things do!"

Callous to much, merciless to more, Strathmore, who had

deemed that nothing in life could ever wound or move him, felt the burning tears gather in his eyes at the simple words and action of this child, so unconscious of his own deep guilt, and of her own great wrong! His voice shook as he stooped to her:

"The dog is yours—none have so great a right; Lucille, if all things love you, will you give some love to me?"

She looked surprised yet wistful, and her eyes dwelt on him earnestly.

"Yes, Lucille, will love you. But not *for* the dog. Tell me your name, that I may say it in my prayers?"

For many moments he made her no answer; and in the silence his loud laboured breathings hoarsely rose and fell. Then his hand passed slowly and gently over her hair, and his voice shook still.

"Ah, in your prayers! God knows I need them from all things innocent. Remember me and love me—I was your father's friend."

The last words were low with a great agony, and seemed to rend and stifle him in their utterance. His hand lingered for a moment in farewell upon her hair; then he turned and left her, bidding the spaniel, which clung to and fawned upon the child, stay with her. Young Caryll was coming swift as the winds towards them. Strathmore passed him without word or sign and went onward, leaving behind him, standing together on the sunny silvery sands, the boy Nello and the young child Lucille, between them the little dog which had crouched in its love upon the dead man's breast, when human friendship had betrayed, and human watchers had forsaken him.

CHAPTER XXXI.

The Whisper in the Tuileries.

MARION LADY VAVASOUR stood in her dressing-chamber, before her Dresden-framed mirror, come from a fête of one

of the leaders of that brilliant set of which she was still the
Fashion, the Cynosure, and the Queen.   The lustrous light
in those superb eyes was not dimmed; the mocking smile on
those lovely lips laughed triumph that was unshadowed; the
fair brow and the delicate bloom wore the brightness of their
youth unmarred. For the world was as ever at her feet, and
remorse had no part and no share with her; it could not
whisper in her golden dreams, nor dog the royal negligent
step with which she swept through life. Remorse! She knew
it not. How could its ghastly cry be heard above the ceaseless
chant of homage about her path?—how could its dread terrors
force their way into the proud and dazzling presence to which
kings bent and princes knelt?

She knew revenge, she knew cruelty, so do the velvet
panther and the painted snake; but she knew not remorse,
neither do they; and that dark tragedy of which she had
been the cause, touched her no more than these are touched
by the death they deal—save that she knew, when the world
babbled of it, it babbled of her power; save that she loved to
learn how deeply a woman's smile may strike, how widely a
woman's loveliness may blast.   True!—till she had wearied
of the fidelity even of a guilty passion, all that she had vowed
to Strathmore had, perchance, not been a lie; true!—there
had come hours when she had thought that had they met
earlier, met when their love might have been pure, and the
breath of the world had not sullied their hearts, she might
have given him such constancy as poets fable and as she
mocked: the fleetest rivers have their deeper waters, the
most heartless amidst us have their better hours. But her
lust was Tyranny, her glory Power, and the evil which she
worked smote not upon her—for her, as for Greek Helen,
brethren warred with brethren, and men cast their lives into
the slaughter! And this triumph was her crown. She stood
now before her mirror, and let her gaze dwell proudly on the
peerless form whose divine grace no living woman rivalled;
then she swept onward to her carriage to go to that world
which was her court. She was the most beautiful woman

of her time. Who shall give me title so omnipotent, sceptre so mighty?

Where she went was to the Tuileries. Here the English Peeress, the beauty of Paris, the leader of Fashion, had ever found her proudest triumphs; here to-night, as countless nights before, Princes coveted her smiles, Queens were out-dazzled by her, and Sovereignties paled beside the sway of the woman whose beauty owned no rival; here, Marion Lady Vavasour was in the height of her brilliance, and her fame. And here, and thus she was watched by the man whom her love had made a slave, whom her lie had made a murderer.

She glittered through the titled crowds that were gathered in the palace of the Bourbons, with the sapphires glancing among her amber hair, and her smile of superb triumph upon her lovely lips, her choice and delicate wit falling like a shower of silver, her resistless coquetries charming to blind-ness all drawn within her circle in the salons of a King. And he watched her—this divine loveliness that had betrayed him with a kiss; this soft and patrician thing that had forsaken him with the vileness of the wanton; those angel lips with their childlike bloom, which had whispered and wooed him to the bottomless abyss of crime. So much the more madly worshipped once—ay, *still!*—so much the more mercilessly was she now doomed, so much the more deeply damned!

The palace was thronged that night. The ball was on the occasion of a royal marriage, and all that was greatest in Europe was assembled at the Tuileries; but as her sapphires outshone all the jewels of royal peeresses and imperial orders, so she outshone all the loveliness gathered there, while she floated through its courtly crowds, now listening to the flat-teries of Princes of the Blood, now to the murmur of velvet-lipped Cardinals, now bending to her feet austerest Statesmen, now seeing bowed before her some proud crowned head. And Memory was far away from her in her superb omnipotence, her cloudless present—far as was Remorse!

She passed down the Salle des Maréchaux on the arm of

the Duc d'Etoile, her perfumed lace floating about her, the sapphires starlike above her brow, the light falling on her dazzling face; and every glance involuntarily turned on her and on her Royal lover, for such he had notably become. But as she went, unrivalled in her omnipotence, unequalled in her beauty, sweeping through the courtly crowds with wit on her lips and conquest in her glance, the eye of D'Etoile, resting on her, saw her face grow pale and a strange tremor seize her.

What was it! Was there poison in that perfumed air—miasma in those royal salons—plague-taint, or subtle death-odour, burning from the lights which gleamed above upon her loveliness, or exhaling from the jewels which glistened in her bosom? No, none of these; we are not in the days of Medici and Sforza, and (grown virtuous from dread of science and of law) we do not slay the body, we only slay by slow and sure degrees the soul, the honour, or the peace of what we hate, because this is a homicide absolved of men.

What was it, then, that, suddenly as she swept through the presence-chamber of the Tuileries, made her lips grow white, her eyes gleam for one fleeting moment with the terror of a hunted antelope, her hand tremble on her Royal lover's arm! It was this only—the whisper of two words, which seemed to float to her from a distance, yet which reached no ear save hers:

"*Marion St. Maur.*"

She glanced on all immediately about her—courtiers, ministers, ambassadors, princesses, peeresses, maids of honour—but she saw that as none of these had heard, so none of these had spoken that whisper of her maiden name. But as she lifted her eyes, they fell upon the face of the man she had forsaken and betrayed; the man who, in the last hour she had beheld him, had hurled her from him because death was too swift and merciful a vengeance.

Strathmore stood at some slight distance, leaning against a console where the light fell full upon his face, which wore

its look of cold and pitiless calm; and his eyes were upon
her, watching her with a steel-like glitter, a dark tiger-pas-
sion, insatiate and without mercy, that the drooped lids did
not veil.

And she who in her light insouciance, her omnipotence of
beauty, feared Heaven and its wrath as little as the most
daring of blasphemers, the most stoic of philosophers, turned
pale even to her laughing lips, and felt the air turn sickly
faint, the lights whirl round her, the crowd grow dizzily in-
distinct, and saw nothing but that gaze, with its mute, and
merciless menace, suddenly met there as a ghost arisen from
the tomb, silently quoting to her the Past, silently threatening the Future.

The weakness endured but an instant, too swift for even
the Prince on whose arm she hung to note it, and he passed
on—passed Strathmore. He did not move; he gave her no
sign of recognition; but his eyes rested on her, and—he
smiled. She knew the deadly meaning of that faint chill
smile; she had seen it on his lips before he went from her to
meet the man whom he had doomed, and she shuddered and
grew sick and cold, and shivered with vague and intangible
terror, as at the chastisement of their mutual sin. In that
single moment, which for the first time smote on her soft and
brilliant life with a ghastly and nameless fear, his vengeance
had begun.

The flatteries had lost their honey, the homage had lost
its glory, the charm of the world was marred, the power of
her sway was broken that night to Marion Vavasour; and
while she reigned in all her radiance in a King's Palace, the
hand of a nameless terror lay heavy upon her, and she saw,
ever pursuing her with its iron calm, that ruthless and unspoken doom.

Henceforth there would be poison in her wine, and canker
in her roses, a ghost beside her couch, an asp within her
bosom. His vengeance had begun.

The Paris Season had commenced, with the marriage-ball at the Tuileries, something earlier than usual, and Lady Vavasour sat in her loge at the Opera, moving her fan with all a Spaniard's grace, lazily listening to Mario and Malibran, or to the whispered worship of her *cohue* of courtiers, while the delicate sandal-wood perfume floated from her rich lace, and some of the brilliant deep-hued tropic flowers of the East lay crown-like upon her lustrous hair.

In the light, in the warmth, with a Prince's homage murmured in her ear, with diamonds of untold price glistening in her bosom, with a proud title of her own, in the sight of a proud Order, surely she, if any, was secured from the evil stroke of bitter fortune; looking on her, it seemed that even Death itself must pass by this beautiful, pampered, imperious thing, as too fair to smite, too full of sovereignty to slay! Yet where she sat, with the sweetness of music lulling her ear, and the gaze of lovers' eyes worshipping her beauty and entreating for its smile, lapped in her own dazzling, voluptuous, victorious Present, like the epicurean she was, the same fear which had suddenly smitten her in the presence-chamber of the Tuileries smote her suddenly here, the same chill ran through her, the same emotion for one brief instant blanched her lips, gave terror to her eyes, made the wit falter on her tongue—for she heard the same whispered words spoken on the air close by her:

"*Marion St. Maur!*"

Yet they were but the words of the name she had borne before marriage.

"Qu'avez vous, madame? Vous trouvez l'air du loge tant soit peu étouffant?" D'Etoile asked, with tender solicitude.

"C'est l'odeur des fleurs qu'on a mises à mon bouquet, prenez-le!" said Lady Vavasour, holding to him the jewelled bouquetière, which Etoile took with such a subtle, graceful flattery in his thanks as only a Parisian can turn; but it fell for once dull and lost on the ear to which it was murmured, as Marion Vavasour pressed her fan against the lips on which she knew their bloom had paled, and thought in her soul, "Who can know it here? Not *he*,—surely not he!"

For the terror on the life of this courted and sovereign beauty who had been used to coquet at her will with Destiny, and rule Fate by a sign of her fan, a *moue* of her lip, was her dread of the man whose love she had fed to madness and goaded to crime, and who had spared her from death only that he might see her live to suffer.

As her eyes wandered, half unconsciously, half restlessly, over the house, in the full glare of the light on the opposite side, she saw him again, saw him as in the Tuileries, with his eyes fixed upon her under their drooped lids, and upon his face that slight, chill smile which struck like the cold touch of steel. A few moments previous he had been in the loge which adjoined hers; now he stood fronting her, looking on her as he had trained himself to look, tranquilly, passionlessly, as in the Question Chambers of the Inquisition the Dominican, with gentle voice and soul of steel, looked on the tortured whom he doomed, and bade the rack be turned.

And Marion Vavasour could have cried out in her dread, and risen and left the Opera House, as though fleeing from some haunting spectre; for she knew then that it had been Strathmore's voice which had whispered her maiden name. But she was too skilled an actress thus to betray herself; though of much cowardice with much cruelty (for her nature was one essentially feminine), she had ever at command finest finesse and calmest self-control: like many of her sex, pusillanimous to the core, she was an actress to the life. She sat there, now that his gaze was on her, with the bloom on her cheek, the smile on her lips, the lustrous languor on her eyes, while her royal lover leaned to her with suavest homage, and the wit, the scandal, the persiflage circled around her. She listened, she laughed, she moved her fan with softest coquetry; she reigned with all her negligence, her brilliance, her grace, her imperious charm. But in the rich harmonies of the music, the courtly flatteries of murmured words, the jeux d'esprit, the wooing homage which filled for her the hours of the *Prophète*, she only heard the single whisper of that name which had told her that the secret of her early life was in the hands of Strathmore. In the glare of light she only saw the face of the man she had betrayed, watching her with that merciless menace of the veiled eyes which quoted to her the unburied past, which foretold to her the shrouded future. Hear what she would, that name sung for ever in her ear; look where she would, that glance for ever followed and met hers; there in the glare of the Opera House, with the light falling on the pale bronze of his face and the dark gleam of his passionless eyes, he stood before her—he whose love had been insanity, whose religion would be revenge.

And when after those brief hours, which had been to her one long-protracted torture—torture which was endured with a smile on the lips, lustre in the eyes, sovereignty seemingly shadowless as of yore, Marion Vavasour was alone in her carriage, she sank back, trembling, quivering, unnerved, dreading evil with the shrinking terror of a delicate woman, shuddering from the fury of the storm whose whirlwind she, the sorceress, had raised from the passions of the man she had tempted and betrayed.

It was thus he ordained that she should suffer first, as the Dominican, with astute calculation, commanded that the torture should be administered gently and by slow degrees, so that each succeeding pang was tasted to the full. To wrench the limbs from out their sockets *at once* were too much mercy. Was it no torture to himself to go into her presence as into the presence of strangers; to look with un-moved calm upon her face; to hear echo on the air the silvery music of her voice; to stand by and watch the gaze of those who had succeeded him fasten on her loveliness, and her eyes look up to theirs? Truly it was such that when it had been endured, and he was alone in the solitude of mid-night or of dawn, when the strain was released, and the un-natural calm broken down, Strathmore's suffering was, as his

love had been, a madness. In the great agony of that last
fooled, cheated, guilt-steeped passion, which even in the riot
of its hate begrudged the breath which whispered to another,
and envied the dog that nestled in her bosom, his misery was
fearful in its strength, fearful in its despair, for he loved
while he loathed her still.

But Strathmore was no coward to *endure;* what he appointed himself, that he would have wrought out, though his
own life had been the penalty at the close. His lust of
vengeance was brutal, but none the less was it immutable as
death, unswerving as destiny. He had the fierce passions
and the profound dissimulation of an Eastern; therefore he
trained himself to meet her thus, and she alone read the
language written in the veiled depths of his eyes. The world
deemed that the liaison of a year before had been dropped
by him among the things of the past; and the world deemed
also that, considering the tragic story which had been interwoven with its rupture, he was something callous to have
forgot so soon; but then, the world remarked, he was a
cold and heartless man, and for the issue of a duel he of
course could not reproach himself. Poor world! great spy
though it be, how surely, how universally it is chicaned!

Strathmore remained in Paris through the whole of that
winter; and through that season, rarely and slightly at the
first, more often and more markedly towards the spring, it
was remarked, chiefly by women, that Lady Vavasour was
losing the brilliance of her beauty, and was looking pale, almost worn. It was the first time that such a rumour had
ever been whispered against her dazzling loveliness, on the
day now eight years past, when she had first appeared as
the Marchioness of Vavasour and Vaux. What wrought it,
was that which has power to shatter the strongest nerve, to
break the boldest spirit, to undermine the most careless insouciance—it was a *hidden fear,* the asp among her couch of
scented roses, the dagger suspended above her head by one
frail thread of hair, which the world could not behold, but
which never quitted her. He had shown her that he knew

her secret, and he let that knowledge—the more bitter because indefinite—slowly and surely eat its poisoned way.

They knew each other's hearts, they whom sin had united,
and sin had severed; and as she read her doom so he read
her suffering, without speech, without disguise. That single
name breathed in her ear told her that she was in his power;
that single glance from his eyes told her with what mercy
that power would be used; though when, or how, or where
the blow would fall, she knew no more than we know when
the stroke of death will descend upon us. And it was this
endless uncertainty, this unceasing apprehension, which wore
and tortured her till her careless, epicurean creeds were rent
by it like filmy gauze, and the woman who had become so
used to sovereignty that she had learned to believe she could
command every hazard of life at her pleasure, grew the perpetual prey of a ceaseless fear and a momentary anxiety,
which gnawed at her heart the more cruelly because concealed from all.

Wherever she went, there Strathmore followed her, till
his presence grew as fearful to her as the spectres which
follow the distempered minds of those in delirium tremens.
In the salons of the Tuileries, in the reception-rooms of ambassadors, in the entertainments of princes and nobles, at the
Opera, on the Boulevards, in the clear noonday as she drove
through the streets, in the midnight glare of light at some
patrician bal masqué, she saw him; always before her, in the
distance and as a stranger whose glance swept over her unmoved, but with the meaning on his face under the cold and
courtly calm, which she had seen there when he went out to
deal death to the man he loved, and with the threat in his
fathomless eyes, which spoke to none but her. He was ever
before her like some avenging fate from which to escape was
hopeless, and which tranquilly and immovably awaited a
chosen hour to strike. He was ever before her, with that unspoken doom in his glance, and that unknown power silently
told in the slight, calm, cruel smile which she knew so well.
And the fear which had possessed her of him, from the hour

when her slave had risen to crush his tyrant, and the passion she had loved to excite to delirium had turned upon her in its madness, grew gradually under this ceaseless watch into a terror unbearable. It made her nerves unstrung, her manner uncertain, her glance like that of the hunted antelope, when it listens for the eager step which gains nearer and nearer through the awful hush of the night in the jungles.

They noted that her bloom paled, that her dazzling insouciance was capricious and depressed, and they noticed rightly; the beautiful hue upon her cheek, which so long had distanced art, now needed, for the first time, to be replaced by art. To regain that repose which had deserted her she had refuge in narcotics, which, however subtle, left their depression on the morrow; and to cover that depression had recourse to stimulants which, however skilfully prepared, left their mark on one, the happy and childlike sunniness of whose nature had been the chief spring of her ceaseless fascination.

The hidden canker in the rose ate at its core, and dimmed its bloom. Marion Vavasour ere this had been a perfect actress, and had never known one pang of pain; but that was when the peace and lives of others hung in the balance. Now it was her own that were in jeopardy; and so strong upon a mind naturally impressionable grew her dread of the vague doom which threatened her, and of the cold, pitiless face which, go whither she would, seemed for ever to pursue her, that she could have shrieked aloud and shrank away when, day after day, night after night, she met the gaze of Strathmore, and could have fled out from his presence trembling, as those who flee from the ghastly phantom of their own imaginings.

That she never thus betrayed herself, was due to her proud and haughty spirit, where dissimulation alone might perchance have broken down, this enabled her so to meet, and brave unflinchingly, what became an hourly torture, that the world should never have title to whisper that Marion Vavasour was agitated by the presence of the lover whom she

had deserted.   To this, also, it was due that she never permitted her dread of Strathmore's power to drive her from the
circles where she reigned.   Once she felt tempted to flee
from him to Nice, Florence, Pau, the Nile, anywhere where
her caprice or her physicians might furnish an excuse; but
she disdained and repelled the temptation; she felt that, go
where she might, there would his vengeance pursue her; she
refused to give to it its first triumph by surrender. Besides,
she knew not *what* he knew; and Marion Vavasour was in her
own epicurean fashion a fatalist. The blow did not fall yet,
the blow might never fall; circumstances might arrest it,
death itself might close his lips with her secret still unuttered. So she reasoned, so she reigned, throughout the Paris
winter.

But in herself she never lost the sickening sense of that
dagger which hung vibrating above her head to descend at
any instant; in her white bosom, unseen by the world, the
asp coiled ever under the freshness of the flowers, under the
brilliance of the diamonds, and ate and ate with its poisoned
fangs.   *He* saw how she suffered—this woman to whom her
sovereignty was her secret, to whom her pride was so dear;—
he saw, and drove the iron farther down into her heart by
every glance with which his eyes met hers, compelling her,
while the eyes of the world were on her, to smile, to coquet,
to scatter her golden wit and her lustrous glances unmoved
and undimmed, while she grew faint and heart-sick with the
terror of that power, vague yet wide and sure as destiny, in
which he held her. Thus he tortured her till the dread of
meeting his gaze grew with her into a morbid agony;—thus
he tortured her until, imperious beauty and accomplished
actress though she was, her cheek paled, her eyes grew
anxious, her health became uncertain;—thus he tortured her,
for he willed that she should taste the full bitterness of vengeance by being forced to watch its slow approach, as the
prisoner chained to the stake was condemned to watch the
gradual onward creeping of the pitiless flame.

And he waited, for the blow of his revenge to fall in the

sight of all assembled Paris, upon the same day in the spring-
tide, as that on which, three years before, they had met at
sunset on the Bohemian waters.

CHAPTER XXXII.

The poisoned Wounds from the silvered Steel.

EARLY in the ensuing Spring the carriage with the coronet
of Vavasour and Vaux upon its panels, its chasseurs, its
lacqueys, its postilions, its outriders, left the court-yard of
her hotel to drive amidst all the other élite of the equipages
of Paris, through the Barrière de l'Etoile, and round the Bois,
and past the site of the ancient ruins of the Abbaye de Longchamps, whose religious rite has passed into a ceremonial of
fashion.

The day was softly bright, the city was in its spring-tide
gaiety, the dense crowds were sweeping down towards the
barrières of the west, Paris was *en fête:* and Lady Vavasour's
cortége, dashing through the streets with its accustomed royal
fracas, bore onwards to join the great stream of carriages
which brought the sovereigns of the Faubourg St. Germain
and the Quartier Bréda, the Royal Highnesses and the Empresses Anonyma, alike to the throng of Longchamps and the
inauguration of La Mode this sunlit day upon the Boulevards.
And she leaned back upon her cushions in her languid loveliness, with the imperial ermine, a Czar's gift, which formed
her carriage-rug, turned aside, for the hour was warm, and
her priceless perfumed point d'Angoulême gathered about her
with that carelessness which was her own inimitable grace.
The carriage joined the row, eight broad, on the Place de la
Bastille, and closed in with it; all eyes turned on her, for she
gave the law of the year and led the fashion, and men surrounded her as her Guards surround a Queen, Princes and
Ministers spurring their horses to approach her, and stoop-
ing from their saddles to seek a word as eagerly as they
would have sought a Crown.

She swept along the Boulevards and down the drives of

the Bois, where the man whom her lie had murdered had been slain when the sun had set; and the past was not remembered nor repented, for remorse had no share in her shadowless life; remorse had no place in her world.

She was alone in her carriage; none were permitted that day to share that throne (of which her barouche-step was the *haut pas*) of the Sovereign of Fashion; her little lion-dog alone occupied the cushions beside her, with his jewelled collar on his snowy fleece, and in the double line of horsemen, on either side the throng of carriages, on every lip there was but one theme—the beauty of the English Marchioness who gave the mode to Paris.

Lady Vavasour drove onward past the site of the old Abbaye, whilst Etoile leant from his saddle, breathing a Prince's flatteries in her ear, until she reached the full stream of equipages, where the occupant of almost every carriage (that was patrician, not lorette) was numbered on her visiting-list; and each one of those delicate *aristocrates* was either her friend for boudoir confidences, or her acquaintance for State dinners. And now in the rich morning sunlight, as she encountered their equipages and received their salutations, she saw that which sent an ice-chill through the warm current of her glad life.

What was it, slight, nameless, intangible yet to be *felt*, that she read in the glance of one or two of the highest women of the French and English aristocracies? Imperceptible to another, *she* caught it—for Marion Vavasour had a secret to guard, and whoever owns a secret always suspects that the world has unearthed it. That which she read, or fancied, in their look was not censure, not inquiry, not insolence, not wonder; it was more vague than any of these, yet to her it spoke them all. She caught it once, twice, thrice on different faces, and her delicate bloom paled: it was that chillness which is marked and felt rather by that which it suggests than by what it does, slight, but intentional as it was unmistakable. Etoile looked surprised; but he was too true a gentleman to affect to perceive what in real truth bewildered

him.   For one brief second her soft antelope eyes lightened
with ill-suppressed anxiety and with unrepressed anger;
there is no glass which reflects so delicately, yet so bitterly
and so surely, every shade of disdain as the faces of trained
women of the world.   The steel with which their scorn
thrusts is silvered, but the wound it deals is barbed, and
deep, and poisoned.   Lady Vavasour caught that disdain,
and knew or guessed its meaning, and her cheek paled under
the sea-shell bloom of her delicate rouge; the thrust of the
silvered steel struck to her soul, for she knew that it struck
to the core of her secret.

The carriages rolled onward, and as yet the coldness lay
but in look, the blow was dealt but from manner, her bows
were returned as of yore, though with a certain distance, a
marked chillness; and Etoile found no constraint in her wit,
no light the less in her luminous eyes; she seemed to note
nothing of the look which spoke so much!   But the asp in
her bosom had fangs not one whit the less bitter because the
smile did not leave her lips, nor the nonchalant grace of her
attitude change: women cover their wounds, but under the
veil they throb—they throb!   The carriages rolled on, and
her postilions threading their way through the throng passed
the stately equipage of her chosen and intimate friend Lady
Clarence Camelot—that cold, proud beauty, in whose veins
ran the "blue blood" of Norman monarchs, and whose social
creeds were lofty if not stringent.   But yesternight they had sat
at the Opera together, rival rulers yet close allies; but yesterday so complete had been their sisterhood, that they were in
private to each other "Marion" and "Ida."   Now, the azure
eyes of the descendant of Plantagenet looked with calm, cold
regard at her, as though regarding a stranger, and, recognising her presence no more than she would have recognised that of a beggar, the Lady Clarence Camelot passed
on round Longchamps.

On Marion Vavasour's lips, which were blanched to whiteness, the smile was arrested as on the lips of those suddenly
smitten with death; and while the smile rested there, into

her eyes came a wild, haunting anxiety as they glanced over the crowd to see whether this had escaped all others. And as they glanced they saw—cold, pitiless, with the brutal menace in the eyes and the slight smile about the mouth, unmoved as though cast in bronze—the face of Strathmore.

He was watching the progress of his work—watching how slowly and surely, drop by drop, his poison fell.

The throng bore his horse backward; her carriage rolled onward with the glittering mass making the tour of the Bois de Boulogne; and once, twice, thrice, again and again, the Queen of Fashion was made to eat of the ashes of the deadly humiliation; and the silvered steel thrust its barbed point farther and farther down into her heart, probing deep to the core of her secret.

She passed the Countess of Belmaine; she passed the Duchesse de Lurine; she passed the Marchioness of Boville; she passed the Vicomtesse de Ruelle; she passed her oldest friend, Lady Beaudesert.

And all these dealt her the same blow, one by one, with the same chill, delicate, unerring weapon; all these gave her no recognition even of her presence.

The procession of Longchamps, which had ever been one long triumphal passage for the proud and dazzling English leader, was one long pilgrimage of shame, worse than that which, in the centuries gone by, the barefoot penitents had made by that same route, when the blind, the sick, and the lame had thronged to the Abbaye altars, to the grave of Isabelle Capet.

On many tongues in that dense throng, among such as could observe it, was but one theme—the insults of her Order to the Marchioness of Vavasour and Vaux.

But she leaned back, not letting the smile even grow constrained on her lip, not allowing even a glance of anxiety in her eyes, a flush of anger on her cheek; but negligent, graceful, tranquil as of old, not seeming to have noticed the thrusts which pierced her to the soul. At last, as her carriage was turned back to Paris, it passed side by side with the equipage of the most notorious adventuress of the demi-monde, Viola Vé, celebrated for ruining a peer of France every trimestre, and whose extravagances startled even "equivocal society;" as her barouche-wheel locked slightly in that of Lady Vavasour, the Lorette smiled and bowed, and said a few careless words to the English Peeress, as though they were of the same world and the same order!—and laughed as her carriage rolled on, as one who gives an insult she knows *cannot be resented.*

The open outrage and insolence were translatable to every looker-on in that dense crowd; the key to it was a mystery which convulsed Longchamps with bewildered amazement, and convulsed Paris similarly in a few hours after. And at this coarse indignity Marion Vavasour turned white to the very lips, and trembled exceedingly; for she was proud, very proud! and she had had her foot on the neck of this haughty and patrician world so long, so long! It was so bitter to have the diadem torn from her brow, the sceptre shattered from her hand!

Once again, as rallying her courage she glanced around in defiance of the insults, she saw in the yellow sunlight the face of Strathmore, watching her with the smile on his lips and the menace in his eyes, watching her as the serpent watches the bird which cannot escape from its fangs. Marion Vavasour knew that it was he who had her secret, and was on her track; his hand which by the silvered steel of these women's indignities, dealt her this poisoned and mortal wound.

With all nonchalance, all hauteur, all easy grace, unchanged, but with her lips blanched and drawn over her pearly teeth, the most beautiful woman of her time returned with that slow and glittering procession from Longchamps to Paris, veiling the quivering nerves and the throbbing pride with calm courage, with admirable artifice— for she was a more perfect actress than any the stage has seen. Yet she ran the gauntlet of a deadly trial; for in those hours which that long pageant occupied, in the dense throngs which fashion gathered, all the eyes of Paris Proper were on her, and the crowd was divided but into two classes, those who passed the outrage on her and those who witnessed it!

As at last she swept up the steps of her own hotel, she did not observe a vagrant woman loitering hard by on the pavement; but the Bohemian had watched there through livelong hours, watched to see her face as she returned from Longchamps, and a smile came on Redempta's lips as her vigil was repaid, and she muttered in Czechen:

"It is begun. I have not lived in vain, beloved! She suffers! she suffers!"

It was true—she suffered! Marion Vavasour had laughed her sweet soft laugh at the mortal agony she dealt to others, but in her own bitterness she, the discrowned, who had known no pain and no remorse, suffered—suffered even as Marie Antoinette when the crown was wrenched from her golden head, and the Dethroned was led out for the gibes of the people.

There was some confusion and agitation in her household as she crossed the great parquet of the hall, but not noting it she swept onward up the staircase, turning to the groom of the chambers:

"Where is my lord?"

The man hesitated slightly, and looked grave; she repeated her question imperiously:

"Where is his lordship? Answer me!"

"Pardon me, my lady, but during your ladyship's absence his lordship was attacked with a—slight indisposition."

An intense alarm and anxiety came into her face—strange visitants there, for the world had never known that she had loved her lord!

"Indisposition of what kind?"

"Something—I believe—of a syncope, my lady."

He was too polite and too elegant a philomath to use so brief a term as "fit," but her fears grasped his meaning, and she bade him send the physicians to her in her boudoir. They came, honeyed and deferential, and from much cream and

verbiage the simple truth gradually oozed that, in plain
terms, the Marquis of Vavasour had been struck by apo-
plexy after a pâté of nightingales, followed by too many
bouchées and rosolios, at his luncheon, and now lay, sen-
sible indeed, but in a state most precarious, of which the
issue was doubtful.

Then she dismissed them with a queenly bow of her
graceful head, and signified an imperative necessity that she
should see her lord alone on family matters of the highest
moment. The physicians, curious, like all of their trade,
vainly strove to represent that their presence was indis-
pensable for every second; all Europe bowed to her will,
and she permitted none to gainsay it; it was obeyed now.
His score of attendants retired from his chamber, and her
husband was alone when she entered it.

With her rich and graceful beauty she came and stood
by the bedside of the sick man, on whose face death had
written its mark out plainly; and, for he was quite conscious
and had every sense left him, he opened his eyes and looked
at her curiously, for it were hard to describe the change
which had come over her features, and she wore no mask
with him.

She leant over him as she sat beside the couch, after a
few hurried words of condolence, speaking low and swiftly:

"Vavasour! All Paris knows it!"

Into the supine face of the old Marquis came a gleam of
malicious amusement crossed with surprise.

"The deuce they do!" he said, with a laboured articula-
tion. "Who told 'em!"

"God knows! What matter *who!*" And she, whom grief
in all its agony, passion in all its fury, had never moved, save
to that gay, triumphant amusement with which a child crushes
its costliest toy, spoke with breathless agitation, her lips
quivering, her fair hands trembling, her eyes filled with tears
of bitterness! "They know it! Even Ida Camelot cut me
dead an hour ago; a score of them passed me as they would
pass a dog! And even that woman Vé, Caderousse's mistress,

dared to insult me—ME! They know it! Nothing less could make them act so, nothing else could give her title with impunity to——"

The sick man chuckled low and with difficulty, as though this were the best joke which could have come to cheer him on his death-bed:

"Gad! I wish I had been there! Deuced pity to have lost it! Eh! bien, ma belle! you can't complain; you've cheated them a long time!"

And where he lay back among his pillows he chuckled still, faintly, for his breath was with difficulty drawn, but with a malicious amusement that was in ghastly contrast with the marks which death had set upon his face.

A passionate anger and misery gathered in hers:

"And that is all the pity that you——"

"Pity!" broke in the Marquis, with a laugh which struggled with a spasm of the breath. "Gad!—the deuce!—what pity do you want? You've had your own way, ma belle, and women love it. I was a great fool to take your terms, for they were confounded high; however, I don't mind it, you've amused me. It was a drawing-room vaudeville, with the fun always kept up; but pity—'fore George! women's ingratitude——"

And the Marquis choked with his disgust at the ill return which was given him, and with his amusement at what roused him even from all the apathy of a moribund.

"But, Vavasour, now—*now*—why not now? If you would, still it might be done—privately, secretly; secresy could be bought, and the world would never know——"

She spoke low, tremulously, incoherently, and in strange agitation for the flattered, courted, proud, omnipotent beauty! Her hands played nervously with the lace and silk of the counterpane, where she leant half kneeling against the bed; her attitude was almost supplication, and her haughty loveliness was abased and dejected; for she had worn her diadem long and proudly, and it was bitter to the Queen of Fashion to have her sceptre wrenched and her purples torn aside for all to see the secret of the discrowned.

"Why not *now*, Vavasour?" she whispered eagerly, while her lips were hot and parched. "It would be so little to you; it would spare me so much. Now—now, before it is too late! I can purchase inviolate secresy——"

The dying man interrupted her with his stifled laugh rattling in his throat, while his sunk eyes leered maliciously, and his hand feebly played with the diamond circlet of her marriage finger—the badge, she had whispered to Strathmore on the rose-terrace of Vernonceaux, as the badge of Servitude and Silence.

"I dare say! and *ma belle veuve* would then win, perhaps, M. D'Etoile, who knows? As it is, she will have to be only his mistress! No! I am not in the mood! You think one *en moribond* ought to lend himself as a lay figure? Ah! there you are wrong, ma belle; you must ask the favour of some one of your old lovers, that man with the Vandyke face, who killed his friend for your beaux yeux; or one of the new ones, perhaps, may pay the price more graciously."

Again the horrid, unfitting laugh, chuckling and rattling in his throat, sounded through the stillness of the death-chamber; Lord Vavasour had eaten his last pâté of nightingales, but he had still palate and power to enjoy what he and most men with him find of still sweeter flavour—the pleasure of Malice. And leaning there against the costly draperies of the bed, in her lace, her jewels, her delicate floating dress which that day had given out the fashion of the year to Paris, in her lovely womanhood, in her haughty grace, Marion Lady Vavasour—who wore no mask with him—sank forwards, thinking nothing of her husband before her, but with her white hands clenched, her teeth set tight, her fair face blanched, her rich hair pushed back in its masses from her temples, eating in all their bitterness of the ashes of Humiliation, tasting in all their cruelty the death-throes of Abdication.

————

CHAPTER XXXIII.

The Errand of the Lost.

THE household was hushed, all moved with noiseless footsteps through the wide marble staircase and the stately corridors and the brilliant-lighted chambers of the Hôtel Vavasour: the presence of death was nigh, and breathed its solemnity even through the gilded halls and the pompous hirelings of that magnificent palace, where wit was usually as rife as in the salons of Rambouillet, and cost was as unheeded in luxury or dissipation as in the days of Vitellius. It was known that his lordship could not recover, and that, Vitellius-like, his goblet was reversed and his last Falernian was drunk, and the Prætorian Guards of Pallida Mors were leading him out, stripped of his purples, and made nothing better or greater than an old, bloated, gluttonous man, to hurl him over the fathomless abyss, where none would mourn him, and down the dark, cold river whence none return.

The household was still and awed through this early part of the spring night, and his wife sat in her own chamber, when her dinner had been served and dismissed, musing and alone. From custom she had dressed for the evening, as habitual, and the delicate shower of costly lace fell about her, and the diamonds and amethysts sparkled in her hair as she sat there, her head leaning on her arm, her lips white and pressed together, her fair proud brow knit in vain thought—thought how to baffle, how to escape from the vengeance which netted her in and held her tight beneath its stifling meshes.

Only five-and-twenty years had passed over her head, and she must lay down the sceptre, and put the crown from off her brows, and pass from the haut pas and the throne, to mingle with the jeered and common crowd. Already! already! She must leave her kingdom in her youth. She had known that sooner or later this must come, that sooner or later this shame and bitterness must fall; but in the royalty of her

omnipotence, the gladness of her power, she had forgotten
her doom. She had believed that it would come, perhaps at
some far distant time, when her beauty was spent, and when
in age it would matter but little; nay, she had at last believed that so happily had fortune favoured her, that her life
would flow on for ever in the sunlight, and that she would
live and die in the honour and odour of the patrician world
she ruled, her secret never guessed, and buried with her in
the grave which would bear the name and titles of Marion
Marchioness of Vavasour and Vaux.

And now—now—in the brilliance of her youth, in the
splendour of her triumphs, the stroke had fallen; and she
must go out, to be the jibe, the mockery, the scorn, of her
rivals and her foes.

The dews stood on her brow, her hands clenched in her
anguish, she shivered and started from her solitary reverie
—it was so horrible!—to stoop her pride into the dust; to be
banned for ever from the haughty, shadowless, patrician life
she loved; to be the scorn and the derision of the women
she had outshone and outrivalled, and made follow the mere
fashion of her drapery, the mere mode that her changing
caprice gave as law.

She started and rose to her feet, and there was a piteous
misery in the eyes ere this so proud, so lustrous, so full of
careless laughter: she had known no mercy for others, but
she knew suffering for herself. As she rose, her lace caught
in and overturned a gold filigree basket filled with the notes
which had come during the past twenty-four hours; one
rested, as the shower fell, upon her dress, and mechanically
she raised it and broke the envelope; they were only a few
lines in French, bearing the date of the previous day:

"MADAME,—Lord Cecil Strathmore has some secret of
your past, with which he intends to take his vengeance on you
to-morrow, in the sight of Paris. I know no more than this,
which I gathered from what I accidentally and unavoidably
overheard between him and Madame de Ruelle this morning.

I acquaint you, that if you deem fit you may seek to avert what seems to threaten indignity, or worse, to you, and I am willing to answer to him for having done so. In this I render you good for evil, but, as you know but too well, I have loved you more faithfully than most.

" *Veuillez agréer, Madame, l'assurance de ma considération distinguée.*

"FALCONBERG."

That note she should have received the night before; and it had lain there in the jewelled basket unnoticed, while the Queen of Fashion had gone out to meet her doom. She, sceptical of all else, believed in that hour in Destiny and Retribution; the writer was an Austrian, a mere boy in years, whose young life the beautiful panther had torn and destroyed for a night's amusement, a coquette's triumph, at one of the gorgeous masked balls of the Viennese Court: and while she read her lips quivered and her hand shook as it clenched upon the paper.

It told her no more than her fears had known before—that the cold and pitiless face she had seen that day had told her without words.

"Poor Falconberg, poor child!" she murmured unconsciously, for in triumph we cast aside human tenderness, but in despair we value it. "His mercy—*his!* As soon seek pity from marble, warmth from ice! As soon ask the vulture not to tear, the lion not to rend——!"

And she sat there with the pallor of terror blanching her lovely lips, which trembled as with cold: she knew that more hopeless than to seek mercy from the beasts of prey was it to seek compassion from the hand which her love and her lie had dyed with blood.

And yet—and yet—her eyes fell on her own loveliness. It had bent him as the wind the reeds; it had melted him as the flames the steel. Might its ancient power not be wholly fled! could he who had been her abject slave gaze on it wholly unmoved! Up from the dread of a great despair grew the sickly shadow of a vain hope, side by side with the mad impulse of an unconsidered resolve. She was so used to her sovereign sway, her proud omnipotence—resistance to her prayer seemed a thing impossible. And hastily, and on the instinct of a misery which made death from his hand look better to be coveted than the living chastisement to which he doomed her, she arose—nerved to a hopeless and desperate purpose.

Late that night Marion Vavasour entered a little brougham by one of the side-doors of her own residence, and was driven rapidly through the few streets which parted her from the Hôtel de Londres. The carriage was hired, the driver a stranger, and she herself was enveloped in long, black, sweeping folds, which concealed her person, while a thick black veil thrown over her head wholly obscured her features. Etoile himself might have passed her at his elbow and never penetrated her disguise; those who would have died for one smile from her eyes would not have recognised her in that veiled and sombre form.

The driver stopped at the hotel, and came to the door for instructions.

"Inquire if Lord Cecil Strathmore be visible?"

The man obeyed, and ten minutes after returned.

"Milord is within, madame, but they doubt if he will be seen so late."

"Very well, let me out."

She descended from her carriage, and entered the hotel. A few moments' conversation with one of the attendants, two louis d'or slipped into his hand, and she followed him up the staircase, along the corridors, and towards the door of one of the great suites.

"Your card, madame."

She handed him one, on which was printed a name, but not her own, and the servant entered the apartment leaving her without, but with the door not wholly closed, so that where she stood she could hear his voice, and that of the one who replied to him.

"A lady entreats milord to see her for a few moments?"

"The 'Countess Lena!' I do not know the name; and what an hour! However, show her in——"

The man returned, threw the door wide open, ushered her ceremoniously into the salon, and retired, closing the door behind him. He presumed this veiled midnight guest, whose voice thrilled him like sweet music, came from the Bréda Quartier, and envied the Englishman who received her.

The door closed, and Marion Vavasour was alone with Strathmore. He rose as she entered, standing under the full light of the chandelier which glittered immediately above his head.

"Madame, may I ask to what fortunate chance I am indebted for this honour?"

As the calm, chill, courtly tones, addressing her as a stranger, fell on her ear, she shivered—could that suave, gentle, immutable voice ever soften to pardon, to mercy? She was silent, pausing in the centre of the chamber; and he moved a fauteuil towards her.

"Be seated, madame. I await your pleasure."

She did not take the chair; she did not answer; and Strathmore, marvelling if his veiled visitant were dumb, awaited her pleasure—leaning his arm on the marble console while the light was shed on the peculiar Vandyke type of his features, with the dark gleam of his fathomless eyes under their drooped lids, and the cold straight line of the calm brows. She looked at him and shuddered, for she knew the fierce passions which lay beneath his high-bred and courtly suavity; she knew the steel gauntlet which was covered with that delicate, velvet, broidered glove of a courtier's manner. All the courage which had brought her hither on a mad impulse failed; the last time that she had been within his reach his hand had been upon her throat seeking her life! She sickened and shuddered with the memory of that ghastly hour, that awful torture, when death had been so nigh;—

noting how she trembled, this stranger, this veiled woman, Strathmore approached her gently.

"Have no disquietude, madame. If I can assist you, command me."

"Strathmore, you can spare me!"

The words rang out almost with a shriek; and as the words smote on his ear, he staggered back, and a spasm passed over his face as at some wound suddenly dealt by a keen knife.

His passion was not dead because it had changed to hate; nay, hate rioted in him *because*, though love abhorred her, love still craved her. For this woman had been to him sovereign, conscience, world, heaven, all that life can hold— all that eternity can offer!

A moment,—and he conquered himself; he held in an iron rein every emotion which could betray him; his face grew chill and passionless, as though it were cut in stone; he looked on her, as he had looked in the Tuileries,—as he had looked in the sunlight of the past day,—and was silent.

He had trained himself to see her thus without a sign, that he might watch her suffer; and she might sooner have wrung tears from a cast of bronze, a moan from a statue of marble, than mercy or weakness from him.

"You can spare me, Strathmore!"

The words rang out hoarse in their bitter supplication; cold and tranquil his answered her.

"I can."

"And you will—you will?"

For all reply he smiled; and that slight smile, as it passed over his face where the gaslight fell white upon it, was more pitiless than any speech which could have condemned her.

A faint cry broke from her lips as she saw it; she cast from her the trammels of her heavy sweeping cloak, and flung back the black lace which shrouded her like a Spanish mantilla. Her loveliness was once more before him, unveiled in all its brilliance, the light streaming down upon her face with its glittering hair and its lovely youth, the sapphires flashing in her snowy bosom, the perfumed lace, half falling off, half trailing round, the divine grace of her voluptuous form. And she stood silent, her head drooped, her eyes soft with lustrous tears, her bosom heaving with its voiceless sobs, the light falling full upon her. This beauty had been omnipotent to tempt him once to cast aside all laws of God and Man—this beauty might tempt him yet again. This had stricken his strength till it was a reed within her hands—this again might give her back her power. And she stood there, while her eyes looked up to his, and her heart heaved where the jewels gleamed; and the lace sank farther down—down —from off her beautiful shoulders, with the diamonds glittering where they nestled in her breast. But his will was iron; his veins were ice—for her; and his eyes did not change, his smile did not alter, as his words fell cold and clear on the silence.

"It is too late for *that!*"

A burning flush crimsoned her face, and she shrank under the blow. She was a woman, and one who glossed her amours with delicate refinement, and one who was used to rule omnipotent, and yield with a sovereign's grace—not to sue and be repulsed. Tears, genuine and bitter, started to her eyes, and her voice thrilled with passionate emotion.

"Strathmore! Strathmore! I am in your power—spare me! I am a woman—be pitiful to me! You loved me so well once—have some pardon for me now!"

He did not change his attitude; he leaned there against the console, with his eyes, under their drooped lids, fixed on her; and his words answered her, falling low and chill on the silence, like the dropping of ice-water:

"I marvel you dare say that to me! Go!—you were always a matchless actress; it is a pity to waste your time, your tempting, and your loveliness!"

She shivered as she heard him: from fiery passion, from menace, from reproaches, she would have hoped to win, to touch, to tempt, to torture him into some mercy. With those cold, measured, inflexible tones, all hope died out. She felt as those who, gliding down into a bottomless abyss upon the Alps, feel the ice-wall they strive to grasp, slide, smooth, and frozen, and shelving from their touch, as they sink downwards to darkness and to death.

With a low cry she threw herself at his feet in all her soft abandonment of supplication; her proud head humbled to the dust before him; her white hands wrung and clenched; her loveliness, thrown there before him like a criminal's who kneels before her judge.

And he looked down on her unmoved, save that his vengeance was dear to him, and sweet: she suffered—at last!

"Strathmore! Oh, God! see, I kneel to you; *I*, who never bent to any mortal thing! I may merit this from you; I do not dare to deny it. You may have much to avenge on me—much!—though I loved you; ay, I loved you as I have loved no other! Women crave conquest, power, cruelty; but we *love*, despite that—love, though we love ourselves first! If I sinned *to* you, I sinned *for* you!——"

"True! It is the trade of the courtesan!"

Where she lay at his feet, prostrate in her loveliness and her abasement, she shuddered under the calm, chill, brutal sneer—she! the woman who had ruled over princes, and to whom kings had knelt! Yet—she would not renounce all hope, she would not give way from all effort: she lifted her head, so that the white light fell on its lustrous hair, and shone in her lovely eyes, with their appealing prayer; and that face, in its blanched pain, its prostrate beauty, its stricken pride, was more resistless than in its most radiant hour of witching sovereignty.

"Shame me! humble me! strike me as you will! I wronged you, and I am in your power, and a woman, and defenceless! Yet hear me: be great enough to forego vengeance—be noble enough to heap coals of fire on my head by Pardon. If I erred, were *you* sinless? If I were guilty, were *you* stainless from crime? See!—you have made me drink the bitterness of humiliation to the dregs! Cannot that content you? Spare me more, for the love of God! Hear me, Strathmore, and have mercy! To-day you have let the world whisper it, but to-morrow's whisper may soon efface to-day's. Lord Vavasour is dying, dying fast; let me bear his name in peace! If you do not reveal the truth to his heirs, none will dare attack, and sift, and search—none will raise the question. I may live in peace; live without shame, and sneer, and jibe from the women I have rivalled, from the society I have ruled. Only spare me this—this! Do not hunt me down to poverty and degradation, do not expose me to the world!——"

She stopped, and a sob choked her voice, for here, if acting still, the actress felt her part and pleaded her prayer in all its acrid bitterness, its keen, imploring pain, for she felt and pleaded for herself. She suffered,—she suffered,—and the burning tears gathered and fell, and under its delicate shroud of lace her form shivered with the physical cold of a great dread, of a convulsive suspense.

She pleaded as the Condemned plead for life. Her future lay in this man's keeping—and he had spared her from death only to bid her live "to suffer."

She had made him in God's sight and in his own a murderer. Could she hope for mercy from him! Could she strike vengeance from his hand!

A death-like stillness reigned between them as her voice ceased, and she lay there at his feet in her abject supplication, her abased loveliness, her stricken pride. He stood changeless, motionless, his face unaltered in its tranquillity, his eyes unfaltering in their relentless gaze:

"If you were drowning before my eyes, and my hand stretched out could save you—you should perish in its need! If you were bound to the stake, and one word of mine could save you—I would not speak it! If you were dying of hunger and thirst, and a cup of cold water from my pity could save you—I would refuse it in your death hour! I have answered. Such mercy as you gave, I give to you; no other."

As his words fell slowly out upon the silence, chill, tranquil, and inexorable as Fate, a shudder ran through her frame,

and a cry broke from her lips wild and piteous, like that of
a woman who receives her death-warrant.

She trembled, shivered, shrank before the iron pitiless-
ness, the icy hate, of this man's nature, on which her own
might fling, and wear, and spend itself for ever, yet make no
more impress than the fretting waves which break upon a
granite sea-wall, and leave no sign of all their feverish travail.
And she lay crouched at his feet in all her fallen loveliness,
stricken and paralysed as by a cruel mortal blow.

His eyes dwelt on her long and meaningly, while not a
muscle of his face changed from its rigid calm, its bitter
exultation; he watched her shudder, and writhe, and crouch
there at his feet with a faint smile playing on his lips—as he
would have watched her strained on the rack or bound to
her funeral pyre; and his voice hissed slowly through his
teeth as he stooped and whispered in her ear:

"Listen! I have what you can never rob me of—I have
my VENGEANCE. You have lived to suffer! And you will fall
lower and lower into sin and infamy, and misery and want;
fall as those fall who trade in beauty, and die as they die
when beauty leaves them: die in the streets—die craving a
crust. Go!—your fate waits for you."

The brutal doom hissed in her ear, maddened her as a
shot a panther, till all its desert nature wakes to life under
its pain. She started, and uprose and stood before him, her
face blanched to the lips, her eyes alight with a tigress-
glare, fearful in her loveliness, ghastly in her brilliance,
dangerous in her weakness and her despair.

"Abase me, expose me, destroy me, work your worst; *I*
plead no more! But, by the God whom we have both outraged, the hour shall come when the mercy you mete out to
me I will mete back to you, when you shall seek in vain of
earth or heaven, Strathmore, for the pity you now deny!"

She stood before him in all her beauty, while the light
streamed down upon her, her face turned towards him with
the glittering hair thrown back, her lustrous eyes dilated,
her form instinct with despairing passion, her voice rising

and quivering in the air till it rang with a menace of the
future, with evil dark and merciless as his own; she stood
there, terrible as Até, prophetic as Cassandra. And thus
they looked on one another, this man and woman, so lately
bound in the close ties of passionate love and mutual sin,
now sundered farther than they betwixt whom oceans roll.
Thus they looked on one another; and in her eyes was the
lurid gleam of a vengeance which soon or late would pioneer
its path and sate its lust; and on his lips sat the calm, chill
smile of a vengeance which would never cease from pursuing,
and never stay its hand for pity or for prayer, which held its
quarry in its grip, and tasted its power slowly, drop by drop,
with thirst which grew the greater with its every draught.

Thus they looked on one another; there was a moment's
silence again, as though she still mutely awaited whether yet
he would not yield to mercy, yet abstain from vengeance,
and bid her go, loathed, abhorred, condemned, but—spared.
There was a moment's silence, in which the very air seemed
pleading for her pardon, and supplicating for the God-like
vengeance of forgiveness. Then she cast one look upon his
face: it was white, calm, chill, inflexible as the features of
the dead, and unmoved as they to prayer, or woe, or menace;
and without word or sign she turned and left his presence.

They had parted.

And, as the door closed, he fell heavily forward, with a
crash, across the marble, weeping a woman's very passion of
tears;—loathing life, longing for death, abhorring himself
while his heart was breaking. He had loved her so utterly;
—he loved her still!

To her he had been as granite, but in his heart he was so
weak. His vengeance had so much guilt, but his life had so
much misery.

"Oh God, I grow a fiend!" he moaned in his great
wretchedness, his added crime. "Oh God, why did they not
kill me in my birth?"

————

CHAPTER XXXIV.
The Core of the Secret.

AT twelve that night, while Lord Vavasour lay dying, and Paris danced and supped, and gamed and laughed, and whirled through the merry hours, a party of some dozen or so were gathered after the opera for a petit souper in the salons of Madame de la Ferriole, the wife of one of those princes whom the Bourse makes in a day. The hôtel was superb; the ameublement would have been deemed marvellous in a palace; figuratively, for its cost, the supper could boast of liquid gold for its wines, and melted gold for its dishes; and the Sèvres on which it was served was rimmed with pink pearls: yet Madame de la Ferriole (genuinely, Madame le Maire) was still on the outskirts of fashionable society, and was at this moment still passing through that transmigratory period which transfers the owners of Capital among the leaders of Ton; and blazons the Or with the Gules. She moved highly, but not with the highest, and therefore her guests around the supper-table discussed the insult of Longchamps without the key to it, which as yet only lay in the hands of the ultra exclusives of one certain set; and, therefore, they hailed with pleasure and empressement the late advent of the single member of that set whom they had yet secured, and who had deigned to come and sup with Madame de la Ferriole, partly because, *en vraie Parisienne*, she respected the wealth, partly because, *en bel esprit*, she wished to satirise the appointments of the roturière. That single member was Blanche de Ruelle.

With all the "languor of good tone," but with all the curiosity of scandal-mongers, the party around the million-naire's supper-table sought the confidence of the haughty and unapproachable aristocrat, who, lying back and slowly breaking her ice, seemed disposed to talk of little but the new opera, and of that only to her own escort, the Vicomte de Chanrellan. Blanche de Ruelle had been the first to whom Strathmore had entrusted the secret of Marion Vavasour's downfall, and bidden deal the poisoned wound with the silver steel; she had been the chief to enable him to mete out revenge and chastisement thus slowly, subtilely, witheringly. And although he in unfolding, she in receiving the story had placed but one motive in sight and surface—to wit, the proud wrath of an insulted Order, and an outraged and patrician Matronage; the chastisement had been the more willingly, the more completely done because she had once loved—hopelessly—where the woman whose abasement she was summoned to carry out had been madly worshipped. The same passions move the world as in older and more transparent days; they are but the more closely veiled.

And now, about the supper-table of La Ferriole, little else but one topic was circulated, if abandoned for the moment, to be resumed the next; and the bored, languid, slander-seeking flâneurs, masculine and feminine, lounging away an hour after the opera over the priceless wines of the Princess of the Bourse, sought its explanation from the first of those who had dealt the deadly thrust that day in the green allées of the Bois. For the insult to the English Peeress was the theme of Paris; and the high station of those who had passed it raised curiosity to frantic wonder and to breathless impatience. Blanche de Ruelle let them babble on about it in her presence, while she spoke of Auber's music with Chanrellan; then she raised her haughty eyes in answer to the questions which turned directly towards her, playing gently with her Spanish fan.

"Pardon, madame! Lady Vavasour! Oh, I pray you drop that subject; society has been grossly outraged, foully insulted. Have you not heard? Indeed! Why, the marriage was fictitious—she was never his wife. The world has been deceived, and we—we have received the Marquis's mistress."

CHAPTER XXXV.

The Abdication of the Purples.

AT twelve of the night the Marquis of Vavasour and Vaux died, and his chaplain, standing by, said unctuously over the bloated body, "Blessed are the chosen who die in the Lord;" for he whose breath had just left his body had had many and rich benefices in his hand, and "died in the Lord," according to all the clergy of the Church of England, which sees no sins in patrons.

"Le Roi est mort, vive le Roi!" and the good chaplain, having said the Last Communion over the past Marquis, went to send the first telegram to the future one. But, rapid as

was his own, one had preceded it to the distant heir, who,
from a nameless Attaché, would become a Personage. Where
the two passions race, Revenge will outstrip Avarice of the
two, though both are hell-hounds fleet of foot.

This latter message ran thus:

"From the Lord Cecil Strathmore, Hôtel de Londres, Paris,
     to William Vere-Lucingham, Esq., British Embassy,
     Constantinople.

"I hear the Marquis, your cousin, died to-night, suddenly
and intestate. See me here as soon as you arrive, or you
will lose the best part of the personalty."

Now, in the absence of all will of any kind, since the
Marquis had ever had obstinate horror of a testament, and
shunned the word of death as utterly as the Romans on their
tombstones, the entail devolved on Vere-Lucingham, sole,
though distant, heir presumptive, and all the rich personalty
would go to his widowed Marchioness. Therefore, when this
telegram came to him with his morning coffee, acquainting
him of the new fortunes which Pallida Mors, best friend of
the Living, had wrought for him, the young Attaché was
bewildered at its latter clause; but knowing well the character of the sender, for he had been under him at Turin, never
thought of slighting or neglecting the strange summons, but
only felt a grateful and wondering eagerness as to its purport.

At twelve of the night the Marquis of Vavasour and Vaux
died—of too much pâté de rossignol and rosolios at luncheon
—not a great death, perhaps, but in the main scarce so harm-
ful an one (to others) as Mithridates' or Hamilcar's, or Julius
Cæsar's, or divers whom we call heroes, because they per-
ished by a weapon with which they had slain thousands ere
their decease, and slew by their legacies thousands after it.
To be gluttonous of nightingales is bad; but it may be worse
for the universe to be gluttonous of nations; a gourmet only
kills himself; a hero fills a larger bill of mortality. The one,
however, has only the restaurants, the other the world, to
chant his *De Profundis*; and, granted, it *is* murder on a larger
scale to kill ten thousand men to make a victory, than to
kill ten dozen birds to make a pâté!

The Marquis of Vavasour and Vaux died, and left the

world a legacy of many inimitable *cuisine* receipts, and one
great wonder. His young cousin, Vere-Lucingham, succeeded to the Marquisate with all its honours, and refusing
to acknowledge her claim to one iota of the rich property
which the law would have allotted to the wife of the deceased,
to one gem of the Vavasour jewels which had so long sparkled
on her brow, the new peer proclaimed to Europe that she
whom it had so long received and honoured had no right or
title to its respect and homage, but had only been the dead
man's mistress. And when the charge was brought, the
condemned could put forward no defence, could allege no
denial: there had been no marriage; and the Law is not to
be seduced by a feminine sophism, dazzled by an actress, or
enslaved by a woman's loveliness, but wrings out one un-
courtly, and coarse thing—truth.

She, whom the world so long had known and worshipped
as Marion Lady Vavasour, had kept her secret well. Who
says that her sex has not the power to guard a secret closely!
Pshaw! they keep one for a life-time, if—their own! She
had kept it, secure that it would never be told by her lord,
and that when he died, with him would die the sole possessor
of it. And now the secret was given to the winds, and hurled
out to the light of the day, and flung to the world where she
reigned, as the deer is flung to the hounds at the curée! For
the hell-dogs of Vengeance had been on her track, and they
never lose scent of the trail.

Years before, cruising among the West Indian Isles, and
lying in a harbour (rarely visited) to have his yacht fresh
coppered, the Marquis had seen her, lovely as the morning.
Her parents, English planters, were dead, and she was fretting at, and wearied of colonial obscurity and insular imprisonment, like a brilliant tropic bird in a cooped-up cage.
She looked at her marvellous loveliness, and knew that while
it could give her sway wider and mightier than the Cæsars',
it must bloom to its full beauty, and fade and die unseen,
like the radiant blossoms of some matchless flower in the
tangled forests and dense swamps of her own island. The
Marquis saw her, loved her, and offered her—the world. She
knew, by intuition in her lovely youth, how great a price such
beauty as hers should fetch, and refused to sell it for less
than his coronet. He declined the payment: she declined
any other. A pause ensued, in which both steeled themselves

from surrender, and each awaited the other's capitulation.
At last the man grew impatient, the woman doubtful: he was
lured by her loveliness, she was lured by the vista of eman-
cipation and conquest which stretched out before her; they
each bent to a compromise. She dispensed with the legalities
of marriage, but stipulated for the semblance; she did not
require to be made his wife, but she required that the world
should hold her so: he, well amused to *joliment jouer son
monde*, and, musing that (unbound) he could end the comedy
whensoever he should have fatigued of it, consented.

She came to Europe with him as the Marchioness of Vavasour and Vaux: it suited his monkeyish malice to play the
trick on his order and on society, and he readily lent himself
to all which might best sustain the delusion. She was received as his wife—and the rest was soon accomplished by her
own unequalled beauty and unrivalled tact. She soon ruled
the fashion, and set her foot on the neck of the world. And
as time went on the old Marquis grew so well accustomed to
her reign, and was so well amused to see society fall before
her and men go mad for her loveliness, that he abandoned all
thought of dissolving their compact; partially perhaps because he did not care to tell the world himself that he had
palmed off a lie upon it, partially because his own weak and
supine character had shown its facile points to her, and was
ruled by her stronger will with facility, and without his being
even aware of the governance. Thus what she appeared to
the world she grew absolutely to regard herself.

Worshipped, courted, obeyed as the Marchioness of Vavasour and Vaux, she forgot that she had no legal claim to
the title and place she filled. One or two obscure persons in
that remote, uncivilised West Indian island were all who
knew her secret; how should these reach her great world, or
her great world reach them? Moreover, they were in her
pay, and bribed to silence; so it was little marvel that Marion
Vavasour—such I must still call her—deemed her position
secure and her single secret safe from revelation; little marvel
that, proud, made to love power and to use it royally,
haughtily fastidious as though a born patrician, with some
blood of an illegitimate Stuart actually wandering in her
veins, and accustomed to the homage of exclusive circles, she
had learned to look upon her rank as unassailable, and felt
the degradation of her deadly fate bitterly, bitterly—as any

queen, who with her crown torn from her brows, and her purples rent from about her, ever was bidden to descend from her throne and come out to the jibes and the hiss of the multitude where yesterday the highest sought her smile, where to-day the lowest could revile and scoff and stone! Strathmore's vengeance would have been more merciful if he had slain her in the glare of that summer morning—a moment's pain, and all had then been over. He had chosen a more lingering and cruel retribution: he had bade her live to suffer.

Her secret was known in Paris, and nothing of the bitterness of her humiliation was spared to the Discrowned. She had outshone the one sex, she had maddened the other; who was there amidst the order she had insulted, the women she had rivalled, the men she had fooled, to break the violence of her fall, to heed how brutally the diadem might be wrenched from the fair, proud head, raised in its lovely sovereignty so long above them?

Her secret was known in Paris: in the cercles, in the salons, in the Tuileries itself, in Galignani's, on the Boulevards; in all the cafés, in all the boudoirs, over fine ladies' chocolate in their bedrooms, over gourmets' five hundred francs' breakfast in the Maison Dorée, it was the theme of the hour, to the exclusion of all else; it flew across the Channel as swiftly as special correspondents' copy could reach Printing-house-square, and filled all the journals, Anglo and Gallic, with its startling sensation-news, its incredible scandal. All Europe knew this beautiful Helen with the antelope eyes, for whom princes and chiefs had been ready to war, almost as in the old days of Hellas. All Europe was summoned as witness and auditor of her shame and her abdication. From the Palace to the Press all Europe arraigned her—and for what mercy could she look in her abasement, when those who found her guilty were the nobility she had insulted, the society she had trepanned, the rivals she had humiliated, the lovers she had fooled? These made judges more pitiless than Alva's Council of Blood.

True, for sake of her loveliness many asylums offered to her, in terms which now she could not resent as insult, and of them she accepted Etoile's. But the protection of a Prince was almost as bitter to her as the obscurity of a convent—she who had reigned in the palaces of Europe to be classed with Viola Vé, she who had shone amidst women of blood royal and visited at St. Cloud and at Windsor to sink amidst lionnes of the Rue Bréda and Enghien toy-villas! It was a bitter change—from the purples of the Patrician to the stained robes of the Hetira.

She suffered—ay! she suffered cruelly, this woman, who had mocked at all human grief with her silvery laugh, and dealt out anguish and death as gaily as a child deals both to the painted butterflies that he slays for his sport. She suffered cruelly; for to the proud and flattered woman there was no chastisement so fearful as humiliation. And it was a scourge of scorpions wherewith he lashed her—he, whose hand, though unseen, dealt every blow under which she shrank.

With the keen cunning and the patience in pursuit, of her vagrant race, the Bohemian had learned the secret of the aristocrat from a quadroon woman whom she had found, by what chain of hazard and investigation combined, matters not. In her hands it was powerless for evil—a gipsy could not be heard against a peeress; but she placed it in those which her shrewd intuition knew would use it most widely, most mercilessly. When Strathmore had taken his yacht, as it was believed, to the Western world, he had gone to pursue every link of the clue given him by the Czechen, in that remote unnoticed colony whence the first thread of his vengeance had to be found. It had needed long and patient search; those he sought were obscure and unknown; but he was patient in the trail as an Indian, and when his gold had bought over their silence and purchased their fidelity to the secret they had in keeping, his vengeance was his. He had returned to deal it—his hand invisible, but his will directing its every step, its every sting.

With his revelation he had bought opprobrium and chastisement for her from the highest; with his gold he bought insult and degradation for her from the lowest. As it had been his intimation which had caused the patrician women to cut her dead in the passage of Longchamps, so it had been his will which had caused the lorette to greet her familiarly in the allée of the Bois—so it was his wealth which purchased every subtle indignity, every suave outrage which, by a cool word or an insolent smile from those in whom womanhood is disgraced, classed her with them, and struck deeper than a dagger's thrust into the heart which, with all its sin, with all its licence, remained haughty, fastidious, refined, aristocratic to its core. A laugh, a note, a bow, the pointing of the monstrari digito, the shame of coarse epigram, or sneering quatrain, or obscene caricatura, the insult of courtesans' friendship, or courtesans' invitation—these were the weapons with which the unseen hand that dealt her doom, stabbed her momentarily, mercilessly, with a retribution as subtle as it was relentless. He had bade her live to suffer! It environed her, it pursued her, it poisoned the very air she breathed; she grew exhausted under it, this unending vengeance, which never slacked its speed, which never slaked its thirst, which, in its subtlety and its power, seemed all but supernatural. My brethren, are not men's passions ever so when they break the bonds of nature, and trample wide the mercy which God yields, but they deny?

He had bade her live to suffer; and she did suffer, this woman, whom no remorse had ever touched, no pity stirred, no tenderness stricken, but who had pride, which suffered deadly agony in its fall. There is a torture of the spirit which is more devilish and more terrible to endure than the shorter and coarser torture of the body; and she—she who had reigned so long!—knew this to its uttermost. She knew it when the men-servants of a household which had used to be obedient to her slightest gesture, could revenge themselves for many an imperious word or haughty command, by the slight and the sneer which the hirelings of the fresh lord had no scruple to deter them from offering to the mistress of the dead. She knew it when the women whom she had scored from her visiting list as beneath her rank, or refused to enter on her invitation-roll as roturières or rococo, could pay her back in whatever coin they would. She knew it when she stood alone, a queen discrowned, in the chambers where she had so long reigned absolute with a crowding court about her, and looked down the long vista of the magnificent salons, where yesterday every art-trifle had been hers, every will had bent to hers, every guest, every servant, ay! even every picture on the walls, or jewel in the tazze, or flower in the conservatories, had been *hers*, and whence now, she passed out with less honour than the lowest hireling who moved about their chambers, with less right, or title, or share in them than the dogs which slept upon their cushions.

The shame of a great sin had never smitten her; she knew it not; but under the shame of a great abasement she writhed, she shrank, she shuddered, as the women of old, who were given over, naked and bleeding, and hooted, to the pillory and the scourge. Is she alone? Surely not, for with mankind it is not the crime which is dreaded, but the scaffold.*

The Duc d'Etoile's carriage awaited her on that day when she passed for ever from the residence and the state of the Marchioness of Vavasour and Vaux. She entered it, sweeping through the great crowd, which assembled to gaze upon her as a notoriety, with all her accustomed haughty grace, now with a shade of defiance in it, and with her teeth slightly set together, for henceforth the world and she were at issue, and would contemn and confront each other. But this was only *for* the world; alone, the fallen empress bowed under the bitterness of her degradation, and writhed as upon a wheel where she was chained for public gaze and public mockery, as the carriage rolled onward to the Duc's villa; Etoile was not with her—some court ceremony detained him at the Tuileries, and he had written that he could not be at Auteuil "jusqu'au souper," in a note, in whose rich compliment already she learned the difference of a Prince's wording to a Peeress of England, and to one of Viola Vé's Sisterhood. She needed the solitude; she was thankful for it. Away from the eyes of the crowd, or from the presence of her lovers, Marion Vavasour's high-strung spirit gave way, like a bow overbent. She who had looked on all pain as her sport, as the young cat claims the agonies of the dying bird for her play, she knew it now for herself.

She was alone; on her arrival the chambers seemed stifling, the very evidences of a prince's wealth prepared for her looked loathsome; they were the insignia of her fall. She needed to suffer in solitude—once—once—for henceforth she would be amongst those whose wealth lies in their smiles, whose livelihood hangs on the brilliance of their beauty, and who must ever laugh—laugh and love, with the rouge on their paling cheeks, and the iron sharp in their souls! She went out into the sheen of the spring sunshine, sweeping

* "Le crime fait la honte et non pas l'échafaud," says Corneille. But the world reverses the poet's dictum; and in the world's eyes and our own, we may sin as we please, provided we avoid the scandal of being gibbeted for it!

swiftly and unheedingly through the grounds of the Duc's villa. The birds sang about her path; she scared them from her; their song was jarring mockery in her ear. A gardener's child asked her for alms; she spurned him from her with a cruel word; she had lived to envy that beggar's brat playing among the roses. A bright-winged butterfly fluttered in the grass at her feet; she trampled it to a brutal death, for daring to be joyous there—that senseless insect!—in the sunny light.

She swept onward swiftly, and unheeding where she went, while in the distance across the stretch of wood, and in the sunny mists of coming evening, uprose the roofs and spires of Paris—Paris, where she had reigned idol of its Court and leader of its Noblesse; Paris, where she had wielded more than a sovereign's sway; Paris, where she had sunk in all the bitterness of her fall. She swept onward, fast and blindly, through the glades and gardens, her lips white, her teeth set, her frame quivering with the shame of that day's degradation, till a branch of one of the early roses struck her across the brow, and recalled her to herself with its sharp physical pain. The flowers swung in the sunlight—the flowers which, with that more poetic element mingling in her nature, she had ever loved and interwoven with her beauty. Now, they recalled a thousand ghastly memories; with a rapid gesture she broke them asunder, and tore and scattered their fragrant leaves upon the earth: she was, even as those roses, a lying loveliness with a canker at the core! And, with a passionate moan of pain, Marion Vavasour sank down upon the stone steps of the terrace to which she had unconsciously taken her way, and, sinking her graceful, haughty head upon her hands, gave free vent—in solitude—to the bitterness of a fallen pride, to the misery of a world-wide degradation.

Yet even this luxury of loneliness she was denied:

"You suffer *now!*"

The words, hissed in her ear in strange ill-spoken French, made her start and rise with her old proud imperiousness, yet with something of fear; for the ruthless vengeance which pursued her had, now that its worst was wrought, left its terror upon her, and in her nature, as in the panther's, something of cowardice ran side by side with cruelty. Bending above her, over the grey ivy-hung coping, she saw the dark figure of a vagrant woman; it was the Bohemian, Redempta,

who had stood there watching her, with a dark hot flush
warming the pale olive of her features, and lending them new
life and light—a flush of thirsty joy. For to the wild, half-
savage nature which had known no duty but its love, no law
but its instincts, revenge looked great and holy: a just peace-
offering to the beloved dead.

To Marion Vavasour she was unknown—her face, though
twice beheld, unremembered—and, in vague alarm, she
glanced around, and saw that she had wandered so far to the
outskirts of the grounds that she was only surrounded by
woodland, with none within call; her hand instinctively sought
for gold, and tendered it in alms to this gipsy, whose gaze
filled her with a nameless terror, thus suddenly met in her
hour of solitude, in her day of dishonour. A smile, mournful in its utter disdain, crossed the lips of the Bohemian,
and she motioned it aside with that calm dignity with which
nature had dowered her:

"Should I touch *your* gold if I were starving? I came for
a richer guerdon than all the wealth of empires—I came to
see you suffer!"

"Suffer—suffer!——"

She repeated the word vaguely, mechanically; in that
moment of abandonment her nerves were unstrung, her
strength beaten down, and the defiance she had assumed for
the world had but left her the more exhausted and heart-sick
with the faintness of despair. She could not resent the
Bohemian's words, but only dimly marvelled at them.

The gipsy looked at her, a smile lighting her eyes, and
breaking up from the immutable melancholy of her face,
while her brown hand clenched on the white, soft arm of
Marion Vavasour:

"Ay! I have toiled, and laboured, and endured for that,
only for that—to see you suffer! You were the murderess of
Marc Lennartson, the slayer of what I loved. Ah! false forni-
catress, did you never hear his blood cry out for vengeance?
—did you think to smile, and sin, and drag men down to hell
with all your loveliness, and never have your crime come
back to you? You slew him—and you laughed at his death.
You slew him—but I have avenged him! I have been on
your trail day and night, and year after year; I burrowed to
your secret at last, and I gave it to Strathmore to destroy
you. You suffer!—your lips are white, your eyes are dim,

your face is haggard—you suffer! You have eaten of such bitterness as you gave; you have fallen from your proud estate; you will die in lowest infamy. God has given me vengeance—God has given me vengeance!——"

The words broke swift and fierce from the Bohemian's lips, with all the ferocious passion of her savage race, her eyes glittering, her voice triumphant, her hand clenching harder on the delicate arm she bruised in her grip, as she watched the woman she had hated and pursued shrink back and shiver, and turn sick under her stripes, as the scourged under those of the lash. Then the glow faded from her dark cheek, the vengeful lust and joy from her gleaming eyes; she loosened her hold and threw up her arms with a wild, piteous gesture to Heaven:

"Oh, God! thou givest me Vengeance, but thou canst not give me back the Dead! She suffers!—she suffers!—but he——"

The shrill, agonised cry died in a broken moan, her arms fell, her head drooped; she stood livid, mute, motionless as a statue. For in this lawless, vagrant woman, born of savage blood and bred by savage laws, brute instincts were outweighed by one great love; and that love turned even the long yearned-for hour of her vengeance to dead ashes, to withered fruit—for vengeance could not give her back her dead!

Her eyes dwelt on the face of Marion Vavasour with a fixed and lifeless gaze of unutterable melancholy, of fathomless pain, and her voice came slowly and hoarsely from her lips:

"I have smitten you, but I cannot make you render back the life that you destroyed! I revenge, but I cannot recall! He is dead, and my youth lies with him in the grave; though I wring you with every torture, I cannot undo your work. Yet—when you live in shame, and die in infamy, you will remember the woman who loved, yet was forsaken by him, avenged him on you, who betrayed and drove him to his death. If you had spared him, you had been spared!"

Then she turned, and moved slowly away with her head bowed, passing out of sight through the leafy aisles of the trees; and Marion Vavasour stood alone, with the chill of a great and nameless terror upon her. Her hands clenched on the stone coping as if for support, her eyes swam, she

shivered in the mellow sunlight, she recoiled under the
chastisement of the great sins which had found her out and
come home to her—fruit of the seed sown.   She shuddered
there, where she stood in the warm evening air, and crouched
down like a thing of guilt, while the dank dew stood on her
fair, proud brow.   And, as though led by the hand of an
avenging angel, her eyes, dim in her bitter, throbbing misery,
unconsciously followed the circling sweep of a white-winged
swallow skimming the surface of the earth; and as they
pursued the bird's flight, fell on the place where it rested, a
block of marble, lying amidst green luxuriance of spring-
tide flowers and the leaves of drooping trees, which bore
the name of the dead below:

BERTIE ERROLL,
AGED 33,
Killed by the Hand of his Friend.

The grounds of the villa touched the cemetery of Auteuil;
beyond, well-nigh at her feet, lay the grave of the man whom
her lie had given to death, with the brief record carved there
by the remorse of his assassin.   And she, who believed in
no God, believed at last in retribution, and stood there
paralysed and stricken with a deadly fear, looking down on
the tomb where the swallow rested and the sunlight played.

Yet, still—still, the soul of this woman knew neither remorse nor repentance, for these, if they take their spring
from crime, yet are holy, and purify while they scathe.   But
only as the panther in its mortal pain grows fresh hungered
for the death-grapple in its blind instinct of revenge, so she
in hers grew athirst for added evil—evil which should smite
him who had been the companion in her sin, yet who had
pursued her as though he were guiltless—evil which should
blast the life that had destroyed her own, and strike to the
dust the iron will that had stricken her—evil in which she
should hiss back into the ear of Strathmore the words with
which he had doomed her: "Such mercy as you gave I give
to you—no more!"

END OF VOL. I.

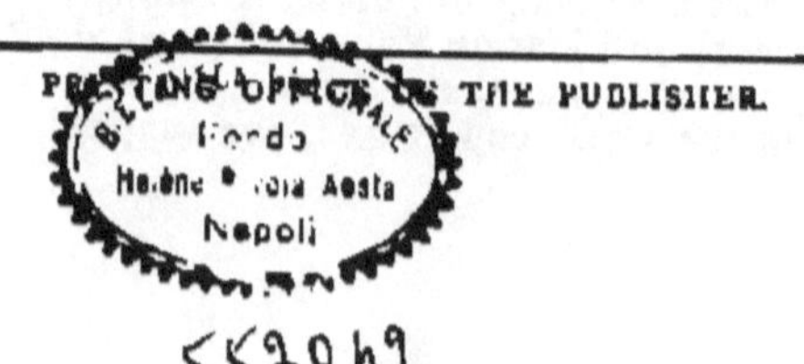

February 1910.

Tauchnitz Edition.

Latest Volumes:

4141. The Happy Prince, and Other Tales. By Oscar Wilde.
4142. Love the Thief. By Helen Mathers.
4143. On Peace and Happiness. By the Right Hon. Lord Avebury (Sir John Lubbock).
4144. Actions and Reactions. By Rudyard Kipling.
4145. Mr. Justice Raffles. By E. W. Hornung.
4146. Mere Stories. By Mrs. W. K. Clifford.
4147. They and I. By Jerome K. Jerome.
4148. Stradella. By F. Marion Crawford.
4149. The Paladin. By Horace Annesley Vachell.
4150. The Glimpse. By Arnold Bennett.
4151. Sailors' Knots. By W. W. Jacobs.
4152. A Reaping. By E. F. Benson.
4153. The Food of Love. By Frank Frankfort Moore.
4154. The Adventures of Captain Jack. By Max Pemberton.
4155/56. The White Prophet. By Hall Caine.
4157. A Woman of No Importance. By Oscar Wilde.
4158. The Lady of Blossholme. By H. Rider Haggard.
4159. Love and the Wise Men. By Percy White.
4160. The Florentine Frame. By Elizabeth Robins.
4161/62. Bella Donna. By Robert Hichens.
4163. Miss Fallowfield's Fortune. By Ellen Thorneycroft Fowler (Mrs. Alfred Felkin).
4164. Glimpses of Unfamiliar Japan. (*Second Series.*) By Lafcadio Hearn.
4165/66. The Lordship of Love. By Baroness von Hutten.